The Unicorn Gentlemen's Club

Nicola J. Grigg

Copyright © Nicola J. Grigg 2016

This novel is a work of fiction. Names, characters, businesses, places, events and incidents are either the products of the author's imagination or used in a fictitious manner. Any resemblance to actual persons, living or dead, or actual events is purely coincidental.

All rights reserved in all media. No part of this publication may be reproduced, stored in retrieval system, copied in any form or by any means, electronic, mechanical, photocopying, recording or otherwise transmitted without written permission from the author and/or publisher. You must not circulate this book in any format. Any person who does any unauthorised act in relation to this publication may be liable to criminal prosecution and civil claims for damages.

For permission requests, please contact: nicola.grigg@yahoo.com

Produced in United Kingdom.

Acknowledgements

I would like to thank my partner Douglas who has endured many hours of my creative ramblings and feverish typing. Also thanks to my mother Connie for her constant love and encouragement to finish my first novel. A very big thank to my editor Alex Matthews who has enriched my story with her excellent editing.

To my readers who are friends, work colleagues, and friends of friends, who have all read each draft of my story from start to finish, many times. A special thank you to Jodi, Sandi, Kelleigh, Sam and Patrick Creamer for providing me with invaluable feedback and much appreciated praise.

Chapter 1

Eva Summers shielded her eyes from the sun and looked up at the elaborate brass sign engraved Unicorn Gentlemen's Club, unaware that her life was about to change forever.

With a dry mouth and heart fluttering beneath her white summer dress, she walked up the black granite steps that led into the club's imposing lobby. A flowery, feminine scent hovered above the faint smell of floor polish; she took a deep breath to steady her nerves.

The sound of her steel-tipped stilettos echoed high into the domed ceiling as she made her way over to the reception desk. This was Eva's second and final interview at one of London's most prestigious lap dancing clubs. She had been chosen from over one hundred girls to be in the final ten.

Recognising the receptionist with heavily applied fake tan and honey-blonde hair extensions from her first interview, Eva gave a small cough. 'Hi. Eva Summers,' she said. 'I'm here for my second audition with Ann Davies and Mr O'Neill.'

The girl looked up and smiled politely, revealing a row of perfectly straight teeth before tapping her manicured nails against the keyboard.

'They're running a little late, so if you could just take a seat, I'll let them know you're here.' She motioned towards a large leather sofa.

Eva sat down and reached into her handbag. Checking her reflection in a compact, she was naturally striking with creamy translucent skin and deep-green eyes. She had applied her make-up with care: alluring smoky grey eyeshadow, just a touch of blusher to accentuate her high cheekbones and a lick of pillar-box-red gloss on her full lips. She hoped her curvaceous figure and perfectly styled red curls, emulating the glamour of 1940s Hollywood starlets, would give her an edge over the other girls. She ran her tongue over her teeth to remove a smudge of lip gloss before dropping the compact back into her bag. It was hard to stop the tip of her heel tapping against the marble floor as she waited nervously.

Eva took a deep breath and got to her feet when she recognised the bespectacled, middle-aged woman walk into the lobby.

'Miss Summers?' said the woman, smiling at her. 'Nice to see you again.'

'Hello, Mrs Davies,' replied Eva politely, wiping her clammy hands against her dress before offering a soft handshake.

'Shall we go through?' Ann Davies beckoned, checking her watch before leading Eva towards a set of double doors into the large dance lounge. 'If you could get changed and do a five-minute routine, then we'll have a chat. Okay?'

With a nervous smile, Eva nodded obediently and felt her high heels sink into the luxurious black carpet. She glanced around at the opulence on her way to the dressing room. Her memory of beautiful ornate mirrors adorning the ivy-green walls and a large crystal chandelier glistening like a crown of diamonds over the main circular podium hadn't faded. With a flurry of goose pimples pricking her skin, she weaved her way through the deep leather chairs and oak tables towards a large door signed Private Staff Only.

In the dressing room stood two rows of white-mirrored tables littered with colourful photographs, which created a fanciful daydream as she imagined her own photographs on display. She dropped her bag on the nearest table and pulled out a tiny black G-string and gold-sequinned bra before slipping out of her dress. Flicking a loose curl over her shoulder, she stood for a second and examined her reflection in the mirror; happy her outfit was revealing enough, she quickly made her way back into the dance lounge.

The main lights were dimmed to a single strobe hovering above the circular stage. The light almost created a divine beam of heavenly illumination against the cold steel bar.

As she glanced towards the phallic dancing pole, adrenalin quickly dissolved the tight knots of nerves in the pit of her stomach. She pushed her shoulders back and swayed past the three silhouetted figures sitting near the stage.

Silence hung in the air. She stepped up onto the podium and gazed momentarily at her distorted reflection in the pole before moving her feet apart and wrapping her slender fingers around the metal bar – her confidence briefly deserted her. *Am I really good enough to work in such a famous club?*

She had excelled at sport in school and enjoyed competing in regional gymnastics competitions for which she had won countless trophies. She knew there was no room for sentimentality in the brutal world of competing; she needed to prove to O'Neill that he should hire her over the other girls she was up against.

Come on, Eva! Don't bottle it now, she told herself. She took a deep breath and rubbed together her glossed lips waiting for the music to start. Slowly swaying her hips in time to the sultry beat, she arched her back sending her long red hair tumbling down to her waist. Her hips gyrated rhythmically as the music gathered tempo; a warm spotlight clung to the soft contours of her hourglass figure. With a provocative pout, she pushed her semi-naked bottom towards her silent audience and elevated her body off the stage with elegant ease. She gripped the pole between her milky-white thighs and gracefully arched backwards; her sequinned bra struggled to contain her large breasts.

Feeling the strain in the small of her back, she reached up and clasped her hand around the steel bar before quickly descending into a freestyle-spinning spiral. Her body looked almost weightless cutting through the air and hair sprayed out like a geisha's fan. She delicately placed the soles of her stilettos on the podium floor and projected a smouldering stare with a seductive, teasing smile. Lifting her body, she quickly rotated until she hung suspended like a Gothic cross. She slowly parted her legs and lowered them into a perfect V to reveal her modestly covered crotch.

She held the pose until her arms began to feel tight. Pulling her body upright, she spun down the pole and glanced out towards the three figures cloaked by darkness. As her feet touched the podium floor once more, she offered another teasing smile before kneeling on the stage to beckon the spectators to join her in a mutual fantasy of lust.

As she slowly unhooked the taut bra fasteners, her ample breasts plunged out of the sequinned cups. Tiny beads of perspiration glistened on her brow – it was time to start her provocative floorshow.

Eva lay on her back, letting her legs fall open slowly, and slipped her slender fingers between her thighs. Feeling the sheer G-string fabric, she lifted her back and pushed her fingers beneath the small triangle of translucent material. Her hips writhed to the motion of her brushing over her thin strip of soft pubic hair, exhaling provocatively with every stroke. Her hand moved from beneath her G-string as she rolled onto her stomach and pushed herself up onto her knees. Her long mane of red hair felt soft and luscious as thick strands tumbled through her fingers while she enticingly cupped her breasts like an eager lover.

Moving into her last position, she knelt and placed her palms flat on the stage floor before lowering her shoulders, leaving her bottom high in the air. The obvious 'doggy' pose was always a favourite with younger men who liked the porn-style view, especially admiring the tantalising view of her modesty through the sheer lace.

The music faded out and light flooded the room. She slowly got to her feet.

'Thanks, Eva. Could you get changed, then join us?' called out Ann. 'We'll go over your CV.'

Eva quickly left the stage and changed back into her dress. She mopped her brow before grabbing her bag and leaving the dressing room.

'Take a seat, Eva,' said Ann, smiling and peering over her glasses.

Eva sat across from a muscle-bound man staring back at her. She immediately felt intimidated by his rugged appearance: he reminded her of a professional boxer, with his slightly crooked nose and a prominent three-inch scar across his left cheek.

God, I hope that isn't O'Neill, she thought, averting her eyes.

'This is Mr Connor O'Neill, the proprietor of the Unicorn,' announced Ann.

Eva followed Ann's gaze and approving smile to see an extremely attractive second man dressed in a pale grey suit and a black open-necked shirt. Trying not to stare, Eva smiled politely and glanced back to Ann.

'And this is Tommy Jakeman who manages the Unicorn's security and casino,' added Ann, indicating to the scarred man who didn't mask his lack of interest in Eva.

'Hi,' muttered Eva, briefly making eye contact.

'So,' said Ann, picking up Eva's CV and pushing her glasses down her nose, 'you worked at Follies for a year, then at the Blue Velvet for two?'

Eva nodded. 'Yes.'

A cloud of spicy aftershave drifted across the table as O'Neill sat silently staring at her.

'Are they real?' Jakeman asked suddenly.

'Pardon?' said Eva.

'It's a simple enough question. Are they silicone or real?'

The bluntness in his voice made her swallow with embarrassment; she shuffled back in her seat and crossed her legs. Her answer would have been sharp if she was propositioned by a punter while in her work clothes, but sitting in O'Neill's presence seemed to subdue her.

'Do you understand the question?' Jakeman asked abrasively, glancing unashamedly at her breasts.

'Yes, they're natural,' croaked Eva.

'Er…shall we move on?' Ann said, noticing Eva fidget in her seat. 'So you've worked at the Blue Velvet for two years?'

'Yes.' Eva nodded again, her clammy fingers interlocked tensely in her lap.

'The Blue Velvet is a good club,' stated O'Neill in a deep southern Irish accent. 'Why did you leave?' He rested his elbow casually on the chair arm in contemplation.

Eva felt momentarily transfixed by his intense stare. 'Er…' she said, trying to compose herself, 'I didn't get on with Mr Thornton's son – you know, after Mr Thornton retired—'

'Richard Thornton?' O'Neill smiled and glanced over at Jakeman. 'Chase you out, did he?' he asked, aware of Richard's reputation.

Eva blushed. 'I guess you could say that.'

O'Neill let out a small chuckle and raised an eyebrow in amusement at her discomfort.

Eva grit her teeth noticing his obvious enjoyment at her misfortune. *Does he think it's acceptable to sexually harass a possible employee just because I take my clothes off for a living?*

'So,' butted in Ann. 'And you've worked at the Rodeo House for the past eight months?'

'Yes, that's right.'

'I thought that degenerate bastard was dead,' barked Jakeman, earning himself a wide smile from O'Neill.

'Now, now, gentlemen…' interjected Ann with exasperation in her voice. 'I'm sure Miss Summers is well aware of her current employer's reputation.'

Eva wasn't surprised at this scathing comment about her boss. Jimmy Booth had worked hard to be unlikeable and untrustworthy. His nickname amongst the girls at the Rodeo was 'Leering Letch'. He was crude and proud of his old-fashioned opinion of women, often proclaiming they were simply not his equal and that their value lay between their legs, not between their ears. It was commonplace to hear him curse other club proprietors especially Connor O'Neill, calling him 'The Irish Inbred'. He would often boast and prophesy that one day O'Neill's dark past would come back to haunt him and ruin his so-called honourable reputation.

Why would such an accomplished dancer like Eva accept employment in Booth's spit-and-sawdust club? It was purely out of desperation. She had a brief but intense relationship with Ryan Steel who was bar manager at the Blue Velvet. The break-up was messy and toxic, so she needed to find another job – quick.

'If you could give us five minutes, Eva, I'll see you in the lobby,' Ann told her.

With one more fleeting look at O'Neill, Eva picked up her handbag and gave Ann a warm smile before walking out of the dance lounge.

Whilst in the lobby she analysed her performance step by step. She didn't think her interview had gone particularly well but tried to console herself with the fact that her routine had been strong and artistic. She imagined telling the 'Letch' she would be leaving his second-rate club because she had a job at the fabulous Unicorn. It was a comforting dream; one she could almost taste.

She waited in the lobby for ten minutes before Ann reappeared. Her poker face didn't convey whether she had been successful or not. Eva felt almost faint and rooted to the spot when Ann walked over to her.

'Mr O'Neill was very happy with your performance.'

'Was he?' Eva blurted out before raising a hand to her mouth.

'Yes. He was full of praise. I think your Celtic colouring appealed to him, too.' Ann chuckled and raised an eyebrow. 'With Mr O'Neill being Irish.'

'Really?' Eva dropped her hand away and smiled.

What Eva didn't know was that O'Neill's right-hand man, Tommy Jakeman, wanted to hire a leggy Swedish girl called Katina and had challenged O'Neill's decision.

'Can you thank Mr O'Neill for me and promise him he won't regret his decision?'

'I'm sure you'll do well here, dear.' Ann smiled kindly. 'We'll see you next Monday, then. I'll send confirmation through the post.'

'Okay,' said Eva beaming, still in shock. *I can't believe it! I'm the one chosen from all those girls. Oh my God! I did it!*

Chapter 2

Eva drove back to her two-bedroom terrace in Hackney feeling triumphant and giddy with excitement. After clumsily clipping the kerb when pulling up outside, she hummed a cheerful melody entering her house. She was immediately greeted by her cat, Mr Jingles, who came bounding down the stairs and circled her legs with a chorus of high-pitched meows.

'Oh, Mr Jingles, I got the job!' she squealed, scooping him up into her arms. Mr Jingles looked slightly startled and wriggled from her tight embrace as she jabbered on excitedly. 'You and me against the world, Mr J. How about a treat to celebrate Mummy's new job?'

After devouring two tuna-flavoured cat biscuits, and sensing there were no more to be had, he walked out of the kitchen with his tail swaying elegantly.

Eva took a shower and towel-dried her long hair trying to ignore the knots tightening in her stomach thinking about Booth's reaction to her working for his nemesis.

She grabbed her workbag and blew Mr Jingles a kiss, which he totally ignored, and stepped out into the late afternoon sun. The smell of honeysuckle and lavender greeted her as she walked down the path. Driving off with an uneasy feeling in her belly she swallowed hard before rehearsing her leaving speech, hoping it would dilute his foul temper if she chose her words carefully.

'Hmm,' she muttered, tapping her fingers on the steering wheel. 'Mr Booth,' she practised, 'even though I've enjoyed working at the Rodeo for the past eight months' —she put on a forced smile— 'I've been offered a job in another club.'

She cleared her throat and deepened her voice to mimic Booth's growl. 'Eh? Another club?'

'Yes, the Rodeo was only really t-t-temporary,' she stuttered, shaking her head. 'I mean…' She composed herself. 'My ambition has always been to work for one of the larger clubs in Mayfair. I think my dancing is good enough to become a principal dancer.'

'Are you saying my club is a shithole?' she snarled, wrinkling her nose. 'Ha – you're an average dancer with ideas above your fucking talent!'

'Average?' she shrieked, her temper soaring. Passing motorists looked on in amusement as she pointed angrily into her rearview mirror.

'Girls like you are ten-a-penny,' she howled. 'I employed your sorry arse when no other club would touch you with a barge pole. If it wasn't for me, you'd be selling your fanny down Docket Lane!'

'How dare you insult me like that?' she barked, hitting the steering wheel with the palm of her hand.

The blast of car horns jolted her out of this one-woman pantomime. Glancing up at the green traffic lights Eva crunched the gearstick into first and sped away, blushing with embarrassment.

In Soho, she turned into Dean Street and looked up at the garish red and green neon sign of a buxom woman straddling a bucking horse. Her mouth suddenly became sand-dry. There was no more time to rehearse. She pulled into the Rodeo car park and took a deep breath.

She was so preoccupied with the upcoming conversation that she didn't hear one of the bouncers shout hello as she walked past. The sound of loud music and raucous voices greeted her as she made her way through the red-lit lobby. Such aggressive baiting quickened her step towards the dressing room. Eva stepped inside and glanced at the mountain of underwear and make-up strewn across the shabby dressing tables. *Just one more week, Eva*, she thought. *Just one more week!*

'All right, Eva?' asked a pretty blonde girl sitting at a cluttered table wearing a pair of black lace knickers and skyscraper heels.

'Hi, Tam,' Eva replied.

'Are you okay, babes?'

'Yeah,' lied Eva, forcing a smile so Tammy wouldn't probe her further. It wasn't that she couldn't trust her, she just didn't want to let slip her plans to one of the other girls before she had told Booth. 'Sounds busy out there tonight,' she said, making small talk as she leaned into the mirror to apply her foundation.

'Bloody Letch has booked four stag parties!' moaned Tammy, plugging in her hair straighteners. 'It's gonna be bloody bedlam in there tonight.'

'When is it not?' Eva bit back.

'Oh yeah, watch out for the group at the front of the stage. Dawn's already had her arse pinched!'

'If anyone grabs me, I swear I'll go for 'em,' warned Eva, snatching a hairbrush off her dressing table.

'That ain't the best of it,' added Tammy. She shuffled around in her seat to face Eva. 'One cheeky fucker only went and offered Dawn a tenner for a blow job – can you fucking believe that? Ten bloody quid! Dawn said round it up to fifty and she'd consider it,' cackled Tammy.

'Scum. I told Booth only last week that we shouldn't have to put up with being manhandled night after night, and you know what he said?'

'Nah, what?'

'That it's a bloody compliment!'

'He's a cheeky fucker,' hissed Tammy, spraying hairspray over her long, straightened hair.

'He's an animal. You would never be molested in a club like the Unicorn.'

'Yeah, true, but the Unicorn is the dog's bollocks of strip clubs. Have you seen the kind of girls they hire there? You know little Lisa? Well, her fella, Nigel, said he knows one of the bouncers at the Unicorn, and he said you won't even be considered for membership unless you're earning a six-figure salary. He said they even have gold taps in the gents. I would fucking saw 'em off and flog 'em!' said Tammy, snorting.

'The girls there are no better than us, Tam,' said Eva, frowning.

'They're in a different league to us, babes. I heard they employ French cabaret girls – you know, your proper high-class show girls.'

'So?' argued Eva. 'We're as good as them.'

'If you say so,' Tammy said softly, shrugging her shoulders. 'I ain't saying we're trailer trash or nothing. You're probably the prettiest girl here, but look at the rest of the girls! Booth knows his market, babes. Can you imagine Sophie with her stretch marks floundering around a city banker with his designer suit and Rolex?' She sneered at the thought. 'The men who come here don't care whether you have cellulite on your arse or how good a dancer you are. They're looking to pay twenty quid to see your average pair of tits and a glimpse of quim – simple as that.'

Grimacing, Eva bit her tongue before she could blurt out her secret. 'Hmmm…' was all she could manage as frustration coloured her cheeks. She quickly changed into a white thong and tasselled, fringed bra from her workbag before slipping into a pair of black stilettos. Sighing heavily, she glanced at her reflection in the mirror before leaving the dressing room for her first dance.

'Get your tits out, love!' shouted an intoxicated overweight middle-aged man grabbing his crotch. 'Come on, love, get your knickers off!' he added, much to the delight of his drunken companions as Eva swung around the mirrored dance pole.

'I'll let you suck my cock for a fiver, gorgeous!' he roared, earning himself another raucous howl of laughter for his crassness.

Eva inhaled deeply and averted her gaze to the safety of an elderly gentleman sipping a pint of beer.

'Come on, love, we ain't got all fucking night!' called out the same man, slamming down his whisky glass.

Gritting her teeth and trying to ignore his constant heckling, she clasped her thighs around the dancing pole and continued her routine.

'Get to the money shot! Come on, get your knickers off! Or do I have to come up there and take them off myself?'

At first Eva wasn't worried by his taunting, but she knew from bitter experience that alcohol and heckling would often accelerate into aggressive behaviour. A loud cheer made her stop dead in her tracks; the man was staggering towards the podium. Frozen to the spot, she gasped out loud and scanned the dance lounge for one of the bouncers. 'Where the f-fuck are they?' she cried.

'I told you to take your knickers off, you stuck-up slag,' shouted the drunk man, tripping up the first step of the podium platform.

'Y-you're not allowed up here,' babbled Eva, backing away from his whisky-sodden breath.

'I ain't shellin' out money to see you prancing round a fucking pole. So – *get* – naked.'

She screamed in panic as his outstretched arm clamped roughly around her slender wrist. 'Let me go!' she hollered hysterically. 'GET OFF ME!'

If it hadn't been for two young men leaping up onto the podium and wrestling the man to the stage floor, she had no idea what might have happened next.

'Where the hell have you been, George?' yelled Eva when a bouncer finally arrived and jumped onto the stage.

'Sorry, Eva, I thought Gary was keeping an eye on things in here. I was out front.'

Storming off, followed by a trail of expletives, Eva stomped back to the dressing room.

'Shit! Where's the fire?' shrieked Tammy as Eva thundered in.

'A bloody punter only tried to attack me on stage!'

'No way!'

'Fucking *yes* way!' retorted Eva. 'And where were Gary or George? Bloody nowhere to be seen, that's where!'

'Where were they, then?'

'Maybe Denise-Marie can answer that one!' Eva folded her arms and stared behind Tammy at a very sheepish-looking Denise whose eyes were locked on the floor, her crimson cheeks confessing all.

'But you're okay, though?' soothed Tammy, walking over to Eva.

'Yeah, but only because two members came to my rescue,' she huffed throwing make-up and clothes into her workbag.

'Where are you going now?'

'To see Booth. I've performed my last dance in his hellhole.'

Seething with rage, she rapped her knuckles hard on Booth's door. Nothing. With increasing irritation, she pressed her ear against the cheap wood grain and heard muffled noises. *Why hasn't he called me in?* She knocked for a second time.

'Yeah?'

Inhaling deeply, she walked into his office and was greeted by a thick cloud of cigar smoke hovering over his desk. The stench of stale sweat hung in the air.

'Yeah, what is it?' he snapped, waving his hand for her to move out of the way.

'I wanted to see you because—' She stepped aside and glanced behind her. Her nose wrinkled with disgust when she saw he was watching a porn movie; the thought of him masturbating under his desk made her feel nauseous.

'Well, what is it? I ain't got all night!'

Clearing her throat, she raised her voice over the grunts and screams coming from the TV, 'I'll be leaving at the end of the week!'

He switched his focus to her; a deep frown lined his sweaty brow. 'What?'

'I think you heard what I said.'

He lowered his cigar and balanced it precariously on the edge of his desk before grabbing a half-empty bottle of whisky. Without uttering another word, he poured a generous measure into a glass and took a large gulp. 'Is this because of the shower incident?'

'Incident,' scoffed Eva, her hands on her hips. 'That was no *incident*, as we both know.'

'I explained at the time that it was an accident,' he said, slamming his fist on the desk, sending his half-smoked cigar toppling to the floor.

Of course he was lying. The 'shower incident', as he put it, was no accident. Eva had taken a shower after her shift. This was something she didn't do often: Booth had a habit of walking into the dressing room unannounced. On this occasion, he'd pretended he was looking for Charmaine. Of course, the only flaw in his story was that Charmaine is black and five foot nine – Eva is white and five foot three.

'Actually, it's not just because of that. I was nearly attacked on your stage tonight!'

'I'm sure you got the situation quickly under control.'

'You really don't give a toss, do you? Your club is a honey-pot for perverts and drunks. All you care about is the money.'

'Look.' Booth grinned to reveal a row of rotten teeth. 'You and me – we're the same. You play hardball, and so do I. Let's cut to the chase here, yeah?' His voice softened as he continued, 'You're a good little dancer, and you're a favourite with the punters. Hey, even *I* like you. Let's say another five pounds an hour – hey? Then we can forget this nonsense about you wanting to leave. What d'ya say?'

Her jaw dropped as she stood speechless for a moment. 'You're out of your mind to think I would spend another hour in this shithole. I'm not leaving because of the money!' she blasted.

'Okay, okay,' said Booth, frowning and waving his hand to silence her. 'Another six pounds fifty, but that's my final offer – plus, this agreement stays between me and you.'

'Have you not listened to a word I've said? I was going to leave at the end of the week, but I cannot stay a minute longer. No amount of money will tempt me to stay!'

Booth wheezed searching the floor for his cigar. 'I know every club boss in London,' he panted, finally locating it.

'So?'

'It would only take one word from me and there wouldn't be any job to drag your arse to, unless you're going self-employed,' he said, grinning.

'Self-employed?'

'It wouldn't be too bad in the summer,' he mocked, 'but you'll freeze your tits off in the winter.'

'Are you suggesting that I'm leaving to become a prostitute?' Eva's mouth hung open in utter shock.

Booth smirked. 'Well...' The wooden chair creaked under his weight as he leaned back. 'I think you've got what it takes, kiddo. Okay, so you're a bit on the fleshy side, but a man like curves on a woman.'

'I would rather be a prostitute walking the streets in a blizzard than work in your *dive of a club* a second longer.'

'Just asking you to rethink, kiddo. I'm happy to forget this whole conversation. I won't even dock your pay for the time you've wasted.' Booth chuckled.

'You're unbelievable! Don't you want to know who my new employer is?' she crowed triumphantly.

'Who is it? Bobby Major from the Honey Trap? He'll drop you like a hot potato after I've been on the blower to him – ha!'

'No.' Eva smirked. 'I haven't been hired by Bobby Major, or Gordon Willis from the Temple of Venus.'

'Who, then?' huffed Booth, taking another swig of whisky.

'Well...let's just say his membership portfolio reads like a celebrity wedding guest list. Famous footballers, well-known actors, rich city traders and men with titles – have you guessed the club yet?'

'You can find all those inbreds in any back-street brothel.' Booth laughed, enjoying his own wit.

'Well, if you can't guess who my new employer is, then I'd better tell you.'

'Go on then, enlighten me with the name of your new pimp.'

'My new employer is...*Connor O'Neill*.'

'Eh?' spluttered Booth, puffs of cigar smoke erupting from his mouth.

'Connor O'Neill.' Eva was enjoying every second of her triumph.

'You're going to work for that Irish bastard?' His sallow, greasy skin turned a mottled shade of purple. 'The Unicorn is just an upmarket fucking brothel. I've heard his own mother was the madam there!'

'Saying it to me isn't the same as having the guts to saying it to O'Neill, you know.'

'Are you saying that I'm scared of that piece of shit?' hollered Booth, making her jerk back with fright. 'I'll make you regret those words!'

She shuffled backwards towards the door and fumbled for the handle.

'Where the fuck do you think you're going? I'll make sure no one wants to look at your face again.' He grabbed the bottle of whisky and hurled it towards her.

Eva flinched and dodged aside as the bottle shattered against the wall behind her. Before Booth could spit another insult, she turned on her heels, flung open the door and bolted down the narrow corridor, kicking off her six-inch stilettos as she ran.

'Get back here, you worthless whore,' roared Booth.

Adrenalin pumped terror through her body as she ran into the dressing room. She grabbed her handbag and raced back out while Tammy and Charmaine looked on in utter confusion.

Booth stood wheezing on the pavement. 'This ain't finished by a long chalk, you bitch! No slag accuses me of being fucking scared of Connor fucking O'Neill!' he thundered.

The coarse gravel punctured her feet as she sprinted through the car park to her blue Vauxhall Corsa. Throwing herself into the driving seat, her teeth began to chatter with shock. She thrust the key into the ignition and crunched the gearstick into reverse. With her bare foot slammed onto the accelerator, she screeched out of the car park.

She drove erratically down the street, constantly checking her rearview mirror for any sign of Booth's silver Jaguar. Her speed didn't slow down through Mayfair. She felt as if she was in the middle of a nightmare and struggled to see the road in front of her through the tears stinging her cheeks. Finally she careered into her own street. Her heart hammering as she braked to a halt outside her house. Feeling utterly drained, she slammed shut and deadlocked the front door before slumping against the frame as Mr Jingles came bounding towards her.

Three large vodkas later, she lay on the sofa in a nervous sleep; her body jerking restlessly with every flash of light from passing traffic.

* * *

Booth's threats replayed continuously in her mind during the following week. She was sure he would have contacted O'Neill if there were any substance to them. But she'd received her contract from Ann Davies, so she assumed his warnings were hollow.

'Oh, Mr Jingles,' she cooed, gathering him up into her arms. 'This time tomorrow I'll be dancing at the Unicorn. I'm so excited!'

Little did Eva know that her excitement would soon dissolve into a dangerous journey of dark desire, devastation and heartbreak.

Chapter 3

Eva pondered for ages at the array of skimpy outfits strewn across the bed. She bought most of her work clothes from sex and fetish shops, with a few stylish pieces from La Senza and Agent Provocateur. She finally grabbed a selection and packed them into her holdall, along with her hair straighteners and favourite black thigh-length PVC boots.

She wondered what kind of reception she would receive from the other girls that night. If experience had taught her anything, it was that she should keep her own counsel. The dressing room was a breeding ground for lies and gossip. She had seen more than one catfight during her three years working the clubs, so she always tried to keep her opinions to herself – but, unfortunately, this didn't always happen.

Whilst sat in the tail end of a long traffic jam, her mind flashed back to her interview with O'Neill and what a few of the girls had said about him behind Booth's back. He was the wealthiest club owner in the southeast and had a reputation as a ladies' man. She'd also heard he had been a professional poker player in his native Ireland before building his property empire and buying the Unicorn.

Researching the club online revealed a long and colourful history: The three-storey building with secret passages was built in 1895 and originally home to Thomas J. Richmond, a notorious judge who sent people to the gallows for pitiful crimes. The property sustained considerable damage during the Blitz and was condemned to be demolished, but an American hotelier, Rhett Carter, bought the derelict building for thirty-four thousand pounds. He restored it to its former glory and created a five-star hotel. It was then sold in 1964 to a wealthy Sicilian businessman called Alberto Mazzola who converted it into a fashionable nightclub, the Golden Kaleidoscope, which became an iconic hangout for film stars and singers. In 2002, the club was sold for almost ten million pounds to Connor O'Neill.

After a hot and wearisome forty minutes she eventually pulled into the Unicorn car park and noticed a gleaming silver sports car with a private number plate that read CON1 OR. She was suitably impressed by her new employer's taste. She sighed heavily and walked away feeling slightly deflated knowing she would never own such a car. She had been saving for six months and was just over two thousand pounds away from owning her dream car, a Mini Cooper in cherry red.

Eva approached the imposing entrance and waited in reception for Ann collect her.

'Hello, Eva. Good, you're on time,' said Ann, glancing at her watch. 'I'll take you through to meet the other girls, then we'll have a quick chat before you start, okay?'

Through the lounge doors they were greeted by a small army of topless waitresses weaving around circular tables making sure each member had a drinks menu and the list of that night's dancers.

'Ready?' Ann smiled as they approached the dressing room door.

Eva took a deep breath and followed her.

'Ladies,' announced Ann, raising her voice over a sea of chitchat, 'this is Eva Summers, our new dancer.'

The chatter faded and a group of pretty faces turned towards them.

Eva instantly noticed a petite blonde girl sitting at the far end of the room frowning at her. She didn't know the reason for her look of annoyance, so she quickly averted her gaze.

'Hello,' said Eva to the attentive group of girls.

'So, to your far left is Tina Jackson,' said Ann, giving the girl a nod.

Glancing over at the pretty, tanned girl who had frowned at her, Eva saw that she still looked sour.

'Hi,' said Eva curtly, returning the girl's stare. She thought the girl was attractive with her honey-blonde corkscrew curls, but her expression spoilt her candy-sweet façade.

'Next to Tina is Donna.' Ann looked at an Afro-Caribbean girl. With her sculptured body softened by feminine lingerie and shimmering make-up, she was more striking than Tina.

'Then we have Roxanne to your right.' Ann nodded towards the stunning raven-haired girl who surprised Eva by offering a genuine smile.

'I just want to go over a few rules and regulations with you,' said Ann after introducing all the other girls. She pointed towards the office at the back of the dressing room.

Eva followed her and sat down as Ann pulled open the second drawer of her desk and handed her a small brass locker key with a handwritten number sixteen on it and a small white book. 'All the Unicorn's rules and regulations are in here. If you find anything not clear, then come and see me. My door is always open.'

Hearing the warmth in her voice, Eva concluded that Ann was going to be a fair but firm manager.

'As for accepting drinks, I'm sure you know what to do.'

'Yes.' Eva knew the rule well. If a client asked to buy a dancer a drink she should request a bottle of the club's champagne, which was marked up by an exorbitant amount. Dancers were allowed to drink a couple of small glasses but were forbidden to get drunk.

'All private dances are to be booked through me. This rule is in place for your safety, and it keeps me informed about what you're doing in the club's time.'

Nodding, Eva acknowledged the serious tone in Ann's voice. She knew a club like the Unicorn would have strict rules in place, and she was glad that the dancers' safety was taken seriously.

Rubbing the bridge of her nose, Ann picked up her glasses and began to clean them. 'Any sexual interaction with any of the club members is totally forbidden. This applies to staff as well. You'll find out soon enough that Roxanne and Mr Jakeman are partners. Tommy is Mr O'Neill's friend, as well as his employee, so their relationship is the only exception to this rule,' said Ann, holding her glasses up to the light and peering through before placing them back on her nose.

Eva was unable to stop her mouth dropping open in shock. She would never have put Roxanne and Jakeman together, not in a million years. Roxanne was stunning, with her jet-black waist-length hair and flawless complexion; on the other hand, Tommy looked like a boxer's punch bag.

'You'll be expected to, what we call, "walk the floor",' said Ann. 'All the girls will be asked to work in the casino from time to time.'

'Oh, but I don't play cards. In fact, I've never set foot in a casino.'

'Eva, you're not there to play cards. You keep the members occupied, so to speak.'

'Occupied?'

'To keep our wealthy customers company and encourage them to place larger bets.'

Eva understood this, of course. She was fine being a commodity, a product, which had to be paid for.

'Every girl is given a dance rota at the start of each week. If you're ill, then let me know before ten o'clock so I can arrange cover for your shift. You won't be paid if you're not in work.' Ann looked at Eva over the rim of her glasses.

'Well, I haven't had any time off sick in the past year. My attendance record should verify that.'

'Well, I think we've covered everything. Is there anything you want to ask me?'

'My rota?'

'Oh, yes,' said Ann, tutting as she flicked through a neat pile of papers. 'Here you go.'

'Thanks.' Eva got up and walked towards the door.

A burst of laughter filled the dressing room as she walked past Tina and Donna. She ignored them and sat down at her table. It was obvious they were scrutinising every inch of her body and face, but she didn't care; nothing could spoil her happiness at being a dancer at the prestigious Unicorn Gentlemen's Club.

'So, Eve, where did you work before?' asked Tina who was backcombing Donna's afro.

'My name is *Eva*, not Eve.'

'What?' said Tina, with more than a pinch of spite in her tone.

'My name is Eva,' she repeated calmly.

'Oh, pardon *me*,' said Tina, a smug smile falling from her face. 'I thought Ann said your name was Eve. So, *Eva*, where did you work before?' she repeated dramatically.

Eva knew embarrassment and ridicule would instantly follow if she answered her question. 'The Rodeo,' she said begrudgingly, waiting for the fallout.

Tina's eyes widened with glee.

Eva inhaled deeply waiting to see what she would say next.

'Really?' said Tina with a wicked smile. 'I heard the Rodeo is a broth—'

'Oh my God!' squealed a heavily tanned, semi-naked woman with cartoon-sized breasts barging into the dressing room. 'Listen to this!'

'*As I was saying*,' said Tina, raising her voice, 'I heard—'

'No, wait, listen to this!' butted in the woman, flapping her hands in the air. 'Apparently that American actor Dan Ward from *Night Stalker* is in tonight. I hope he chooses me for a private dance!'

Grinding her teeth, Tina knew her chance to probe Eva further had passed. There was no way she could compete with the avalanche of questions being thrown in the air; she silently accepted defeat and turned her attention back to Donna's hair.

It was all too clear this was just a reprieve for Eva. She took an array of colourful sequinned bras and G-strings from her bag along with a selection of black stockings and suspender belts and placed them in her drawer. She then took out three photographs and smiled broadly looking down at the first picture of two giggly, happy girls – Eva and her best friend at school, Susanna. The photo was taken in 2009 at Glastonbury Festival. They had spent the whole weekend in a psychedelic, hedonistic haze as they smoked pot, danced drunkenly to Lily Allen and Lady Gaga, and had sex with strangers, which even made her blush to this day.

The second photograph was of two older people standing on a golden beach with their tanned bodies silhouetted against a blue sky. This was her mother Patsy and partner Dennis Tindal who met on holiday in Spain four years ago. He was a down-to-earth cockney with a zest for life who sang in the local tavern.

The third picture, which was old and faded, was of a young man – her father, Thomas McCoy. Her mother told her he had died in a motorbike accident a week before she was born.

She pushed the edges of the photographs under the plastic rim of her dressing table mirror and started to get ready for her first dance. Dabbing foundation onto her pale skin, she glanced at Tina who instantly cut her a look of annoyance and flicked a long blonde curl over her shoulder. Eva stared back before looking in her mirror. Sighing with exasperation, she dipped a soft bristled brush into a pot of face powder. She had decided to darken her almond-shaped green eyes with grey eyeshadow and false eyelashes before finishing her dramatic look with blood-red lipstick.

She stood naked in her bare feet fishing out her blue negligée and matching knickers. She could see out of the corner of her eye that Tina and Donna were watching her every move, probably making a mental note of every dimple of cellulite on her thighs. She was sure they would be irritated by the fact she was more than happy with her naturally curvy figure and pert breasts. A rush of adrenalin quickened her breath as she weaved through the semi-naked dancers in the dressing room. Loud chatter, a fusion of expensive colognes and dance music pumping out of the stage speakers greeted her as she stepped into the dance lounge. She pushed back her shoulders and swung her hips – trying not to look at the sea of shadowy faces ogling her skimpily dressed body as she swaggered through the testosterone-filled air.

As she reached the podium, a lustful wolf whistle pierced the air before being quickly silenced by the start of Prince singing 'Purple Rain'. She stood on the podium with her legs a foot apart and pushed herself up onto the balls of her feet before elevating her body and gripping the pole between her thighs. Circling around, she stopped and lowered her shoulders to hang horizontally, her legs parallel with her upper body, suspended in mid-air. The spotlight hovered above her. She held the pose for a couple of seconds before lifting herself upright and pushing the back of her knee against the cold steel. Her chiffon negligée billowed out revealing a glimpse of her pert naked breasts as she spiralled down the full length of the pole. With her six-inch heels on the podium, she stood facing the crowd and placed her hands above her head then swayed from side to side and shimmied down into a crouch. She brushed her delicate hands down her pale neck before caressing her breasts and seductively pouting.

'Hey, gorgeous,' called out a young fat man, in a more diluted heckle than she was used to hearing at the Rodeo. 'This is for you, honey,' he shouted, waving a note in the air.

Smiling at him, she rested her hands on her knees and pushed her legs apart before sliding back up the pole, letting it brush against the soft skin of her bottom.

Her audience sat captivated and submerged in their own personal fantasies. She knew lust would be swelling between their legs. The older men would usually be more conservative and fidget in their seats while discreetly slipping their hands into their tailored trouser pockets.

Reaching for the pole again, she pushed her body close against it and swung her legs out into a perfect right angle. She slowly parted her legs in a horizontal scissor movement, giving the members who sat to her left a snapshot of her modestly covered crotch. Slowly bringing her legs together, she wrapped them around the pole and glided effortlessly down. She stepped away when her feet touched the floor and glanced out at the ocean of faces staring back at her.

Every man in the room stared at her lustfully. She ran the tip of her finger along the soft curve of her stomach before slowly touching the silky blue bow that held her negligée together. With a slow, teasing movement she pulled the strands of ribbon apart before lowering her provocative gaze and letting the feather-light fabric glide down over her large breasts.

An American accent bellowed over the music, 'Bring it home to Uncle Sam, baby girl!' shattering the trance hypnotising the inner circle of men sitting around the podium.

Pouting like a schoolgirl, she knelt down with her knees apart. Cupping her breasts, she mercilessly teased the men while they watched her gently squeeze her erect nipples and fantasised about being her lover. A flurry of fifty-pound notes littered the stage. She slowly lowered one of her hands, guiding it into her sheer knickers.

'Oh yeah, baby,' shouted a Scottish accent, followed by a high-pitched whistle.

Her hand moving back and forth simulated masturbation before positioning her body in several explicit sexual poses before slipping out of her sheer knickers.

She designed her routine so it had a burlesque flavour, rather than a hard-core sex show. She had no moral issue with stripping naked and showing her all, but she didn't do the 'money shot', which was the full frontal, open legs, porn shot. Most strippers did, but she thought it gratuitous and favoured more sensual poses that left a little something to the imagination.

For her final pose she stepped down from the podium and lay seductively on the circular stage. Her favourite rock track by Chris Isaak 'Wicked Game' belted out of the speakers. A table of boisterous German men got to their feet, not wanting to miss a second of her performance.

Her body glistened under the spotlights; the tiny beads of perspiration on her skin shone like diamonds. Writhing and arching her back, she lay on the floor caressing her breasts.

Slowly parting her legs, she gave the men in the front row a glimpse of her naked sex. The table of German men became more and more raucous, with one of them getting up from his chair and grinding his hips to the music. Such behaviour would have gone unnoticed at the Rodeo, but she felt tension building amongst the other club members who began to frown and turn around in frustration until one of the bouncers intervened and told the guy to sit back down.

Eva got to her feet and turned her back to the men. She gathered her hair up above her neck and swayed as she parted her legs and moved her hips. She moved into her final pose, letting her hair cascade down her back. Pushing her weight onto her arms, she lifted her body into a handstand and slowly lowered her legs to give the men a fleeting glimpse of what they craved. Their carnal baying indicated she would be handsomely rewarded for her erotic floorshow.

As punters threw money onto the stage, a middle-aged man with heavy-framed glasses made his way over. He was unattractive but smartly dressed in a navy suit and tie. Making eye contact with him, she stroked his ego by offering him a sensual smile as he pushed a bundle of twenty-pound notes into the top of her thigh-length boot. It was all an act on her part. She was a successful stripper and knew the more unattractive the man, the more likely he was to be generous.

She noticed Donna standing in the shadows watching her gather the money spread like confetti. Eva could tell she wasn't amused at this very lucrative first dance and smiled smugly walking past, fanning herself with a wad of banknotes to take to Ann.

'Well,' said Ann smiling, 'I take it your first dance went well?'

'Yes, I'm really happy with what I took,' Eva said beaming.

Ann followed Eva back into the dressing room to make an announcement. 'Right, girls, a little bit of hush, please. With the grand opening of the newly refurbished casino tomorrow night, Mr O'Neill has invited the local press to cover the opening.'

Tina raised her arm in the air and bobbed excitedly in her seat. 'What time is Mr O'Neill arriving tomorrow?'

'Around lunchtime,' said Ann impatiently. 'So, I want a couple of girls to walk the floor for the press photos.'

'I'll do it!' squealed Tina, punching her hand in the air again. Her feverish excitement made everyone turn around; Donna prematurely congratulated her on being chosen.

Ignoring Tina's outburst, Ann proceeded, 'So Donna, Roxanne and…Eva.'

'*Me?*' said Eva, looking at Ann.

Tina jumped to her feet. 'No!'

'Pardon?' said Ann, frowning.

'Why have you chosen her?' argued Tina indignantly. 'She's only been here two minutes!'

Ann released a weary sigh and continued, 'Anyone who is not on stage can join us in the casino to have their photo taken – no one needs to feel left out.'

A chair went flying as Tina stormed out of the dressing room with Donna in hot pursuit.

Eva sat in astonishment at Tina's dramatic outburst while the other dancers sat and stared at her. She knew Ann had unwittingly made her a target of jealousy. She turned to look at Roxanne who seemed the friendliest when she was introduced to the girls.

'Roxanne,' said Eva, making her way over.

'Call me Roxy. Only Ann and my mother call me Roxanne.'

'Wow, your tattoo is amazing.' Eva gasped in admiration at the large black and grey dragon tattoo covering her back.

'Thanks. It hurt like fuck!'

Eva was a little surprised by her crudeness. She had – naively – expected the dancers at the Unicorn to be more eloquent, but it seemed they were normal girls just like her. Although, she had to admit, they were all more attractive than the girls at the Rodeo.

'Er...is Tina always like this?'

'You'll get used to tedious Tina and her sidekick – or learn to ignore them.'

'She didn't look happy when I walked in, so she's really going to hate me now I've been chosen for the press photos!'

'She thinks she has movie star qualities but apparently couldn't get past the director's casting couch. I wasted ten minutes of my life once hearing about her being offered the chance to become a Hollywood Playboy Bunny.'

'Did she?'

'Did she fuck!' scoffed Roxanne. 'The only time that woman has ever worn a cottontail was in a school pantomime.'

Roxanne's dry wit made Eva laugh. She was blunt and her sense of humour stung like a slap in the face, but she liked her slightly brusque manner.

Roxanne beckoned Eva closer while lowering her voice. 'The silly mare is in love with the boss, I reckon,' she said with a smirk. 'I know he's not screwing her, but she has given him a BJ!'

'Really?' said Eva.

'Well,' whispered Roxanne, lifting a strand of hair away from Eva's ear, 'it was caught on the club's security camera!'

'Oh my God!'

'Shhhh, keep your voice down,' warned Roxanne, glancing up to see if there were any eavesdroppers. 'Tommy was checking one of the security tapes but had to take a call, so I carried on checking through.'

'Yeah,' whispered Eva, licking her lips at the delicious gossip.

'Let's just say, her hand technique was lacking because he had to finish what she'd started,' she said with a chuckle.

'Is that why Tina stomped out? Does she think O'Neill has chosen me over her?'

'I guess so. It'll be interesting to see her sulk around him tomorrow. It's worth a laugh if nothing else.' Roxanne gave a wicked smile.

Their gossip-filled giggles were short-lived when Tina came bounding back in. 'Well, I'm going to talk to Connor tomorrow!' she bellowed sulkily, flashing a seething look over at Eva and Roxanne.

'See you later, Roxy.' Eva walked back to her table and purposely blanked Tina's death stares. Tina took great delight in whispering indiscreetly every time Eva walked past her for the rest of the evening.

Chapter 4

'Shit! Am I late?' gasped Eva walking into the dressing room.

'Don't panic, Tommy and I came in early. He wanted to make sure everything was on schedule upstairs,' explained Roxanne, sitting in a short black cocktail dress.

Eva draped her collection of dresses in suit carriers over the back of her chair.

'Blimey, have you brought your entire wardrobe?' Roxanne teased.

Running her fingers through her short fringe, Eva sighed. 'I'm not sure any of them are suitable.'

She quickly changed into a purple maxi dress and turned to look at Roxanne. 'No...?' said Eva, reading Roxanne's frown.

'It's nice, but too casual,' replied Roxanne, crinkling her nose.

Eva unzipped the second bag, pulled out her pillow-box-red diamanté dress and stood rigid like a shop mannequin.

'Is it a bit over the top, hun?'

'Over the top?' repeated Eva, looking down at the clingy fabric. 'Well, I only have one more dress to try on. It's either that or go naked!' she said flippantly.

Eva changed into a blue-fringed dress. 'What do you think?' pleaded Eva.

'Hmmm... Turn around.' Roxanne looked deep in thought. 'Sorry, but it's a bit lampshade-ish, don't you think?'

'You think I look like a lampshade?'

'The fringe at the bottom looks naff.'

'Naff!' spluttered Eva. 'This is from Zara and cost me sixty-five quid!'

'Maybe we can cut the fringe off?' added Roxanne, trying to find a solution.

'*I am not cutting it up!*' Eva cried out.

'Okay, sorry, just trying to help.' Roxanne held up her hands in defeat before turning away.

'Sorry...' said Eva sheepishly. 'But what the hell am I going to wear?'

'Look, I've brought another dress with me as I couldn't decide what to wear either,' said Roxanne, turning around and offering Eva a sympathetic smile.

'You're a size eight, Roxy!' scoffed Eva, resting her hands on her curvy hips.

'It's a black tube dress that stretches. You could fit me *and you* in it,' reassured Roxanne before suddenly realising what she'd just said. 'I didn't mean it like that. You have the perfect hourglass figure, Eva. Women pay to have a body like yours,' she said, aiming to soothe.

With her spirits elevated, Eva tried on the dress. 'Is it a bit clingy?'

'No, you look fit,' said Roxanne approvingly. Slipping into her five-inch silver stilettos, Eva checked her appearance in the mirror before spinning around when the dressing room door flew open.

'Bloody hell, Tina, you'll have the door off its bloody hinges!' barked Roxanne.

'Evening to you as well,' Tina fired back, closely shadowed by Donna holding a milkshake.

Within twenty minutes the dressing room was heaving with semi-naked women engrossed in mindless chatter.

'Well, don't you both look nice,' praised Ann, walking out from her office in a tailored two-piece suit.

'Thank you.' Eva smiled. 'I was a little worried about showing too much cleavage,' she added, tugging at the low neckline.

'Ann?' Tina interrupted rudely. 'I need to speak to Connor?'

Ann turned to look at her. 'What do you need to see him about?'

'It's private. Can you let him know I'll be up in about five minutes?'

Ann watched Tina flounce out of the dressing room like a petulant teenager.

'Ladies, be ready by seven thirty, then make your way up to the casino,' said Ann curtly walking back to her office.

Noticing the length of time Tina was gone, Eva wondered if she had persuaded Connor to let her take her place. By what means of persuasion – she had a fair idea.

Eva glanced up at the clock again after checking her figure for the umpteenth time. It was just approaching ten past seven when Tina came waltzing through the dressing room door with a large, smug smirk.

'Is Ann in her office?' Tina said with a triumphant, devious smile. Eva could almost hear her crowing as she strutted past.

'What the fuck is up with Silly Knickers now?' snapped Roxanne, throwing her hairbrush onto her table and knocking over a large can of hairspray.

'I think Mr O'Neill has been talked round,' said Eva, stepping out of her high stilettos.

'You can leave them on because there's going to be trouble if she has,' fumed Roxanne, getting to her feet.

Within seconds Tina came swaggering out of Ann's office flicking her long honey-blonde extensions over her shoulder.

'Oh, *Eva*,' she purred. 'You can take your dress back to the charity shop. Connor said I can take your place.'

Eva stood up trying to think of a suitable retaliation. 'W-what did you just say?!'

'Are you deaf as well as fat?' snarled Tina.

'Oh, you pathetic cow!' bellowed Roxanne.

'And who the hell are you calling fat?! You emaciated bimbo!' yelled Eva.

'ENOUGH!' shouted Ann, striding out of her office on hearing the commotion.

The room suddenly became silent.

'Tina. Eva. My office now!' snapped Ann.

With neither woman taking the first step, Eva returned Tina's trance-like stare.

'If either of you think you're going to cause trouble, tonight of all nights, then you're both very much mistaken. My office now, BOTH OF YOU!'

Both women stood rooted to the spot, refusing to be the first to move, like a shoot-out in a cowboy movie.

'You have two choices, ladies,' warned Ann, 'follow me, or go home and wait for your P45.'

Eva stood with her hands clenched down by her side and anger permeating her powdered cheeks.

'Time is ticking, ladies. Roxanne can go upstairs. I'll be up shortly,' said Ann.

'But—' Roxanne started, pointing at Tina standing with her arms folded and lips pinched.

'No "buts", Roxanne. GO!'

Roxanne glared at Tina, then turned on her heels and stormed out of the dressing room.

Tina and Eva stood like reprimanded schoolchildren in front on Ann in her office.

'I don't see why I've been called in. Connor said I could replace her tonight. If she has a problem with that, then tough!' wailed Tina.

'Er…excuse me,' Eva roared back, 'you're the one with the problem!'

'I don't think so, you—'

'Enough!' yelled Ann. 'I've just spoken to Mr O'Neill, and his version of events don't tie in with yours, Tina.'

Tina blinked away tears of frustration realising Ann was no fool and had checked out her story with Connor.

'Yeah, well…he said I can be in the photos too! You can't seriously choose her over me? She looks dreadful in that cheap bin bag thing she's wearing. Connor wants classy!' screeched Tina, her face contorted with fury.

'That's why you haven't been asked!' yelled Eva. 'Plus, I don't appreciated being called fat!'

'That's enough from both of you. I'm going to make this crystal clear so everyone understands what's happening tonight. *Eva* will walk the floor with Roxanne.'

'But—'

Ann made a 'talk to the hand because the face ain't listening' gesture to Tina.

'I've been here four years. It's not fair!' protested Tina, stamping her feet.

'Well, life isn't, my dear,' patronised Ann.

With that, Tina thundered out of Ann's office, slamming the door behind her.

'You can make your way up to the casino now, Eva,' Ann said brusquely.

Eva followed her orders and walked upstairs still shaking.

'What did Ann say?' quizzed Roxanne as she stood outside the casino double doors.

'Just that she'd spoken to O'Neill and Tina had lied through her teeth.' Eva grimaced. 'I just hope she stays out of my way tonight – otherwise, I'll wipe that spiteful pout off her inflated lips!'

The casino was already heaving and noisy with jaunty chatter. A large group of suited men were gathered in a semicircle around a marble unicorn while sporadic camera flashes lit up the room like a firework display. A rather stout, unattractive man stood scribbling in a little notebook, occasionally glancing across the room towards the buffet table.

Feeling slightly claustrophobic, Eva followed Roxanne to the bar. 'You okay, babes?' soothed Roxanne.

'Yeah. Tina said I look like I'm wearing a bin bag!'

'Cheeky bitch!' cursed Roxanne. 'I got that from H&M – it cost over forty quid.'

'I need a large vodka!' announced Eva. 'And quick!'

'All right, gorgeous?' Darren the barman winked at them. 'What can I get you sexy ladies?'

'A double vodka and lemonade, and a rum and coke?' said Roxanne. Turning her back to the bar, she looked over at Tommy who was gesturing for them to join the group.

'Here you go, ladies.' Darren placed their drinks on the brass countertop.

'Where's Connor?' asked Eva, quickly taking a large gulp of her drink.

Roxanne pointed to the reporter. 'Standing next to that fat bloke.'

Eva took another large mouthful and held the cold glass tightly in her hand as she followed Roxanne back through the crowd towards the perimeter of the group.

'So what's your next venture? World domination?' joked the stocky reporter, propelling his question into the centre of the group. 'Is there another project in the pipeline, another club, Connor?'

'Actually, there are plans to open another club in Birmingham and don't worry Garry, I'll lay on another free buffet just for you,' replied Connor dryly in a smooth southern Irish lilt.

The witty reply caused a ripple of laughter amongst the men, with the stocky reporter not taking offence at his comment.

Eva wasn't listening to the banter being thrown around like a beach ball. She was too busy guzzling down her drink.

'Roxy,' called out Tommy, beckoning her again to join him in the inner circle.

'Come on, Miss Bin Bag…' said Roxanne looking to her side. 'Eva? Where the hell have you gone?' Roxanne stood on her tiptoes and followed Eva back to the bar. 'What are you doing?'

'Just getting another drink. It's so hot in here…' She huffed, fanning her face with a drink coaster. 'I'm dreading Tina joining the party in case she's hell-bent on continuing her "I hate Eva" campaign in front of everyone,' she added in a hushed tone.

'She wouldn't dare, O'Neill would sack her bony ass on the spot. He hates all that "screaming banshee" stuff, so chill-lax.'

Eva felt the strong vodka sting the back of her throat, and then grunted in agreement as they made their way back to the group.

'Hey, babe,' Roxanne said smiling. She raised her chin so Tommy's lips could reach her mouth.

Eva looked up at Tommy and scrutinised his appearance. He looked even more unattractive under the shimmering light radiating from the crystal chandelier. Standing by his side stood a suited man with his back to them. The material of his black dinner suit looked expensive and perfectly tailored to fit his broad square shoulders and slim waist. Eva couldn't avert her gaze from the man's bottom. There was a masculine scent of warm sandalwood and hints of musk and vanilla mingled with a spicy undertone. It wasn't the first time she had smelt such an aromatic scent. She went to take a swig of her drink but realised she had already finished it when a piece of ice clinked against her teeth.

'Connor,' said Roxanne, gently tapping the smartly dressed man's shoulder.

'What?' He turned around to Roxanne briefly before looking directly at Eva.

Feeling her eyes locked into his stare through a vodka haze, Eva had forgotten how handsome he was. His mesmerising steel-blue eyes, framed by ink-black lashes, complimented his smooth sun-kissed skin. Her mind stole a photograph of his face before he turned away. Capturing his chiselled cheekbones and well-shaped mouth – he was exquisite to look at. He spoke clearly and articulately. His passionate laugh penetrated the air with confidence, engaging everyone in his company. She guessed his age at late thirties. Her prediction was purely based on the fine lines around his eyes and his black hair with slight speckles of grey gathering at the temples. He was what every fairy tale required: a tall, dark, dashing prince. But knowing he was a womaniser blemished his Hollywood looks. She couldn't let herself feel attracted to such a man.

'Excuse me, please! Can I get past?!'

Eva's anger resurfaced watching Tina push her way to the front of the group and unashamedly drape herself around Connor's arm like a cloak.

'I haven't missed the photos, have I?' quizzed Tina with childlike excitement.

Eva turned away, unable to watch Tina's desperate attention seeking, and tapped her fingernails against her empty glass. She looked longingly at the bar and seized the chance to slip away from the group to replenish her drink.

'There you are!' growled Roxanne, grabbing Eva by the arm. 'I hope you're not pissed!'

'I'm f-fine,' slurred Eva, talking another large mouthful of vodka.

'Look – I know Tina is as irritating as a bout of thrush, but is she worth losing your job over?' Roxanne took the half-empty glass out of her hand.

'I-I'm fine.' Eva tutted. 'But can I pinch a cigarette?'

'I didn't know you smoked?' Roxanne frowned, not impressed with the state Eva was getting herself into.

'I just fancy one, that's all. Oh, go on…*pleasssee.*'

'Perhaps the fresh air'll sober you up,' grumbled Roxanne scratching the back of her head. 'Come on then, hurry up! The photographer will want to start soon, and Connor will get the right arse if we keep him waiting.'

They stepped out into the small courtyard at the back of the club. Eva closed her eyes and lifted her face to feel the warm rays of the evening sun against her skin.

Roxanne reached for the hem of her dress and slipped her hand up her thigh to reach a concealed packet of cigarettes nesting in the top of her black stocking.

'Where do you keep your lighter?' Eva asked, giggling and swaying slightly.

'Here,' said Roxanne, offering her a cigarette. 'You'd better sober up, and quickly. No more alcohol. Just stick to soft drinks from now on,' she ordered.

'Honestly, Roxy – I'm not d-drunk.' A grinning Eva placed the brown cigarette filter between her lips.

'Yeah, and George Clooney is one of my regulars!'

'He's bloody gorgeous him,' said Eva, producing an unattractive grunt as she inhaled the bitter tobacco before coughing out a plume of smoke.

Roxanne shook her head and raised her eyebrows in dismay.

'So, come on then, spill the Heinz. Has Tina been bad-mouthing me to O'Neill?' probed Eva.

'No, she's on her best behaviour – unlike you, may I add. Mind you, her tongue is so far up his backside, I'm sure she can taste what he had for dinner last night!' cackled Roxanne, stubbing out her cigarette.

'That's where she's going wrong.' Eva laughed and made a suggestive bulge in her cheek. 'She's licking the wrong side!'

'Oi!' growled Roxanne. 'For fuck's sakes, don't blab that out. I told you in confidence! Anyway, come on, we need to get back.'

Eva discarded her half-smoked cigarette on the black tarmac and trudged behind Roxanne back into the club. Once in the casino they quickly made their way towards the photographer.

'Right, hush, please. If I could have the young lady with the long black hair.'

'Me?' asked Roxanne, pointing to herself.

'Yes, you darling. If you could stand to the right of Mr O'Neill. Then we'll have…'

Before he could finish, Tina quickly linked arms with Connor posing with her tanned leg showing through the revealing high split in her dress.

'Wait a minute, Norman,' said Connor, unlinking his arm. 'Red…get in the photo,' he said abruptly.

Looking to her side, then glancing behind her, Eva looked away in puzzlement.

Connor flashed a look of annoyance towards Ann.

'Quick, Eva – join Mr O'Neill!' demanded Ann, practically shooing her over towards him.

'Here,' directed Connor, nodding to where Tina stood open-mouthed in disbelief.

Eva did as she was told.

'Take the photo,' instructed Connor, placing his hand onto Eva's waist.

Mirroring Tina's gasp, Donna watched her friend raise her chin in the air while her bottom lip quivered with betrayal. Tina marched away from the group and out of the casino.

Roxanne's sniggering luckily went unnoticed when Donna ran after Tina sobbing loudly in the casino lobby.

Eva stared ahead feeling her whole body stiffen under Connor's grip. The heady aroma of his aftershave washed over her like a sea mist. The warmth of his body against hers made the tiny hairs on the nape of her neck stand to attention.

'If we could just move in a little?' asked the photographer.

Eva yielded to Connor's side as he pulled her in further.

'Lovely, maybe one by the roulette table as well?' suggested the photographer, reaching into his bag for another lens.

Connor removed his hand from Eva's waist and nodded as the group slowly made their way across the room.

Roxanne nudged Eva. 'Did you see her face?' she scoffed. 'Now that's what I call a picture!'

'I'm not impressed with being called "Red",' snorted Eva.

'Don't read anything in it,' assured Roxanne, thinking she was being a bit sensitive.

'Roxanne, Mr O'Neill wants you and Donna in the next photo. So chop-chop. Mr Connor's in a rush to get the photos done,' Ann ordered briskly.

Eva watched the photographer click away until her gaze wandered over towards the overweight reporter lingering near the buffet table.

'Thank you, ladies and gentlemen.' The photographer smiled in Connor's direction.

The group quickly dispersed towards the banquet of food.

'You've got to try the crab cakes with the lime and chilli mayo,' insisted Roxanne, her cheeks bulging with food. 'Oh, don't look now, but I think the entertainment is just about to start,' she added, cramming in another crab cake.

Eva stood on tiptoes peering over to a group of men but spotted Tina standing next to the boss with tear-stained cheeks. Connor's body language confirmed his annoyance as he rudely turned his back to her.

'No blow job for him tonight,' scoffed Eva, shoving a cheese cube in her mouth.

Roxanne pointed towards an untouched prawn and sweetcorn fritter on Eva's plate. 'You eating that?'

'Nah.' Eva exhaled, puffing out her cheeks. 'Oh God, don't look now!' she whispered.

'Eh?' mumbled Roxanne, trying to dislodge a piece of sweetcorn from her teeth.

'Oh shit! He's coming over!'

'Who is…?' asked Roxanne, rubbing the trapped piece of sweetcorn with the tip of her tongue. 'It's only O'Neill and Tommy.'

Eva stood rooted to the spot.

'Hi, babe,' said Roxanne, still picking her teeth.

'Hi.' Tommy winked and offered Roxanne a warm smile before casually glancing at Eva.

'You have something there,' said Connor looking down at Eva's chest.

'What?' Eva felt her cheeks blush. She glanced down at a blob of mint yoghurt sitting on her barely covered left boob. Quickly wiping it away with a paper napkin, embarrassment kept her gaze low, her crimson cheeks revealing mortification.

'Nice buffet, Boss,' said Roxanne, trying to lift the uncomfortable silence.

Connor acknowledged Roxanne's compliment with a small nod and returned his gaze to Eva. 'Are you enjoying the food?'

'Er, yes. It's okay… Excuse me, please,' spluttered Eva, quickly walking away from the group still holding her plate. She rushed into the ladies toilets and saw her flushed reflection in the oval vanity mirror. Her mottled cheeks and stained dress made her cringe as she tried to remove the rest of the yoghurt with a wet paper towel. Eva sighed and closed the toilet cubicle door. She was tugging up her dress when she heard someone come in.

'Why did he ask that fat cow to be in the photo?'

'Dunno, T.'

'I can't believe he did that to me, how could he do that to ME?'

Holding her breath, Eva listened to Tina and Donna obviously taking about her.

'Do you think he fancies her?' wailed Tina petulantly.

'What, over you? No way. Have you seen the size of her arse? It's massive! I reckon he's just in a bad mood. You know he blows hot and cold. I bet he asks to see you tonight,' reassured Donna

'He hasn't seen me in months. I really thought the last time we were, you know, actually going to do it, but no. I think he's lost interest.'

Feeling a twitch in her nose, Eva quickly pinched her nostrils to muffle a sneeze.

'Remember his last girlfriend? She was fat, too,' added Tina.

'Well, you're a size zero and fabulous. It's clear he fancies you – not *Fatty Arbuckle* out there,' scoffed Donna, earning herself a chuckle of agreement from Tina.

Hearing this stunned Eva into a silent rage; she repeated the words under her breath, 'Fatty Arbuckle!'

'She's no threat to you, babes,' proclaimed Donna. 'He would never be interested in a ginger-haired fatty whose backside could eclipse the sun!'

'I know, but Connor must've thought her pretty to hire her,' sobbed Tina, blowing her nose loudly.

'Look, just go back in there and be your amazing self. He won't give Fat Tits a second look, come on.'

As their voices faded, her fury quickly manifested into thoughts of revenge. Eva pulled down her dress, unlocked the door and sauntered back into the casino. Noticing the savoury buffet had been cleared away and replaced with an array of mouth-watering deserts, she quickly made her way over.

Roxanne sighed in an almost orgasmic-state of enjoyment pushing a forkful of soft lemon sponge and blackberry buttercream into her mouth. 'Hmmm, this is so good.'

'Oh, should I have any?' Eva hesitated to salivate over the large vanilla cheesecake sitting under a bed of fresh plump strawberries.

'I hope you haven't taken to heart what Tina said about you – you're not fat,' reassured Roxanne, shoehorning another large forkful of cake into her mouth. 'You need to be happy in your own skin, babes.'

'Yeah, you're right – sod it.' Eva nodded while cutting herself a large slice of cheesecake.

'Someone's got a sweet tooth.'

Hearing Connor's voice made Eva drop the cake knife onto the table. She waited for him to bait her about a lack of self-control. But, before she could think of a witty comeback, she smelt a waft of pungent perfume and instantly identified the wearer.

'Wow, are you eating for two!' Tina giggled, trying to mask her intentionally cruel remark.

Inhaling deeply, Eva knew she could let Connor and Tina jab her with words of spite; or, she could unleash her quick temper and volleyball insults back to them.

'Well, we can't all be pencil thin and have the body of an under-developed ten-year-old, can we?' she said, releasing her temper.

Roxanne grunted like a pig sniffing for truffles. 'God it's only a bit of cake, leave her alone!'

'An under-developed wha—'

Before Tina could reload, Connor picked up Eva's fork and pushed it through the layer of strawberries and down into the soft biscuit base. Everyone watched in astonishment as he lifted the fork to his mouth.

'You don't eat sugar and cakes,' Tina wailed sulkily.

Ignoring her childish pout, Connor stared down deliberately at Eva and directed his answer solely to her, 'I can resist everything but temptation.'

'So, that would make you flawed like the rest of us,' said Eva, smirking.

'Of course. Life without temptation would be…insipid and tasteless. So if that means I have moments of weakness, then, yes, I'm flawed like everyone else,' replied Connor with confidence.

'But don't you find,' added Eva, 'temptation can be like a disloyal friend. It can persuade and coerce you, but in the end when the desire has lost its taste, it abandons you like a heartless lover,' she said, almost poetically.

Little did Eva know that Connor felt sexually aroused by her annotations. It was a game of chess played with words, with the final move being 'checkmate'.

'I think we should mingle a little, Connor. Your guests must be feeling neglected,' complained Tina, reaching down to touch his hand.

Pulling his hand away, he glanced down at the rounded contour of Eva's breasts before looking back up at her glossy red lips. He narrowed his eyes and a closed smirk spread across his face. He walked away without saying another word, but not before glancing back at Eva one more time.

'Be careful there,' advised Roxanne, watching Connor disappear into the crowd.

'Why?' said Eva, proud of expressing herself so articulately while under Tina's contemptuous frown.

'I think you've intrigued someone's interest – just be careful. He can be charming when he wants something, or rather someone, then boom, he loses interest, just like that,' warned Roxanne, clicking her fingers together.

'You are joking.' Eva laughed and widened her eyes in shock. 'I'm not interested in having my name put on his conquest list!' she proclaimed, wrinkling her nose.

I've known him for four years, and in all that time I've never known him to have a monogamous relationship with anyone. I don't think there's a woman who can hold his interest for longer than a couple of months.'

'Oh, a womaniser.' Eva sniffed, wrinkling her nose.

'I guess the "playboy" label suits him well. He's got millions in the bank. He's good-looking. He enjoys the company of *uncomplicated* women,' scoffed Roxanne.

'Men like that don't fall in love,' Eva commented.

'Sounds like you've met a few *O'Neills* in your time, then?'

Eva's silence confirmed what Roxanne was thinking. It was true – she had met no other type of man.

'Hey, it's your night off tomorrow as well, isn't it? If you're not doing anything, we could go clubbing at the Funky Buddha and try to get our drinks paid for all night!' said Roxanne.

'Count me in, I'm up for that!' said Eva.

Connor didn't speak to her again for the rest of the evening, but his words lingered in her mind during the taxi ride home that night. Their brief but intense conversation would not abate until she drifted into a restless sleep.

Chapter 5

'Where are you, Rox?' Eva frowned, clutching her mobile to her ear.
'I'm just round the corner. Are you there yet?'
'I've just got here. You wanna see the queue – we're gonna have to wait at least an hour to get in!'
'Don't worry. I'll be there in two ticks.'

Eva dropped the mobile into her clutch bag and tutted as she sidestepped out of the queue to look at the long line of people waiting to get into the club. There was no way she was going to wait an hour to get into a bloody nightclub.

'Hi – I wonder if you'd like to join me and my friends, were nearly at the front of the queue?'

She glanced up and smiled flirtatiously at the good-looking man dressed in dark grey trousers and a white open-necked shirt.

'Well, I'm just waiting for my friend, she won't—'

'Sorry I'm late. My poxy hair dryer decided to overheat!' ranted Roxanne, using her hand as a fan.

'Roxanne,' Eva said turning to look at her and smiling, 'this gentleman said we could join him and his friends at the front of the queue.'

'We're fine thanks,' said Roxanne, dismissing the man rudely by turning her back on him.

'Why did you say that? We could've used him to us get in, then ditched him,' moaned Eva.

'I've got something to tell you, so please don't be mad. I swear I didn't ask them to come.'

'What are you going on about? Who—'

'Evening, ladies…'

Roxanne bit the inside of her cheek and averted her eyes as Eva stood open-mouthed in shock.

'You look amazing, Miss Summers.' Connor grinned and let his gaze travel down the full length of her body.

'What are you doing here?'

'Well, that's a nice welcome, isn't it, Tom? Anyway, why are we standing at the back of the queue?' asked Connor impatiently, reaching for his mobile in his trouser pocket.

'You see the line of people in front of you?' said Eva, raising her eyebrows mockingly, 'it's known as a "queue". We're all waiting our turn to get into the club.'

'Don't they say sarcasm is the lowest form of wit?' baited Connor, pressing his mobile to his ear.

'Yes, I believe dull people are fond of saying that,' responded Eva, flashing Roxanne a look of annoyance.

'Yeah, just outside,' said Connor talking on his phone. 'Right, let's make a move.' He left the queue and walked straight past the line of people towards three smartly dressed bouncers standing at the main entrance.

'I swear I didn't know they were coming,' pleaded Roxanne, offering Eva a half-smoked cigarette. 'I was just leaving when Tommy said Connor fancied a night out, too. I couldn't say that they shouldn't join us because his best mate, and let's not forget *our boss*, is getting his dick sucked by your nemesis, could I?'

Eva inhaled deeply on the cigarette and blew out a long line of smoke. 'Just tell me one thing?'

'What?'

'Are we to expect "suck the Thames dry" Tina as well?'

'No fucking way – it's just us four,' promised Roxanne.

Eva sighed heavily and nodded before dropping the cigarette butt on the floor. 'Well, I guess we have no choice now they're here.'

Linking arms, Roxanne pulled Eva closer and whispered excitedly, 'Silver lining situation – at least we won't have to buy any drinks tonight.'

That may be true, but Eva would have preferred to buy her own drinks and not have the company of her boss all night.

'Mr Knowles is waiting in the VIP area for you, Mr O'Neill,' said the tallest of the three bouncers unclipping a dark burgundy security rope to let them walk straight through.

'What's going on, Roxy?' whispered Eva.

'Looks like Connor just got us VIP access,' said Roxanne with glee.

'Oh…' Eva felt slightly awkward when a group of young men voiced their annoyance on seeing them queue jump. 'So who is this Mr Knowles?' she probed as they followed Connor and Tommy into the dance lounge. 'The owner?'

'Yeah, all the club bosses know each other. Knowles sometimes comes to the Unicorn.'

'Connor, great to see you again,' said a short, bald man getting to his feet.

'Derek, how's tricks?' Connor smiled shaking his hand firmly.

'Great! Please sit.' Derek smiled at a young waitress bringing over a large bottle of champagne and six glasses on a tray.

'You remember Lisa, don't you?' Derek introduced the slender blonde woman half his age sat next to him.

Eva looked at the stereotypical blonde bimbo wearing a low-cut dress and giggling as though hooked up to a bottle of helium. Her dark tanned skin reminded her of a Peperami stick. Mean of her to think it – but she did look she'd been dipped in a vat of creosote.

'What's wrong with her mouth?' whispered Eva.

'Too much lip filler.' Roxanne sniggered thinking how the woman's mouth bore an uncanny resemblance to a pair of horse's lips that had been attacked by a swarm of wasps.

'You remember Tom, and this is Roxanne his partner, one of my best dancers,' explained Connor, looking over at Roxanne who smiled graciously on hearing such a compliment.

'Lovely to meet you. I think I've had the pleasure of seeing you dance, if my memory serves me correctly,' said Derek grinning and offering his hand.

'And this is Eva Summers – she used to work at the Rodeo,' added Connor.

Eva glared up at him. *Why did he have to mention that?* His comment seemed to warrant some sort of sympathy from his unattractive friend who raised his eyebrows in a look of pity.

Eva forced a smile. 'Hi.'

Staring out beyond the VIP area, Eva sat and gulped down a glass of champagne while Connor dominated the conversation. His voice grated on her as she sat pondering her introduction to his friend.

'I'm going to the loo,' said Eva in a huff, getting to her feet.

'I'll come too, wait for me,' said Roxanne quickly following her out of the VIP area.

'Why did he have to tell the Oompa Loompa Twins that I worked at the Rodeo? And did you see the look he gave me, like he was judging me,' she roared, slamming the toilet door behind her.

'I don't think Connor said it purposely to hurt your feelings,' reasoned Roxanne.

'Why else would he have said it, then?'

'I don't know. Men don't think, do they?'

With the sound of the toilet flushing, Eva unlocked the door. 'I'm so pissed off. He's ruined the night for me now,' she moaned. 'I might go home. I can't even bear to look at him for a second longer.'

'Oh, please don't – look, we can sit somewhere else, we don't have to sit with them, we can still have our girly night,' pleaded Roxanne.

Eva stood and thought for a second as other women jostled past her to use the loos. '*I guess* we can sit somewhere else, then.'

'Okay. You find us a seat and I'll nip back and grab my bag.'

'Hmm – okay,' murmured Eva, pursing her lips.

Eva found a couple of empty seats and wondered what was keeping Roxanne. She wanted to go to the bar but didn't want to lose their seats by getting up.

'Can I have word?'

'Jesus…' spluttered Eva, raising her hand to her chest as Connor suddenly appeared from nowhere. She averted her gaze towards the heaving dance floor and remained indifferent as Connor sat down uninvited. Sighing with frustration, she quickly shuffled her bottom across the seat as his thigh brushed against her leg. She could smell his cologne and minted breath when he leaned over towards her.

'Why have I offended you by telling the truth?' he asked, raising his voice over the din of the music.

Eva crossed her legs and ground her teeth together; anger bubbled in the pit of her stomach. 'Won't Hugh Hefner and his playmate be wondering where you are?' she fired back, fidgeting to pull down the hem of her short dress.

'*What?*' asked Connor. 'Let's go somewhere more private. I can't hear what you're saying.'

He wrapped his hand around her slender wrist. She felt his strong arms effortlessly pull her up and lead her out of the noisy dance lounge.

'Can you let go of my wrist, please!' she commanded.

'In a minute,' said Connor. He led her towards a flight of stairs where she saw two smartly dressed bouncers nod to Connor and wink.

He walked her into a plush office and released her wrist before closing the door behind them.

'Roxanne says I've upset you? I don't understand why – you did work at the Rodeo?'

She stared at him defiantly with arms folded.

'So?' Connor glanced at the neckline of her dress.

Unfolding her arms, Eva reached into her handbag and took out her cigarettes.

Connor stepped back and frowned as a ball of smoke drifted up towards his face. 'You're not allowed to smoke in here.' He took the cigarette from her fingers and stubbed it out in an empty glass sitting on a large desk.

Eva pursed her lips together in annoyance.

'I didn't say it to imply—'

'Imply what? That I worked in a club where sex is offered with every bottle of champagne. Implying, that by working in such a club, I might have offered my body for money?'

'What?' Connor looked perplexed. 'Are you accusing me of calling you a prostitute?' he retaliated forcefully. 'I wasn't suggesting—'

'Actually, I don't have a problem with women who do,' interrupted Eva. 'It's not up to me judge anyone, but what I don't understand is why you couldn't have introduced me as one of your dancers. I may not be your *best* dancer, but—'

'You're as good as Roxanne.'

'So, doesn't that make your comment even more derogatory?' fired back Eva without fear.

Connor ran his hand through his short, thick black hair at a loss for words.

'Why are you even here tonight? This was supposed to be a girls' night out, or was my embarrassment pre-planned to amuse you?'

'Are you always like this?' he said eventually.

'Like what?!' bellowed Eva.

'A screaming banshee!' He threw his hand up in the air dismissing her outspokenness as merely a childish tantrum.

'A *screaming banshee!*' she repeated, raising her eyebrows. 'And what are you…eh?' she snorted childishly while looking him up and down. 'An arrogant, self-opinionated, lothario!'

'I think you've said enough,' growled Connor, his eyes darkened with rage. 'No one, but, NO ONE talks to me like that. Take my advice, and take it very seriously, I don't want some *prima donna* stirring tension within my club. I can fire you as quickly as I hired you, so be very careful what you say next. I suggest you keep your head down and your nose out of my business – have I made myself clear?'

Eva's eyes pricked with tears and her whole body trembled with resentment. 'Yes,' she said, understanding the severity in his voice and blinking back tears.

Her mobile suddenly rang out as she left the plush office. It was Roxanne cheeking where she was. Apparently Connor had stormed back to the VIP area with a scathing grimace across his face broadcasting his sudden change of mood.

'I'm so sorry, Eva,' grovelled Roxanne, quickly joining her in the club foyer. 'He just asked where you were and before I could warn you, he just got up and went to find you. What did he say?'

'I think he's just given me a verbal warning.'

'Oh, shit,' said Roxanne, worried for her friend. 'Look, let's go back to yours – yeah?' We can talk there in private.'

* * *

'It must be handy having an off-licence just round the corner – two decent bottles of wine for just under a tenner,' announced Roxanne, looking at Eva slouched in the back of the cab. 'Look, don't worry, Grumpy Balls will soon simmer down. He's just throwing his toys out of the pram. You challenged his ego, that's all. Remember he's not used to a loud…er, I mean, strong woman. He likes his women to "toe the line". Look at Tina, she doesn't question his conscience. He's like most men,' she added, raising her voice so the Indian taxi driver could hear, 'they can't deal with a woman's emotional issues. That's why they bark so aggressively. Their brains haven't evolved like ours.'

'He's not even a bloody Neanderthal! He's still a fucking ape!' sneered Eva.

'All men, apart from my Tommy,' said Roxanne.

The young taxi driver glanced through his rearview mirror as they pulled into Eva's road.

'You grab the wine, and I'll pay the fare,' said Eva, sighing and fishing in her purse for a twenty-pound note.

'So, this is the famous Mr Jingles, then?' Roxanne beamed at Eva's cat dashing over after they walked through the front door.

Taking two large wine glasses out of her cupboard, Eva turned around and smiled at Roxanne who stood fussing Mr Jingles as he sat purring on the kitchen worktop.

'I need a cigarette.' Eva opened her kitchen door whilst holding a bottle of wine. 'Can you bring the glasses, Roxy? We'll sit outside.'

They sat under a large cream garden parasol on Eva's small patio as the humid air sat heavy on their skin.

Roxanne shook her head and declared, 'What a bloody night! Don't worry about your verbal warning; Connor was just in a bad mood.'

'Hmmm,' replied Eva, chain-smoking in between frequents gulps of cold white wine. 'I've found there are two types of men,' confessed Roxanne.

'Yeah?'

'You know the scenario – little wifey at home with the kids, oblivious that hubby is bankrolling his little tart in a swish apartment in Mayfair.'

'And the second?' asked Eva.

'Then there's your "average Joe", hard-working but dull as dish water. He thinks spoiling the wife means a bunch of half-dead weeds from the local petrol station and a two-minute fumble on a Saturday night.'

'What a choice – a cheat or a bore! Which is Tommy?'

'He's the exception to the rule,' crowed Roxanne. 'There are a few men out there who are, but not many.'

'Well, you're lucky,' moaned Eva. 'I'd like to find a "Mr Exception to the rule"!'

'So, are you saying our boss is rotten to the core, then?'

'I didn't say he's rotten,' explained Roxanne, taking another large swig of wine.

'Oh, but—'

'I'm just saying he's a walking hormone.'

'But Ann thinks a lot of him, though?'

'Oh, yeah. Well, Ann's grandson, Charley, was diagnosed with a rare form of leukaemia, and Connor paid for his treatment in America.'

'Oh right.' Eva was surprised to learn about his softer side. 'So, what do you know about his past?'

'Actually, I don't know that much before he met Tommy,' confessed Roxanne, flicking a long line of ash onto the ground. But Tommy did mention once that he was engaged before he came over to England. Apparently the date was set and everything.'

'Huh, engaged,' scoffed Eva, finding such a revelation hard to believe.

'No, it's true,' stated Roxanne.

'So, what happened?'

'She cheated on him, I think.'

'He probably drove her to it, I shouldn't wonder, with his *high and mighty* attitude.'

'I dunno,' answered Roxanne, shrugging her shoulders.

'So how did Connor and Tommy meet?'

'They've been good friends for over twenty years – like brothers, really. Tommy knows everything about O'Neill, but he would never betray his trust.'

'But do you know how Connor made his millions?' probed Eva, refilling Roxanne's glass, hoping the alcohol would loosen her tongue.

'Connor was, and still is, the most skilled poker player I've ever seen,' proclaimed Roxanne, taking a large gulp of wine.

'Really?' said Eva, stubbing out her cigarette and relighting another one.

'Yeah, of course he never played for pennies. He made his money betting thousands in unregulated illegal games. It's no secret. He needed protection, and that's where my Tommy came into the equation.'

Listening eagerly, Eva leaned forward as Roxanne painted a picture of Connor's life.

'Connor is a shrewd businessman. He invested in property and owned his own construction company before buying the Unicorn. He's a jammy bastard. He sold everything before the market crashed and walked away with millions, I reckon.'

Eva slumped back in her chair. Booth had often ranted that O'Neill had more skeletons in his past than a pauper's grave. So, being incredibly nosey, she couldn't help feeling intrigued by her present boss's past.

'Look, I'll tell you something,' slurred Roxanne, 'but if you ever rat me out, then you and me are finished for good – understood? Plus, I'm not going to go into any specific details, so don't even bothering asking!'

Eva's eyes widened with curiosity. She drew an invisible cross over her chest. 'Cross my heart, hope to die,' she whispered.

'Connor met Tommy in prison twenty-three years ago.'

'In prison!' This revelation made Eva gasp causing a swirl of smoke to billow out of her open mouth. 'What for?'

'I can't tell you that, but he did a two-year stretch.'

Narrowing her eyes, Eva pondered for a second. 'Two-year stretch, eh? Well, it must've been something serious.'

'No. No more questions on O'Neill. I've said too much already.' Roxanne hiccupped loudly. 'Anyway, this conversation is becoming boring. Let's change the subject.'

'Oh,' said Eva, deflated, wanting to know everything. She sat back in her chair wondering what sort of man was hiding beneath the polished veneer of money and cashmere suits. So far, all the evidence was leading to a lawless man with a violent past. 'I think I've got more drink here somewhere.' Eva wobbled back into the kitchen and burped as she slumped down onto her hands and knees. 'I am s-sure I've got a bottle of brandy in h-here,' she slurred as pots and pans flew across the kitchen floor.

'Er, why do you keep brandy in your pan cupboard – are you expecting burglars?' Roxanne laughed when Eva's head disappeared inside the kitchen cabinet.

'Aha!' said Eva, holding a slightly dust-covered bottle. 'Cooking sherry!'

'God, this is a new low for me – cooking sherry!' cackled Roxanne slumped against the kitchen door.

Stumbling back outside, they both lay on the parched grass and looked up at the row of empty bottles accumulated on the garden table.

'H-how many b-bottles are there,' said Roxanne, squinting, 'because I can see f-fuckin h-hundreds,' she scoffed, spilling a mouthful of wine.

* * *

'God, you were wasted last night.' Roxanne chuckled watching Eva walk slowly into the dressing room wearing a large pair oversized sunglasses.

'I think one of those bottles of wine was off, you know, Roxy.'

'Hmmm… not convinced,' said Roxanne looking bemused. 'Could have been that half bottle of cooking sherry and that coffee liqueur you threw down your neck, though?'

'Oh, don't.' Eva tried to stifle a belch.

'Mr O'Neill is on his way down, ladies,' called out Ann from the back office.

None of the girls made an effort to cover up, apart from Eva who glanced at Tina sitting in a pair of red silk French knickers and drenching her wrists with strong perfume. Eva quickly laced up her black and gold chiffon negligée and made her way to the ladies toilets. She hoped that lingering in the loos for a few minutes meant Connor would have left by the time she returned.

After hiding for what felt like five minutes, she went back into the dressing room.

'Good, you're back, Eva,' said Ann, standing next to Connor who casually glanced down at her legs when she walked past to her dressing table.

'Now everyone is here, Mr O'Neill would like to talk to you about this year's PGCG.'

A surge of excited squeals engulfed the room as the girls clung to Ann's every word.

'For the new ladies here who don't know about the PGCG, it's a charity gala organised by some of the private gentlemen's clubs, of which Mr O'Neill is chairman,' said Ann smiling like a proud parent. 'It will be held at Claridge's in two weeks on the ninth of August.'

Roxanne had briefly mentioned this charity event to Eva. It was a night of pomp and glamour with all the money made going to a local children's hospital. Being the chairman, Connor received free tickets which he raffled off to members of staff.

'First name,' said Connor, unfolding the small piece of paper he pulled out of a moneybag Ann was holding. 'Darren Jacobs.'

A low groan rippled through the room before quickly becoming silent again as Connor plucked out the second recipient.

Eva couldn't take her eyes off Tina who was staring over at Connor willing him to call out her name.

'Rebecca Law.'

'I'll tell her when she comes in,' said Ann, knowing that the young nineteen-year-old waitress would be thrilled to go to her first gala.

Eva quickly averted her gaze down to the floor as Connor glanced over at her.

'Tina Jackson.'

A loud gasp came from the back of the dressing room as Tina sprang to her feet and rejoiced loudly.

'Hmm...' Eva sighed with boredom. *This is such a fix.*

'Fourth name is David Woodstock.'

David was one of the bouncers on the main doors. He was married with two young kids but was having an affair with Charlotte, one of the topless waitresses and more than fifteen years his junior.

'I can tell him when I go back upstairs,' said Connor, dipping his hand back into the cloth bag.

Donna sat disgruntled, but Tina didn't seem to care that her friend's name hadn't be called out.

'Last name,' called out Ann, looking around the room.

'Rosie Locksley,' announced Connor.

Ann smiled warmly towards Rosie being congratulated by a couple of the other dancers who knew her violent drunk of a husband was behind the purple marks blemishing her skin.

'Congratulations.' Connor smiled and gently touched Rosie's shoulder before leaving the dressing room.

'Oh well, looks like one of the ugly sisters will be going after all,' quipped Eva, perching herself on the edge of Roxanne's dressing table.

'It's a shame your name wasn't picked,' said Roxanne.

'I'm not fussed. It wouldn't be any fun without you there anyway,' Eva said with a shrug. 'Plus, imagine if Booth was there!'

'There's little chance of that. You're forgetting that Connor is the chairman. Booth has never been invited as far as I'm aware.'

'Oh well, maybe our names'll be called out next year,' added Eva, philosophically.

'Funny you should mention that.' Roxanne cringed and raised her eyebrows apologetically. 'Connor always keeps two tickets back for me and Tommy, so I will be going to the gala after all.'

'Oh…' Eva blinked trying not to sound a little jealous.

'Well, it's only a meal, comedian and disco,' explained Roxanne, trying to play down what was going to be a fantastic evening of fine dining and great entertainment.

Chapter 6

The two weeks leading up to the charity gala went quickly. Tina dedicated every possible moment crowing over the other girls.

'Are you looking forward to tomorrow night, Roxy?' asked Eva, brushing her hair.

'Yeah, guess so. I wish your name had been picked. You're so funny when you're drunk,' teased Roxanne.

'Hey, I wasn't drunk, I'll have you know. I was slightly merry.' Eva giggled knowing full well she had been pissed as a fart.

'Ann wants to speak to you, Eva,' Tina said walking past her table in a huff.

'What about?'

'I dunno. Do I look like a mind reader?'

Eva knocked on the door of the back office and walked in to find Ann sitting at her desk.

'Rosie just phoned. She needs to take a couple of day's holiday and won't be attending the gala tomorrow night, so I thought you'd like to go in her place,' said Ann, handing her a fancy black and white embossed ticket.

'Oh right,' said Eva, nodding and taking the ticket from Ann. 'Hmm… Booth won't be there, will he?'

'No,' said Ann, turning back to her computer. 'Mr Booth is not on the guest list, I can assure you,' she added, glancing back at her.

Eva instantly felt relieved and began to get excited about the gala. She couldn't wait to tell Roxanne.

'Great!' Roxanne said, beaming. 'We're gonna have such a fucking laugh,' she added, giving Eva a high five.

'I hope I'm not sat by "Mr Dual Personality",' groaned Eva. Her excitement started to subside at the thought of sitting next to Connor all evening.

Roxanne laughed. 'He can be an arrogant so-and-so but cut him some slack. He put all this together for charity – so he's not a total heartless bastard. I'll try and make sure you're sitting next to me.' She winked to reassure Eva.

* * *

'Where are you, Eva?'

'I'm stuck in traffic. Can you believe it's raining? Weeks of dry weather, then tonight of all nights there's an effing thunderstorm!'

'How long are you going to be?'

Eva wiped her hand across the misted cab window and peered through the heavy beads of rain. 'We've just turned into Brook Street, but it looks like there's a bottleneck outside the hotel. I might get out here and make a run for it, what do you think?'

'Yeah, go for it. See you in a couple of minutes.'

Eva swung open the taxi door and jumped out into a barrage of dense droplets falling onto her powdered face. A deep rumble of thunder made her sprint towards the shelter of the hotel as she weaved through the congested traffic. The concierge barked instructions to irate taxi drivers as they sat beeping their horns. Trying to protect her pinned-up hair with her clutch bag proved to offer little protection before reaching the sanctuary of the hotel's canopy. She shimmied through the revolving doors, trying to dab the rain from her face, before stepping onto the white and black chequered floor. The grandeur of the sumptuous art decor interior made her gawp in amazement.

She scanned the throng of men in black tuxedos and elegantly dressed women in search of Roxanne. 'Where are you, Roxy?' she grumbled, standing on tiptoes in her new emerald-green knee-length cocktail dress.

A young waiter approached her with a tray of glasses filled with chilled Bollinger champagne. 'Champagne, madam?'

'Yes, please.' Eva smiled and took a fluted glass, then spotted Roxanne coming towards her.

'Where have you been? I've been looking for you,' said Roxanne, embracing her. 'Oh good, you've got a glass of champagne. This stuff's over a hundred bloody quid a bottle, so get it down your neck, babes!'

Eva replied, 'That's the plan!'

'Come on, let's go in,' said Roxanne leading the way into the French Salon.

The opulent dining room was arranged to accommodate a hundred diners. There was a small platform positioned at the back of the room with a tall wooden stand and microphone. The lighting was soft and intimate, with beautifully dressed circular tables draped in white linen each with a small centrepiece of cream and pink roses.

'We're table four, I think,' said Roxanne checking her ticket.

Quickly taking a seat next to Roxanne, Eva watched Connor sit next to Ann whilst leaving three seats empty to his left. She was surprised to see that Tina was quite happily sitting next to Tommy – not the object of her desire.

'Who are the empty seats for?' enquired Eva, placing a napkin onto her lap.

'His folks and brother.'

'Ohhh…' said Eva, raising her eyebrows in intrigue.

'You'll like his father. His wit is as dry as Tina's split ends!' Roxanne said, giggling at her own joke.

'What's his mother like?'

'See for yourself. They've just walked in,' said Roxanne, glancing over towards the door as Connor quickly got up to greet them.

Eva sat back in her seat to peer from behind Roxanne at Connor's parents. She thought it sweet that Connor offered his arm attentively to escort his mother to the table.

'For those who haven't met my parents before, this is my mother, Norah, and my father, Shamus – so watch your language,' joked Connor pulling out a chair for his mother.

Studying his behaviour, Eva watched Connor hand his mother a copy of the menu and instruct the waitress to wait on her before attending to the other guests at the table. The 'arrogant Connor', who so cruelly dismissed her feelings at the nightclub two weeks ago, was nowhere to be seen.

She thought his mother attractive. The lines creasing her skin betrayed her age, but they were softened by pretty almond-shaped eyes and a small tilted nose. Her long, greying hair styled up away from her face displayed a beautiful pair of diamond and pearl drop earrings. Eva assumed correctly that Connor had bought them for his mother; they were expensive and suited her perfectly.

'What are you having?' asked Roxanne, running her finger down the lavishly embossed menu.

'Where's his brother?' asked Eva.

'Connor,' Roxanne called out, not lifting her gaze from the menu. 'Is Gabriel joining us?'

'I told him to turn it off, so I did, but the boy kept on watching,' said Connor's father, pushing his wine glass to one side as the waiter placed a cold pint of Guinness in front of him.

'Why, is there a big boxing match on tonight, then?' asked Roxanne, glancing up.

'Ay – Lemont Peterson and Amir Khan. It's going to be a mean dance between those two, for sure.' Shamus grinned and rubbed his hands together excitedly. 'We're recording it, son, aren't we?'

'Yeah. He'd better get himself down here, quick,' said Connor frowning at his platinum Rolex.

Eva's attention was drawn back to Connor's father and it was plain to see, under his weathered complexion, that he had been a handsome man in his youth. Connor had inherited his mother's eyes, but he had his father's masculine jaw line and slender stature.

'May I take your order for your starter, madam?'

Eva looked at the waiter and instantly grabbed one of the menus from the table before quickly scrolling down the list. 'Hmmm, I think I'll try the lobster ravioli, please.'

'Very good, madam.'

'Forgive me, miss, but you have the most wonderful red hair,' Connor's father said from across the table. 'Would you be having some of the Irish in ya?' he added, smiling.

Eva blushed as Connor glanced over to her. 'My father's family are from Scotland,' Eva replied while kicking a sniggering Roxanne under the table who was obviously reading a more lurid meaning into Shamus's question.

'Oh, Roxanne…'

'Yes, Shamus,' replied Roxanne, composing herself.

'You know I still enjoy sex at seventy-four – I live at seventy-five, so it's no distance at all!'

His humorous quip was acknowledged with a light ripple of laughter around the table as a small army of waiters began to serve the starters.

'Sorry I'm late, everyone,' apologised Gabriel, his eyes dodging the look of annoyance from his elder brother.

'Cute isn't he?' whispered Roxanne. She nudged Eva's arm, sending her fork laden with plump ravioli straight past her mouth and smearing her cheek with lobster sauce.

Wiping her face, Eva agreed but secretly thought he wasn't as handsome as his brother, even though they both had the same dark hair and striking blue eyes.

'What did you order for your main, Rox?' asked Eva, glancing over at Connor.

'Venison with wild garlic and asparagus spears. What have you ordered?'

Eva wrinkled her nose at Roxanne's choice. 'The pan-fried monkfish with celeriac puree. I hope it's not too bony.'

The conversation around the table was almost non-existent as everyone sat and enjoyed their meal. Eva glanced over at Tina chewing her food. Her white peroxide hair, heavy false eyelashes and red pouty mouth reminded her of a cheap synthetic sex doll.

'Hmmm…pudding,' said Roxanne, grinning. 'Peach and almond tart with vanilla and pistachio ice cream. Delicious!'

Eva looked down at her rich chocolate sponge drenched in a warm hazelnut and chocolate sauce. After three mouthfuls, she released a deep bloated sigh and pushed her plate away.

'The auction is about to start,' said Roxanne looking down at Eva's half-eaten dessert. 'Are you not eating that?'

'Nah… I'm totally stuffed.'

'Oh well, if you're going to waste it,' said Roxanne, eagerly relieving Eva of her plate.

The auctioneer tapped the microphone before saying, 'One-two, one-two.'

Eva watched in disbelief as more food appeared. Large silver platters of fine cheeses and an assortment of crackers and fruit were placed onto each table. She pushed her chair back to escape the pungent smell of stilton cheese.

'Good evening, ladies and gentlemen,' said the auctioneer in a clear and jovial voice. 'Firstly, may I say how wonderful you all look this evening, and secondly I hope you're all enjoying your evening so far. If you would care to look to my right, you will see an Aladdin's cave of splendid items that will be auctioned off this evening. As you know, all the money raised tonight will be donated to Great Ormond Street Hospital. So let us all dig deep and try to topple last year's total of ninety-four thousand pounds. Can I have the first item please, Jane?'

With only a hundred pounds in her purse, Eva feared, judging by the expensive jewellery draped around the ladies in the room, that her measly amount would be swallowed up in just one bid.

The first lot was a box of Cohiba Behike cigars, which didn't interest her at all, but sold for a staggering three hundred and sixty pounds.

'Lot two – one for ladies, I think,' joked the auctioneer, holding aloft a beautiful Chanel jewellery case.

'Twenty pounds!' called out Eva, raising her arm in excitement.

Tina punched her hand in the air. 'Forty pounds!' she shouted, flashing Eva a false smile.

'Sixty pounds!' bellowed Eva glaring back at Tina.

'A hundred pounds!' yelled Tina, taking a large bundle of twenty-pound notes from her purse.

Eva hissed under her breath, 'Roxanne, can you lend me fifty quid?'

'Six hundred pounds!' called out Connor, turning around and smiling over at Eva.

'You can't jump from a hundred pounds to six hundred pounds!' challenged Eva, complaining that his bid was outrageous.

'I can and I have.' Connor laughed at her protests as she glared at him from across the table. She slumped back heavily in her chair with arms tightly folded under her chest.

'Yes!' squealed Tina, as Connor's bid of six hundred pounds secured him the designer jewellery box.

Slamming down her empty glass on the table, Eva got up and flounced out of the room. *It must have been one hell of a blow job to be worth six hundred pounds*, she fumed to herself.

Eva stood outside the hotel inhaling deeply on her cigarette and watching the traffic whizz by. She was in no mood to re-join the group and watch Tina clap like a performing seal while Connor lapped up the attention like a dog on heat. But at least the mystery of Tina's all-year tan had been revealed: she must have been topping up her orange glow from the proverbial light shining out of Connor's backside.

Once back inside she made her way to the loos. *Hiding in the toilets is fast becoming a habit*, she thought with a rueful smile. She leaned over the tiled vanity unit and peered into the mirror. After reapplying her lip gloss, she heard her mobile beep in her clutch bag and checked the message.

Hi Eva, sorry for being a bitch when we spoke last – dumped the loser. You were right as always! Text me when you have a mo. Lot of love Suz xxx

A rush of joy quickened Eva's fingers as she quickly texted back, *Hi Susanna, I am so sorry for upsetting you, really glad that you have texted. Are you still coming over to the UK for my 25th?*

Susanna and Eva had been best friends since they were five years old. Susanna had encouraged Eva to try out pole dancing because of her talent for gymnastics. Susanna, on the other hand, went on to become a wealthy escort living in Las Vegas. She had a circle of regular clients and a weakness for controlling boyfriends. The thought of seeing her again filled Eva with happiness; it had been over seven months since they had last seen each other.

'What are you doing, Eva? Connor is asking where you are!' snapped Roxanne, storming into the ladies toilets.

'I just went outside for a smoke. Sorry, I won't be a minute. I'm just going to send this text.'

Roxanne gave Eva a look of exasperation and issued her with a five-minute reprieve before walking back out.

I am at a boring charity thing so I have to go, text me when you're free and I'll phone. Lots of love Eva xxx

She dropped the mobile back in her bag and slowly made her way back to the auction.

'Nine thousand pounds, going once, going twice.'

Eva glanced over at the auctioneer and sighed heavily before slumping back into her seat. She would have enjoyed the auction if she had hundreds of pounds to spend. She really wanted that jewellery box.

'Whoa, slow down there,' warned Roxanne, watching Eva gulp down a whole glass of champagne.

'Can we have some more water, please,' asked Connor, clicking his fingers at an attentive waiter.

Eva flashed Connor a look of irritation. 'I'm fine!' she replied.

'Well, ladies and gentleman, before the disco we have the celebrated comedian Gavin Jenkins, so please give him a warm welcome – Mr Gavin Jenkins!'

A subdued applause ushered the cheery-faced comedian onto the small podium as he picked up the microphone and mockingly thanked everyone for their 'rapturous welcome'.

'My father said to me on my wedding day, "Now you're married, son, you can forget all your mistakes – there's no use in two people remembering the same thing"!'

A rumble of laugher hovered in the air as the men in the room chuckled under the scornful eyes of their partners.

'I went to the cemetery yesterday to lay some flowers on my old mother's grave. As I stood there, I noticed four gravediggers walking about with a coffin. Three hours later, and they're still walking about with it. I thought to myself, *they've lost the plot!*'

Eva chuckled. She took a drink of water and noticed Gabriel looking at her.

'I've always thought that politicians and nappies have one thing in common – they should both be changed regularly, for the same reason.' The comedian earned himself a more appreciative applause.

'Roxanne?' whispered Eva, nudging her elbow.

'What?'

'Do you fancy coming out for a cigarette?'

'No, I'm listening,' she said nodding towards the comedian.

Releasing a deep sigh, Eva looked down at the empty champagne glass in front of her.

'My mother was never really the brains of our family. She could never see the irony in calling me a "son of a bitch". But I always looked up to Father. I had to, he was taller than me – no, please don't clap,' said the comedian laughing and holding out his hand in front of him, 'you've already paid for your ticket.'

'I might go for one, then,' whispered Eva already getting to her feet.

'Shhh,' ordered Connor, glancing over at her and frowning.

'Just sit back down and hold on for another half an hour, then we'll go out together,' hushed back Roxanne.

Eva flopped back down in her seat and pursed her lips together as she stared back up at the comedian.

'My neighbour knocked on my door at two thirty this morning. Can you believe that – half two in the morning! Luckily for him, I was still up playing my bagpipes!'

Eva reached for her handbag and slid her chair back. 'I'll just pop out for a quick puff. I'll be back in two ticks.'

'Hmm,' replied Roxanne, dismissively.

A ripple of disgruntled murmurings followed her as she weaved through the other guests and slipped out of the room. She fumbled for her cigarettes while making her way across the foyer when a familiar throaty smoker's rattle stopped her dead in her tracks.

'Well, look who it is!'

A wave of anxiety paralysed her body; she stood motionless in the middle of the foyer. Surely her mind was playing tricks on her. *It couldn't be HIM?*

'Cat got your tongue?'

She struggled to breathe hearing the heavy footsteps getting nearer. The pungent smell of his aftershave could not disguise the stench of stale cigarette smoke and sweat. There was no mistaking who it was: Booth.

Fear forced her to look across at his bloated face before her gaze wandered to the menacing pallid-looking man standing next to him – he looked like a ghost, with his pure white hair, deep-set bloodshot eyes and skin that looked vacant of any pigmentation.

'Eva?'

Gasping for air, she spun around on hearing the deep Irish accent pierce the tense atmosphere.

'What going on?' asked Connor, stepping in front of Eva to shield her from Booth's glare.

'Just saying hello to an old friend. What's it got to do with you, O'Neill?'

'I don't think the lady wants to speak to you,' replied Connor coldly.

Phlegm echoed in Booth's throat as he released a deep malevolent laugh. 'Did you hear that, Patrick – *she is a lady!*' He sneered and turned to look at the pale man who stood motionless with fists clenched down by his side.

'Why don't you go back and join Roxanne,' said Connor, reaching behind him to gently push Eva away.

'What, and miss our lovely little reunion,' interrupted Booth. 'How about a kiss for your old boss, then?'

His words made her feel nauseous and unclean. Eva slowly concealed herself behind the width of Connor's body and instantly felt sheltered and protected.

'What are you doing here, Booth? No one invited you, *or him*,' fumed Connor, glancing over to the pale man as he squeezed Eva's hand gently offering her reassurance.

'Him? Please, I think we're all on first name terms here, don't you think?'

'I think it's time you dragged your fat, bloated body out of here.'

'He did time for hitting a woman and killing her unborn child – did you know that, Eva?'

'Why don't you shut your diseased, feral mouth,' Connor barked back, releasing Eva's hand as he took a step towards Booth. 'Or, if you don't, I'll make sure you take your last breath where you stand!'

Noticing the man called Patrick enjoy the verbal jousting between Connor and Booth, Eva thought the whole situation was going to explode as the receptionist quickly phoned for the manager.

'I thought I could smell dog shit,' shouted Tommy, walking into the foyer, 'and here they are, two sinking turds dropped out of the arse of life!'

'Look who it is, Patrick, it's the child killer's rent-boy,' goaded Booth.

'You wanna say that to my face, old man? Cos I can promise you one thing, it'll be the last thing that comes out of that rancid, decaying body of yours,' vowed Tommy.

'Stay out of this, Jakeman,' snapped the ghost-like man in a thick Irish accent. 'This ain't any of your business.'

'Is everything all right, Mr O'Neill?' enquired a worried looking manager as he slid his glasses up the bridge of his nose. 'Shall I fetch security, sir?'

'*Shall I fetch security, sir?*' mocked Booth. 'He makes his money the same way I make mine, isn't that right, O'Neill – off the backs of whores!'

'It's okay, Robert, I'll take care of this – Booth and St Clair are leaving.' Connor grimaced and a deep V creased his brow.

Booth snarled and turned towards his sidekick. 'Don't worry, we're going. Your past has come knocking, O'Neill. Watch your back!' jeered Booth, walking towards the revolving doors followed by St Clair. 'Your past has come a knocking, ha…ha…ha.'

Eva stood dazed and confused. With thoughts flying around her mind, she couldn't pin the truth on O'Neill, Booth or St Clair. She knew Booth was a liar and a fantasist, so why would his so-called friend be any different? But she also knew Connor had been to prison – was it for hitting a woman?

'What the fuck were those maggots doing here?' asked Tommy.

'Who knows what goes through a degenerate's mind? Booth knew I'd be here, he's just come looking for trouble and brought along St Clair to hold his hand?' said Connor, turning around and reaching for Eva's hand.

Feeling disoriented and frightened, Eva flinched away from Connor's touch. Her withdrawal left him in no doubt that she believed the accusations thrown at him.

'Tom, can you ask Roxanne to take Eva up to my room? I'll be up in a minute.'

Before Eva could refuse, she was being ushered into Connor's private suite by Roxanne, who unknowingly made her anxiety rise with her probing.

'I told him I'm fine – I just want to go home,' explained Eva wearily.

'I can't fucking believe Booth had the brass neck to show his face here tonight and with that bastard albino. How did Connor react when he saw St Clair?' she asked, spotting a half-empty bottle of French brandy. 'Here, drink this,' she instructed. 'It'll help with the shock.'

Eva winced as the strong brandy took her breath away. 'I thought it was all going to kick off! You know what Booth called him? A murderer! He said Connor attacked a woman and that she had lost her unborn child because of it. If that's true, then that makes him a monster, and there's no way I'm going to work for someone like that!' wailed Eva, shaking her head.

'Look, calm down. I know it sounds fucked up, but I can promise you, it isn't as black and white as Booth would have you believe. You know how Booth can twist and turn things to his own advantage. I can't say anymore, but I can reassure you that you don't have to fear O'Neill – I can promise you that on my life.'

'Tommy seemed to know the man with the white hair too,' explained Eva.

'St Clair. He's scum just like Booth,' proclaimed Roxanne. 'Look, just lie down for a minute until Connor and Tommy get here.'

'Don't leave me here on my own,' pleaded Eva, climbing on the bed.

'I won't, I promise. Now just rest for a minute.'

The strong brandy numbed Eva senses a little, making the countless questions in her head muffled and distanced.

'Just five minutes,' murmured Eva, bringing her knees close into her body as a drowsy calmness washed over her.

Gingerly closing the door behind them, Connor glanced over to his empty bottle of brandy then over to Eva who was now snoring in long, slow grunts.

'Shhh...' whispered Roxanne, pressing her finger to her lips.

'Do you want me to sling her in a cab, Connor?' asked Tommy.

'I can't believe you've just said that!' fumed Roxanne in a whispering growl. 'So, we're going to "sling" her drunk and frightened into a cab in the middle of the night on her own then, are we? Tommy Jakeman – I swear I don't know you at all!'

Tommy shook his head. 'For fuck's sake! It was only a suggestion, babe,' he fired back.

Connor looked tired as he ran his hands through his hair. 'Okay, leave her here – I'll take her home in the morning.'

'I can take your parents to the airport tomorrow morning, if that helps? You know, if you're tied up with this mess,' suggested Tommy, securing himself with another furious glare from Roxanne.

'Thanks, but I should have enough time if I drop her back early. Anyway, I'll see you both tomorrow – yeah,' said Connor, glancing at his watch.

As the door closed behind Roxanne and Tommy, Connor dimmed the lights and sat quietly mulling over what Booth had revealed. He wasn't relishing addressing Eva's probing questions in the morning. Booth's allegations were indeed damning and held more than a little truth in them. His past was creeping up on him, and there was little he could do to silence the accusations.

Chapter 7

Eva's eyes flickered open hearing noises coming from the bathroom. She looked anxiously at across the bed, then towards the indented pillow on the large leather sofa with relief.

He came into the room dressed in a white short-sleeved T-shirt and tight-fitting jeans. She tried not to stare at his toned physique.

'Morning, do you want to freshen up or have some breakfast first? I can ring room service,' he offered.

'No, I'd like to get home if that's okay. I've got things to do?' said Eva.

'Fine,' said Connor and went back to the en suite to let her to get dressed.

'You look a right mess, Eva,' she moaned to herself, straining to look in the dressing table mirror. Trying to smooth down her unbrushed hair with her fingers was a pointless task. The remnants of smudged mascara proved stubborn to remove as she gently rubbed under her eyes. She quickly put on her dress and scrambled into her stilettos. 'I'm ready,' she shouted.

With his car keys and wallet, he led them out of the room. After locking the door behind them, Eva eyes widened hearing a familiar Irish accent from down the corridor.

'Connor…!'

Connor turned around quickly, then sighed.

'Connor…!'

'Dad, go back to your room. Its only seven o'clock – I'll be back later,' he rebuked as his father peered down the hall at Eva whose cheeks were glowing with mortification.

Praying that the floor would open up and swallow her, she knew what his father was thinking by the deliberate wink he so indiscreetly flashed at Connor.

'Mr O'Neill,' said Roberts the hotel manager who walked over to greet them when they entered the hotel foyer.

'Roberts,' said Connor shaking his hand firmly.

'I trust your suite was to your satisfaction, sir? I hope last night's unpleasant events did not spoil your evening too much. I have informed front of house and our concierge that under no circumstances are either gentlemen allowed to step foot in Claridge's again. They were not guests staying at this hotel.'

Eva stood awkwardly feeling dishevelled and uncomfortable in front of the immaculately dressed hotel manager. She lowered her gaze to the chequered floor wishing she had taken the time to shower and straighten her hair.

'I would like to apologise for any strong language heard by any of your staff last night,' Connor said with a concerned frown.

Roberts nodded courteously. 'I hope you and your companion come back to Claridge's soon, sir,' he said with a smile and bobbing his head towards Eva.

'We will,' said Connor, glancing at his watch.

'Then I'll say good day, Mr O'Neill.'

Humiliation didn't even describe how Eva felt at that particular moment. She had found herself in the unfortunate 'Pretty Woman' scenario! The wild red hair and handsome middle-aged millionaire sneaking her out of a posh hotel. The only thing missing was her work thigh-length boots.

She was finally relieved to step outside in the morning sun. They stood in silence, as though strangers, waiting for his car to be brought around to the front of the hotel. Eva took out her mobile and turned away as the hotel concierge's tuneful whistling started to annoy her. She checked her messages and raised an eyebrow noticing the voicemail symbol. She quickly dialled to listen.

'Hi, it's Roxy – I hope you're okay? You were out of it last night, so we all thought it was best to let you sleep. I hope Connor explains a little about what was said last night. He isn't as dark as Booth portrayed, so try to have an open mind about the whole thing. Anyway, I know you're not in work tonight, so I'll speak to you Monday. Oh yeah, in case you were wondering, I underdressed you last night.'

With a sense of relief Eva dropped the mobile back into her clutch bag. Even though Connor had seen her semi-naked at the club, she would have been upset if he'd removed her clothes while she was intoxicated. She glanced over at Connor when his silver Maserati approached.

'Get in,' he said curtly.

Charming as ever, she thought getting into the passage seat. She surveyed the general hubbub of activity through the window to avert her attention from Connor and twirled the delicate metal chain of her clutch bag tightly around her fingers as he pulled away from the hotel.

'There is some truth in what Booth said last night,' he said impassively.

Eva started to chew her lip and sat rigid waiting for Connor to continue.

'Her name was Maria. I'd known her since I was five. She used to tease me about my dimples, saying they were from my mother, over squeezing my cheeks as a child – you know, kid's stuff.'

Eva looked over at him. She couldn't believe he was sharing such intimate, childhood recollections with her. She couldn't ignore the tenderness in his voice as he relived the happy memory.

'We started dating in our teens. I guess it wasn't ideal. We were so young, and I was travelling all over Ireland trying to make money to give us a future. I knew she was lonely, but what could I do?' he confessed, his voice deepening. 'She wanted me to give up my dreams, my ambitions, and find a nine-to-five job. I watched my father break his back to line another man's pockets – I wasn't prepared to do that. I told her to have faith in me, and the plans that I was making were for us.'

The chain from Eva's handbag dropped into a pool of silver links in her lap as she sat in shock at his openness. She was completely engrossed in his narrative of the only woman he had ever loved.

'I came home one night to see her and St Clair together,' said Connor before suddenly accelerating and making them jolt in their seats. 'He was, and is, the lowest kind of scum you can imagine, a two-bit poker player and a loan shark. So I kicked her out and let her live with her gutter rat. Six months later she came looking for me,' he continued as they pulled up to a set of traffic lights.

'What – to ask you to take her back?' asked Eva.

'No, she knew I would never take her back, but she did ask for my help. She was seven months pregnant with St Clair's kid and looked like she'd taken a beating. She was frightened and needed money to get to the London.'

'Did you help her?' Eva asked gently.

'I wanted her to suffer – she had betrayed me,' said Connor coldly, speeding away from the traffic lights. 'But I couldn't send a kid back to that lowlife, so I gave her a thousand pounds. I didn't do for her. She could've rotted in hell for all I cared,' he added bitterly.

'How did she lose her baby? You don't have to tell if you don't want to.' Eva averted her gaze, not knowing if she could bear witness to the possibility of him being a woman beater and murderer.

Connor inhaled deeply.

Eva covered her mouth in anticipation.

'St Clair found the money. He was making a scene and throwing threats around. Too much of a coward to say them to my face, so he openly threatened my mother in the street,' he said, his voice faltering slightly. 'He signed his fate there and then. But things got messy and out of control,' reasoned Connor, as though he was still arguing with his conscience after all these years.

'Did you fight with St Clair?'

'I think that's pretty obvious, don't you? I wanted to kill the bastard. He had stolen everything from me and threatened my family, but somehow Maria got in between us. I must've knocked her over, I guess, I don't know. Anyway, in court she said that I attacked St Clair, and that I hit her making her lose the kid. I got five years for GBH with intent but was released on probation after two and a half.'

'She said that you had hit her!' argued Eva. 'So after you tried to help her, she betrays you for a second time – I'm speechless!' She gasped in outrage. 'But,' she continued, trying to fit the pieces together, 'if St Clair had been knocking her about, who's to say that she didn't miscarry before the fight?'

'I think he probably put pressure on her testify. Perhaps it was in exchange for her freedom – who knows?'

Eva gave directions to turn into her road.

'Which is your house?' he asked, looking at the row of terraced houses thinking they looked small and ugly.

'Number nineteen,' said Eva, lingering in her seat for as long as possible, trying not to make it too obvious that she was keen to hear the rest of his story. 'Well, would you like to come in for a coffee?' she spluttered, her cheeks tanning instantly dreading the embarrassment of his refusal.

'Is my car going to be safe here?'

His comment made her laugh out loud, until she realised he was being serious. 'I may not live in Kensington, but it's not a slum area – thank you. Your car will be perfectly safe here. My car has never been broken in to,' she announced, not quite grasping the fact that her four-year-old Vauxhall Corsa was probably not worth stealing for parts.

Connor walked up her small garden path looking impressed at the borders of scented flowers revitalised by the rain.

She pushed open her front door and walked down the hall into the kitchen leaving Connor to close the door behind them.

'So, do you live here on your own?'

'I live with Mr Jingles.' Eva beamed, glancing down at the two cat bowls on the floor.

Connor nodded. 'So, no boyfriend, then?'

'Well, there aren't many men who would choose for their girlfriend to be a stripper,' she retorted.

'I guess not. How long have you been single for?'

Sensing the tables were turned, she felt a little coy at Connor probing into her private life. To admit the truth, which was nearly seven months, would have been too humiliating, so she embellished the truth a little.

'A couple of months now, I guess.'

'Don't you miss having sex?' asked Connor brazenly.

'I think I can control my urges for a couple of months, but I can appreciate *some people* have the morals of a tomcat,' she preached, glancing up at him.

'Are you calling me a "lothario", Miss Summers?' said Connor, grinning.

'I wouldn't be surprised if your bedstead hasn't been whittled down to a matchstick, Mr O'Neill,' whipped Eva, returning his grin.

'You don't think much of me, do you?'

'I'm not judging anyone. Casual sex is something I'm not interested in,' she stated, conveniently forgetting about her hedonistic weekend at Glastonbury. 'Shall we go through to the lounge?' she asked, handing over his black coffee.

She waited until Connor sat down before she put down her drink and sat in the leather armchair opposite.

Connor glanced at the large mirror hanging above the cream fire surround silently approving of her taste in decor: it was uncluttered and not overly feminised with flowers and ornaments.

'Hello, baby,' cooed Eva as Mr Jingles came sprinting into the lounge meowing loudly before arching his back on seeing Connor. Padding over gingerly, he sniffed his hand before brushing his body against his leg.

'He likes his chin rubbed.' Eva smiled watching Mr Jingles like a proud parent.

'Hello, little man,' said Connor, reaching under his chin. 'I have two dogs, but my mother has a cat called Bailey, mind you, he's an old boy now.'

'What are your dog's names?'

'Bodie is a two-year-old black Labrador and Doyle is a six-month fox-red Lab. I named them after *The Professionals*?' Connor said with a grin and brushing the cat hairs off his trouser leg.

Eva looked on blankly. 'So…' she said, raising her eyebrows and gently blowing on her hot coffee, 'you haven't seen Maria since the court case?'

Connor reached over to pick up his drink. 'That would be a bit difficult,' he replied curtly.

'Oh…?' Eva frowned trying to work out the reason why.

His relaxed demeanour fuelled her confidence as she practised the next question in her head. 'So – er, Maria eventually left Ireland and moved to England, then?'

'Yes – that's where they found her body,' said Connor without a flicker of emotion.

'Her body! Oh my God, Maria is dead?!' Eva gasped and jolted forward. 'What happened to her?'

'She was found in a canal in Birmingham with her throat cut. The police said she was a well-known prostitute and drug user, so it could've been a punter or a mugging – the case was never solved.'

Eva clamped her hand over her mouth and shook her head in disbelief. 'Murdered, oh my God – how did you feel when you heard?'

'Feel?'

'Yes, when you heard that she'd been murdered?'

'I didn't feel anything.' Connor shrugged and glanced at his watch. 'Anyway, I'd better be making tracks. I've got to take my folks to the airport, and try to convince my father that we didn't have wild sex last night,' he said with a smirk, enjoying her instant blushes. 'See you Monday, "Red",' he added teasingly.

Eva pressed her lips together into a forced smile and closed the door behind him. She was intrigued by his past, egotism, charm and how different he was in a one-to-one situation. *It's just as well I'm not attracted to him,* she thought, in complete denial.

* * *

The next day Eva still hadn't got over her 'Pretty Woman' scenario – she hoped she didn't have to see Connor's father for a while, and she wasn't going anywhere near Claridge's ever again. She carried out her household chores with incessant questions swarming around her mind and trying to analyse Connor's lack of emotion. *Surely he must have felt something knowing the one woman he loved was murdered.*

After finishing her laundry, her mobile phone beeped on top of the microwave. It was Susanna. *Hi, what u up to?*

Glancing at her watch Eva wondered what time it was in Las Vegas. Working out it would be late evening she decided to phone instead of texting back.

'Hi, Suz!'

'Hi,' Susanna whispered back.

'Are you okay?' asked Eva, wondering why Susanna was whispering.

'Yeah – I'm with a client, but he's in the shower – how are you?'

'I'm working in a new club now – the Unicorn. It's one of the best clubs in London. The money is really good, so I can start saving again.'

'You? Save?' scoffed Susanna. 'Money is like water through your fingers!'

'Well, I'll just have to find myself a rich sugar daddy,' Eva said giggling. 'There are plenty of them at the club.'

'What are the girls like?'

'One is really nice – Roxanne, but there's a girl called Tina who's a complete bitch!' ranted Eva. 'She took an instant dislike to me the very moment I stepped in the dressing room. Plus, she's in love with the boss.'

'Oh yeah, what's he like?'

'Arrogant, good-looking, could be a murderer—'

'WHAT?' shrieked Susanna so loud it made Eva remove the phone from her ear.

'It's a long story, and I don't know all the facts to be honest, so I could be letting my imagination run away with me.'

Susanna chuckled knowingly. 'Yes, you do have a very vivid imagination.'

'Anyhow, who's your client? A bronzed horse-riding cowboy?'

'I wish,' sneered Susanna, lowering her voice further. 'No, he's a regular. Overweight, bald and boring.'

'Ewww…' said Eva, wrinkling her nose.

Susanna quickly added, 'But fifthly rich!'

'Have you seen your lowlife ex around?'

'Er... How's your mom? How's the bar in Spain going?'

Eva could see straight through her change of subject. 'Suz, tell me you're not back in contact with him?'

There was a short silence before Susanna cleared her throat. 'Look, I've got to go, Eva, my regular is calling me. I'll see you for your birthday, okay – love you. Bye.'

Eva heard the line click dead and pressed the mobile to her mouth as she stood thinking. She felt disappointed and annoyed with her best friend. Eva hadn't met Susanna's ex in person, but she had managed to piece together enough information from numerous sob-filled phone conversations to realise he'd had been violent towards her. Eva had convinced Susanna to call the police after she'd suffered a broken wrist, but within hours the charges were dropped, saying everything was sorted out and they were fine again – infuriating Eva to the point where their friendship was nearly put on the line. She decided to bring the subject up again when Susanna came over for her birthday in December.

* * *

'Evening, Eva,' said Roxanne brushing her hair and sitting naked at her dressing table.

'All right, Roxy.'

'Fancy a cigarette?' asked Roxanne pulling on a silk kaftan.

'Yeah, okay.' Eva knew she wanted an update on whether Connor had explained about Booth's revelations.

Once outside she brought Roxanne up to speed. 'He explained about his ex doing the dirty on him with that guy St Clair, and that she must've got in the way of them fighting and lost the baby. It's terrible that she lied in court, though.'

'She's a fucking evil bitch to do that, and after he tried to help her too. Karma always comes back to bite you on the arse,' stated Roxanne, flicking her cigarette ash on the ground.

'Even so, no one deserves to be murdered,' challenged Eva, thinking Roxanne's comment was harsh.

'She nearly broke him and got him put away for two an' a half years! You reap what you sow, is what I say.'

'Hmmm, anyway, remember I told you about my best friend in Vegas – Susanna? Well, she's coming over in December for my birthday, so I hope you're up for a boozy night?'

'Count me in. Guess I'll have to buy you a present now,' teased Roxanne.

'Yes – but don't go crazy – a Ferrari or Lamborghini will do,' she snorted, stubbing out her cigarette. 'I guess it's back to work to earn those pennies to buy my dream car!'

'Good, cos I ain't buying you a bleeding Ferrari, Mrs!'

'Actually,' said Eva, linking arms with Roxanne as they walked back into the club, 'my dream car is a red Mini Cooper. I always fancied an original, but you wanna see the new Mini Cooper S type,' she gushed. 'Hatchback with alloy wheels…'

'Calm down.' Roxanne giggled pushing open the dressing room door. 'Oh, before I forget, its Tommy's forty-fifth birthday a week on Saturday. Well, his birthday is on the Wednesday, but we're having a little barbecue on the Saturday, if you fancy it? I'm sure one of the girls will swap their shift with you?'

'I don't think Tommy actually likes me. I doubt he'll want me to be there?'

'Don't be silly, what's not to like,' Roxanne said with a grin, knowing that Tommy had let slip he thought Eva was a drama queen after their girls' night out.

'I'm not sure anyone'll want to swap.' 'Look, I'll ask Carol, she owes me a favour. So it's sorted, then – you're coming.'

Chapter 8

'Oh, you look nice,' cooed Roxanne taking a poorly gift-wrapped bottle of whisky and card from Eva.

'I forgot to ask, does Tommy like Jack Daniels?'

'Is the Pope a Catholic?' Roxanne laughed as she led her down a flight of stone steps to a beautifully tended garden.

Eva lifted the hem of her long yellow dress and gingerly made her way down the sandstone steps. 'Wow, this is lovely.'

'Thanks, I know I don't seem the green-fingered type,' explained Roxanne, 'but I love my garden and vegetable patch.'

Weaving their way around a circle of guests, Roxanne smiled warmly at one particular woman in the group.

'Let me introduce you to my mum, Barbara.'

'Hello.' Eva smiled as she shook Barbara's hand and complimented her on her bohemian multicoloured patchwork skirt.

'Hello,' replied Barbara warmly.

'My mother's an old hippy, aren't you, Mum?' Roxanne laughed, wrapping her arm around her mother's shoulder and kissing her affectingly on the cheek.

'Yes, dear,' Barbara replied, chuckling.

'Let's get a drink – my throat's as dry as Ghandi's flip-flop,' quipped Roxanne.

'Where are all the men?' asked Eva, glancing around and noticing a lack of men under the age of fifty.

'Tommy converted the cellar into a "lads den". I think they're just finishing a game of snooker. Here, get this down your neck,' she urged, handing her a large vodka and lemonade.

She took a sip and reached for the sunglasses sitting on the top of her head. 'So, is Connor here – are you expecting him to join us?'

'He's not here yet. He said he'd only be able to stay half an hour.'

'Didn't you say he was off to the States?'

'Yep, and for two whole weeks too,' said Roxanne. She led her over towards two garden chairs nestled under a white parasol.

Taking shelter in the shade, Eva turned in her seat hearing voices behind her. She saw three bouncers from the club and Tommy make his way over.

'Won't be a minute.' Roxanne got out of her chair and walked over to Tommy who was now placing a line of raw beef burgers on the hot barbecue grill.

Eva was intrigued by their relationship. She couldn't understand their connection at all. She found Tommy unattractive with an unpleasant demeanour; whereas, Roxanne was stunningly attractive and could have her pick of men.

With an expression she hadn't seen on Tommy's face before, his hard features instantly softened when Roxanne approached him. Eva sat immersed watching their conversation littered with small kisses, affection and devotion.

'Help yourself to the cold buffet, burgers and sausages,' called out Roxanne, unwrapping large foil trays of smoked salmon, salads and potatoes.

'Burger, please,' said Eva, trying not to make eye contact with Tommy who stood behind a thin blanket of smoke.

'Onions?' asked Tommy, flipping a beef burger onto a fresh bun.

'You've got to have onions on a burger, surely?'

Eva's eyes widened hearing Connor's voice behind her. Still not sure what to make of the revelations about his ex, reliving her humiliation at Claridge's was the last thing she wanted. 'Sorry-yes-okay,' stuttered Eva, almost apologetically. A sudden dryness swelled in her throat. Trying to balance the food on her plate, she quickly walked across the manicured lawn towards a small cluster of white plastic chairs sitting by a large hydrangea bush. Dragging one of the chairs out of view, she glanced over at Connor talking to Tommy and two young women.

The brunette was short, petite and openly flirtatious. Her blonde and curvy friend stood next to her posing.

Eva positioned her plate on the chair arm and lit a cigarette before pushing aside a pastel-pink flower head to peer at Connor happily chatting to the voluptuous blonde.

'*Complete womaniser,*' she snorted under her breath, watching Connor's hand brush against the blonde's waist, not noticing a long line of cigarette ash fall down her dress. Feeling the filter burn her lips, she quickly dropped her cigarette to the ground and gently brushed off the ash. A loud burst of laugher made her quickly peer back over to Connor. '*Desperado!*' she huffed, taking a huge bite out of her burger as she watched the blonde touch Connor's arm and flick her hair, yet again, over her shoulder.

With her cheeks bulging like a gluttonous hamster, she briefly became distracted by Roxanne who was busy ensuring everyone had a drink and a plateful of food before glancing back towards Connor. With food nearly tumbling out of her mouth, she saw him approaching the hydrangea bush. *'Fucking Hell!'* she mumbled, emptying the half-eaten contents out of her mouth onto a paper napkin.

'Eva, are you in there?' asked Connor, walking behind the bush and seeing a pair gold wedges poking out from under a flowered skirt of pink and blue hydrangeas.

'Oh, there it is.' Eva appeared red-faced holding aloft a bright yellow pashmina. 'The wind must have blown it off the back of my chair!' she gabbled.

Connor glanced up at the windless sky and looked back at her in disbelief. 'Why are you hiding in a flower bush, and why are you avoiding me? Grab your stuff and come and join everyone!' he instructed firmly.

'Oh, I'm sorry,' snapped Eva sarcastically, 'I must have misread the terms and conditions on the back of the invite. I didn't realise that I *had* to mingle with you and your *harem*.'

Connor frowned. 'Harem?'

'Yes, your little *harem* over there. What will Tina say?'

Connor looked bewildered as her words assaulted him like a slap to the face. 'I insist that you come out from behind this darn bush and join everyone, and stop this bizarre behaviour,' he snapped.

'Bizarre?'

'Yes, bizarre. Unless, you have an unhealthy obsession with hydrangea bushes?'

'Oh *pleasssse*, you'll be making me laugh next,' scoffed Eva. 'Quick, you'd better scuttle back before they wonder where you are. If you're lucky, they might agree to a threesome!'

Connor's lips spread into a wide smirk. 'Oh... I see now,' he said with a nod.

'See what?' questioned Eva frowning up at him.

'You're jealous...'

'Jealous – ha! I don't think so,' she rebuffed while her crimson cheeks betrayed her.

'There's no need to be, Eva – you put them all in the shade. You must know that I think you're stunning,' said Connor, cheekily glancing down at her breasts.

'Put them both in the shade?' she berated. 'Is that supposed to be a funny "fat joke"?'

'What *are* you going on about? Are you just playing at being dense or does it come naturally?' replied Connor, his frown intensifying further.

'Oh great, so now I'm bizarre, fat and dense!' sulked Eva. 'Please don't worry about my feelings – no, feel free to carry on. May I suggest the hair next? Surely you have an opinion – look, GINGER!' she sneered grabbing a long strand of curls.

'Can you just shut up for one moment – just one second, that's all I ask,' said Connor, raising his voice. 'Don't you understand what I'm trying to say? And if you mention the words "fat" or "dense" again, I will carry you over to that pond and throw you in!' he added sharply.

Eva swallowed hard glancing over towards the large ornamental pond at the bottom of the garden.

'I am not insulting you – why can't you understand that. I think you're beautiful.'

'One of many, no doubt,' mocked Eva, releasing a sarcastic grin.

Taking a step back, Connor inhaled deeply and ran his hand through his hair. 'Okay, so you want me to say it – I fancy you, ginger hair an' all!'

Eva's expression confirmed her boredom. 'Did Tina fall for the same line?'

'As well as being stunning and breathtakingly sexy, you are infuriating, outspoken and judgemental!' Connor added quickly, grabbing her waists.

Eva tilted her head back and sulkily tried to avoid Connor's mouth, but he snared her tightly in his arms and forcefully pulled her towards his body. With a petulant stare, she sucked in her cheeks and turned her face away from him. This action only seemed to intensify his frustration – and determination.

'Let me go, I can't breathe!' Eva's wriggling made Connor instantly slacken his grip.

'*You* are *beautiful!*' he announced, forcefully cupping her face with his hands so she met his gaze. 'You could drive a man insane! I believe that with every fibre of my body – but you have a natural beauty, and a body that could destroy a man's soul,' he declared.

Eva blinked slowly gazing up at him. She hadn't noticed the faint freckles on the bridge of his nose partially disguised by his golden tan, nor a small scar trailing off his top lip as she focused on his mouth.

He sounded so genuine, but could she actually let her guard down and be honest about her attraction to him? With her pupils dilated like two pools of black ink, Eva's arms fell down by her side.

Moving his mouth slowly down to meet hers, he wrapped his arms around her waist and gently probed his tongue inside her mouth.

It was the sweetest kiss she had ever experienced. She felt completely intoxicated by his passion; the tension in her body quickly dissolved. Closing her eyes, her body felt weightless as his kiss produced a pulsating urge between her legs. Her mouth felt slightly numb when she broke away from his kiss, only for him to urgently cup her face with his hand and pull her back to his mouth again.

'I wish I didn't have to go,' admitted Connor, letting her take a much-needed breath. 'I would love to whisk you away to a quiet hotel and make love to you all night,' he whispered, slipping his hands down the small of her back and caressing her bottom firmly while nuzzling her neck with soft kisses. 'As soon as I get back, I'll arrange something, somewhere romantic.'

'What?' muttered Eva, trying to make sense of what was happening. 'Meet up?'

'Yes, when I come back,' said Connor, gently swaying her in his arms, stirring her from her serenity. 'Eva – are you listening?'

'I-I'm…' said Eva, blinking rapidly. 'I'm not sure… Maybe, I guess—'

'No "maybes". When I come back from New York I'll organise a night away for us,' he insisted, talking over her.

'Er…' mumbled Eva, sounding unsure.

'Look – I've got to go,' said Connor checking his watch. 'This is my mobile number – text me tonight.'

Eva stared down at the white and black business card.

'I'll see you in two weeks,' Connor said smiling. He wrapped his arms around her waist and lifted her off her feet before planting another passionate kiss on her lips.

Feeling the soles of her gold wedges return to the ground beneath her, Eva stood holding his card and watched Connor disappear back to the party. Within moments he was walking up the sandstone steps towards the house. She glanced up at him as he turned around and winked at her before disappearing from view.

She opened her hand and looked down at his business card.

'There you are!' said Roxanne walking over towards her. 'Hope you're up for a bit of karaoke later?'

'Yeah – if you want,' said Eva, still reeling from Connor's declaration.

'Are you all right? You're not coming down with something are you? You look very pale.'

'No, I'm fine…' said Eva curling the business card in the palm of her hand.

'Good, because my friend Grant, him over there,' said Roxanne pointing over to a Gothic looking man with shoulder-length black hair and tattoos covering his arms, 'he fancies you.'

'Oh…' Eva glanced over at the tattooed man.

'"Granted",' said Roxanne, nudging Eva and laughing at her own wit, 'he isn't Brad Pitt, but he's a nice bloke and has a big knob!' she said grinning.

'How do you know?' Eva asked with a chuckle.

'My friend Lisa shagged him and she said he's hung like a horse, so go and say hello.'

* * *

An hour later, Roxanne found Eva sitting alone smoking a cigarette.

'Making a call?' she probed, seeing Eva holding her mobile.

Eva quickly dropped her phone and Connor's business card into her bag. 'No.'

'Did you speak to Grant?'

'No – sorry, he's not my type.'

'Well, Lisa did say she couldn't walk properly for a day or so after – so maybe you're wise. Well here, drink this.' Roxanne handed Eva a large vodka and lemonade. 'For Dutch courage.'

'Dutch courage?'

'For the karaoke!'

'Oh, yes – s-sorry,' spluttered Eva, shaking her head.

'Well, there's no time like the present.' Roxanne turned around and belched loudly. 'Right, everyone, it's karaoke time. Follow me into the lounge!'

A chorus of loud, drunken cheers erupted as everyone made their way inside.

'Come on, time to get in the party mood,' insisted Roxanne, handing Eva a microphone.

'What are we singing?' she asked wearily.

'What else?' Roxanne shouted to everyone in the room. '"Dancing Queen"!'

Eva couldn't concentrate as she fluffed and missed out most of the words to the song. She was quite relieved when playful boos urged her to stop while Roxanne carried on singing tunefully.

She slipped outside into the cool night air and sat on the bottom garden step. After pulling her pashmina over her shoulders, she reached inside her bag for her mobile and Connor's business card before quickly lighting a cigarette. Inhaling deeply, she stared down at her mobile.

Hi, it's Eva, she texted, before quickly deleting the message.

Hi, it's me, she typed. Her heart beat hard against her chest as her finger hovered over the send button.

'BOO,' yelled Roxanne, reaching down and grabbing her shoulders. 'Every time I turn round you've gone. What are you doing so secretively out here?'

'Nothing!' replied Eva quickly pressing her mobile against her chest.

'Hmmm… Well, crash us a fag, Tommy keeps hiding mine. He's so desperate for me to give them up,' she babbled on drunkenly.

'Here…'

'Wh-who loves you, then?' hiccupped Roxanne, taking a deep drag on her cigarette as Eva's phone beeped.

Oh, fuck! thought Eva, realising she must have accidently pressed the send button.

'Aren't you going to see who it is?'

'It's just my mum,' Eva quickly lied.

There is no way she could confess her secret to Roxanne. She knew she wouldn't approve, especially after she'd warned her about Connor's reputation.

Roxanne stubbed out her cigarette and started to make her way back into the house. 'Coming?'

'Yeah, in a minute,' called back Eva. She opened her message.

Who is this?

She gasped reading Connor's reply.

It's Eva! she texted back, lighting another cigarette.

I know – just kidding! So are you drunk yet?

Funny. No I am not drunk ☺

Good. I wouldn't want you doing anything you might regret in the morning.

'Too late,' Eva muttered to herself, now realising what a dangerous situation she was walking into.

So tell me, what colour knickers are you wearing?

Shocked by his direct question, she thought it a little crude. *What colour are you wearing?* she texted back.

I'm not wearing knickers! Black boxers!

Are you normally this forward?

No, but I'm guessing we have passed first base?

What are you doing in New York? she texted quickly, deliberately changing the subject.

Roxanne stepped out onto the patio again and shouted, 'Eva – come on! What are you doing out here?'

'Yes, I'm just coming,' called back Eva, quickly sending Connor another text. *I have to go, Roxanne is wondering what I'm doing outside. I haven't told her anything!*

Connor didn't reply.

The party didn't finish until two thirty in the morning.

***

'Oh God…my head,' whined Eva lying face down on Roxanne's sofa. 'What time is it?'

'Quarter to eleven,' croaked Roxanne whose smudged eye make-up bore an uncanny resemblance to Alice Cooper.

Eva lifted her head slowly and glanced at the carnage of intoxicated bodies littering the floor. She somehow managed to sit upright and ring for a cab.

She still felt drunk with bile clinging to the back of her throat as the taxi driver pulled up outside her house. After throwing up in the kitchen sink, she knew downing ten shots of gin with Roxanne last night was a bad idea. Groaning like a dime hooker, her ghoulish moans and wails startled Mr Jingles who quickly disappeared back through his cat flap.

The tranquillity of lying on top of her bed was disrupted when her mobile pinged on the bedside cabinet.

'For fuck's sake, go away,' she whimpered, turning over and covering her head.

With each ring amplifying tenfold in her head, she rolled over and grabbed it. '*Yes…!*' she grumbled down the phone

'Wow, you sound rough.'

'Oh, it's you,' said Eva, reaching for a glass of water sitting by her bedside lamp.

'That's a nice way to greet someone,' teased Connor.

'Sorry, I've got the hangover from hell,' explained Eva before gulping down the water with raspy groans.

'I thought you said you weren't drunk?'

'I wasn't then, but Roxanne decided to hand out shots – the rest is history.'

'Drinking to excess isn't good for your liver,' warned Connor. 'You're not a teenager anymore, you should realise what you're doing to your body.'

'I'm sure when you were *my age* you drank to excess.' Greeted with a deafening silence, Eva instantly regretted her quip.

'I am older,' replied Connor. 'But with age comes wisdom and a wealth of sexual experience,' he boasted.

'Does everything come back to sex with you?'

'I like sex,' replied Connor confidently. 'In fact, what's better than passionate sex? Plus, *you* haven't had sex in a while, so I'm expecting you to be extremely eager, Miss Summers,' he taunted.

'Well, the next time I have sex, I'll make a point to phone you,' said Eva with a wicked smirk across her lips.

Connor's laugh made her momentarily forget her hangover as she lay her head back down on the pillow.

'Well, I'm hoping I'll be there,' he teased.

'Anyway, what are you doing in New York?'

Sensing her awkwardness, he let her change the subject. 'Looking at a few properties. I might open a club over here.'

'Oh, right. So you'll be spending a lot of time in America, then?'

'Yeah – but I'll make sure I make time for you.'

'You're so confident, aren't you? Do all women say "yes" to you?'

'Yes…'

'Well, I haven't agreed to anything yet.'

'Hmmm… Playing hard to get? It only makes me try harder,' he baited.

Chapter 9

Connor was true to his word and continued his pursuit through daily texts over the next two weeks.

As his returned loomed, Eva felt more than a little anxious. Every fibre in her body was warning her against entering into any sort of relationship with him. First and foremost, he was her *boss;* secondly, he had the reputation that would make Casanova look like a monk.

Hi, I should be at the club in about forty-five minutes. I was thinking, I've got a poker game later but should be finished by midnight, so you could invite me back to yours?

Eva stared down at Connor's text as she walked over to her dressing table.

Roxanne suddenly stormed into the dressing room. 'Can you believe it?! I've just got a fucking flat tyre,' she moaned.

'Oh, what a nuisance,' said Eva, not really paying much attention as she sat pondering how to reply to Connor's text.

'*Nuisance?*' mimicked Roxanne. 'Fucking pain in the ass, more like!'

'Yeah…' said Eva, starting down at her mobile.

Sorry had time to think. Don't think it's a good idea, she texted back.

Ten seconds later a reply pinged back. *I am disappointed Eva. You played your part in this too and now you're calling it off?*

Sorry – you have nothing to lose, while I have everything!

Connor didn't reply. It was obvious he was angry with her. She felt strangely annoyed that he hadn't tried harder to change her mind. Perhaps it was for the best if his interested cooled so easily.

After sweeping on green eye shadow, she carefully glued on a pair of black false eyelashes. Blinking rapidly, she waited for glue to dry as thoughts of Connor swirled around in her mind. She reached down into the top drawer of her dressing table and pulled out a pair of pink and black lace knickers with matching silk bra. As she stepped out of her underwear, standing naked in front of her mirror, she glanced over to Tina's empty seat. It was a refreshing to be able to strip bare without Tina and Donna sniggering like two inbred hillbillies.

'Eva,' called out Ann from the back office.

'Yeah?'

'Mr O'Neill has asked that you and Roxanne join him and his guests tonight.'

'Oh…?' said Eva, scratching the back of her head and looking perplexed.

'Mr O'Neill is entertaining five clients with a private poker game upstairs in his penthouse apartment. You'll be expected to wait on the gentlemen. Roxanne knows the ropes, so she'll tell you want to do. You both need to be there in twenty minutes.'

Eva returned to the dressing room with a knot of apprehension in the pit of her stomach.

'I guess we'd better change, then,' said Roxanne picking up her gold PVC hot pants and bra. I have a couple of bits here if you want to borrow something.'

'Thanks…' said Eva, forcing a smile. The last thing she needed was to see Connor after what had happened. Perhaps he asked her to join them so he could ridicule her in front of his rich friends.

Roxanne grinned at Eva's choice of sapphire blue mini dress. 'You look hot, babes.'

Eva followed Roxanne through a side door and up a narrow stone staircase to the top floor with apprehension, but also intrigued to see Connor's bachelor pad.

'Why didn't we use the lift in the lobby?' asked Eva out of breath.

'One of O'Neill's many rules. We're only allowed to walk around front of house if we're accompanying a club member to the casino on the second floor.'

'Oh, so we know our place, then,' Eva said sarcastically. She followed Roxanne down a small hallway.

'Oh yes. I'm surprised Ann didn't tell you?'

Eva frowned before replying, 'No, I don't think she did.'

'Well, we're not allowed, so make sure you remember. Always use the back stairs otherwise *His Lordship* will have your guts for garters!'

'OK,' said Eva, making a mental note.

Taking in a deep breath, Eva stood behind Roxanne as she knocked on the large oak door of the penthouse.

'Come in,' said Connor opening the door.

Eva entered the apartment and looked around in awe at the fine furnishings, oil paintings and beautifully dressed panelled windows. She quickly averted her gaze to the floor and caught a waft of Connor's aftershave as she walked past him.

'Gentlemen, *Messieurs, permettez-moi de vous présenter Roxanne sur votre droite*,' said Connor fluently to introduce Roxanne. The group of gentlemen bobbed their heads in acknowledgement. '*Et cela est Eva*,' presented Connor while staring down at her flushed cheeks. 'Ladies, from your left, Monsieur Darl Morin, and Monsieur Louis Charbonneau from France. Larry Anderson is our guest from the States, Scott River is from the UK and Herr Markus Schmidt from Germany.'

'Hello.' Roxanne smiled, revealing her small sapphire tooth stone.

'Hello,' parroted Eva, noticing one of the French gentlemen smiling over at her.

'*Bonsoir, mademoiselle, parlez-vous Français?*'

Not understanding a word he said, Eva glanced over to Connor.

'He is asking if you speak French – I take it you don't?'

'No,' replied Eva, feeling more than a little embarrassed at her lack of linguistic skills.

'*Non, elle ne parle pas Français*,' said Connor, curtly.

'Then we will all speak English for you, mademoiselle,' said the portly Frenchman smiling over at her warmly.

Eva blushed. 'Thank you.'

'Shall we take our seats, gentleman?' Connor ushered the group towards a circular card table.

'Are we supposed to serve the drinks straight away?' whispered Eva to Roxanne.

'No, just wait until they're all sat at the table.'

Eva glanced over to a smartly dressed man stood by the table wearing a burgundy and gold Unicorn identification badge. 'Who's that?'

'Alan Parking, he's the club's senior croupier,' explained Roxanne.

'I don't know anything about poker, Roxy.'

'The basic rules are simple. The dealer, who is Alan, will ask the two French guys sitting to his left to place a blind bet – one small bet and one big bet. The small bet is half the value of the big bet – yeah?'

Eva blinked heavily as Roxanne tried to educate her on the basic rules of poker.

'Gentleman, the game will start in three minutes,' said Alan, placing five unopened packs of playing cards on the table.

'So…' whispered Roxanne, 'Alan deals two cards to each player face down. No one but the player will see these cards.'

'Right…' Eva replied, frowning.

'So, on the strength of the two cards, each player will decide if they want to bet or fold. Once everyone has placed their bets, Alan will place three cards face up in the centre of the table – this is called the "flop".'

'A flop?'

'Yes, a flop. Basically, each player is trying to secure the best hand using his two cards and the three "community cards" – the flop.'

Eva smiled weakly in confusion.

'Connor always insists on a "no limit". I've told you before, he isn't a cent and nickel kind of guy. Thousands of pounds can exchange hands during a private game, and sometimes the guys give the girls a tip – and best of all,' Roxanne said with a grin, 'Connor lets us keep it!'

'I like the sound of that,' Eva said smiling.

'Thought you might. So smile and stick those puppies out – tits equal tips!'

Eva flashed a big smile and pushed out her chest, making her ample bosoms spill over the tight bodice of her dress.

Connor was the last man to take his place at the table. 'Drinks,' he ordered, nodding over to Roxanne.

'If you can ask everyone what they want, I'll help you serve,' instructed Roxanne, turning towards an oblong table stacked with an assortment of wines, champagne and bottled beer.

Eva swayed sexily over to the table and took everyone's order.

Connor didn't look up to ask for a whisky with no ice.

'I believe the opening bet has been agreed, gentlemen – a thousand pounds sterling,' said Alan. 'Monsieur Morin, if you can place the small blind bet, please,' he added, opening a pack of playing cards.

The handsome Frenchman nodded as he pushed five hundred pounds into the centre of the table.

'I wouldn't kick him out of bed – would you?' whispered Roxanne as she turned her back towards the betting table.

Eva glanced over at him. His sandy-coloured hair sat neatly combed in long layers against his bronzed skin. She guessed his age was about thirty-eight and his friend, who was grey-haired and unattractive, about fifty-two.

'Yeah, he's not bad. I've never been out with a French guy,' she said. 'I wonder if it's true, you know, what they say about French men?'

Roxanne grinned. 'Yes, it is.'

'Oh – so you've dated a French guy?'

'Yeah, *for a night*,' Roxanne answered with a titter.

Trying to muffle their giggles, Eva filled three glasses with chilled champagne. 'I wouldn't say no. I like an older guy with an accent,' gushed Eva, pulling a dreamy face.

'That's Connor isn't it?' Roxanne's chuckle silenced Eva instantly.

'Shhh,' hissed Connor, flashing them both a look of annoyance.

Both Frenchmen pushed their bets into the centre of the table to begin the game.

Eva tried to concentrate, but boredom quickly set in watching the dealer deal two cards to each player. The room resembled an undertaker's Christmas party the men sat in silence gingerly curving the corners of their cards.

She looked at a large oil painting of a Pre-Raphaelite siren hung above the imposing white marble fireplace. She found it amusing that they were quite similar in appearance: both with flame-red hair, generous hips and large breasts. She then studied Connor's face. He reflected no emotion as he stared straight ahead; it was impossible to tell if he had a strong or weak hand.

'I'm out,' said Connor, turning his cards over and getting to his feet. 'Roxanne, why don't you show our foreign guests your full personality?' he said dryly – basically asking her to flirt and distract the other players as Tommy was still in the game.

'Okey-dokey,' answered Roxanne with a grin and a swagger to the poker table.

'Come with me,' Connor told Eva as he walked away from earshot of the group.

'You look amazing tonight,' he said broodingly whilst looking at her heaving bosoms.

Eva blushed trying to push her protruding flesh discretely back into the confines of her dress. 'Thank you.'

'So, you've obviously had a change of heart since the barbecue? I didn't realise your dislike for me ran so deep?'

Eva blinked up at him. 'Dislike?'

'Yes, you were just playing with my feelings. It's obvious to me now – you don't like me. I would even go so far as to say that I repel you!'

'No...' muttered Eva, lowering her voice and looking at the floor, 'that's not true.'

'I think you're just saying that because of who I am. My affections repulse you – I repulse you!'

'I explained why,' answered Eva, lowering her voice to a whisper. 'I have everything to lose, and you have nothing…apart from the price of an advertisement.'

'I promise you, here and now, I would not fire you if something happened between us – you have my word. I am not the cold bastard you think I am.'

'If I had a pound for every promise I'd been made,' scoffed Eva, 'I wouldn't need to play the lottery.'

'How can you be so cynical at what? Twenty-three—'

'I'll be twenty-five in December,' interrupted Eva. 'So I'm not a naive sixteen-year-old. I know how things go.'

Connor held her gaze. Her resistance and strength not only aroused him, but also heightened his intrigue. He knew he wouldn't be able to rest until his lust for her was quenched. 'Well, I can be a patient man…'

Eva smiled beneath the coyness of her lowered lashes. His pursuit was intense and she liked that. She couldn't halt the sexual effect he had over her.

'Thank you, gentlemen,' roared Tommy, followed by a squeal of delight from Roxanne, as he won with an ace of clubs.

'I'll speak to you later,' said Connor, brushing his fingers against her hand before returning to the table.

Roxanne skipped over to Eva beaming. 'Tommy has just won twelve thousand fucking pounds!' she squealed.

'Oh my God, that's amazing!' said Eva, genuinely happy for her friend.

'What did His Lordship want?'

'He just asked me to keep everyone's glass topped up.'

'Tommy reckons he's seeing someone because he's always secretly texting.'

'Seeing someone?' said Eva, swallowing hard.

'Yeah, he loves the thrill of the chase!' scoffed Roxanne pouring them both a drink.

'Who's this mystery woman, did Tommy say who she is?'

'Even if he knew, he wouldn't say anyway,' Roxanne said with a shrug and muffling a belch. 'I told you, Tommy would never betray Connor's confidence, not even to me.'

Eva took a large gulp of her drink and looked at Connor who returned her stare with a perplexed frown.

'I'm out,' said Connor casually folding again without a word of disgruntlement towards the dealer. His indifferent mood resulted in glances of shock and confusion from his guests. Tommy noticed Connor give Eva a lingering look as he left the table.

'Can you pour me a whisky, Miss Summers?' Connor smirked and purposely blocked her so she had to brush past him to reach the bottle.

She inhaled the pungent fragrance of whisky mingled with the masculine aroma of his aftershave. 'Ice?' she murmured.

'Yes, thanks. I like my drink like my women, hot and fiery and distilled for about twenty-five years,' he added softly so Roxanne couldn't hear.

Lowering her gaze, Eva felt the tips of his fingers brush against hers as he took the crystal tumbler from her hand.

'Just popping to the ladies,' said Roxanne, oblivious to the mounting tension between her boss and Eva.

'*Spend the night with me,*' implored Connor urgently.

Eva swallowed hard and bit her lip. The temptation of being ravished by him was proving increasingly difficult to resist.

'What, just one night?' asked Eva.

'Whatever you want,' answered Connor quickly, sensing her resolve was beginning to weaken. 'I promise it won't affect your employment – you have my word.'

One night of passion, thought Eva, *then we could just carry on as if nothing had happened. We'd never mention it again; it would all be forgotten.*

Connor instantly latched onto the glimmer of hope of a one-night stand. 'As I said, you have *my word* on it, Eva,' he repeated.

'And you promise?'

'Absolutely, I promise on my life!'

'Then, my answer is…'

'Is…?' badgered Connor eagerly.

'Yes…'

'When?' Connor's urgency intensified.

'I-I don't know.'

'When's your next night off?'

'I'm not sure… Wednesday, I think, but—'

'I fly out to Ireland tomorrow morning, but I can come back early the next day – on the Wednesday. Shall I book a hotel room?'

His questions bombarding her like a flurry of hailstones left her feeling dazed and anxious. 'Wednesday's the day after next!'

'I don't want to leave it any longer in case you change your mind,' confessed Connor.

A faint smile curved Eva's lips as Connor's honesty sent a shiver of anticipation down her spine.

Seeing Roxanne returning, Eva took a step backwards increasing the gap between them. 'Yes – okay, but not in a hotel,' she quickly whispered.

'I'll text you later for details,' said Connor, swiftly walking away when Roxanne approached them.

'Let's have another drink.' Roxanne sighed. 'Connor can go on all night!'

Eva couldn't help but smile at her comment.

Chapter 10

Eva looked down at the fresh linen covering her bed and held her stomach to steady her nerves. She had spent the last two hours polishing and vacuuming the whole house.

Connor reassured her through hourly texts of his desire.

Having ran a bath, she sat immersed sipping on a cold glass of wine as scented candles flickered around her.

The water was almost cold by the time she got out. She glanced at her alarm clock in her bedroom, it was six o'clock – another two hours until Connor was due to arrive. Her stomach groaned through lack of food as she dried her hair, but she couldn't face eating anything.

She opened her wardrobe door and pondered whether to wear demure or revealing. The choice was proving to be too over whelming and panic started to set in.

'I need a cigarette,' she muttered, quickly going down into the kitchen. She stepped out into the garden when her mobile beeped in her dressing gown pocket.

Will be early, see you in an hour – Connor x

'*Fuck!*' cursed Eva, taking a deep drag on her cigarette.

She took her third glass of wine upstairs and looked at the array of outfits lying on her bed. Frowning with indecision, she slipped into a pair of silk and lace red knickers and matching bra, and sprayed a cloud of perfume over her body before finally deciding on her black mini dress.

For the next hour she paced her bedroom taking sporadic guzzles of wine in between peering out of her window every two minutes. '*Ohhh, shit, he's here,*' she gasped, jumping back from the window. Brushing her glossed lips together, she tried to compose herself by exhaling deeply through her mouth. Slight nausea washed over her as she closed her eyes for a second before opening the front door.

'Evening, Miss Summers,' Connor said beaming, holding a beautiful bouquet of flowers and a bottle of champagne.

'Hello.' Eva blushed instantly. 'They're beautiful – thank you,' she added, clumsily taking the flowers from him.

'Champagne, too?' Connor smiled holding up a bottle of Bollinger champagne.

'I already have some wine opened, unless you want to open this?' she gabbled on nervously, closing the door behind him.

'Actually, I thought we could go straight to bed?' Connor said brazenly.

'P-Pardon?' stuttered Eva, stopping dead in her tracks.

'Yes, a drink would be good, Eva,' Connor said, laughing. 'I'll open the champagne, shall I?'

'I forgot you had a sense of humour,' mocked Eva, following him into the kitchen.

A brief moment of awkwardness descended as they sat down in the lounge.

'So, what have you been doing all day?' asked Connor, filling the silence.

'Nothing exciting,' replied Eva, taking a sip of champagne. 'So how was your trip to Ireland?'

'I went to see my family.'

'Do you have a large family?'

'Four sisters and one brother, Gabriel. You met him at the charity gala,' said Connor.

'How about you – any sisters or brothers?'

'No, just me,' said Eva, offering an anxious smile.

Eva cheeks darkened to a rosy hue as silence filled the room again. 'S-sorry would you like cheese and crackers?' she stammered.

'No thanks,' said Connor, raising his eyebrows. 'Why don't you come and sit next to me?'

Taking a large gulp of champagne, awkwardness pinned her to her seat.

'Do you fear me?' Connor said frowning.

Eva crossed her legs. 'No!' she insisted.

Connor studied her uneasy body language and softened his approach.

'So tell me, what did you want to be when you were growing up? I wanted to be an astronaut. Well, actually, between you and me, when I was three, I wanted to be a dolphin.' His laughed revealed two deep dimples.

'A dolphin?' Eva giggled and leaned forward. 'I don't believe you.'

'I swear – a dolphin. My dad was a fisherman, and during the school holidays he would take us out to sea to watch the dolphins. So I wanted to be one. What about you?' he asked, reaching over and refilling her glass.

'I don't know…' Eva wrinkled her nose in thought. 'It wasn't to be a pole dancer, that's for sure.' She giggled and noticed for the first time how dashing he looked in his black tailored suit and deep burgundy shirt.

'No, I guess not.'

'I've always liked animals, but I never got the grades to go on to uni,' she quipped as she watched him get to his feet and walk over to her.

Gently lifting her out of the seat, he pulled her close. 'We don't have to do anything if you don't want to,' he said softly, reaching under her chin and tilting her face up towards him. 'If you've changed your mind?'

Staring up at his handsome face, Eva closed her eyes and parted her lips as she felt his hand cup her cheek tenderly.

His warm lips manipulated her mouth. She felt his hand slide beneath her short dress and caress her bare thigh.

'SHIT!' called out Connor, quickly releasing her.

'Naughty boy!' bellowed Eva looking down at Mr Jingles whose sharp claws were hooked into Connor's trouser leg. 'Sorry…' she offered while quickly detaching her cat's paws.

'Don't worry,' said Connor, brushing cat hairs off his trousers, 'but perhaps you could put him outside?'

'*Perhaps* we could go upstairs?' said Eva, her cheeks burning.

'Well, Miss Summers, how can I refuse such an offer,' retorted Connor, beaming.

Standing on the landing, Eva told Connor to go through to her bedroom while she nipped into the bathroom.

'Shit, *this is it*,' she muttered to herself, staring into the bathroom mirror. '*THIS IS IT!*' Quickly undressing, she left her clothes in a pile on the bathroom floor and fluffed her hair into messy layers. After squirting another cloud of perfume, she took a final look at her reflection. *Just enjoy it, then forget about it, Eva*, she told herself.

Opening the bathroom door, she was greeted by Mr Jingles meowing loudly outside her bedroom door.

'I won't be a minute,' she called out before sprinting downstairs in her underwear followed by Mr Jingles. 'Go on, go and catch some mice,' she said, shooing him out of the cat flap.

Back upstairs, she fluffed her hair again before gently pushing down the door handle and walking into her bedroom.

'Hello, gorgeous…' said Connor, grinning.

Eva lowered her gaze and felt her cheeks blush as she glanced up at Connor sitting naked under her cream duvet.

'I hope it was okay to…'

'Y-yes of course,' stuttered Eva, averting her gaze from his tanned naked chest.

'Why don't you come and join me,' Connor said gently, letting his gaze wander down the full length of her body.

A coy smile shaped her lips as she looked down at the refilled glass sitting on the bedside table. Quickly slipping under the duvet, she suddenly felt a bit tipsy as Connor rolled onto his side to look at her.

'Are you drunk?'

'No, just a little merry.' Eva smiled as her hair sprayed across the pillow.

'Good.' Leaning over, he kissed her gently on the lips.

Running her fingers through his hair, she felt his kiss intensify as his tongue probed deeper into her mouth. Feeling his hand reach behind her, he gently pulled her onto her side and unclipped her bra with one swift movement of his fingers.

Eva's body jerked when he suddenly threw off the duvet cover, sending it crumpling to the floor as he lay naked and aroused by her side.

'Your skin is so soft,' he whispered nuzzling her breast while gently stoking the inside of her thigh.

Feeling him gently brush over her lace knickers, Eva let her legs fall open. Connor eagerly slipped his fingers underneath.

With breathy sighs, Eva writhed under his touch as his fingers controlled the intensity of her pleasure.

'Connor…' gasped Eva, on the brink of ecstasy.

'Not yet,' groaned Connor, moving down the bed. 'I want to taste you…'

Watching in almost tunnel vision, Eva saw Connor's face slowly sink between the soft flesh of her thighs. She gasped in ecstasy as the warmth and firmness of his tongue brushed against her swollen clitoris.

Jolts of bliss shuddered through her body while Connor's head bobbed rhythmically between her thighs.

'Eva…!' called out Connor, slipping his index and middle finger into her writhing body; her hips twisted to find his mouth once more.

'Con-nor…' croaked Eva clawing at the bed sheets – an intense orgasm pulsating through her body.

'Hmmm…' groaned Connor, small beads of perspiration sat in clusters on his temples. He planted small kisses up her body until he reached her mouth.

Tasting her own orgasm on his lips, she felt Connor's erection pressing against her thigh as he kissed her.

Moving down the bed, Eva's hair lay in folds across his groin as she touched his penis. His thick erection felt like a baton of steel beneath a warm silk sheath.

'No, I want to see your face,' insisted Connor, leading her to the edge of the bed and motioning her to kneel down in front of him. '*Yeahhh*,' he said breathlessly, gathering up her hair as her slender fingers moved up and down the shaft of his penis. '*E-va…*' he panted, feeling her warm mouth envelope his erection.

His cries of pleasure moved in sync with the gentle thrusting of his pelvis as Eva sucked and caressed eagerly, until he suddenly pushed her away.

'On the bed!' ordered Connor impatiently. He reached over to the bedside cabinet, ripped open a box of condoms and pulled out a silver packet.

Eva watched memorised as he tore apart the foil with his teeth before rolling the latex sheath over his impressive erection. *Oh my God…* she thought, remembering Roxanne's comment about her friend Grant.

Connor knelt between her legs with pure lust in his eyes. Orally pleasuring her once more, her wetness moistened his lips as he padded up the bed on his hands and knees. Letting his arms take his weight, he lowered his body onto her.

Enthusiastically wrapping her legs around his waist, Eva watched with bated breath as Connor reached down to his penis, slowly guiding himself into her body. She placed her hands on his broad shoulders stroking down to his biceps bulging like two orbs of granite.

Eva dug her nails into his taut flesh with the full length of his erection deep inside her.

Deep groans of pleasure fell from Connor's mouth onto her flushed cheeks as his thrusts became harder and quicker. The bed shook beneath their weight making the bedside lamp wobble with the movement of the bed knocking against it.

'I want to see your body – I want you to fuck me, Eva,' insisted Connor, withdrawing and rolling on his back.

Eva straddled his muscular thighs and guided his penis into her body. Her long red hair swaying as she rocked back and forth.

Cupping her breasts, Connor greedily nuzzled her nipple as ecstasy pulsated through his balls.

'Connor...!' exhaled Eva, almost incoherently as a third orgasm engulfed her body.

Cradling her tight against his chest, Connor attentively brushed stands of damp hair away from her flushed cheeks as her breathlessness subsided.

'Get onto your knees...' whispered Connor.

With her palms flat on the bed, she felt Connor kneel behind her. Enjoying the smoothness of his hand gently caressing her bottom, she shrieked with shock when his hand struck her flesh.

Hearing her cry out sent a feverish pulse of lust straight to his penis as he thrust relentlessly into her body. So urgent was his passion, she wondered that he might physically push off the edge of the bed.

'On your back, Eva!' said Connor, growling with frenzied lust, forcefully flipped her over. He grabbed her legs and lifted them over his shoulders as he thrust deep inside, filling her.

Her whole body felt damp and hot as her feet bobbed above his head. So energetic was his love-making that the headboard knocked violently against the wall like an impatient debt collector.

'*Jesusss...*' cried out Connor before his body jerked and shuddered to a halt. His contorted face suddenly softened as his orgasm abated. He rolled onto his back and lay silently catching his breath before reaching down and removing the used condom. After dropping it into a small wicker basket by the side of the bed, he turned to look at Eva. 'Any regrets?'

'No, why have you?' asked Eva, quickly bringing her legs together.

'None at all.' Connor grinned, gently brushing his hand across the softness of her stomach.

Only now, lying naked, did she feel slightly exposed. Lust had overridden her senses, but now she had to confront the fact that she'd just had sex with her boss.

'Your body is delicious, Miss Summers,' said Connor in his deep Irish drawl, brushing his fingertips over her nipple.

'Thanks...' Eva blushed as her nipple rose under his caress.

'I know you said this would be a "one-off",' said Connor with a grin, 'but does that mean we can only have sex once, or can I make love to you again – just to clarify things.'

His comment made her laugh. '*To clarify,*' mocked Eva.

'Are you taking the mickey out of me?' Connor asked with a smirk.

She giggled. 'Er…that would be a *yes*.'

'Well, Miss Summers, do you know the punishment for such subordination.'

'Subordination?' she scoffed.

'Yes – laughing at the boss.'

'Hmmm… I think I can probably guess…' Eva blushed, letting her legs fall open.

For a second time that night, she enjoyed multiple orgasms through his experienced hands.

Connor quickly fell asleep after their second love-making session.

She picked up the crumpled duvet cover off the floor and gently draped it across his body after admiring his manhood one last time. She lay on her back looking up at the ceiling. The smell of his warm body consumed her with sexual yearning. She pressed her thighs together as a surge of pleasure throbbed deep inside.

*   *   *

A gentle tapping noise woke her; a cool breeze chilled the room. Looking across at the empty space next to her, she brushed her hand across the cold bed sheet unsure whether she had dreamt the whole thing. Her alarm clock read 8:05 a.m.

She threw the duvet off her naked body and grabbed her dressing gown before shoving her feet into a pair of novelty hedgehog slippers. After shuffling into the bathroom, she held a warm flannel up to her mouth and stared into a small vanity mirror sitting on the windowsill.

'Well, things that I might live to regret list,' she said flippantly. 'Sleeping with the boss – tick.' She sighed staring back at her reflection.

She plodded downstairs and nearly jumped out of her skin when she walked into the kitchen. '*SHIT!*'

'Sorry, I didn't mean to startle you,' said Connor smiling. 'I thought I'd make us some breakfast.'

'I thought you'd left,' said Eva, quickly trying to flatten her hair with her hand.

'Well, you thought wrong,' he said, grinning.

Mr Jingles watched patiently hoping the thin strip of smoked salmon dangling from Connor's fingers was for him.

'Do you want orange juice or coffee?'

'I'm easy...' said Eva. '*I mean*, I don't mind – either,' she corrected herself quickly and averted her gaze by peering over to a pan of poached eggs.

I know what you're thinking,' added Connor, handing her a plate of fresh salmon and a poached egg on granary toast.

'*Can you?*' said Eva, worried that he actually could.

'You're thinking not only is he a considerate lover, but he can cook, too,' he quipped boastfully.

'I am a little surprised,' Eva said, cheekily. 'I didn't think you were the type to stay around for breakfast.'

Connor replied dryly, 'Shut up and eat.'

'Hmm...delicious,' Eva said smiling before wetting the tip of her finger and scraping a dribble of egg from her dressing gown.

'Hope you don't mind, but I grabbed a shower earlier. *I could* be persuaded to take another, though?' teased Connor, taking her empty plate and placing it down on the coffee table.

Eva blushed. 'I thought we agreed it was just going to be a one-night stand.'

'I guess it doesn't count until I leave – right?' Connor glanced down at her bare legs through the opening of her dressing gown.

'*Actually...I was* thinking of taking a shower.'

'I am also very good at washing hair,' said Connor, pulling her up from her seat and wrapping his arms around her waist.

'Your aftercare service is five star, Mr O'Neill,' mocked Eva playfully. 'Are you always so attentive?'

'No...' said Connor pulling her close into his body. 'I am not always this nice, so I suggest you take full advantage of my good mood.'

'Take full advantage, eh?' Eva enjoyed their flirtatious banter.

Connor swept her up in his arms and carried her upstairs.

With a cloud of warm steam circling them, Connor reached down for the large bow holding Eva's dressing gown together. 'I remember the first time I saw you.'

'My audition...' Eva smiled at him as her dressing gown fell from her shoulders.

'The way you swayed past me with your delicious heart-shaped ass,' said Connor walking behind her. 'You made my dick hard,' he soothed, lifting up her hair.

His warm breath on the nape of her neck sent a shiver of excitement down her spine. She felt his hand brush against the soft curve of her stomach up to her breast.

'You came between me and my sleep that night,' whispered Connor, slipping his other hand down towards her groin. 'I knew I wouldn't be able to rest until I had you.'

Reaching behind her, Eva brushed her hand over his budging erection pressing through his trousers; she panted heavily under his intoxicating, lustful words.

'*Oh God…*' whimpered Eva as his fingers manipulated her clitoris. '*Connor,*' she murmured, feeling her legs buckle under sheer ecstasy.

'Not yet, baby,' groaned Connor, quickly reaching up to unbuckle his belt.

His mobile suddenly rang out.

'Please don't stop…!' Eva cried out.

'Let me quickly get rid of them, baby,' gasped Connor, reaching for his phone.

On the brink of orgasm, she pressed her thighs together as Connor mercilessly removed his fingers from her sex.

'Yeah?' snapped Connor down the phone. 'Why, what's been said?' He frowned, looking down at Eva bending down to grab her dressing gown. 'Okay, I'll be about twenty minutes. Don't do anything until I get there – yeah?'

'Oh, you have to go?' asked Eva, disappointed he couldn't stay to ravish her for a third time.

'Mm-hmm…Yeah – pity because I'm good at making lunch, too,' he teased, zipping his trousers and buckling up his belt.

'It's nothing serious, is it?' asked Eva, following him out of the bathroom.

'No, but it's something I have to deal with.'

'Oh, okay… So…' she said with a soft smile. 'I'll probably see you at the club later?'

'I might pop down and see you – if that's allowed?'

'Allowed?'

'Well, you're the rule maker. I just do as I'm told.'

His dry sense of humour made her laugh.

'Until later, then,' said Connor, kissing her passionately on the lips.

Chapter 11

'Evening, Eva,' Roxanne said with a sigh before popping two painkillers.

'Headache?'

Roxanne grimaced. 'Hangover, actually.'

'Fancy coming for a cigarette to take your mind off it?' said Eva, shaking her cigarette packet at her.

'Yeah, okay,' Roxanne muttered.

Eva made her way outside with Roxanne wincing as she followed her.

'I didn't know fucking peach schnapps was so bloody strong,' she moaned, taking a deep drag on her cigarette. 'Mind you, mixing it with vodka probably wasn't a great idea…' she said before releasing a belch. 'So, how's you?'

Instantly blushing, Eva wet her lips and looked at the floor. 'Yeah, fine.'

'Oh, yeah, before I die of this fucking hangover,' exaggerated Roxanne. 'Halloween is next Friday, and we always dress up. I've got loads of stuff, so you can borrow something, if you want?'

'Cheers, Roxy.' Eva smiled. 'I don't deserve you. You're such a good mate.'

'Oh, shut up,' mocked Roxanne pretending to be bashful.

Back in the dressing room, Eva sat at her table checking her mobile for the umpteenth time. She hadn't heard anything from Connor since he left that morning.

'Can I have a bit of quiet please, ladies?' Everyone turned to look at Ann holding a black clipboard. 'We have two corporate parties in tonight. Yin and Chu Steel Corporation, and Patterson-Clark Solicitors. As some of you know, Mr Chu is an enthusiastic member of the club.'

'He's a bloody octopus that smells like a damp dog!' exclaimed Tina, knowing Chu would make a beeline for her.

'Yes…' Ann frowned knowing that, for once, Tina was telling the truth. 'Well, Mr O'Neill will be joining them this evening, so I'm sure he'll keep an eye on our guest. So, Tina, Rebecca and Scarlet can you all be ready by seven thirty. Please don't keep Mr O'Neill and his guests waiting, girls.'

They nodded in agreement.

'Right, Donna and Lyn, you can accompany Patterson-Clark in the casino.'

'Ricky Patterson is well fit?' announced Donna excitedly.

'Yes, quite,' said Ann. 'That's all, ladies, so please watch your language and try to sell the Moet champagne because we're holding too much stock,' added Ann.

'Great!' whined Rebecca, clipping a layer of hair extensions under her shoulder-length bob. 'A night of being pawed by that slimy bastard!' she cursed. 'You do know he offered me a grand to suck him off! I wouldn't have minded if it had been Patterson – but Chu, I'd rather eat a dog turd!'

The dance lounge was swarming with punters. Every table was occupied with an overspill of men at the bar.

Eva waited until Rosie walked to the edge of the stage before swaggering past, letting her long mane of copper red hair swing in heavy layers down her back.

A cluster of high-pitched whistles greeted her from a group of men sitting at the front of the stage as she stepped onto the dance podium.

She noticed Connor was sitting by Chu who was happily sandwiched between Rebecca and Tina. She would have pitied any other girl, but Tina, who was grinning like a Z-list celebrity opening a supermarket, deserved no such sympathy.

Eva held the pole between her thighs and spun her body up and down as though riding a carousel. Letting her body fall into a perfect arch, she tried to concentrate on her routine as she held the pose for a couple of seconds. Pulling her body upright, she glanced back over to Connor.

'What the hell!' she muttered, watching Tina brazenly drape herself all over Connor, who didn't seem to be in any rush to block her advances.

After dismounting the pole, Eva couldn't help feeling betrayed by Connor's lack of sensitivity. He knew that she and Tina disliked each other, yet he let Tina slobber all over him in front of her.

Eva knelt on the stage and started her floor routine. A volley of cheers from Connor's guests circled the stage as she reached for the small silver zipper holding together her black leather waistcoat. With anticipation filling the air, she held the zip between her fingers and slowly undid her waistcoat to Queen's rock track 'Fat Bottomed Girls'.

Out the corner of her eye she could see Chu pointing towards the stage. He flapped his arms excitedly as Connor nodded over towards her.

After letting her waistcoat fall to the floor, she lay on her back with her legs apart and slipped her hand down between her thighs. Brushing her fingers over the silky triangle of her G-string, she arched her back.

Admiring glances and prolonged open-mouthed leers washed over her body, followed by a flurry of high-value notes littering the stage.

'Lucky you,' said Rebecca beckoning Eva to the edge of the stage. 'Old man Chu has took a liking to you, so Connor wants you to join us.'

Staring over at Connor, while Chu waved at her excitedly, Eva tried to conceal her reluctance to join the group. She grabbed her waistcoat from the stage and quickly made her way back to the dressing room to hand in her money before changing into a white boob tube dress.

'Aren't we going for a fag, then?' asked Roxanne seeing Eva rush towards the door.

'No, Connor wants me to join him and Chu!' she huffed before disappearing out of the room. She pursed her lips and inhaled deeply on her way over to Connor and Chu.

"Ello, please join, bootiful lady! We have champagne!' said Chu grinning like a demented clown.

Connor frowned and nodded at Eva to quickly do as Chu instructed.

'Drink!' barked Chu, shoving a glass of champagne in her hand, his bulbous cheeks glistening under the hot spotlights. Gratefully, at least, she couldn't detect the smell of damp dog.

'Name again, please?' Chu asked with an enthusiastic nod.

'Eva—'

'Miss Summers has only been with the club a couple of months,' said Connor, clicking his fingers at one of the topless waitresses to replace their empty champagne bottle.

'Here, sit!' instructed Chu, dismissing two of his flunkies who quickly gave up their seats for her.

Eva crossed her legs and tried to discreetly edge away from his infatuation with her, or rather her breasts.

'You bootiful wred hair, lade,' gushed Chu, clumsily draping his arm around her shoulders.

Feeling his clammy fingers touch her bare skin propelled Eva to jerk forward in her seat before flashing Connor a look of utter contempt. She was used to men leering and ogling her body, but not in such close proximity. *Why is Connor letting this odorous man brazenly molest me?*

'Hmmm, smell good – yes you, E-va.'

Eva, ignoring his comment, stared ahead at Tina busily occupying the other two men in the group by thrusting out her breasts and pouting like Marilyn Monroe, much to the pleasure of her two slightly inebriated admirers.

'Drink, drink!' barked Chu, refilling her glass to the brim.

Eva glared at Connor again hoping he would tell his 'guest' to back off, but Connor seemed incapable of reading her grimace – or chose to ignore it.

'Fire!' swooned Chu flicking Eva's hair over her shoulder.

Not being able to persuade her mouth to form a civil reply, Eva mustered a fake smile through gritted teeth at her obnoxious suitor.

'Shall we make our way to the casino?' said Connor, eager to maximise Chu's good mood by keeping him intoxicated.

Eva tugged at the flimsy material of her dress and pulled it high over her breasts as they entered the casino. She looked underdressed next to Rebecca and Tina, who wore stylish cocktail dresses. She thought about asking Connor if she could change, but the thought of speaking to him made her feel nauseous.

As they made their way towards the first roulette table, Eva tried to distance herself from Chu by falling back from the group.

'Look, I know his behaviour is a little indelicate, but can't you try a little harder?' whispered Connor, grabbing her arm.

'Try harder!' growled Eva. 'You're lucky I haven't spat in his face!'

'Stop being so sensitive and start acting more professional,' seethed Connor. 'He's a degenerate gambler when drunk – so smile and encourage him to drink more!'

Eva looked up at him with a sarcastic smile. 'Of course, money is what makes your heart beat, doesn't it, Connor?! Everyone has a value to you,' she goaded, jerking her arm out of his grip.

'For fuck's sake, I'm not asking you to screw the guy – just do your job and get him to bet!' snarled Connor with a furrowed brow.

'Tell me one thing, before I'm forced to sell my pride,' quipped Eva, 'would you let such a man paw one of your sisters? You're no better than Booth!'

Such a comment made Connor clench his teeth in anger. He wasn't used to being spoken to like that by anyone, especially not a member of his own staff.

'Don't you walk away from me!' fumed Connor, trying to grab her again.

Eva quickly flinched her hand away and strode over to Chu who was standing at the roulette table with a large stack of multicoloured betting chips.

'Maybe I can be your Lady Luck?' she offered with a grin, not having the guts to implement any of her high principles.

'Yes, yes, you Lade Luck! You win for me, ha-ha.' Chu laughed and quickly removed his hand from Tina's waist while grinning longingly up at Eva.

'Shall we play?' purred Eva, snatching a large handful of chips.

'You choose, prease,' said Chu, nodding at Eva. 'You choose lucke numba!'

'Place your bets, please,' called out the croupier.

Looking down at the mosaic of black and red squares, Eva knew as much about roulette as she did about poker: practically zero. Randomly choosing ten black and sixteen red, she stacked a tower of chips on each square.

'Good... Yes,' rambled Chu, glancing down at the table, then quickly back up to her cleavage.

'No more bets, please,' said the croupier, dropping a small wooden ball onto the wheel.

Connor stood at the side of the group staring at Eva under a deep frown.

'Number four black,' called out the croupier, gathering all the betting chips from the chequered board.

'Oh, no! You lose me mone!' Chu said in a high-pitched wail. 'You do betta now!' he added, pushing a pile of high-value chips over to her.

Feeling her skin crawl under Chu's touch, Eva flashed Connor another look of disbelief as he callously averted his gaze.

'Nine red!' called out Eva, grabbing the chips with both hands.

'No!' said Chu, grabbing her hand. 'Too many!'

'But we could win?' argued Eva, forcing a smile.

'Hmmm...' Chu smiled as he wet his lips and narrowed his eyes. 'Kiss if win, ha-ha!'

The croupier glanced up at Eva, then across to Connor who nodded for the bet to be honoured. Both Connor and the croupier knew the club would stand to lose double the original bet if nine red won – it was worth thirty-four grand.

'No more bets, please.'

Eva prayed for the wooden ball to drop on nine red. She wanted to hurt Connor where he would feel it: in his wallet.

'Twelve black,' called out the croupier, placing a small brass weight on the winning square.

'Ohhhhh, you lost mo-ne!' cried out Chu, slapping his hand hard against her bottom. 'Vary bad girl!'

'How dare you slap me!' roared Eva, sending her hand crashing against Chu's cheek. 'You disgusting creature, you repulse me!'

Chu's lackeys inhaled in unison.

A stunned Connor gawped in disbelief.

Tina and Rebecca held their hands over their mouths in shock.

As the angry commotion unravelled behind her, Eva could hear Chu's voice echoing around the room. She ran to the casino foyer before storming angrily into the ladies toilets with her heart pounding.

'Eva, STOP!' barked Connor, rushing after her.

'NO!' she cried out.

Connor charged in after her, his quick reflexes stopping the door from hitting him in the face.

Eva spun around and glared at him. 'I don't have anything to say to you!'

'Well – I have plenty to say to you!' shouted Connor. 'You've embarrassed me in front of an important guest. I told you to ride it out. Chu is worth millions, so go back in there and apologise!' he seethed, baring his teeth in anger.

'I'd rather crawl back to Booth on my belly than apologise to that creep!' she fired back.

'Careful what you wish for, because you're seconds away from that becoming a reality!'

His vicious warning made her blink back tears as she stood trembling with rage.

'Why are you the only one acting the diva tonight? Tina and Rebecca aren't complaining – they're just getting on with the job!'

'Diva!' Eva grimaced, taking a step backwards. 'He's a filthy pig! I don't care about Tina and Rebecca. If you want to pimp them out, then that's up to you. I'm a dancer, not bait for sexual predators like him!'

'*A pimp?*' scoffed Connor, shaking his head.

'You're making us lead him on – that's not fair,' she argued, her cheeks crimson with anger.

'So?' yelled Connor, shrugging his shoulders. 'The Unicorn is a business. Do you think that taking your knickers off is enough to run this place? We need people like Chu to lose big.'

'His hands were everywhere! He's a lecherous slimeball!'

'I've been watching him all night. All he's done is put his arm around your waist and tap your backside – hardly a hanging offence!'

'So you think I'm overacting?' disputed Eva.

'Yes! You're not bloody Mother Teresa; you're a stripper for Christ's sake. I'm sure you've had to deal with worse!'

His words were cold and void of any tenderness or respect. He couldn't have made her feel more worthless and degraded.

'Where are you going?' roared Connor when she charged past him.

Eva reached for the door but stumbled backwards as Tina thundered in.

'Chu is livid. I think he's going to leave, Connor,' she warned, flashing Eva a look of disdain. 'I *can't believe* she lashed out at him. You could be done for assault, you know,' she added, jabbing her finger at Eva. 'Chu could be phoning the police right now!' she crowed theatrically.

'That's all I need, the Old Bill crawling all over the place. Right, get out of my sight, Eva!' snarled Connor, his eyes dark with rage.

She flounced past Tina, trying to disguise her quivering bottom lip, and strode back into the dressing room with fury oozing from every pore. She dried her eyes after five minutes of intermittent crying.

Roxanne walked in. 'Where have you been?'

'Hiding,' muttered Eva, keeping her face low so the light wouldn't show her swollen red eyes.

'I heard something happened in the casino?'

'Have you spoken to Connor, then?' asked Eva dabbing her eyes with toilet issue.

'No, but Rebecca told me what happened. She said Connor was trying to calm Chu down. I think you've caused quite a stir, babes.'

'Shit, I'm going to get the sack, aren't I?' whimpered Eva.

'Look, we don't know anything for sure yet. Chu's a prolific groper. You're not the first and certainly won't be last to fall fowl of his sweaty little mitts. A few of the girls have complained about him, but you're the first to have slapped him one, so respect for that,' said Roxanne grinning.

'Eva…? My office NOW!' called out Ann.

'Good luck,' mouthed Roxanne as Eva glanced anxiously up at her.

'Shut the door,' ordered Ann. 'Do you realise the seriousness of your actions this evening? Physically assaulting a member of the club! What were you thinking, Eva?'

'He assaulted me first!' she stressed. 'He slapped my bottom! Surely that's classed as physical assault?'

'Look, Eva,' Ann said impatiently. 'You've worked the clubs; you should know how to handle situations like this in a professional manner. Mr O'Neill was with the group, so surely you must've known you were perfectly safe.'

'You'd think, wouldn't you?' huffed Eva sarcastically. 'Am I going to get the sack?' Eva asked, snivelling into a tissue.

'Mr O'Neill has not instructed me to do that, but such behaviour is not acceptable here, even if you're provoked. Violence is *never* acceptable.'

Eva bowed her head as Ann sighed with exasperation.

'You're a good dancer and popular with the club's members, but you keep finding yourself in trouble.'

'Sorry, Ann,' she mumbled.

'Mr O'Neill doesn't want to risk Mr Chu seeing you again tonight, so he wants you to go home.'

'Maybe I can do a couple of private dances, no one—'

'No, Mr O'Neill wants you off the premises.'

'Oh, okay…' muttered Eva walking out of her office.

'What did Ann say?' asked Roxanne looking worried.

'Connor wants me off the premises,' she said with a sniffle on her way to her locker.

'Shit, has he sacked you then?'

'No, well, not yet, but I think he will. I'll text you tomorrow and let you know,' she said with a sense of doom.

'Yeah, okay. Look for what's it worth, you're a good dancer and Connor knows that. He won't sack you lightly. Look, if I hear anything I'll let you know. Try to stay positive, babes.'

'Yeah,' said Eva. She mustered a weak grin and choked back more tears as she clocked out.

The cool night air soothed her reddened eyes as she walked down the black granite steps towards the public footpath. Glancing up at the starry sky, she felt very small under the vast darkness above her.

She slumped down into the driver seat and switched on the ignition while fishing out her mobile from her bag. She was numb driving through Mayfair as her mind teased her with the many consequences facing her. Would she be sacked? Would she be issued with her final warning? Could she rely on Connor's lust to save her?

She pulled up in front of a set of traffic lights just as her mobile phone lit up in her lap.

Be at the club for 6 tomorrow and come to see me straight away.

Eva re-read Connor's text with fear. *Are you going to sack me?* she replied.

What choice have you given me? Give me one good reason why I shouldn't fire you?

Eva heard a car horn blare behind her and glanced up to see the traffic lights had changed to green. She pulled away and parked up at a bus stop. *Because it wasn't all my fault! That creep put his hands on me and because I'm just a stripper, YOUR WORDS, I'm the one who has to pay the price because I'm expendable.*

You were never in any danger! came the reply.

I'm not a piece of meat to be pawed at. I told you I felt uncomfortable and you did NOTHING! she retaliated, cursing him under her breath and dropping the phone back in her lap.

With no immediate reply, her temper got the better of her. She grabbed the phone and threw it down into the passenger foot well.

'Arrogant, unfeeling bastard!' she cussed loudly before driving off again.

Chapter 12

'Hmm... What?' croaked Eva waking abruptly. She fumbled for her phone and squinted to scroll down her messages.

You still haven't apologised to me, perhaps if you did, it would soften my mood!!

She dropped her phone down on the bed and rolled onto her back. She had only been asleep for twenty minutes, and now Connor had woken her up asking her to apologise.

'Oh, go away,' she said, groaning.

Her mobile pinged again.

She turned onto her side and stared over towards the yellow hue of the street lamp shining through her window. She grabbed her phone and sighed reading Connor's second text.

You can't be asleep already. Don't ignore me Eva!

Actually I was asleep, but I'm awake now, thanks... texted back Eva, now quite irritated, before adding, *I am sorry for demonstrating my feelings tonight. I felt violated, but I understand I shouldn't have reacted the way I did!* 'There,' she announced, 'happy now! Dickhead!'

You have a very quick temper. You need to learn to control it! Connor texted back.

Eva sat bolt upright. *I know, but you haven't mentioned why I did – that's not fair! Anyway, I've apologised now. I shouldn't have physically retaliated so publicly, it won't happen again – I apologise again!*

If you had apologised earlier instead of throwing a tantrum, you could have saved yourself a night's wages.

Eva released an infuriated growl; it took every ounce of self-control not to throw her mobile at the wall. 'What does he want, a written apology, in blood!' she shouted, making Mr Jingles raise his head and stare at her.

Well I'm sure Mr Chu will be more than happy when he hears that you've sacked me, so is there anything else you would like to say before I go back to sleep? she replied, her face contorted into a jaded grimace.

Yes, there is...

Releasing a long impatient sigh, she quickly texted, *??????????!*

Even though you infuriate me with your tantrums, you still turn me on!

'Eh...?' scoffed Eva. 'Talk about Jekyll and Hyde!' she declared out loud.

After a couple of seconds of silence, her phone began to ring. The continuous sound of her ringtone made her chew her lip as she hesitated to answer.

'Yes...'

'Hi,' replied Connor.

An awkward silence hung in the air while Eva waited for him to speak again.

'So, you're in bed then?'

Eva frowned and shook her head in exasperation. '*Well, yes!* I told you I was asleep when you texted!'

'Oh, yeah,' said Connor, in a casual tone.

Another pause followed.

'I was thinking...' he said.

'What...?'

'That I could pop over...'

'Why? So you can deliver my P45 in person?'

'Would save me the price of a stamp,' Connor said dryly. 'I thought we could talk.'

'It's late – I'm in bed.'

Connor laughed softly. 'I don't have a problem with that.'

'You told me to see you at the club tomorrow, so we can talk then, can't we?'

'No, I want to talk now. I'll be there in twenty minutes.'

'But... Hello? *Hello, Connor?*' said Eva, but the line clicked dead. She continued to churn out expletives on her way downstairs. She lit a cigarette in the back garden and pondered whether Connor was coming to see her in the hope to bed her one last time before sacking her tomorrow.

After stubbing out her cigarette, she locked the door and flicked on the kettle. She made a hot chocolate, tossed the spoon into the sink and stood staring through the window. She checked the clock and blew on her steaming drink before going into the lounge and switching on the TV.

Suddenly jerking, she realised she had nodded off. Her lukewarm drink sat untouched in her novelty Minnie Mouse mug on the coffee table. A wave of anxiety washed over her hearing a gentle rap on the front door. She tightened the cord on her dressing gown and unbolted the door.

'Hi,' said Connor, studying her expression after stepping into the hallway.

'*Morning*,' huffed Eva.

Connor gave her a wide smile and walked straight into the lounge.

'So…' said Eva, folding her arms. 'Have you come here to sack me?'

'I don't know yet, it depends how nice you are to me,' said Connor in a deadpan tone. 'Have you got any decent whisky?'

'S-sorry,' stuttered Eva.

'Well, that's a start,' added Connor, playfully baiting her. 'Okay, a decent bottle of wine. A Sauvignon Blanc or Shiraz?'

Eva looked dumbfounded as Connor walked into the kitchen and opened her fridge.

'Pinot Grigio will have to do then, you having one?'

'It's ten past twelve, Connor.'

'I'm well aware of the time,' he said, opening her cupboards in search of two wine glasses.

'Dare I ask what happened with Chu?'

'I cleared his losses,' he said casually, handing her a large glass of wine.

'Cleared his loss?'

'Well, you didn't leave me with many options, but I'll get it back on his next visit,' said Connor nonchalantly.

'So he doesn't want to cancel his membership, then?'

Connor laughed. 'The Unicorn isn't a gym. As I said, he is a degenerate gambler, so he'll be back.'

'Oh…' said Eva feeling genuinely relieved. 'So…' she paused to clear her throat, 'do I still have a job, or have you come here to give me my P45?'

Connor took a sip of wine and glanced down at her shapely legs. 'Do you deserve a second chance?'

'I have apologised,' murmured Eva.

'Yes, but I had to prompt you.'

'I don't like being groped by perverts… But,' added Eva, finding all this quite difficult, 'if you give me a second chance, I promise nothing like that will happen again.'

'If I do, there will be conditions. You are to keep out of trouble, and that means getting on with the other girls, too.'

'You mean *her*!' Eva shrieked, glaring at him. 'Tina!'

'Do you want this second chance, or not?' asked Connor in a berating tone.

'Yes…' Eva replied meekly.

'And secondly,' said Connor, stepping towards her, 'start being nice to your boss.'

'I thought I had been.' Eva was flippant but unable to stop her cheeks from blushing. 'So...I don't have to meet Chu again?'

Connor coughed, almost spitting out his wine. 'I can guarantee you that! I can't afford to keep on clearing his debts!' he teased sarcastically. 'Look, I admit, I was a little abrasive tonight, you certainly know how – and in what order – to push my buttons.'

'But—'

'Just let me finish,' said Connor, now getting irritable. 'I keep my work separate from my personal life. When you're working, you'll be treated like any other employee. I expect you to you do as you're told.'

'Okay,' conceded Eva.

'Then,' Connor continued, softening his tone, 'when we're alone, you can have my full attention, and you'll probably get your own way on occasions – when it suits me, of course,' he said with a grin.

'Well I haven't actually agreed to be your "secret" mistress.'

'There's no denying that we *fit* together sexually, plus I like to spoil my *mistresses*,' he teased.

Eva couldn't help but feel a sense of sexual power over Connor. He was prepared to give her a second chance purely on his hunger for her.

'So, "friends" again?' added Connor, taking a step towards her.

His schoolboy grin persuaded Eva to return his smile. 'Okay, friends again, well for now, anyway.'

'Just friends?' probed Connor.

'I'm not sure. I've dated someone from work before, and it all went sour,' she admitted. 'Remember, I told you? I have everything to lose, and you have nothing.'

'Yes, because you're "you", and you didn't keep your relationship separate from work.'

'No, it was because he was a lying, cheating scumbag!'

'His loss is my gain,' said Connor, choosing his words carefully.

'You're smoother than melted chocolate – do you know that?' Eva grinned feeling his hands cup her bottom.

'Didn't you know I have shares in Cadburys?' Connor said smirking and bending down to nuzzle her neck. 'Anyway, enough talking... I want you here and now,' he demanded, lifting her onto the kitchen worktop.

'Now...?' Goose bumps pricked her skin.

'Yes, now...!'

With breathless haste, Connor unravelled the tight knot of her dressing gown cord, then reached for the buckle of his belt. 'Lean back!'

Eva watched in a startled daze as Connor manically unzipped his trousers and quickly knelt down on the kitchen floor. Lifting her legs over his shoulders, he raised her bottom off the worktop and pulled her naked sex to his mouth making Eva squeal with shock.

Eva gasped with ecstasy as his tongue manipulated her clitoris, gliding up and down with firm sporadic flicks making her whimper and gulp for air.

Such noises brought Mr Jingles bounding in through his cat flap and up onto the table top. Eva turned her face away as an orgasm pulsated through her body. She tried to cover her naked body making Connor glance up.

'Out!' he bellowed, sending Mr Jingles scuttling back towards the door.

Before her orgasm had subsided, Connor quickly got to his feet and forcefully pulled her down off the work surface.

'I'm going to fuck you so hard...!' declared Connor, spellbound with lust, almost slamming Eva over the kitchen top.

Seeing an empty condom packet fly past her, Eva held her breath as she felt the side of Connor's leather shoe shove her feet further apart.

Biting down on her lip, she closed her eyes. Connor's hard erection plunged deep into her body making her sting with the thickness of his penis.

'Baby...you're so tight and wet...' gushed Connor, reaching underneath to cup her breasts.

His love-making was fuelled by an animalistic hunger. He brushed his hand across her milky-white flesh before making her cry out as he slapped her bottom hard.

'Did you like it?' asked Connor breathlessly, caressing the soft pink hue on her right buttock.

'I'm not sure.' Eva blinked, slightly anxious as she glanced over her shoulder to look at him.

'Would you like me to do it again?' His face ablaze with desire.

Her flushed cheeks confessed her coyness as she nodded and pressed her fingertips down hard onto the surface to steady herself.

Watching Connor raise his hand, she held her breath again and closed her eyes. The second strike felt sharper than the first.

'So?' asked Connor eagerly. 'Nice, or not?'

'Er – not...' Eva added quickly.

'That's fine,' said Connor as his hips moved back and forth.

Eva wondered if she was going to be bruised tomorrow.

He withdrew from her body and scooped her up into his arms. 'Enough talking for now, I need to concentrate,' he added, slightly breathless from carrying her upstairs to the bedroom. Connor eagerly lowered his body onto hers. His kisses were forceful and passionate.

Feeling his penis fill her, his slow thrusts became urgent and untamed as the headboard pounded against the wall with Connor's unbridled lust. Hearing Eva's cries of satisfaction fuelled his lust as his muscular thighs slammed against the softness of her flesh.

Calling out his name, as her orgasm pulsated around his penis, quickly resulted in Connor climaxing instantly as his body shuddered to a halt.

"*Jezzuss...*' he yelled out as his body slumped on top of her.

Feeling Connor's hot breath on her neck, she draped her arms around his shoulders and cradled him as his rapid breathing slowly settled.

'Hmm...' murmured Connor, lifting his body off her and rolling onto his back.

Eva felt a little disappointed that Connor's attentiveness waned straight away; it wasn't long before he quickly fell asleep. She liked nothing better than a good snuggle or a bit of spooning.

* * *

Connor woke her early with a sexy grin, and a very impressive erection. 'I didn't realise it was so late?' he said glancing down at his watch. 'I've got a meeting with my accountant—'

'Kiss me, Connor,' growled Eva, reaching up for his face and pulling his mouth to meet her lips. Her heart beat like an enthusiastic schoolgirl tasting her first kiss.

'Babe, I've got to go,' said Connor, gently moving away her hands. He felt his penis twitch as Eva monopolised his lips, pushing her tongue deep into his mouth. With her passion fevering his blood, he couldn't stop his erection.

'Fuck me hard, Connor.'

'*Jesus Christ...!*' he gasped before turning her over roughly. 'We can't go all the way, I don't have any more condoms with me,' he groaned with bated breath.

'I'm on the pill,' Eva replied quickly, pulling his hips down to hers.

'Will you let me come in your mouth?' pleaded Connor, thrusting his erect penis into her wet sex.

Lost in the urgency of lust, Eva groaned heavily feeling Connor plunge deep inside her.

'Will you…?' gasped Connor, cradling her tightly while slamming his groin between her fleshy thighs.

'Oh God…!' Eva dug her fingers into his muscular back he obliged by fucking her hard. '*Connor*…!' panted Eva – her climax shuddered through her entire body.

Feeling Eva's intense orgasm throb around his penis made Connor instantly lose control; his handsome face contorted with ecstasy as he came inside her. '*Shit*, I meant to pull out,' cursed Connor, wiping beads of perspiration from his top lip.

'It's fine, I'm on the pill,' soothed Eva, sliding her hands over his chest and washboard stomach.

'I don't like surprises,' Connor said coldly, brushing away her hands and sitting upright. 'I like to take care of things myself,' he added, quickly gathering his clothes to get dressed.

Eva frowned at his unwarranted cautiousness. She had already explained twice that she was on the pill, so unless he had 'super sperm', then there was less than one percent chance of her getting pregnant.

'And you've made me late…' said Connor impatiently, reaching for the door. 'If I've got time tonight, I'll try and pop down to see you at the club. But I've got a meeting with my architect tomorrow, so I won't be back at the club until Friday?'

'I'm sure I'll be able to survive without seeing you for a day or two,' replied Eva flippantly, making sure he noticed her annoyance.

Connor held her stare for a couple of seconds before opening the bedroom door and walking out.

'*I don't like surprises!*' mimicked Eva in an unrecognisable Irish accent as she heard him go through the front door.

She stepped into the shower, closed her eyes under the jet of warm water, then tutted under her breath before announcing, 'Does he think I want to trap him? Eh? My aspirations reach a little higher than being a single mother at twenty-five!' She quickly got dressed, her mind still in overdrive. 'Womanising. Money obsessed. Workaholic.' The words were so loud in her head that she felt compelled to say them out loud. But one question sat on her lips: *am I slowly falling for Connor?* Even though his moods were challenging, and the sex addictive, was the reason she took everything to heart because she was falling in love with him?

She went downstairs and glanced at her mobile sitting on kitchen worktop. The same worktop where, just last night, Connor had pleasured her. With no text of apology for his unwarranted comment, she wondered if her feelings would even register in his unemotional mind.

Standing in her back garden, she lit a cigarette and looked up at the sky. The air felt cooler and her silver birch had started to shed creating a carpet of amber over her small, parched lawn.

She checked her phone again. In a way she wished that Roxanne knew about her and Connor; at least she would have a confidant to talk to. She could phone her mum, Patsy, but she would question her to within an inch of her life, making an SAS interrogator look like children's entertainer. That just left Susanna, but after her lecture on 'bad boyfriends' she feared Susanna would berate her for not following her own principles.

After flicking on the kettle she heard her mobile beep.

Hi.

Looking down at Connor's one-word text made her grimace with annoyance until a wicked thought crossed her mind.

Gosh, the price of pregnancy tests – £15!

I don't understand?

Pardon? texted Eva, enjoying her childish game.

I think you're trying to wind me up. I was only inside you this morning and now you're testing to see if you're pregnant – not funny.

Sighing heavily, she texted back, *Ok, so I'm not funny* ☹

I agree. Anyway, let's start the conversation again. Hello ☺

Eva stared down at the smiley face on her text. She didn't have Connor down as a 'smiley face' kind of guy.

Connor texted again. *Are you not talking to me?*

Eva pondered her reply with puckered lips. *Do you believe I'm on the pill or not?*

Yes — but accidents happen. You know marriage and kids don't interest me. Maybe I can swing by tonight?

'Un-bloody believable!' muttered Eva before quickly texting back, *Maybe another time, haven't you got to travel to Birmingham tomorrow to see your architect?*

I can leave from your house. I might even let you make my breakfast this time ☺

Gasping at his galling confidence, Eva was determined to make him work a little harder for her affections. *Enjoy your trip!*

Fine…

'Eh?' said Eva out loud, grimacing and feeling deflated that Connor wasn't willing – or interested enough – to woo her over.

Fine then, she texted back.

I'm busy – bye.

Bye? Eva gulped as her mind raced to rationalise his text. Was he saying 'bye' ending their affair, or 'bye' until he got back? *He never ends his texts with 'bye'!*

She couldn't bring herself to ask for clarification in case he found her pathetic or needy. *Sorry*, she texted, before quickly deleting it.

A sense of melancholy hung over her like a rain cloud for the rest of the day.

Perhaps it's best if he ends it now rather than a year down the line, she said to herself half-heartedly, not really wanting to believe that her refusal of sex had made Connor callously dump her.

Chapter 13

'Watch where you're going E-va!' barked Tina, shoving past her as she flounced out of the dressing room.

'God, it's heaving out there tonight,' announced Donna, striding in wearing a miniscule gold G-string. 'What's up with you?' she asked, briefly glancing over at Eva.

'Nothing, I'm fine,' lied Eva, rubbing small blobs of pale foundation on her cheeks, forehead and chin.

'Well, try telling your face that!'

'I need my red dress!' squealed Tina, rushing back into the room. Such uncontainable excitement made everyone look up and stare as she practically skipped over to her table.

'Connor wants me to join him and Samuel Black!' she gushed, stripping naked and pulling on a poppy-red Lycra mini dress.

'Who's Samuel Black?' asked Eva with a curious grimace.

'God, you know nothing,' said Tina with a sniff. A cloud of pungent mist appeared as she drenched herself in perfume.

'Samuel Black is Connor's bank manager – he gets VIP treatment and, of course, Connor wants me there because I am a *professional*. I don't go around slapping important clients in the face,' goaded Tina. 'That's why he hasn't asked for *you*!'

'I guess if he wants a slack-mouthed airhead, then he's asked the right person,' Eva fired back.

'You causing trouble again, Tina?' said Roxanne hearing Eva and Tina sparring again.

'Well, *I'm* not. I haven't got time to bandy words with her because Connor's waiting for me!' With a whip of her head, Tina strutted back out again.

'Are you up next, babes?' asked Roxanne

'Yeah, but I don't feel like dancing tonight.' Eva sighed zipping up her knee-length boots.

'I know. It can get to you like that sometimes. I'll meet you at first break, yeah? Let's hope the time goes fast!' huffed Roxanne.

With a spray of perfume, Eva left the dressing room. She weaved her way around the crowded tables and sashayed towards the dance podium. After walking up the small flight of steps onto the stage, she turned around and glanced out to the sea of faces looking up at her.

Forcing a teasing smile, her gaze suddenly zoomed in on Tina sat grinning like the cat that got the cream next to Connor and a grossly overweight man wearing a dinner suit. It took a table of boisterous corporate bankers' wolf whistles to snap her out of her trance.

Eva pressed the soft flesh of her thighs against the steel pole and swung her body letting it free fall effortlessly. With the grace of an Olympic gymnast, she made every move count. Technical poses saturated with sexual tension, high kicks, twirls and the exotic allure of burlesque created breathtaking sensuality.

She tried to concentrate on her performance, but her snatched glances convinced her that Connor was revelling in Tina's amplified devotion. She believed, rather than feared, that he would be in Tina's bed come the morning.

Blinking her eyes wide open, Eva watched Tina strategically sit on Connor's lap. Connor's reluctance to remove her was the catalyst for Eva's next dramatic move.

With jealousy and anger quickening every stride, she stomped down from the podium and leapt up onto the nearest table. Such an unexpected move sent the men into a frenzy as she sauntered across the tables like a circus lion. Standing directly above Connor, Tina and Mr Black, Eva held her nerve staring down at them in a dominatrix stance.

With no care for the bottles of expensive champagne knocked over like skittles, Eva listened to the fevered jeers as two young suited men helped her jump down.

She swaggered over towards Connor before walking behind his chair. Leaning forward, her long hair fell down over his face and she dragged her fingernails down the soft fabric of his burgundy open-necked shirt.

'*What do you think you're doing, YOU MAD COW?*' hissed Tina, getting to her feet before being told to sit down by a group of middle-aged men behind her.

Witnessing total disregard for the rule of no physical contact provoked the men to whoop and cheer wildly.

Strutting around to face Connor, adrenalin provided Eva with invincibility as she pushed back their table with her bottom before swaying her hips in front of him. His deep frown and narrowed eyes warned her of his dark mood, but it was too late to walk away now – she had to finish what she'd started.

Straddling Connor's thighs made him blink in disbelief as the provocative Pussycats Doll's 'Don't Cha' remix boomed through the stage speakers. She gyrated her hips and squatted inches above his crotch before pushing her breasts up against his face, forcing him to jerk back his head.

Roars of lustful baiting sucked the oxygen out of the testosterone-filled air.

Purposely striking his cheek with her nipple tassels, Eva glanced over at Tina sitting open-mouthed like a cheap sex doll while Black sat captivated by her alluring and aggressive routine.

'You are so sacked, you stupid bitch!' shrieked Tina, before spinning around in her seat and telling a young man to piss off when he excitedly suggested that she join in and make it a threesome.

Eva got to her feet with flushed cheeks and a defiant stare. Pursing together her glossed lips she quickly shoved the tip of her boot an inch away from Connor's groin, exposing her shapely stockinged leg.

'Put some money in her stocking!' shouted a man over the music.

Connor's face darkened to a scowl and he snapped his head to the side on hearing someone fire a drunken insult at him.

Eva raised her hands in the air and started to clap along to the beat of the song. With her adoring public joining in, Connor fidgeted in his seat as she pushed the tip of her boot further into his balls.

She knew this would seal her fate. There was no going back. If she were going to be sacked that night, then she would bow out in blaze of adulation.

'Pay...pay...pay,' chorused the men, many of which were now standing on seats and tables.

Connor lips snarled. He glared up at Eva while reaching inside his jacket. Snatching a fifty-pound note from his wallet he held it up between his middle and index finger ready for her to take as the room erupted into a rapturous applause. But Eva wasn't finished yet. She was not going to let another arrogant lover humiliate her.

Her thigh hovered an inch from Connor's face as she lifted her leg over his shoulder.

'Put it in her stocking!' cried out the members, some of them laughing at Connor's obvious displeasure and humiliation. '*In her stocking! In her stocking!*' came the avalanche of pantomime cries completely drowning out the loud dance music.

Connor forcefully grabbed Eva's leg, making her reach out and clutch the side of Black's chair, and shoved the fifty-pound note into her stocking before pushing her leg off his shoulder and getting to his feet.

Eva snatched the money from her stocking top and raised it triumphantly into the air to a burst of raucous cheers and whoops.

Connor stormed out of the dance lounge without a backwards glance.

'May I, miss?'

Eva looked down at the bloated, sweat-sodden face of Mr Black whose dark beady eyes sat behind a pair of thick untrimmed eyebrows.

'Sure,' smiled Eva, offering him her thigh. He placed two fifty-pound notes into her stocking and money fell like confetti around her from the other members.

Tina stood rooted to the spot. She knew Connor would be furious if she left Black with Eva after such a display. 'I'll stay here with Mr Black until Mr O'Neill returns, Eva.'

'But won't Mr O'Neill be expecting you, Tina? She follows him around like a bitch on heat – bless her,' quipped Eva acidly direct to Black.

'That won't be necessary,' said Connor, suddenly appearing behind her. 'I suggest you collect the rest of your money and hand it in.'

Swallowing hard, Eva pressed her glossed lips into a thin line as Connor's delicious aftershave found the tip of her nose. 'Okay...' she said, glancing up at his stunningly handsome face scowling down at her.

Eva was greeted by Roxanne looking anxious as she walked into the dressing room.

'Fuck me, Eva!' roared Roxanne. 'What the hell were you thinking making a show of O'Neill like that? Are you off your bloody nut?' she ranted. 'We all watched you. I was going to step in to stop you, but feared I'd get fucking lynched by the punters. It's a good job Ann had to leave early; her daughter has just gone into labour.'

'I still can't believe it!' Scarlett called over in excitement. 'No one has ever pimped their ass at the boss before,' she said, sniggering. 'You've got balls – I'll say that for you. You do know he's going to fire your ass, don't you? You've just kissed goodbye to your job at the Unicorn,' she added, just in case she hadn't made herself clear.

All the anger and adrenalin that had fuelled Eva's temper suddenly abandoned her. After dropping the bundles of curled up notes onto her dressing table, she brushed her hand over her stomach. 'Actually I feel sick,' she muttered, rushing towards the loos.

'What made you do it?' probed Roxanne, following her.

Eva retched as she leaned over the toilet. 'I don't know... It just snowballed into a—'

'Your fucking leaving party, Eva,' wailed Roxanne.

'I don't know what's wrong with me.' Eva sobbed as she unlocked the toilet door. 'He was whispering and laughing with *her*...and...'

'Who? Tina?'

'Yes, and I know they were laughing at me, so—'

'Whoa...' said Roxanne, 'just breathe,' she added. 'You're letting this whole Tina thing take over your life. You're getting fucking paranoid. You do know he won't let this go, don't you? He ain't gonna turn a blind eye to being publicly humiliated in his own club. I'm fucking worried for you, babes... You've taken this way too fuc—'

'*Eva?*' said Scarlett, poking her head around the door. 'O'Neill wants to see you upstairs in his apartment in ten minutes.'

'Well, this is it,' Eva said, snivelling.

'Look, I can ask Tommy to speak to him, maybe—'

'No...' said Eva, 'I'm so sorry, Roxanne, I've let you down. I am so stupid; you're such a good mate. I don't deserve a friend like you. Anyway...' added Eva, wiping her eyes, 'I just want to get it over and done with. I'll hopefully see you before I go.'

'Oh, mate...' said Roxanne, holding back her own tears.

Eva felt numb making her way up to the penthouse. There was no game plan, no excuse, no thoughts of begging for her job. She had accepted her fate, and the realisation that she was going to be sacked.

Wrapping her knuckles against the door for a second time, she waited until she heard Connor call her in.

'Oh...' said Eva, looking over at Connor and Mr Black.

'Mr Black wants to book a private dance with you, so take him down to one of the booths,' Connor said coldly.

Eva blinked over at Black who looked ashen in the light, apart from grey shadows underneath his beady, puffy eyes.

'He hasn't got all night,' barked Connor, clicking his fingers at her.

'Y-yes – sorry,' croaked Eva in confusion. 'If you would like to follow me, Mr Black,' she continued, watching him heave himself off the sofa wheezing and coughing.

Eva plastered a fake smile listening to the lift groan under Black's enormous bulk. She was relieved when they safely reached the lobby on the ground floor.

Hearing Black struggling to breathe behind her was alarming, so she purposely walked slowly to one of the private booths. Waiting for Black to shuffle past her, she turned around and watched uncomfortably Black shoehorning his expansive backside into the leather chair by a small circular drinks table.

'Mr O'Neill said there's no charge,' said Black, pulling a white handkerchief from his breast pocket and mopping his glistening brow.

Eva nodded and cringed hearing Black clear his throat of phlegm. She reached for the dancing pole still wearing her red nipple tassels and knickers. She was grateful for the soft lighting that masked Black's grossly unattractive face and sweat-drenched shirt. She hoped Black wouldn't realise she was rushing through parts of her routine to block out his panting and deep groaning.

'Can you dance nearer, my sweet? My eyes are not what they used to be,' grunted Black, replacing his sodden handkerchief with a clean one.

Hesitating with repulsion, Eva could now smell his damp body as he indiscreetly slipped his bloated hand into his front trouser pocket.

'Um... Ok-k,' she agreed reluctantly. *Maybe he'll report back favourably to Connor if I please him.*

His breathing became raspy and shallow ogling her breasts while his hand twitched in his pocket. 'Hmmm...' croaked Black, brushing the tip of his tongue over his top lip. 'Move closer, my sweet, will you?'

'Arghhh!' Eva yelled as Black's head came crashing towards her chest. Frozen in shock, she fell backwards when he tumbled out of the chair, landing on top of her.

'GET OFF ME!' she screamed, almost hysterical with the weight of Black's body crushing her legs and pelvis.

Black's breathing suddenly became intermittent as Eva tried to reach out for the panic button.

'HELP!' screeched Eva, 'SOMEBODY HELP ME!'

Black was now motionless. A horrifying deep rattle gurgled in his throat. Eva realised he was having a heart attack.

'*Oh, please God, let somebody hear me,*' whimpered Eva trying to roll Black off her abdomen.

Feeling his warm saliva drip onto her skin made her scream. Black started to convulse violently before releasing one last gravelly breath.

'HELP ME...! SOMEBODY PLEASSSE HELP ME!'

The booth door flung open.

'TOMMY – THANK GOD!' she cried out.

With loud dance music flooding the booth, a startled looking Tommy and Marcus, one of the other bouncers, came rushing in.

'What the fuck has gone on here?' gasped Marcus, helping Tommy lift Black off Eva.

Eva rolled onto her side and let out a raspy cough and frantically pawed at her skin trying to wipe off Black's saliva sitting in frothy blobs on her breasts.

'What happened?' barked Tommy, lying Black on his back and unbuttoning his saturated shirt. 'For fuck's sake, Eva, what happened?!'

'Shit – I think she's gone into shock,' said Marcus. He knelt on the floor and wrapped his arm around Eva's trembling shoulders as she sat with her knees pressed up against her chest.

Tommy felt for a pulse and quickly started CPR after shouting at Marcus to call for an ambulance.

Roxanne rushed in after seeing the commotion from the stage. 'Oh my God!' she cried.

'I think he's dead,' said Tommy.

'No—' gasped Roxanne, placing her hand over her mouth as she knelt down by Eva.

'The ambulance should be here in four minutes,' said Marcus. 'They want us to carry on giving him CPR until they get here, Tom.'

'Has anyone told Connor?' asked Roxanne, looking up at Tommy.

'I'll go and fetch him!' Marcus rushed out of the booth.

'Try and get her to tell you what happened, Roxy!' yelled Tommy, continuing to pump Black's chest.

'Maybe the paramedics can shock his body back to life?' pleaded Roxanne.

'A thunderbolt couldn't bring this guy back,' replied Tommy, using his shirtsleeve to wipe the sweat from his brow.

'Oh, Eva…' whispered Roxanne, holding her close. 'What happened, babes?'

'What the fuck's happened here?' boomed Connor, charging into the dance booth.

'Looks like a heart attack,' said Tommy, glancing down at Black's lifeless body.

Connor quickly knelt down to feel for a pulse. 'There nothing,' he said, glancing over at Eva.

'Mr O'Neill, the paramedics are here,' said Beverley, the receptionist, showing the two paramedics into the booth.

'If you could stand aside please, sir,' said the older paramedic. 'Can someone tell me what happened?'

'He…he…he was making a funny noise,' stuttered Eva, before starting to cry again.

'We found him on top of her,' said Marcus.

'He asked me to m-move closer t-then he fell forward out of the chair,' explained Eva through deep sobs.

The younger, ginger-haired paramedic asked Eva if she was hurt.

'Just my hips, he was so h-heavy.'

'Oh my God! What's happened!' shrieked Tina running in, promptly followed by Donna and Scarlett. 'Has she killed him?' asked Tina. 'I told you she's unhinged, Connor!'

'Can we clear this area, please?' asked the older paramedic, shining a small torch-like instrument into Black's eyes.

'Tina, Scarlett, Donna – out!' barked Connor over his shoulder.

'If you can lie on your back, Miss…?' asked the younger paramedic softly.

'Eva Summers,' she answered, sniffing.

'Well, Eva, I'd like to check your pelvis area, if that's okay?'

Eva's body jerked with every deep sob as Roxanne held her hand.

'Unfortunately, this gentleman has passed away. It looks like he's had a cardiac arrest. The police will need to be notified,' explained the older paramedic.

'Tom, can you make the call?' asked Connor, watching the ginger-haired paramedic check Eva's abdomen and legs.

'She will be okay, won't she?' asked Roxanne.

'Yes – there'll be some bruising over the next couple of days.'

'T-thank you,' mumbled Eva, averting her eyes from Black's dead body.

Tommy helped the two paramedics roll Black onto a stretcher and cover his huge body with a blanket.

Roxanne gently guided Eva back into the dressing room as Connor and Tommy waited for the police to arrive.

'What'll happen now?' asked Eva, dabbing her swollen red eyes with a tissue.

'I heard Connor tell Tommy to close the club early and send everyone home. I think the police will want to speak to you, though.'

'I'll never forget this night as long as I live,' Eva murmured. 'I've never had someone die on me before!'

'He was grossly overweight, babes. He was a ticking time bomb, sad to say,' reassured Roxanne.

After the police had taken Eva's statement, Roxanne offered to take her back to hers.

'It's okay, I'll take her home,' said Connor.

'But I don't think she should be on her own tonight, she's still in shock,' argued Roxanne.

'I'm fine. I just want to go home to my own bed.' A dull headache pounded as Eva wept.

'Are you sure, babes?' soothed Roxanne, rubbing her hand across her shoulder.

'Roxy...' interrupted Tommy. 'She said she's fine, babes.'

'I'm just making sure – thank you!' snapped Roxanne, flashing Tommy a sour grimace.

'I'll be fine, honest, Rox,' said Eva weakly.

'Boss, can I have a word?' asked Tommy, motioning Connor towards the dressing room door. 'I can deal with this mess, if you want. I know you're travelling up to Birmingham tomorrow.'

'No, I need to deal with it. I need to find out what happened, then phone Black's family.'

'Okay – if you're sure,' said Tommy, shaking his head. 'But if you ask me, she's a walking fucking disaster. First Chu, now Black.'

'This is hardly her fault,' said Connor, sighing and glancing over his shoulder at Eva.

'She's a fucking liability. I warned you at her interview. Anyone who works for that fucking lowlife Booth is gonna be trouble, whether she's easy on the eye or not.'

Connor's eyes narrowed in thought. There were no lies in Tommy's synopsis of Eva's short employment at the club. Her arrival had created a sense of chaos, which followed her around like a lovesick teenager, but Connor secretly found her unharnessed energy and volatile passion annoyingly arousing.

Tommy, over the years, had witnessed many of Connor's conquests. All the women were stunning, passive and forgettable. He knew Connor's only true love – Maria – had been fiery and unpredictable like Eva. Even though he hadn't told him directly that Eva was his lover, Tommy could see the change in him, which made him fear for his best friend. Would history repeat itself and a woman bring Connor to his knees again?

Leading her out of the club, Connor gently held onto her waist as they walked to the car park. Eva sniffed continuously into a paper hankie. He unlocked his Range Rover and helped Eva climb into the high seat, draping his suit jacket over her.

'I don't feel well,' mumbled Eva, her body giving way to an involuntary shiver.

'I'll turn the heater on,' said Connor, starting the engine.

Eva sank down into the seat as deep exhaustion forced her eyes shut. Within moments she was fast asleep, but flashbacks of what happened with Black made her groan and fidget in her seat until she stirred and squinted through the darkness.

'Where are we?' asked Eva, turning to look at Connor.

'I thought it best not to wake you, so I've brought you back to my house.'

'Oh,' said Eva, peering through the window.

Turning down a dark country lane, they arrived at a pair of black wrought iron gates lit by two Victorian style street lamps. The soft hue shone down over a modern looking surveillance camera.

Connor pulled up alongside the intercom and lowered his window.

'Evening, Mr O'Neill.'

'Evening, Andrew,' said Connor, waiting for the gates to open.

Eva's head still felt fuzzy as she stared at the leafy shadows cast by the neon moonlight. She glanced up at the two imposing stone pillars flanking a large white door as they drove up the long gravel path towards an impressive neo-baroque manor house.

'Do you need me to carry you?' asked Connor, unclipping his seatbelt.

'No, I can walk,' said Eva wearily, pushing open the passenger door.

Following Connor up to a large stone porch, she held together the lapels of his jacket as she shuddered again. Her hips and back felt sore; a painful reminder of the nightmare that had taken place that evening.

'Do you want a brandy or something?' asked Connor, closing the door behind her.

'Actually, I'm really tired,' croaked Eva, rubbing her fingers against her temple.

'I need to ask you what happened tonight.'

Eva sighed heavily and winced with fatigue before recounting again what happened.

'Okay,' said Connor, brushing his hand across his mouth.

'Where can I sleep?'

'You can have my room,' said Connor, looking at her pale complexion and puffy eyes.

Too tired to notice the plush surroundings, Eva followed Connor towards a large oak staircase. Letting his arm circle her waist, she walked slowly up the stairs to a long, wide landing to his bedroom.

'The en suite is through there if you want to take a shower or bath,' said Connor, nodding over towards a large oak door leading off the spacious bedroom.

'Okay,' said Eva, turning back to look at the large beautifully dressed bed in front of her.

'I'll be back in a couple of minutes,' said Connor softly, leaving her to undress.

The wooden floor felt cold as she slipped out of her high heels. She took off the jacket, and slipped out of her jeans and top. After dropping them into a pile on the floor, she pulled back the cotton sheets and got into Connor's bed.

She snuggled down into the jasmine-fragranced linen, just leaving her face exposed. Within seconds she was asleep.

Chapter 14

A warm chink of sunlight woke Eva. She saw the indented pillow next to her but the bedsheet on that side was cool. The time on her phone read 7:15 a.m. She felt warm and comfortable but knew she had to get up and look for Connor.

Looking around the room stood only in her bra and knickers, she noticed her clothes in a neatly folded pile on a large walnut sideboard. She slowly made her way to the en suite to change. The heated floor tiles warmed her feet as she glanced around at the dark masculine decor. After quickly using the loo, she washed her hands and face.

Holding her shoes in her hand, she walked out of the bedroom and down the expansive landing towards the top of the large staircase. She stared in awe at the sumptuous oil paintings decorating the high walls and the array of beautiful antique furniture adorning every available floor space.

She came across a pair of heavy wooden doors. Once opened, they revealed a bright, sun-drenched room. Three large windows stood swathed in rich embroidered cream drapes as a thick stream of light shone over a beautiful oatmeal sofa and square footrest the size of a coffee table. A vast stone fire surround dominated the room and a large tapestry displaying a coat of arms hung proudly above the carved stone mantle.

She turned back and hesitated for a second with no idea where Connor could be. The only way to find him in such an enormous house was to phone his mobile.

'Morning, miss.'

'Oh!' Eva jumped at the greeting from a tall, rosy-cheeked gentleman.

'Sorry to startle you, miss. My name is Andrew Campbell. I am Mr O'Neill's butler.'

'Can you tell me where Mr O'Neill is please?' asked Eva, coyly.

'Mr O'Neill left early this morning, miss.'

'Oh.' Eva stood awkwardly holding her shoes. 'Hmm, is there a train station nearby?'

'Mr O'Neill said I am to drive you home when you are ready. Would you like some breakfast before you go?'

'No, thank you,' she said politely, 'I'd need to get home.'

'If you wait here, I will bring the car round,' instructed Mr Campbell after walking her to the front door.

With little conversation on the journey back, Eva replayed every detail of Black's death in her mind. 'Thank you, Mr Campbell,' she said, grappling for the door handle as he pulled up outside her house.

'Okay, miss.' he nodded and waited until she slowly walked up the garden path with her key ready.

With a quick backwards glance, Eva waved and opened her front door before quickly slamming it shut behind her.

After feeding a very disgruntled Mr Jingles, she ran a hot bath and lay in it for a good half an hour. Her mood was numb as the cloud of hot stream enveloped her. Hearing her mobile beep, she dried her hands and reached down to grab it off the floor.

How are you? Roxy xxxxxx
Yes I'm fine. I've just got back home.
Eh?
Yes, Connor's butler dropped me home.

Her phone suddenly rang in her hand.

'You went back to Connor's house?' probed Roxanne sounding shocked.

Eva paused for second realising she wouldn't have known that Connor had taken her back to his house.

'Yes, I fell asleep in his car, so he took me back to his house or, should I say, mansion.'

'Yeah, it's fucking amazing. Six bedrooms, a library, swimming pool and stables. Tommy said it's worth about five million quid!'

'Bloody hell – five million?' Eva shook her head.

'Well…I did offer to take you back to mine, but he wouldn't hear of it?' explained Roxanne.

'If I'm honest, I wasn't aware of what was going on around me. I don't think he really knew what to do with me,' mused Eva. 'It was such a crazy night with everything that happened. I feel like I've been in a train crash or something,' added Eva, looking down at her bruised legs.

'Well, I guess that was nice of him to look after you, especially after…you know.'

'What – humiliating him in his own club, then probably contributing to his friend's death!'

'I guess you could look at it like that. But for what it's worth, Black was on borrowed time. He must have been twenty-three stone, at least. I know it sounds harsh, but I doubt Connor will have the heart to fire you now, not after his friend died on top of you!' reasoned Roxanne.

'I'm not sure,' said Eva sighing heavily.

'I guess it's just a case of sitting tight and hoping it all blows over,' soothed Roxanne softly. 'Are you coming in tonight?'

'Connor hasn't said not to,' said Eva, brushing her toe over the bath tap.

'Okay, well I'll see you later, babes. We can talk tonight.'

'Thanks for phoning, Roxy, it means a lot.'

'What are friends for?'

As the line went dead Eva wondered if she should text Connor. He was so attentive last night; maybe he has forgiven her in the light of Black's death.

Hi, she texted, slightly apprehensive.

How are you feeling? replied Connor promptly.

Bruised...and worried.

I guess you would be bruised.

Are going to sack me?

I have every right to.

Eva didn't know how to reply. She got out of the bath and wrapped her cotton dressing gown around her before texting back, *After the 'pill' comment and seeing you and Tina together, I admit my temper got the better of me – I can give you your fifty pounds back?*

Forget about the money – you need to control that fiery temper of yours. The pill comment wasn't meant maliciously. I am very careful, and also upfront about what I want in my life and what I don't. Tina is just an employee as I've told you before. Is that why you didn't want to see me, because of the pill thing?

Yes – I have no wish to trap you Connor. The thought of being a single mum horrifies me. I am very careful too! When I'm upset, I bite back without thinking (as you know).

So you acknowledge your faults?

Eva exhaled loudly in response to Connor's comment. *We all have faults and yes, mine is not thinking before I speak!*

I'm glad we both agree on that. If Black hadn't asked you for a private dance, I would have fired you last night – without a second of hesitation. Your performance on stage will no doubt be spoken about for months amongst the men.

'Shit,' muttered Eva under her breath. *Sorry,* she replied.

Losing a good friend has mellowed my mood. Life is short, so if you promise never EVER to embarrass me like that again, I'll downgrade your sacking to a written warning. You step out of line again, and I will fire you on the spot without a reference! You have my word on that!

I promise – I will make sure I stay out of your way from now on.

You should be trying hard to please me, not hack me off!

Eh...? I don't understand.

When I want to see you privately, don't refuse me again! I will text you when I want to see you – do you understand?

Yes, replied Eva thinking that if arrogance were a nugget of gold, Connor would be in possession of his very own goldmine.

* * *

'And here's the psycho killer,' roared Tina when Eva walked into the dressing room.

'Is that the best you can come up with?'

'Nah, I'm just warming up,' said Tina, grinning. 'Well at least the mystery of Black's sudden heart attack has been solved. It was the sight of all that ugly cellulite – ha-ha. He probably went into shock, then BANG! Dropped dead of fright!' she cackled, glancing over at Donna who winked at her.

'Yeah, yeah,' replied Eva. She replayed Connor's words of warning in her mind: '*Control your temper and make an effort to get on with the other girls!*'

'Perhaps someone should tell the boss how disrespectful you're being, Tina. Black was a good friend of Connor's,' baited Roxanne.

'W-what? No...! I'm not being disrespectful!' stuttered Tina.

'Cigarette?' Roxanne asked Eva with a smile as the other girls sniggered behind Tina's back.

'So what did you think of Connor's gaff?' asked Roxanne, turning her back to the chilly wind to light her cigarette.

'Yeah, nice, if you like a millionaire lifestyle,' scoffed Eva.

'It's funny. Connor didn't mention to Tommy that he'd taken you back to his place.'

'Does Connor tell Tommy everything, then?'

'Well, yeah, pretty much,' replied Roxanne, nodding and inhaling on her cigarette. 'I told you, they're like brothers. I bet you felt uneasy crashing at his place – I know you don't like the boss.'

The deep crimson hue colouring Eva's cheeks must have told Roxanne she was keeping something from her. 'I…er…can't remember much, if I'm honest. It's cold, shall we go back in?' Eva shuddered stubbing out her half-smoked cigarette.

Once back in the dressing room she texted Connor, *How is Birmingham?*

I'm in my hotel room alone and very bored!

Bored? Why don't you watch a movie? ☺

Let's start the conversation again… I am bored, so entertain me.

A slow grin shaped Eva's lips. *Black-seamed stockings, suspenders and thong*, she texted.

Hmm, I actually prefer white briefs…

Do you? She replied, surprised by his preference.

Not every man's taste conforms to red or black skimpy underwear. Does that surprise you?

I suppose not…

Anyway, where were we?

Pondering her next comment, Eva thought she would spice things up a little. *What would you do if I was there with you?*

Smack your backside hard for humiliating me the other night!

Eva swallowed hard. She knew Connor wasn't going to forgive her easily, or quickly.

Then… I would peel your underwear off with my teeth! pinged the next text.

A wave of relief and excitement made Eva fidget in her seat. *Continue*, she replied, grinning.

Just the thought of your firm heart-shaped backside makes my cock hard!

Muffling her schoolgirl snigger, Eva blushed as her fingers moved with speed over the keypad of her blackberry. *So are you aroused then?*

Semi.

What can I do to make you hard?

Sit on my face, texted Connor crudely.

Being so engrossed in her sexting, Eva wasn't aware of the attention gathering around her as she squealed and giggled with arousal. *Maybe just wearing a pair of white knickers?* replied Eva, hoping her comment would provoke a lust-frenzied reply.

FUCK, YES! I wish you were here right now. You wouldn't be able to walk properly tomorrow!

Connor's direct and graphic text created a deep throbbing between Eva's thighs.

'What's up with her?' jeered Tina, peering over.

'She's texting her new beau…Chu!' Donna laughed hysterically.

Hearing Donna's remark made Eva glance up momentarily. 'It's none of your business *actually*,' she replied curtly. She quickly got to her feet and went to the ladies toilets.

Locking the cubicle door, Eva felt overwhelmed to pleasure herself. *I'm in the ladies loos with my hand down my knickers – OMG!* she texted back.

Her phone immediately started to ring.

'Are you teasing me?' croaked Connor.

'*Well, yes*, but I'm doing what I said in my text,' purred Eva.

'Fuck! That turns me on!' growled Connor excitedly. 'Are you wet?'

'*Very*—'

'Are your fingers inside you?'

'No, not yet,' replied Eva, as her voice trembled with excitement.

'Slide two fingers inside very, very, slowly,' instructed Connor.

'Okay,' said Eva, putting down the loo seat and perching on the edge.

'Have you done it?'

Biting down on her lip, she did as she was told and groaned with pleasure. 'Yesss…'

'Right, start moving your hand back and forth – slowly,' said Connor as his breathing became raspy. 'Describe to me how you feel?'

'Warm and wet…' gasped Eva.

'*Jesus Christ…!*' panted Connor.

'It feels so good,' moaned Eva with her knickers below her knees and her mobile wedged between her cheek and shoulder.

'You're driving me *crazy*! I wish you were sitting on my cock right now!'

Hearing his crude yearning sent a surge of ecstasy flooding through her groin as her legs began to buckle.

'Ohhh…' whimpered Eva, pushing her fingers deeper and faster inside her.

'Don't come yet…I want you to do something for me!'

'I-I don't think I can wait!' pleaded Eva.

'Scold me!' ordered Connor in a harsh tone.

His bizarre request took her by surprise; her mind raced for a response. 'Y-you are very naugh—'

'No… Harsher!'

Scrambling for words, Eva blurted out the first thing that came into her mind, 'Don't backchat me you…you arrogant pig!'

With no immediate reply, she listened to Connor's shallow breathing.

'You disgusting man – *you repulse me!*' she continued hoping to get a constructive response.

'*More…*' came Connor's muffled reply.

'Did I ask you to speak!' blasted Eva, slipping into her best dominatrix persona. 'You only speak when I tell you to – *understand?*'

Hearing Connor groan with pleasure gave way to a surge of pulsating ecstasy, nearly resulting in her dropping the phone.

'What are you doing?' demanded Eva. She frowned at the silence and pressed her mobile closer to her ear. 'Connor?' she added. 'Oh yes,' she said, grimacing, 'you can answer!'

'*You're sitting on my cock and fuck-ing me hard!*' murmured Connor, his voice barely audible with lust.

'How close are you…? You can answer.'

'My balls feel like they're going to explode… I-I'm going to…'

With her legs trembling, Eva slumped forward as her orgasm erupted deep within making her pant loudly. With her mouth void of moisture, she couldn't utter a single coherent word.

'*Fu…ck, yeahhh,*' whispered Connor.

As her heavy gasping abating, Eva sat sprawled across the loo seat. Reaching down for a handful of toilet tissue, her hips and back hurt due to the bruising and awkwardness of her position. She definitely wouldn't be recommending masturbating on a toilet seat any time soon.

'*Hi,*' said Connor in his deep southern Irish drawl. 'I think I need to call housekeeping to come and clean up this mess. It's everywhere…' he said laughing.

'Did I say the right thing, then?' asked Eva, flushing the loo.

'Hmmm… Not bad for a beginner,' teased Connor. 'You know what they say, "practice makes perfect".'

'Well, I guess I need to pract—'

'EVA – are you in there?!' shouted Scarlett.

'Y-yes,' stuttered Eva, cutting Connor off and unbolting the door.

'You're late, you should have been on stage by now. It's not my job to go searching for people, you know!' She tutted before disappearing back through the door.

Chapter 15

For Eva the next two weeks went slowly waiting for Connor to return from Birmingham.

'Tommy said the boss is back,' said Roxanne, patting on her face powder.

'Oh, is he?' said Eva, trying to sound casual and checking her mobile hidden in her drawer.

I can't wait to see you. Tell Ann you're ill or have some sort of emergency to deal with.

No! I can't lie to Ann. She already suspects something's going on, fretted Eva.

Remind me who Ann's boss is? Plus, what did I say? Don't refuse me.

I am NOT refusing you...she won't believe me.

Eva – think of something, go home and wait for me. I have a surprise and want to give it to you – pun intended!

'So, was it Weight Watchers?' jabbed Tina.

'Shut up! You're becoming a bore,' said Roxanne with a sigh before returning to straighten her long black hair.

Knowing she had an audience gave Eva the perfect opportunity to put her loosely cobbled plan into action.

'Are you okay?' asked Roxanne noticing Eva drop her face into her hand and rest on her dressing table

'Actually, I feel a little off. I think I might've eaten something dodgy. I'm just going to the loo,' she said quickly striding towards the toilets. She decided to hover in the cubicle for a couple of minutes and then tell Ann that she was sick and needed to go home.

Practising her 'sick face', she knocked on Ann's door.

'Yes, what is it?'

'Sorry, Ann, but I don't feel well.' Eva hoped her Oscar performance of a deep frown while rubbing her belly might convince Ann of her fake illness.

'What's wrong with you?'

'I, er...think I've eaten something that's upset my stomach.'

'Mr O'Neill is back this evening,' said Ann, trying to analyse the situation.

Eva blinked feeling her cheeks instantly burn. 'Is he?'

'He's leaving the club in an hour and won't be back this evening – so here you are, needing to go home.'

Eva stared down at Ann and crossed her fingers behind her back. 'I swear I know nothing about Mr O'Neill plans. I just feel unwell,' she muttered.

'Don't forget to clock out,' said Ann in a dismissive tone before turning back to her computer.

'Yes, of course...' Eva replied, hating herself for lying.

Roxanne watched Eva clock out. 'I hope you feel better soon, babes.'

'Well, I hope it's nothing catching!' moaned Tina, wrinkling her nose, 'I thought you looked more pasty then normal!'

'I'm sure it's just a twenty-four-hour thing,' babbled Eva, avoiding eye contact with Roxanne. 'I'm sure I'll be fine tomorrow – night!'

After leaving the club, Eva checked her watch before texting Connor. *God I feel horrible! I've just told Ann a barefaced lie!*

Don't worry – Ann is well paid. I'll leave in an hour, so see you then my little liar.

Knowing Ann was slowly losing respect for her still wasn't enough to stop Eva from halting her affair with Connor. He was now under her skin, in her mind and slowly taking control of her life.

Once back at home, she hurried inside and sprinted upstairs to the bathroom. She quickly took a shower and slipped into pair of white full brief knickers along with a matching bra. Next, a pair of nude sheer stockings before slipping her feet into her six-inch blue stilettos. Standing under a cloud of perfume, she smiled at her reflection when she heard the doorbell ring.

'*Oh*... Mrs Simms,' she said, hiding her half-naked body behind the door.

'Hello, Eva dear. Can I interest you in buying a raffle ticket for Hackney Community Centre? They're a pound a ticket,' she said smiling, dressed in a pink mac and see-though rain hat.

'Er...' said Eva, feeling her mobile beep in her hand. 'I'll just go and get my purse.' She smiled sheepishly leaving the door ajar while unhooking her handbag off the banister and glancing down at her text.

Something has just come up so might have to take a rain check.

'You have got to be joking!' shrieked Eva.

'Is everything all right, dear?'

'I've just told a blatant lie for you, and now you can't bloody make it!' Eva grabbed her purse from her bag. 'I don't believe this!'

'Believe what, dear?' asked Mrs Simms, trying to peer around the door.

'Nothing,' Eva grunted. 'How much – a pound, did you say?'

'A pound a ticket or five pounds a strip. First prize is a food hamper from the local Co-op, so well worth buying a strip, dear.'

'Er… Yes, okay, I'll take a strip.' Eva forced a smile shoving a five-pound note into Mrs Simms' mitten-covered hand.

'Thank you, dear, here are your tickets.'

Hearing her mobile beep again, Eva quickly grabbed her tickets and shut the door leaving Mrs Simms standing on the doormat.

Might still be able to make it, not as serious as first thought, but will be late.

Without a moment to filter her reply, Eva shot off a text, *I've lied through my teeth for you tonight! What is sooo important that you're going to be late?*

My grandmother has taken a fall and is at the hospital, is that IMPORTANT enough for you?

Covering her mouth with her hand, Eva felt terrible. 'Oh shit, he's going to think I'm a complete bitch now,' she uttered out loud. Panicking, she quickly fired off a grovelling apology, *Sorry ☹ I didn't mean to sound harsh. I hope your grandmother is ok xxxxx*

An hour later Connor still hadn't replied.

Looking at her watch it was ten past twelve. *Ok, going to bed. Sorry again x*

As soon as she turned off her kitchen light, she heard her phone beeping in her dressing gown pocket.

Just pulling into your road now.

Her stomach churned with apprehension. His text hadn't revealed what kind of mood he was in.

The beam of light shining through her lounge window announced his arrival. Unlatching the door, she swallowed hard watching him walk up her garden path.

'How's your grandmother?' she asked quickly, noticing his deep frown.

'I need a drink,' growled Connor, stepping into her hallway carrying a large white box under his arm.

Eva closed the door and followed him into the kitchen.

'How is she?' she probed again.

'She cut her leg and needed four stitches… You having one?' asked Connor bluntly, taking a bottle of white wine from her fridge.

'Yes please… Sorry for being a bit—'

'Demanding and childish!' Connor finished her sentence for her.

'You didn't give me a reason why you were going to late, so I assumed—'

'Assumed what? That I was lying – seeing someone else? I don't lie, Eva. When I say I can't make it, then I can't make it!'

Looking down into her glass of wine, Eva felt his severity. She didn't like his 'demanding and childish' remark but didn't want to escalate the tension between them.

'Sorry, I shouldn't have been so offhand,' she relented.

'You need to work hard to sweeten my mood,' warned Connor, wrinkling his nose at her choice of wine.

'I know…' Eva said passively.

'I've brought your surprise, but I'm not sure I'm in the mood to enjoy it. I'm going to take a shower. I need to wash the day off me.'

'Yes, okay.' Eva nodded and glanced over at the large white box sitting on the kitchen table.

'I'll take the box up, you bring the paint stripper,' quipped Connor, describing her mid-range wine.

Looking down at the box sitting on the bed, Eva gulped at her drink while Connor took a shower. There were no labels to say which store it was from. With her intrigue building, she poured herself another glass of wine – Connor hadn't given her permission to look inside.

'Hmm…' Eva mulled to herself. *By his choice of virginal white underwear, I reckon it must be a sexy schoolgirl outfit.* She grinned, fancying herself as a bit of a sleuth.

Licking her lips, she leaned forward and slipped her fingers under one of the corners of box. *Gosh, perhaps I'm wrong?* she thought, puzzled by the weight.

'You need to take off what you're wearing, apart from your knickers,' instructed Connor, walking into the bedroom and making her jump back from the box.

Staring up at Connor's naked tanned body, Eva's eyes were automatically drawn to his flaccid penis. Even in such a relaxed state, it hung down heavily from his well-trimmed groin.

'And wash off your make-up, too.'

Eva giggled nervously. 'What?'

'You won't do that for me, then?' said Connor, frowning.

'If that's what you want, then – yes.' Eva nodded compliantly.

'Good, change in the bathroom.' He pulled back the bed covers and lay down.

Blinking curiously, Eva picked up the heavy box and turned to Connor whose face was serious with tense anticipation.

She placed the box on the bathroom floor. Crouching down, she gingerly lifted the lid. Parting the white tissue paper, her mouth fell open. Folded neatly was a black woollen robe with a simple white headdress and a small gold crucifix.

An anxious laugh dropped from her mouth as she lifted out the authentic nun's habit. She found it ironic that a man who made a fortune selling provocative fantasies preferred an image of purity and virtue to turn him on.

Removing her bra, she stood in her knickers while removing her make-up. The long shapeless tunic felt slightly coarse against her skin and disguised her shapely figure completely.

Looking into the mirror, she hardly recognised herself. A wave of nervous giggles engulfed her as she had the urge to sing 'The hills are alive with the sound of music'!

As she opened the bathroom door, a startled Mr Jingles sprang to his feet and arched his back before hissing with fright and bounding downstairs.

Inhaling deeply, Eva walked into her bedroom.

She thought of cracking a joke about trying to kick the 'habit', but the look of sheer captivation etched on Connor's face electrified the air as his steel-blue eyes gazed down the whole length of her tunic.

'Come over here,' he purred, slowly getting to his feet, his flaccid penis quickly thickening. Circling his strong fingers around her delicate wrist, Connor pulled her close into him. He slipped his index finger under her chin to tilt her face towards his. 'Do *not* tell anyone of this. This is something I do for private pleasure – *understand?*'

Eva felt the threat in his voice, but his soft, lustful gaze took the sting out of his warning.

'What do you want me to do – sing?' asked Eva, suppressing a smile.

'No...' Connor said bluntly. 'But I guess you're curious...'

'I understand the fantasy side, of course, but this,' said Eva, sweeping her hands down the woollen fabric, 'goes a little deeper than titillation, I think.'

A wide smile spread across Connor lips as two large dimples sunk into his tanned cheeks. 'Nuns played a big part in my youth.'

'Hmmm... Fancied one of the pretty young nuns, did you?'

'It was definitely a "love-hate" relationship, or "lust" should I say.'

'I don't understand? Did one of the nuns touch you inappropriately?'

'Not the kind of touch you're imagining.'

'They hit you?'

'"Discipline" they called it,' explained Connor, stroking his fingertips against the material of her robe.

'So why am I dressed like this if they represent such a horrible childhood memory? Surely you despise nuns now?'

'There lies the question,' said Connor, lowering his voice and taking hold of her hand again. 'I can't explain the enjoyment I get from being overpowered by this image. But the truth is, it brings me intense pleasure.'

'So you want me to hit you?' asked Eva anxiously.

Connor smiled reassuringly. 'Hit – no, dominated – yes.'

Raising her eyebrows, Eva nodded. 'Okay... Have you done this with many women?' she probed.

'Shall we start?' said Connor, brushing off her question.

Clearing her throat, Eva tried to process Connor's secret pleasure. 'What was the nun's name?'

Inhaling deeply, Connor stared down at her intensely. 'Sister... Mary... Bernadette...' he said in a slow southern Irish drawl.

'Right...' Eva swallowed, quickly racking her brains what to say. 'Er... It has been brought to my attention that you, *Connor O'Neill*, have been disruptive in class!'

Connor seemed underwhelmed by her first attempt at scolding him.

'She was more formidable than that – I'm sure you can do better, Eva.'

Hold on a minute, she thought, *who's scolding who?*

'What have I told you about speaking without permission?!' Eva barked quickly.

Her second attempt seemed to satisfy him; his large erection twitched spontaneously in front of her.

'Get on your knees and look down at the floor,' she added aggressively. She blinked in disbelief as Connor dropped to his knees without hesitation and felt strangely aroused as he averted his gaze to the floor. 'Hmmm... What punishment is suitable for a dammed soul,' mused Eva. She hooked her index finger under his chin, lifting his gaze.

Connor's expression was immersed as he stared up at her beneath his thick black eyelashes. 'I don't know, Sister.'

'Sister...what?!'

'Mary Bernadette...' added Connor quickly, lowering his gaze again and slipping his hand down to his thick erection.

Latching her fingers firmly on either side of his cheeks, Eva roughly pulled his face up to meet her stare. 'Repeat after me...' she growled slowly. 'I am... an evil... worthless boy!'

Her vicious words transported Connor instantly back to his childhood. With shallow breathing, he pleasured himself urgently as his breath hissed through his teeth. '...W-worthless boy.'

'Yes,' Eva said coldly, bobbing her head. 'So, what punishment is fitting for such a creature?'

'I-I don't know, Sister...' whispered Connor.

'Kiss my feet!' ordered Eva, perching herself on the edge of the bed.

Watching spellbound as Connor slowly pushed the fabric of her tunic up over her ankle, she revelled in the situation as he took her foot in his hands. His well-defined lips gently pressed against her pale skin, sending a shudder of excitement down her spine as his warm breath settled on her painted toes.

Having her toes sucked was not a new experience for Eva, but under such intense circumstances – this was.

Feeling the wet confines of Connor's mouth enveloping her big toe, she relished every swirl of his tongue. Lifting the hem of her gown to expose her shapely leg made Connor masturbate with fevered urgency as he glimpsed the tantalising triangle of her white cotton knickers.

'*Fuc...cckk.*' Intense pleasure in his balls and penis made him gasp out in spasms.

'Kiss me here,' purred Eva, letting her legs fall open.

Kissing her sex over her knickers, Connor's eyes widened with time-aged memories clouded with lust as the small crucifix shimmered against the darkness of Eva's gown.

Sister Mary Bernadette was ingrained in his mind. She was a domineering and unemotional woman of great beauty. His hunger to touch her hidden flesh diluted the physical pain of her daily punishments. He almost resented her abuse wasn't sexual. Even to this day, the fantasy of taking her virginity as a fourteen-year-old boy was as sexually potent now as it was then – a fantasy that had lasted twenty-six years.

'You may remove my underwear – boy,' commanded Eva.

Restraint fuelled the air as Connor tried to control his eager passion from violently ripping Eva's knickers from her curvy hips.

'What would you like to do to me – boy?' asked Eva, her words drenched in yearning to be ravaged by him.

'T-taste you...S-sister,' whispered Connor as he watched Eva lie back on the bed.

With an urgent frenzy he sunk his face between her thighs, flicking his tongue firmly over her clit greedily.

Feeling his fingers sink into her body, Eva felt overwhelmed with yearning as his tongue and fingers pleasured her in perfect unison.

'*Connor!*' she gasped, her body writhing on the bed as though she lay on a blanket of burning coals.

'*Ohhh fu-ck!*' Connor's body shuddered to a halt as his orgasm sprayed into his cupped hand. Kneeling back, he exhaled deeply as his body surrendered to the overpowering ecstasy.

'Con-nor...' moaned Eva, slipping her fingers down to her swollen sex.

'Baby...' Connor quickly reached over to slip his glistening fingers deep into her body.

As Eva's cries of pleasure filled the room, her orgasm merged with his over his long tanned fingers. She sat up with rosy pink cheeks and looked down at a very contented Connor. 'Shall I take this off?' she asked, slipping out of character.

'Not yet...I want you to fuck me wearing it.'

After mopping her brow, she ordered Connor to lie on the bed as she hitched up the long robe and straddled his thighs. She glanced over to her bedside cabinet looking for his box of condoms. Giving him a perplexed look, she glanced back over towards the cabinet again.

'I trust you,' soothed Connor, caressing her chest over the gown.

Eva smiled down at him and tapped his hand away from her breast. 'Don't touch Sister without permission – boy!'

Rewarded with a slow, wide smile, Connor watched expectantly as Eva guided his penis into her.

'*Oh Jez...*'

'Shush...!' berated Eva, pressing her finger firmly over his lips.

Rocking her body back and forth, her cheeks darkened with exertion as the small gold cross swung down in front of Connor like a hypnotising pendulum.

'You are such an evil child!' she cussed, digging her nails into his smooth chest making him groan and clench his teeth.

Stilling her hips, she grabbed the hem of her robe.

'Why have you stopped?' panted Connor.

'There you go again, O'Neill, speaking without permission,' she hissed, playfully slapping his clammy cheek with her hand. 'This will be perfect,' muttered Eva, walking over to her wardrobe and taking out a black silk scarf.

'Sis—?'

'Shssh – sit on the edge of the bed!' instructed Eva. Using the scarf as a blindfold she whispered into Connor's ear, 'Roll onto your stomach.' She reached into her beside cabinet and took out a black leather paddle she had bought because Connor was so keen on spanking. Caressing his toned bottom with her fingertips sent a shiver of excitement through her body.

'Hmm…' mumbled Connor, feeling the warmth of her tongue brush against his tanned right buttock cheek.

'*Is that nice*?' purred Eva seductively.

'Yeahhh,' said Connor, his voice tight with lust.

A wicked smile spread across her lips. 'Good.'

'*JESUSSSS Christ!*' hollered Connor as she struck the leather paddle hard against his flesh.

'How dare you curse!' she roared, raising the paddle into the air again.

'*SHIT*…not so hard, Eva!' cried out Connor, digging his fingers into the pillow.

Stifling a nervous laugh, she said theatrically, 'Well, let that be a lesson to you!'

'I think it's time,' he panted, easily untying the loose knot of the blindfold.

Eva raised her eyebrows with intrigue. 'For what?'

'It's time I took back control,' he said with a menacing grin.

He gently pulled the heavy robe over Eva's head and dropped it to the floor. 'Come here.' Connor grinned, patting his thighs.

'Sit or lie across?' asked Eva narrowing her eyes.

'What do you think I would like?'

'Hmm…this?' She giggled, lying across his muscular legs.

'I'm impressed,' teased Connor, looking down at her smooth domed bottom.

Not feeling particularly comfortable, Eva closed her eyes waiting for the sharp sting to colour her flesh. Her body jolted in anticipation of a sharp strike; instead, Connor trailed the silk scarf across her pale bottom. A low laugh left his mouth as he swept the silk scarf over again. '*Argh!*' squealed Eva, feeling a blunt slap. 'Sneaky,' she said, knowing his soft touch was just a decoy from what was coming next.

'I don't know what you mean.' Connor laughed bringing the paddle down again.

'*Argh…!*'

'How far can I go?' he asked, placing his hands onto her hips, gently pulling her bottom towards his erection.

'I don't want to do that,' said Eva.

'Have you tried it?'

'Yes – I didn't like it,' she added quickly.

'That's fine,' reassured Connor, sliding his hand up underneath her belly to touch her breast.

Feeling Connor enter her, his slow thrusts suddenly quickened to urgent plunges as his hips relentlessly slapped against her bottom. His deep pounding quickly brought Eva to orgasm as she cried out with rasping groans.

'*FUCK!*' panted Connor. The bed shook violently beneath them as his second orgasm poured into her.

'That was…' gushed Connor breathlessly, withdrawing from her body, 'fucking memorable!'

Eva sighed with bliss.

Connor kissed the red indentations colouring her pale buttocks. 'I think we'll use something softer next time,' he remarked, smiling.

Chapter 16

As Halloween and Guy Fawkes Night passed quickly, Christmas adverts monopolised every child's thoughts as Eva's twenty-fifth birthday loomed. She had booked a long weekend off and intended to celebrate her birthday in style with her two best friends, Susanna and Roxanne.

'Oh, you shouldn't have, Roxy, they're beautiful,' said Eva beaming.

'I know your birthday isn't until tomorrow, but I thought you'd be rushing around, so…'

'You shouldn't have spent so much. They must have cost a small fortune.'

'So you like them, then?'

'Absolutely!' squealed Eva, holding up the nine carat white gold and amethyst earrings.

'I hate purple,' crowed Tina walking past.

'Well it's a good job they're not for you then, isn't it!' sneered Roxanne, glaring up at her.

'Oh, take no notice of her,' said Eva.

'So what else did you get?'

'Money from my mum and family, oh yeah, and Yardley talc from my elderly neighbour, Mrs Simms!' Eva chuckled.

'What time are you picking up Susanna tomorrow?'

'Her flight arrives at ten thirty in the morning. What time are we meeting outside the Cuckoo Club – half nine?'

'Yeah…'

'Is it still okay to stay at yours tomorrow night, babes?' asked Roxanne, pulling on a pair of tiny gold hot pants.

'Yes, no worries,' Eva said smiling and rubbing her hands together in excitement. 'I can't wait for you to meet Susanna – you'll get on like a house of fire!'

'It's buzzing out there tonight!' said Donna, storming into the dressing room wearing a pair of red French knickers and a garter above her knee.

'I love the hustle and bustle of Christmas,' said Eva before being distracted by her mobile beeping.

I have a gift for you x, read the screen.

The mind boggles Mr O'Neill ☺ texted Eva, walking back to her dressing table.

Come up in an hour and you'll see – don't be late!

Eva had acclimatised to Connor's complex and domineering personally. She had fallen in love with his tender and attentive core while accepting the sharp edges of his temper.

Glancing up at the clock, she felt like an impatient child waiting for the hour to lapse.

'So how old are you?' asked Scarlett, securing the attention of Donna and Tina.

'Twenty-five,' replied Eva, not looking away from her vanity mirror.

'I guess with your pale skin you'll probably age quicker,' Tina retorted. 'Where as I'm still asked for ID when buying alcohol,' she crowed.

'Oh Tina,' Eva said, laughing. 'I would rather be me than a vain, lemon-lipped bitch like you! Nastiness runs through you like a cheap stick of seaside rock – nah, I would rather be me, thanks.'

'That's harsh,' said Scarlett, glancing at Tina who sat open-mouthed at Eva's accurate description of her.

'Who's harsh?' Roxanne glanced up.

'Eva just said Tina was. What did you say? A lemon-lipped bitch,' repeated Scarlett.

'Tut-tut,' mocked Roxanne. '*More* like a soulless, lemon-lipped bitch.' Roxanne smirked and winked at Eva.

A ripple of laughter provoked Tina to get to her feet in protest. 'Why do you always have to side with her, Roxanne? If anyone's a bitch, then it's *her*. But no, I'm an easy target. Let's all pick on the petite pretty one. I've told Connor, you know, that you and *her* pick on me!'

'Get over yourself, Tina, you're like a squealing bagpipe. Everyone sitting here knows you're rotten to the core!' announced Roxanne unapologetically.

With tears pricking her eyes, Tina jumped to her feet and strode towards the toilets, quickly followed by Donna and Scarlett.

'Where you going, babe?' asked Roxanne, watching Eva head towards the dressing room door.

'Er…I won't be long. I just need at quick word with Beverley on reception.'

'Okay, I'll meet you outside for a cigarette in five minutes!' called out Roxanne as the door clicked shut.

Eva raced up to the penthouse fluffing her long hair and knocked on the door.

'Come in…'

'Hello.' Eva grinned as she entered.

Connor sat cross-legged on the sofa with a bottle of champagne cradled in a silver ice bucket on the large coffee table in front of him.

'Hmmm champagne!' Eva giggled sitting down beside him.

'Well it's not every day you reach a quarter of a century.'

'Saying it like that makes me sound old!'

Connor poured two glasses of chilled champagne amused by her retort. 'Here's to you, Eva, "Happy twenty-fifth birthday",' he toasted, handing her a drink.

Clinking her glass, the fizzy bubbles quickly found the tip of her nose as she casually scanned around the room for her gift.

'Do I get a birthday kiss, then?' asked Eva, hoping to spot signs of a lavish present.

She closed her eyes and felt his soft lips press firmly against her mouth. His spicy aftershave sent a tingle down her spine.

'I guess you'd like your gift?' asked Connor, reaching into his jacket pocket.

Eva's eyes widened in anticipation as she nodded excitedly.

'Well, I know you love cats…' Connor smiled handing her an envelope.

'Oh…' said Eva, opening it. 'A cheque for the Hackney Cat Sanctuary, that is…so kind of you.' She said, sounding underwhelmed. 'Thank you.'

'I know you got Mr Jingles from a cat sanctuary, so I thought I'd make a donation for your birthday present – look,' said Connor, 'you get a car sticker, too.'

'Wow, a thousand pounds is amazing. I-I don't know what to say…'

'I didn't get it right, did I?' Connor frowned at her response.

Eva's cheeks darkened at feeling ungrateful; his gift was so thoughtful and heartfelt.

'You got it perfectly right,' she gushed, leaning over to kiss him.

'So you're abandoning me this weekend for your American friend,' grumbled Connor.

'She isn't American, she's English – she just works in Vegas.'

'Is she a dancer? I pretty much know all the clubs in Vegas.'

'Actually the name of the club has completely gone out of my head,' lied Eva, quickly taking a large gulp of champagne. She felt a little apprehensive revealing Susanna's profession in case he disapproved. 'Anyway, I'm not *abandoning* you.'

'Yes you are. We could've spent the night together, but you've chosen your friend over me,' he continued. 'Is she single?'

'Why?'

'I take it you'll be going to a club and getting drunk! You'll be an easy target for men on the make.'

Eva suppressed a smile and brushed her hand up his leg towards his groin. 'I won't be looking. I'm more than satisfied with my rampant, handsome Irishman,' she crowed, caressing Connor's ego.

'I want you to text me regularly until we see each other Monday afternoon,' he instructed.

'Okay, Boss,' she said with a giggle.

'Eva…' Connor inhaled sharply and brushed away her hand. 'Don't patronise my feelings.'

'Sorry.' Eva blinked, suddenly realising his mood was darkening at the thought of other men wanting to hit on her.

Connor got to his feet and gently pulled her up from the sofa. 'Well then, I'd better make sure you're fully satisfied so you won't be tempted to go off with a young chancer.' He wrapped his arms around her waist and kissed her passionately.

Eva smiled coyly. 'You do that every night.'

'I have a high sex drive which you satisfy perfectly, Miss Summers,' assured Connor, sliding down his hands to cup her bottom.

Connor's love-making was energetic and feverish as they had wild sex on the soft cream carpet.

'I'd better go before Ann asks where I am,' said Eva, flattening her hair and straightening her black sequin top.

'See – you can't wait to get away from me,' complained Connor, zipping up his flies.

'You hired me to make you money,' Eva quipped.

'Oh, of course, "money makes my heart beat", doesn't it?' replied Connor in a deadpan tone, quoting her words from the casino's reopening party.

Eva ran back into his arms and stood on tiptoes to drape her hands around his neck. 'I didn't mean it. I know you have a heart, somewhere, deep inside,' she baited and earning herself a slap on the bottom.

'There's an element of truth in what you said,' agreed Connor. 'I am driven by the need to be successful and wealthy, which, I might add, I've achieved through hard work and being a hundred percent focused. Then this sexy little redhead walks into my life and distracts me.'

'So, I'm just a distraction for you?' asked Eva, suddenly looking forlorn.

'Hmmm…' Connor thought about his reply. 'No – but nevertheless a very welcome one.'

Eva's heart jumped a beat hearing his softly spoken words. She was beginning to see many layers of emotion under his, at times, cold harsh exterior.

'So you see, Miss Summers, I do have a heart to bruise and wound. So look where you're treading – don't stamp on it carelessly,' warned Connor, kissing the tip of her nose. 'Go on, then,' he said, tapping her bottom again, 'go and earn me some money.'

'See you Monday afternoon, and thank you for my present and the great birthday sex,' said Eva, turning to leave.

'Oh, "Red",' called out Connor.

'*Yes…*' Eva turned and raised her eyebrow on hearing her epithet.

'Don't forget to text me – I don't manage rejection well!'

Eva blew him a kiss on her way out of the penthouse.

* * *

Eva's joy at seeing her friend in Arrivals soon subsided after seeing the dark shadow under her left eye. She didn't believe the excuse of her falling over in new stilettos while drunk was the true cause. But her concern quickly melted as Susanna's excitement spread like a virus until they were chatting, squealing and giggling like teenagers again all the way back to Eva's.

'Your home's lovely. You've done well for yourself,' praised Susanna, glancing around her lounge.

'All thanks to you and your wise words. If you hadn't suggested dancing, I wouldn't have been able to afford my own place,' she said, handing Susanna a large glass of wine. 'The mortgage and bills take most of my wages, but it's all mine, babes!'

'Here's to girl power!' Susanna smiled, raising her glass.

After lunch, they giggled their way through the entire afternoon reminiscing about their school years and wild parties.

'So,' asked Eva gingerly, 'are you still seeing that guy in Vegas?'

'Boyfriends are off limits,' insisted Susanna. 'This is a "girl only" weekend!' she said, shaking her head with a mouthful of wine.

Eva guessed her reluctance to discuss boyfriends, and the ugly bruise under her eye, meant she was still seeing her deadbeat boyfriend. She couldn't understand why an intelligent, beautiful woman like Susanna would let such a man into her life, but she knew if she pressed her it would sour their short time together.

'Oh – I'll just get that,' said Eva hearing the doorbell.

'Hello, Miss Eva Summers?'

'Yes,' said Eva, looking at the short middle-aged man reading from a blue clipboard.

'Can you sign this delivery note for me please, love?'

'What am I signing for?' asked Eva, looking for a parcel.

The man turned and looked towards the road. '*That*,' he said, pointing to the unloading of a red convertible Mini Cooper.

Eva stood speechless as Susanna came to the front door.

'Wow, that must've set you back a bit?' quizzed Susanna, peering over the man's shoulder.

'I think you've made a mistake,' said Eva, handing back the clipboard and unsigned delivery note.

'Eva Summers? Nineteen Normandy Close? That's what it says here, love,' said the man impatiently.

'Yes, I can see what's printed on the sheet, but I haven't ordered it.'

'There's an envelope inside the car,' said the man, holding out a set of keys.

'A secret admirer!' squealed Susanna shoving Eva out onto the garden path. 'Go and see what it says – go on!' she added, following her to the car.

'What does it say?' said Susanna watching Eva reach for a red envelope sitting on the dashboard. 'Oh my God! There are about twenty shoe boxes in here!' She gasped, grabbing one. 'Shitting hell, they're all Louboutins!'

'What?' shrieked Eva, ripping open the envelope.

Did I fool you? Happy Birthday! Lots of sexy thoughts, C x

'Who's "C"?' probed Susanna, looking at the handwritten note.

Reading the words again rendered Eva mute.

'Someone is giving some quality "boo-ty",' scoffed Susanna, opening a second shoebox. 'Oh, these are beautiful. Can I borrow them tonight?' she pleaded, pawing at a pair of black and gold red-soled shoes.

'So if you could sign for it, then? I am on schedule,' the man said bluntly.

'Y-yes, sorry,' stuttered Eva, taking the pen from him.

Susanna grinned and plonked herself in the passenger seat. 'So…who is this mystery "C"?'

'Actually, it's a bit complicated,' Eva said, blushing. She crouched down and peered into the car.

'*Married* complicated?'

'No!' protested Eva strongly. 'It's just no one knows, that's all – not even Roxanne, so keep it to yourself.'

'Intriguing…' mused Susanna, getting out of the car clutching a handful of shoe boxes. 'All this secrecy can only mean one thing,' she stated watching Eva lock the car. 'You're seeing someone you shouldn't. I know you said he isn't married, but—'

'He isn't married,' snapped Eva, walking back to the house with Susanna hot on her heels.

'So?'

With her cheeks turning crimson, Eva quickly shut the front door behind them. 'He's… Er…'

'A wealthy punter?'

'No…'

'Not your manager again!'

'Er…no…'

'For God's sake, put me out of my misery – who is he?' badgered Susanna.

'My boss!' Eva blurted out.

'Your boss!' Susanna dropped the boxes on the stairs. 'Have you forgotten how difficult it was working with Ryan – your last manager, after you spilt up? You used to text me every night saying how depressed you were seeing him every day. And now you're making the same mistake again?!'

'No – we're just enjoying each other's company, that's all. We have an understanding. He doesn't want a serious relationship and has promised things will stay professional at work.'

'Yeah right, and I've got a billion pounds in the bank!' berated Susanna. 'You don't do casual sex, Eva. Well, excluding that one time at Glastonbury, and even then you had to be drunk!'

Eva exhaled sharply. 'I know what I'm doing, don't worry.'

'You're gonna get hurt!' warned Susanna sternly. 'You don't do friends with benefits. You've always been a traditionalist since school – marriage and kids. I've no doubt he's turned your head with great sex and expensive gifts, but what happens when he gets bored of you – and he will!'

'I don't want to discuss it anymore!' barked Eva. 'I'm not sixteen!'

'Fine,' Susanna snapped. 'I don't want us to fall out over a guy. Just saying that you're beautiful and funny, you don't need to be some guy's trophy shag – you're better than that.'

'I know I am!'

With a deafening silence wedged between them, Susanna quickly softened. 'I'm only saying this because I love you. It's your birthday and I'm only here until Monday. I don't want us to fall out,' she coaxed, reaching out to hug her.

Returning Susanna's embrace, Eva smiled before saying, 'Okay, a truce. No men talk!'

Chapter 17

'Eva! The taxi is here – come on!' bellowed Susanna up the stairs.
'Okay, I'm just coming!'

Eva slammed the front door shut and followed Susanna gingerly down the garden path in her new electric-blue skyscraper designer heels to the taxi. She glanced over at her new sleek Mini sitting under the street lamp and reminded herself to text Connor once Susanna was out of view.

Once outside the Cuckoo Club, Eva tapped excitedly on the window and waved seeing Roxy. She handed the driver thirty pounds. 'Keep the change!' she squealed, flinging open the door and jumping out.

'Happy birthday, Eva!' Roxanne said excitedly, hugging her tightly.

'Thanks!' Eva turned to Susanna. 'This is Susanna, my best friend from school.'

'Hi,' said Roxanne, smiling and bobbing her head in Susanna's direction. 'I take it you two have already started drinking!' she scoffed.

'Yep – time for another one, or ten,' said Eva, laughing. 'The first round is on the "birthday girl"!'

Within half an hour they had finished their three Blue Hawaiian cocktails and three tequila slammers and were well on their way to getting drunk.

'I love Florence and the Machine,' shouted Roxanne over the loud music as she got to her feet.

'You've got the love! You've got the love! Yoouuu've got the loveeeee!' they all sang at the top of their voices grabbing their handbags and weaving their way through the crowds towards the dance floor.

Feeling hot and smelling of tequila, thanks to Susanna spilling the entire contents of her fourth tequila slammer down her dress, Eva shouted over to Roxanne, 'I'm just nipping to the loo, can you look after her?' she mouthed, pointing at a very drunk Susanna.

'Okay,' yelled Roxanne, sticking up her thumb.

Eva followed the sign to the ladies toilets and sighed heavily joining a long line of boisterous, intoxicated women. She reached into her handbag for her phone. '*Oh shit!*' she cursed realising she had left it at home. *Maybe I can get Roxanne to text Tommy and hint that I've forgotten my phone?* she pondered, not sure how she could orchestrate such a plan without arousing Roxanne's suspicions.

Her gaze moved away from the queue and suddenly fear chilled her to the core. *What the hell is he doing here?* Standing in the foyer was Patrick St Clair, the ghost-like creature she met at Claridge's. Under the neon light, his pallid skin looked almost alien-like. His unemotional stare sent an ice-cold shiver down her spine as one question screamed in her head, *if St Clair was here, where the hell was repulsive Booth?!*

She quickly left the queue and leapt in front of a group of girls who were walking back while constantly peering over her shoulder.

'There you are! I think this one is hammered,' scoffed Roxanne, propping Susanna up in her seat.

'Roxanne! I've just seen St Clair!' gasped Eva, looking over her shoulder again.

'Where?'

'In the foyer – he looked straight at me.'

'Did he say anything?'

'No, I didn't give him the chance, I just came back here. I don't want to stay if he's here with Booth!'

'Okay, calm down,' said Roxanne, getting to her feet. St Clair hasn't got a grudge against you, it's with O'Neill. And as for Booth, well he's just all talk.'

'Yes, but we work for Connor!'

'Look, just keep a lid on that imagination of yours! If you feel uncomfortable, then we'll go,' said Roxanne reaching down and grabbing Susanna's arm.

'Do you think we should tell Tommy and Connor?' wheezed Eva, trying to keep Susanna upright. 'I would've text myself, but I forgot my phone!' babbled Eva.

'You haven't got Connor's number though?'

'W-well no, but…'

'Anyway, I texted Tommy about an hour ago. They've only gone and flown out to Ireland!'

'Ireland? Did Tommy say why the sudden trip?'

'He said it was a spur of the moment thing. Connor's been in a dark mood all day, so no doubt he's gone looking for a bit of "pussy",' said Roxanne with a chuckle.

'Oh…' replied Eva, feeling her heart sink into her belly, knowing her absentmindedness was probably the cause of his 'dark mood'.

Eva shoved Susanna into the back of a cab and flopped down next to her. She felt winded replaying Susanna's words of warning like a film reel in her head.

'How many women do you think there are?' asked Eva, sounding sullen.

'God knows…' Roxanne yawned loudly.

'Where to, love?' asked the Indian taxi driver.

'Eva…'

'What?'

'What's your address?' asked Roxanne.

'Oh yeah, sorry…nineteen Normandy Close, Hackney.'

'I think Tommy said Cara's with them,' added Roxanne, reaching for her mobile.

'Cara?'

'Yeah, he's mentioned her before. She must be his favourite bimbo!' mocked Roxanne. 'I told you he likes uncomplicated women.'

'Well, if she's his *favourite*, maybe he'll marry her, then?' Eva seethed looking out of the cab window and tried not to cry.

'O'Neill will never love another woman, not after all that business with his ex. Tom said he'll never trust anyone else, so the poor cow will always be "just another shag".'

With her mind spinning, and Susanna's incoherent grunts, the twenty-minute journey back to Eva's house went slowly.

'Are we putting this one to bed, then cracking open a bottle of wine?' asked Roxanne, prising her handbag from underneath Susanna's thigh.

Eva sighed heavily. 'Definitely.'

After paying the taxi driver, Eva and Roxanne struggled to hold up Susanna as they made their way indoors.

'Right,' instructed Roxanne, 'if you can pull her up the stairs, I'll push from the back.'

After much heaving and shoving, they slowly guided Susanna into the spare room and gently lowered her onto the bed.

'I'll get a glass of water and a sick bowl in case she wakes up,' said Eva, walking out the bedroom.

Being away from Roxanne and Susanna gave her the chance grab her phone and check her messages. '*Holy shit!*' she cursed, glancing down at the four texts from Connor.

09:07: *Happy Birthday gorgeous – hope you're in around 1pm today? xxx*

13:25: *Has something arrived for you… where's my text? X*

14:27: *Why haven't you text me Eva?! You don't like the car?*

'Oh fuck.' Eva frowned quickly scrolling down to his last text.

16:43: *If this is some sort of mind game, then you lose because I'm not interested in second guessing what you're thinking! I let you into my private life and shared personal things with you only for you to make me feel like a fool! It won't happen a second time!*

'Eva!' Roxanne called out. 'Where are you with that bowl!'

'Yeah, coming!' Eva yelled back, quickly firing off a text. *I am sorry Connor! Today has been a whirlwind with my friend arriving then receiving your gifts, which I am totally overwhelmed by! Susanna is drunk and Roxanne is here too, so I haven't had a moment to myself. Feel like a fool – who is Cara?*

'C-an we can go for a drive tomorrow i-in your new car,' Susanna garbled in between hiccups. 'And bring your s-secret admirer!' she slurred drunkenly.

'Shhh, sleep now,' hushed Eva, putting down a large bowl and glass of water by the bed.

'Secret admirer – who's got a secret admirer – you?' quizzed Roxanne.

'Oh, she's drunk,' said Eva. 'Give me a hand to undress her, will you?'

'Woah—' Roxanne gasped, stepping back. 'What the fuck's happened here?' she said, pulling up Susanna's red jumper dress. 'Has she been in an accident or something?'

Eva's eyes widened in shock looking down at a cluster of angry bruises colouring Susanna's skin.

'Shit, there's more,' said Roxanne, rolling Susanna onto her side.

'Oh God.' Eva held her hand up to her mouth.

'Do you know who's done this to her?'

'Her bastard of a boyfriend, I'm guessing!'

'Why do women put up with this shit. If Tommy ever raised his hand to me, that would be it!' she announced, shaking her head. 'Have you met this scumbag?'

'No, but we fell out a few months ago when she hinted that her "then boyfriend" had physically hurt her. I told her to dump him, but she wouldn't, and ever since she won't mention him or discuss their relationship. I don't know how to help her,' whimpered Eva.

'There's nothing you can do. She has to figure it out for herself, and one day she might see him for what he really is – a fucking bully,' raged Roxanne. 'Come on, let's go and get a drink,' she added, wrapping her arm around Eva's shoulder.

'Well, this is a birthday I'd rather forget! Seeing St Clair, then finding out my best friend is being beaten to a pulp – I can't wait until midnight!' Eva sighed and flopped down on the sofa.

'Listen, babes,' Roxanne said softly. 'What we can't change, we have to find a way of dealing with. St Clair is scum and just hanging around to annoy Connor. I think it was coincidental he was at the club tonight. Even deadbeats like him like to drink and have a dance, you know,' she said wearily.

'Yeah, I suppose.'

The sound of a text alert made both women reach for their mobiles.

'It's me,' said Roxanne, reading her message.

'Oh…' mumbled Eva, checking her phone. '*Oh shit!*'

'What is it?'

'Oh nothing, sorry…' said Eva, realising to her horror that her text to Connor was sitting in her draft box.

'It's Tommy, looks like His Lordship is on form tonight.'

'What do you mean?' asked Eva, glancing up from her mobile.

'I mentioned Cara earlier, didn't I?'

'Er…yes.' *The Irish tart!* she thought spitefully.

'Well, looks like Connor is spending the night with her; Tommy's gone back to their hotel on his own.'

Eva guzzled the rest of her drink and quickly refilled their glasses. 'Perhaps you're wrong about him not trusting another woman. She could be "the one"?'

'Nah, she just fits the criteria – easy, has a pulse, a vagina,' cackled Roxanne.

'Oh, right,' said Eva, forcing a smile. 'I guess some people never change.'

'Have you got anything to eat? I'm fucking starving.'

'Oh yes – sorry, I bring in some nibbles,' said Eva quickly getting to her feet. She brushed a tear from her cheek carrying her wine into the kitchen.

'Do you want a hand?' called out Roxanne.

'No, I can manage,' said Eva now with salty tears streaming down her cheeks. Swigging down her second glass of wine in two large gulps, she wiped her mouth with the back of her hand and slammed down her empty glass. '*SHIT!*'

'What is it?' cried out Roxanne rushing into the kitchen. 'Bloody hell!' she shouted looking at the shards of sharp glass spread across the kitchen top.

'I'm so clumsy!' said Eva, chastising herself and carefully placing the broken glass onto a lime-green tea towel.

'Look, forget about the snacks, I'm knackered so I might go up,' Roxanne said yawning, not noticing Eva's tear-streaked cheeks.

After Roxanne had gone up upstairs to bed, Eva stood outside in the cold night air for a cigarette thinking about Connor. She only smoked half her cigarette before locking the back door and going back into the lounge. With copious amounts of alcohol fuelling her increasingly dark mood, she wrestled with her temper goading her to send Connor a provoking text. Her temper won.

I take it you're with her – Cara. I saw your old friend this evening…St Clair! He didn't send his best wishes by the way! Eva smirked with sour satisfaction.

She turned off the lights and took her mobile and a glass of water upstairs to the bathroom. Her thoughts would have been vocal if she had been on her own, but she didn't want to mutter away in case Roxanne woke up and heard her eccentric rambling. The beep of her phone made her jump.

Did he speak to you?

Clenching her teeth in rage she fired off a reply, *Are you with her?*

Did he say anything? Where did you see him?

She stamped her foot in frustration, incensed by his obvious reluctance to answer her. *I will repeat my question again! Are you with her?*

Eva! Are you going to tell me if he said anything or not?

With her cheeks burning, she grimaced quickly replying, *I didn't text earlier because I had forgotten to take my phone out with me. SORRY!*

She cursed under her breath when there was no instant reply and flushed the loo. Tiptoeing into bed, trying not to disturb Roxanne who was fast asleep, tears dampened her pillow as she tried to push away all thoughts of Connor making passionate love to another woman.

* * *

'You were tossing and turning like a fish out of water last night, babes,' moaned Roxanne when Eva walked into the sunlit lounge.

She looked down at Roxanne lying on the sofa. 'Sorry, did I disturb you? Have you been down here all night?'

'Most of it – what time is it?'

'Early,' called out Eva, walking into the kitchen.

'How's Susanna?' enquired Roxanne yawning, following her.

'Sleeping like a baby. Coffee?'

'Yes, please.'

Eva flicked on the kettle feeling miserable and lethargically made her way over to the fridge. Making a milky sweet coffee and a strong black coffee for Roxanne, they went outside in the garden and smoked a cigarette.

'I'll shoot off after this,' said Roxanne, taking a deep drag on her cigarette followed by a spluttering cough.

'Don't you want to stay for breakfast?' asked Eva secretly relieved; she was finding it difficult to muster enthusiasm for idle chitchat with Connor monopolising her thoughts.

'I won't, if you don't mind. I've got loads of stuff to do at home, plus Tommy is on his way back.'

'Tommy and Connor?'

'Yeah, but Tommy sounded pissed off.'

'Why – have you spoken to him?'

'No, he texted, but it was short and blunt, which isn't like him. Maybe he's had words with Connor.'

'I thought they were supposed to be *best buddies*?' mocked Eva.

'They are, but like all men they have enormous egos! I've seen both explode at each other before now.'

'What – words or physical?' asked Eva.

'Just words, they didn't speak for a couple of days, though.'

'Tommy is a giant meat-house,' said Eva, believing no man could overpower his enormous stature.

'Connor didn't get a body like that by doing a couple of hours down the gym,' explained Roxanne. 'He's into martial arts, jujitsu and taekwondo, so don't assume anything. Connor has earned his reputation.'

'Reputation?'

'As I've said before, don't be fooled by the Armani suits and polite chitchat. Even Tommy said he wouldn't like to be on the receiving end of his fist. Connor can handle himself, be sure of that.'

'Hmmm,' sneered Eva, 'a common thug under all that finery and charm.'

'W-what time is it?'

'Morning,' said Eva looking at a very pasty and dishevelled Susanna shuffling into the kitchen.

'Oh my head!' winced Susanna, resting her hand against her forehead. 'I feel so rough. I think I might've had my drink spiked, you know.'

'Or maybe it could've been all those tequila slammers and cocktails you knocked back?' reasoned Roxanne.

'I need painkillers,' murmured Susanna. 'Can you bring some through, Eva?' she whimpered, walking slowly into the lounge.

'Right, I'll shoot off, then,' said Roxanne. 'Nice meeting you, Susanna, take care – yeah,' she added.

Lying on the sofa, Susanna raised her arm into the air and groaned inaudibly, 'Eva...I need painkillers, now!'

'Yeah, okay.' Eva sighed, shutting the front door behind Roxanne.

Susanna's hangover pinned her to the sofa all day, so she had no real opportunity to probe her about the bruises while she drifted in and out of sleep. With her phone as silent as a muzzled dog, Eva felt utterly miserable mulling over Connor's texts.

'Sorry I got so pissed last night, Eva. I didn't ruin your birthday, did I?' croaked Susanna, stirring from her restless nap.

'Don't be silly.'

'Have you heard from "C" today?'

'Er...no.' She pressed the TV remote and flicked on a home improvement programme. 'I think it's finished anyway. As you said, he's got bored.'

'I'm not going say "I told you so",' winced Susanna, slowly heaving herself upright.

'So...' said Eva, not moving her gaze from the television. 'How's work? What are the men like over there – do they treat you okay?'

'Yeah,' said Susanna convincingly.

'Just, I noticed your bruises when I undressed you last night.'

'I told you, I fell over,' Susanna said curtly.

Turning away from the television, Eva forced a smile as she replied, 'Okay, just as long as you're all right.'

Susanna frowned. 'I'm fine, stop fussing.'

Eva knew from her tone it was futile to press her any further.

By four o'clock sheets of heavy rain pelted against the windows as Eva ordered a pizza delivery. Twenty minutes later a large Meat Feast and Hawaiian were being devoured.

'So he died right in front of you?' asked Susanna, listening to Eva's account of Black's death.

'I will never forget that night – ever,' explained Eva, taking a bite of her pizza.

'What did Knobhead do?' asked Susanna, referring to Connor.

'Actually, he was great.'

'I should think so, it was hardly your fault!'

'I know, but he was really caring. It's hard to explain, one minute he's like *Mr Perfect* –attentive, caring and approachable, then within a heartbeat he's cold and patronising!'

'A proper Jekyll and Hyde, eh?'

'I think all men are,' huffed Eva. 'One minute they can't wait to get into your knickers, then the next, they can't wait to escape! I'm done with men.'

'You should become a lesbian,' scoffed Susanna.

'Sounds very appealing at the moment.'

'It's a big fantasy with most of my clients, you know. Hey, come into business with me. We could make a fortune putting on a girl-on-girl double act,' she said, giggling.

Eva wrinkled her nose. 'Hmmm, not for me, I'm afraid. But *he* does have a weird, I don't know if you would call it, fantasy or fetish.'

'Really?' said Susanna excitedly. 'What is it, cross-dressing? Likes to wear a nappy?'

'Ugh, no, nothing like that. He likes me to dress up.'

Susanna looked unimpressed. 'A lot of men like that kind of thing. A sexy nurse, nun, schoolgirl, that's pretty basic stuff, hun.'

'No, it's a proper nun's habit. A long woollen robe – gold cross and everything!'

'Hmm interesting, and you don't mind?' asked Susanna, suitably amused with Connor's unusual inclination.

'Well, no I guess, but he likes me to dominate him, you know, belittle him…' said Eva, lowering her voice. 'Or he used to anyway,' she added bluntly.

Susanna burst out laughing. 'I get asked all the time to spank or restrain my clients. I've noticed the more successful they are, the more degraded they like to be. I was asked once to piss on a guy.'

'I guess it makes a change from them pissing on us?' proclaimed Eva sulkily.

'Ain't that the truth,' added Susanna nodding in agreement. 'Men are such bizarre creatures!'

'That's why I've decided to become celibate,' announced Eva adamantly. 'I can't be bothered with all the mind games and cheating. If I get desperate, then I've got a vibrator!'

Susanna guessed that Eva's affections for her mystery 'C' went deeper than she was going to admit.

Chapter 18

Eva slammed off the alarm feeling as if she had only been asleep for ten minutes.

'I won't miss this weather,' said Susanna, running to Eva's Mini.

Sitting in her new car made Eva smile momentarily until she realised Connor would probably want to take his gifts back.

After finally finding a parking space, Eva walked with Susanna into the airport departure lounge. 'Thanks for my birthday money, Suz.'

'Sorry it wasn't a lot, hun.'

'Don't be silly, just seeing you has made my birthday.'

'Your Christmas box wasn't ready in time, so I'll post it on.'

'Don't worry about a gift if you're short of money,' assured Eva. 'But here, don't open it until Christmas morning,' she added, handing Susanna a square packaged gift.

'Love you. Merry Christmas.' Susanna smiled, her chin started to wobble with emotion.

'Love you, too, Suz. Take care of yourself – promise me,' pleaded Eva, not letting go of her hand.

'I will – see you soon. Bye…'

Eva released her and watched until she disappeared into the crowds. Her mobile buzzed as she got back to her car and slumped into the driver seat.

I'll get the car collected – keep the shoes.

Being in no mood to accommodate Connor's spitefulness, she fired back a seething text, *Are you sure Cara wouldn't like the shoes too? She's welcome to everything you've bought me!*

Her confidence was fleeting. She couldn't face Connor yet; her feelings were too raw. She sat wondering if Ann would let her extend her holiday.

'This is very short notice, Eva, but luckily Becky has asked for more hours this week, so she can cover your shift tonight. Next time I need at least a couple of days' notice,' warned Ann.

'Yes – sorry,' she said cringing, pressing her mobile to her ear. 'Thanks, Ann.'

During the drive home she knew her extended break was only a short reprieve. She was going to have to face Connor at some point.

Locking her beautiful red Mini, a wave of self-pity washed over her as she walked up her garden path. She slammed the front door shut and dropped her handbag at the bottom of the stairs. There was only one way to ride out her dark mood – a large bar of chocolate and her *Pride & Prejudice* DVD.

'Oh, Mr Darcy…' Eva sat on her sofa inhaling deeply with melted chocolate swirling around her mouth. Her stomach churned feeling her mobile vibrate in her lap.

EE Network: You can now view your bill online.

Dropping her phone back down, she yawned and broke off another square of chocolate. Her mobile pinged again.

The car will be collected tomorrow at 3pm – will you be in?

The sweet taste of chocolate quickly lost its favour as she despatched a goading reply, *I'm not sure. I might be busy.*

Be in!

'Argh…!' seethed Eva, clutching her phone and storming into the kitchen. 'Who does he think he is? "*Be in*"!' she mimicked with a grunt. Lighting a cigarette, her mobile pinged again.

By the way, you can't just tag on extra holiday at a moment's notice. I've overridden Ann's decision, so I expect to see you Tuesday evening as per your rota.

With her mouth resembling a Venus flytrap, Eva stood motionless with a swirl of cigarette smoke billowing from her mouth. *Ann said it was ok, so I've made plans now!* she quickly texted back.

Within a few seconds Connor replied, *Un-arrange them. Be in or be sacked. The choice is yours!*

You can't sack me for booking holiday! Eva mouthed the words through gritted teeth as she typed.

I can do whatever I want. I AM THE BOSS!

His cold bullying made her burst into tears. 'Well…*fuck you*…Connor O'Neill!' she said, in between loud sobs.

* * *

The next day Eva made sure she got up early and went out for the day. With her mood mirroring the grey and miserable weather, not even the glow of the Christmas lights illuminating Oxford Street could lift her spirits while she jostled amongst the throngs of shoppers to buy all the presents on her list.

Two hours later Eva struggled laden with shopping back to her Corsa. She checked her phone for messages, hoping by now Connor would have confirmed the Mini had been collected.

She chain-smoked all the way home and was horrified to find it still parked outside her house. 'You've got to be kidding me!' she hissed, parking behind it.

Why is the car still here? she texted after dropping her bags on the sofa.

Bring the keys into work tonight. I didn't have time to arrange a collection.

'*Arrrgghh*,' fumed Eva. 'You know I'm not coming into work tonight you annoying, stupid man!' she cried out. *I've booked tonight off, as well you know! So I will bring them in Wednesday. I suggest if you cannot wait that long, then send someone around to collect them, as you said you would!*

If you're not in work by 6.30 with the keys — I WILL COME AND COLLECT THEM AND YOU!

'Arrogant, selfish *pig*!' yelled Eva, stomping up the stairs.

Having a shower did little to wash away her blues; her mood shifted from self-pity to petulance as she wrestled with her feelings. 'Fine,' she snapped, stomping heavy-footed into her bedroom. She threw a few clean work clothes into her workbag and started to dry her hair.

'*You can have your bloody car back!*' she barked to herself, racing downstairs with Mr Jingles weaving in and out of her legs.

'*Fuccck!*' she cried out, catching her foot in the strap of her handbag and tumbling down the last three stairs.

Lying sprawled out flat on her belly, she whimpered manoeuvring herself to look down at her ankle. 'Bloody bag!' she cursed, throwing it towards the front door.

She hopped into the lounge and took a deep breath to sit down slowly on the sofa. She looked down at her ankle but couldn't see any visible signs swelling. '*OW, SHIT!*' she gasped trying to wiggle her toes.

'Pain killers!' she muttered, hopping into the kitchen. Gobbling down two pills, she now saw that her foot was starting to swell.

'Argh, you are joking!' she muttered when her mobile pinged in her jeans pocket.

Are you on your way?

She hobbled slowly back into the lounge wincing with the throbbing pain. *No!* she promptly replied.

Eva, I told you what I would do if you didn't get yourself into work, are you deliberately trying to provoke me?

If you MUST know, I've hurt my ankle!

You're lying!

With rage diluting her pain, she pressed her mobile to her ear. 'Come on pick up, you arrogant prick!'

'What!' barked Connor.

'How dare you!' she yelled, 'I might've broken my ankle, and all you care about is getting your bloody car back for your tart!'

'It all very coincidental isn't it. I tell you to come into work, then all of a sudden you've *hurt* your foot!'

'Ankle!'

'Ankle, then!'

'Well, if you don't believe me, come and see for yourself. Then while you're here, you can pick up your precious car keys!' she ranted. 'Hello…? Hello, Connor…? *He's put the bloody phone down on me!*' she roared. A bewildered looking Mr Jingles cocked his head at her scream of frustration.

She wrung out a wet tea towel and wrapped it around her ankle. She was beginning to panic that she wouldn't be able to get out of her skinny jeans because of the puffiness. After elevating her leg, she thought about phoning Roxanne to see if she could drive her to hospital.

Eva chose to ignore a knock at the door and wondered whether to call an ambulance instead. 'Oh, go away!' she growled as pain engulfed her. 'GO AWAY!' she shouted, hearing the persistent knocking getting louder and faster.

Blinking back tears, she slowly hopped to the front door only to be greeted by a sour-faced Connor.

'*Oh great!* If you've come to have a go at me, then don't waste your time because I'm in absolute agony!' she said without drawing breath.

'Are you going to let me in?' demanded Connor, standing on her doorstep dressed in a smart navy pinstriped suit and open-necked mauve shirt.

Eva shuffled backwards and sat down heavily on the stairs to let Connor step into the hallway.

'For God's sake don't knock my ankle!'

'What happened?'

'I fell down the stairs!' shouted Eva, deliberately omitting the fact that she had carelessly tripped over her own handbag.

'Let me take a look,' he said, bending down and unwrapping the damp tea towel.

'Ouch, careful! Eva hissed through gritted teeth while holding onto the stair banister.

'I think you'll need to get an X-ray. I'll take you.'

'I've already left a message for Roxanne to take me,' Eva lied. 'I assume you've come to collect the car keys? They're over there in that envelope. I'll wait here until Roxanne arrives.'

'Martyrdom doesn't suit you. Roxanne's off ill, so she won't be coming – let's go!'

Begrudgingly Eva knew she had to accept.

He ignored her churlish refusal to be carried to his Range Rover parked outside and quickly swept her up in his arms and marched down the path.

'You can just drop me off at the entrance, I'll be fine,' Eva muttered in a huff.

'Don't be ridiculous, you can hardly stand up!' reasoned Connor, shaking his head with exasperation. 'I'll take you in. I know one of the doctors at Homerton Hospital.'

'What's *her* name?' sneered Eva sarcastically as they pulled away from the kerb.

'*His* name is George Peterson!'

Eva stared out of the window in a brooding sulk, only breaking her silence to curse loudly as they hit a pothole at the end of her road.

'Thanks. I'll be fine from here,' said Eva swinging open the passenger door and looking anxiously down at the coarse tarmac.

'Stop being so obstinate, let me carry you into reception.'

'I can manage!' Eva said stubbornly with a scowl.

Connor watched with bemused irritation as she struggled to get out before he lost his patience. 'Just sit there!' he snapped, getting out of the car and walking around to the passenger door.

Sweeping her up into his arms, Eva clamped her teeth together as the throbbing pain in her ankle reverberated down to her toes.

Once inside the hospital she growled at Connor to be careful weaving his way towards the reception desk.

'Yes, can I help you?' asked the receptionist looking bemused at Connor's gallantry as he stood cradling Eva in his arms.

'I think she might've sprained her ankle,' said Connor looking at the plump grey-haired woman.

'Can I take some details, please?'

'Yes,' winced Eva, 'and my ankle might be *broken*!' she added, flashing Connor a look of annoyance.

Not wanting to enter into a spat in the middle of a crowded waiting room, Connor suppressed his anger as the receptionist told them to take a seat.

'So how long do we have to wait to see your friend?'

'I'm not sure,' said Connor gently lowering her onto an orange plastic chair.

'My foot is turning a funny colour!' Eva moaned theatrically. 'What if it starts to turn gangrenous?!'

'It won't turn gangrenous!' Connor said sharply. 'It's probably no more than a bad sprain.'

'So you have X-ray vision now!' goaded Eva with tears starting to form. 'Where are you going?' She snivelled pathetically watching Connor turn to leave.

'Just going to make a call, I'll be back in five minutes.'

Brushing a tear away from her cheek, Eva glanced around the waiting room and saw an old man with a cut above his eye. She felt sorry for him sitting alone with a trail of blood staining his cheek.

Hiding her relief on seeing Connor return, she waited until he spoke first.

'You're lucky, he can see you.'

'Okay...' said Eva, feeling a twinge of guilt as she glanced back over at the old man.

'Connor O'Neill...!'

Eva turned to look at the tall balding man dressed in a white doctor's coat. She found his nasally upper class accent instantly irritating.

'George,' said Connor with a smile and shaking his hand warmly. 'How are Marianne and the two kids?'

'That would be three, now,' replied George. 'Have you settled down yet?' he asked, looking at Eva.

'Marriage and kids?' Connor laughed before adding, 'Definitely not...'

'Eternal bachelor, eh...?' George congratulated Connor on escaping the responsibilities of monogamy and parenthood with a playful slap on the back.

'And this is Eva Summers,' said Connor. 'She's one of my dancers. I think it might just be a sprain.'

'Give me a couple of minutes to find an empty cubicle,' said George.

'So he is your doctor friend, then?'

'Yes, he's a consultant here,' replied Connor, slipping his arm around her waist and lifting her out of the chair.

Eva clenched her teeth until they reached the cubicle.

'So what happened?' asked George, looking down at her bruised ankle.

'I fell down the stairs at home,' Eva explained sheepishly.

'I think we'll start with an X-ray, but unfortunately we'll need to cut off your jeans to the knee.'

Eva whimpered, shaking her head. 'But they cost seventy pounds! Can't I leave them on?' she pleaded.

'Sorry – no.'

'Just cut them off, George,' instructed Connor brusquely.

Eva lay back feeling sorry for herself as a very overweight female nurse began to cut away at her jeans.

Within fifteen minutes Eva was back from having an X-ray.

'Well it's not broken, and you haven't torn any ligaments,' confirmed George looking at her X-ray. 'Just looks like a nasty sprain.'

Feeling relieved but also utterly pig sick that Connor's diagnosis was correct, Eva felt embarrassed that she had caused such a fuss over a sprained ankle.

'I'd suggest complete rest for four to five days, then introduce some gentle movement. Nurse will bandage your ankle to reduce the swelling.'

'How long will it be before she can walk on it?' asked Connor.

'At least two weeks before full movement is regained, but for complete recovery it could take anything up to eight weeks.'

'Well, I appreciate your time,' said Connor. 'You must swing by the club one night. We've just reopened the casino.'

'Not sure I could convince the wife on that one.' George chuckled turning to look at the nurse. 'Nurse, can you arrange some pain relief and a pair of crutches, please?'

Eva refused Connor's offer of being carried back to his car after leaving the crowded A&E department; instead, she opted to hobble clumsily with a petulant pout.

'Well, thanks for taking me to hospital,' murmured Eva as they pulled up outside her house. 'I won't keep you. I suppose you have places to go – tarts to see!' she added childishly.

'I want to talk to you before I go!' said Connor sharply. He locked his car and roughly grabbed her handbag from her shoulder. 'I'm not discussing my business in the street for everyone to hear!' he added, rummaging for her front door key.

'I can manage – thank you!' snapped Eva, wrestling back her bag, sending the contents rolling down the path. '*Argh!*' she growled, anger souring her pretty face.

'Here!' Connor shoved her purse and make-up back into her handbag before opening the door. 'Just get inside.'

With her cheeks flushed with frustration, she shuffled past him into the living room letting her crutches clatter to the floor before collapsing on the sofa.

'I'm making myself a coffee, do you want one?' he called out on his way into the kitchen.

'A glass of water would be *greatly* appreciated!' whipped Eva, searching for her box of painkillers.

Sitting opposite Connor, she swallowed two tablets as he sipped on an unsweetened black coffee.

'Why are you annoyed with me when you're the one who broke your promise?' he asked, putting down his hot coffee. 'A simple "thank you" for the car would've been nice.'

'I know what I promised, and I had every intention of texting, but the time went fast. Then Susanna and I had words after your gifts arrived,' explained Eva curtly.

'Words?'

'She said I should stop seeing you.'

'Why? She doesn't even know me!' stated Connor, perplexed. 'I can only guess she's made her assumption on what you've told her – which is…?'

'That you're my boss!' Eva fired back.

'Who is she anyway? Bloody Mother Teresa!'

'No, she's a loyal friend who cares about me.'

'Looks like she's succeeded in her objective, then,' snarled Connor dismissively. 'You said you saw St Clair, are you sure he didn't say anything to you?'

'I think I would've remembered, Connor. Anyway, we left after I saw him and came back to mine. Then my birthday celebrations really started,' Eva said glumly. 'First, I discover my best friend's boyfriend is using her as a punch bag, and then you're sleeping with another woman – so excuse me if I didn't find the time to text and say "whoopee"!'

Connor pondered before replying, 'Who told you about Cara? I guess it must've been Roxanne?'

Exhaling loudly, Eva cocked her head to the side. 'No, I heard it on the news actually!' she quipped sarcastically, staring at him. 'You didn't like the idea that I was going to a club in case I was tempted to go off with another guy, and there you are up to your dick in Baileys!'

'What?' Connor asked looking puzzled.

'Irish Cream!' Eva grimaced. 'I *know* I'm not your girlfriend, but we've been having unprotected sex. This Cara woman might be riddled with God knows what.'

'You promised me you were on the pill. Are you now saying you're not!' choked Connor, leaning forward in his seat.

'The pill won't protect me against sexually transmitted diseases!'

'Well, I haven't got anything!' snapped Connor indignantly.

'How do you know? You could've picked up something from *one* of your cheap conquests!'

'The only woman I don't use condoms with is you, so unless you're telling me that you have something, then there's nothing to worry about – is there!'

Pausing briefly, Eva's braced herself before asking, 'Who is Cara?'

'She's just someone I see when I'm over in Ireland – it's nothing serious.'

'So how long has "nothing serious" being going on for…months…years…decades?'

'I don't know.' Connor shrugged with indifference.

'You're lying…'

'Okay – maybe five years, I guess… Does it matter?'

'Five years…!' mumbled Eva in shock.

'I told you it isn't serious,' added Connor, seeing her reaction.

'How can it not be serious? You can't be involved with a person for that length of time and have no emotional attachment. Does she know about your opposition to marriage, babies and monogamy? Poor cow has probably got the vicar on speed dial.'

'I don't love her, so why would I want to marry her?' said Connor gesticulating moodily.

Eva halted her interrogation briefly and studied Connor's body language. 'So you have no feeling for her whatsoever, then?'

'She's a nice woman,' replied Connor with a casual air, 'what else do you want me to say?'

'How does she feel about you?'

After pretending to survey his spotless polished shoes, Connor looked up to meet her stare. 'You're right, she said she has feelings for me, but...*BUT!*' pronounced Connor sternly, 'I've already explained to her that marriage and kids are not on the cards for me.'

'While you're still enjoying each other's company, never say never, Connor,' said Eva sourly.

'I didn't have sex with her on Saturday night.'

'Well, you're a free agent, you can do as you please,' declared Eva breezily, folding her arms under her chest.

'I admit, I probably wasn't capable with the amount of whisky I'd had, but the truth is I didn't want to fuck her. I only wanted sex with one woman that night, a woman who promised to text me – but didn't!'

'Oooh, it's like a Mills and Boon love triangle,' goaded Eva sarcastically. 'Who should he fuck or chuck?'

'Okay,' said Connor, sighing, 'enough of this silliness. I will – in your words – "chuck" her.'

'What – just like that?' squawked Eva, clicking her fingers.

'You make it sound as if I'm planning to jilt her at the altar!' Connor laughed, flashing her a dazzling white smile.

'I'm glad it amuses you?'

'Why do you always take everything I say the wrong way?' rebuked Connor, the two deep dimples in his tanned cheeks melting away. 'What I'm trying to get across to you, *if you'll listen*, is I prefer to have you in my bed as opposed to her or any other woman, so if that's means being *exclusive*, then that's how it'll be.'

'I don't know whether to feel flattered or disgusted!'

'*Disgusted?*' repeated Connor, looking bewildered.

'Yes – disgusted! How could you be so cruel to someone who's *obviously* in love with you?!'

'Why should it play on *your* conscience if it doesn't play on mine?!'

'Because I've been on the receiving end of *unrequited love* and it hurts like hell!'

'Look, Eva,' said Connor, leaning forward and pausing briefly before continuing, 'why are we going around in circles? You know I like you, and forgive me for stating the truth, but haven't I always treated you well?'

'Hmmm…let me think…' Eva smirked as spite flavoured her reply, 'You reprimand me in front of Tina when I refused to be molested by Chu, then you accuse me of lying when I said I was on the pill, and of course let's not forget your latest romantic gesture – taking your gifts back. I don't think Disney will be banging down my door for the film rights – do you?'

'You can keep the car!' fumed Connor. 'It was a knee-jerk reaction because you hadn't texted. What was I meant to think? I react to situations passionately. I am not a middle-of-the-road type of guy. You should know this by now.'

'You mean you have a fiery temper!'

'Okay, I'll concede that because it's true, but in the same vein you're responsible for pushing my buttons and firing me up. If you'd text me as promised we wouldn't be sitting here, drinking this atrocious coffee.'

'I'll have you know it's "Taste the Difference" coffee!' Eva said defensively.

'I can taste the difference, all right,' Connor bit back with a grimace. 'So where are we, then? And don't quote your address because I swear I'll have cross you over my knee, sprained ankle or not. Are we both reconciled to putting this down as a misunderstanding?'

Eva pouted and raised her eyebrows. 'Maybe.'

'I'll take a "maybe" over a "no" anytime,' said Connor, grinning.

'Well, I can't decide right now. My head is pounding, so I'm going to bed.'

'Well in case Disney *are* watching,' said Connor smirking boyishly, 'allow me, madam.' He stood up and scooped her into his arms.

Gently laying her onto the bed, Connor made sure she had her pills and a glass of water within easy reach. He promised to return later to check on her and took the spare front door key hanging in the kitchen before going back to the club.

Chapter 19

The morning sun filtering through the partially drawn curtains brought Eva out of her slumber. She turned over, wincing with pain, and glanced at her alarm clock. She noticed her glass had been refilled with water sitting next her mobile along with a handwritten note.

Juliet… I didn't want to disturb you, so I've left your crutches by the bed and mobile on the bedside cabinet. I will pop back round about 2pm with something to eat. Ann knows about your accident, so your wages will be paid into your account as normal. Phone, if you need me… Romeo!

Connor's 'Romeo and Juliet' comment made Eva smile. Carefully pulling back her duvet, she gingerly lifted her leg over the edge of the bed. She used her crutches to hobble out of her bedroom, but then started to curse looking down the flight of stairs and decided it would be safer to shuffle down on her bottom.

'Hello, baby,' she cooed looking down at Mr Jingle's full water bowl and remnants of fresh food on the floor. *Connor must've already fed him,* she thought.

These small actions of thoughtfulness redeemed Connor from his intolerant and, at times, dictatorial personality. She loved the fact that he liked and cared for her cat.

Drifting in and out of sleep for most of the day, she only woke properly hearing her front door being slammed shut.

'Is that you, Connor?'

'Yeah – sorry I'm late. I was stuck in a meeting till three.'

She sniffed the air as a waft of fried chicken awoke her senses.

'I'm assuming KFC is to your liking?' Connor smiled walking into the lounge with a box of fried chicken and hot salty fries.

'You assume correctly,' teased Eva, realising she hadn't eaten anything all day and grabbing the box off him. She munched her way through the fattening feast with enthusiasm and satisfaction.

'So we're okay – yeah?'

'What do you mean?'

'You know what I mean, Eva, stop playing with me.'

'And *Cara*?'

'There is *no* Cara – only you.'

'You're very good at manipulating a situation to suit your own conscience,' quipped Eva, enjoying her provocative teasing.

Connor smiled over at her. 'So am I still welcome in your bed?'

'No…'

'*NO!* Connor blinked and bolstered himself forward in the chair. 'You don't want to be my lover – why not?'

'Be your *lover*?'

'Yes, be my lover,' repeated Connor.

'Are you sure you have the correct terminology – not "fuck buddy" or "bit on the side"?'

'Where's this going?' Connor frowned and indiscreetly checked his watch.

'Sorry, am I keeping you from something?'

'No, but I want an answer.'

'The only way I'll welcome you back into my bed is if we start a proper relationship, no hiding me away. Plus, I want to tell Roxanne.'

'What is a *proper relationship*?' remonstrated Connor moodily.

'I want to be introduced as your girlfriend, not someone who danced at the Rodeo!' said Eva, pouting. 'I want mini-breaks, romantic meals…'

'You can have fancy meals,' said Connor smiling confidently.

'I'm not talking about *fancy* meals. I'm talking about romance and love.'

'*Love…!*' Connor shook his head.

'Yes – love, don't you ever want to fall in love again?'

'Love is overrated. Let me enlighten you. Loving someone doesn't necessarily bring happiness. When has love ever brought you any happiness?'

'Only because I haven't found it yet, it doesn't mean I'll stop searching.'

Connor brooded in silence, lost in his thoughts and avoiding her gaze. 'Well I'm not looking for love, Eva. It holds no allure for me. It's a superfluous and time-consuming emotion.'

'*Superfluous and time-consuming?* Why – all because you had your heart broken twenty years ago! I've had mine repeatedly broken, but I haven't given up hope.'

'Maybe love has on you!' stated Connor harshly, getting to his feet.

His words cut through her like a steel blade. If he wanted to make her feel like a failure and fool, then he had succeeded.

'Just go, Connor!' snapped Eva.

'I didn't mean…'

'Just go, there's nothing more to be said!'

Glancing up towards the ceiling, Connor exhaled sharply as his gaze fell back down to a very forlorn looking Eva. 'One piece of advice for the future,' he warned. 'Don't let the idea of "love" blind you from something that is real and tangible – what we had was good. All because it was missing the arbitrary "in love" label doesn't mean it had no chance to flourish.'

'At least I'm not scared of falling in love, Connor. It's obvious we want very different things – bye.'

'Fine, have things your own way,' said Connor, briefly hesitating before putting her spare front door key on the side dresser and walking out of the lounge.

Hearing the front door slam behind him, Eva shuffled off the sofa and peered behind curtains watching his sports car roar down the road. Her deep, breathy sobs filled the room and a feeling of hopelessness engulfed her as she hobbled back over to the sofa.

* * *

Misery and pain were her only visitors over the next two days. She couldn't stomach eating anything and only managed small sips of coffee during the day. But as soon as the dark bleakness of night approached, she would consume glass after glass of wine.

Receiving an apologetic text from Roxanne explaining that she herself had been unwell and bedridden for the last three days, she also revealed Tommy had mentioned Connor's despondent mood at the club. Eva offered no interest in Roxanne's observation as she sank lower into a state of depression.

After three days of not eating, Eva managed to force down a small bowl of cereal which she conceded was only to silence the gnawing sound of starvation echoing in her stomach.

On the fourth day of confinement she stood in the bathroom with lank, unwashed hair and stared up at the shower. Her despondency had manifested into impatient anger as she battled against her own self-pity and incarceration.

'You don't need anyone, Eva!' she muttered to herself with steely determination. She clumsily clambered over the edge of the bath with expletives choking the air. After her much-needed shower and making herself a milky coffee, she heard her mobile ping on the windowsill.

I was going to visit you today, but I didn't think I would be welcome?

A dull ache in Eva's stomach made her delete Connor's text instantly. She was never going to heal herself if she let him back into her life again.

You must know by now that I like you a lot. Okay, so I'm not the type of guy to shout my feelings from the rooftop! Catholic's are born into suppression! I am, I admit, missing you though.

Brushing away a salty tear, she deleted his second message. Knowing that Connor was incapable of even trying to fall in love made her cry.

Why won't you text back?

Eva grabbed a tissue as she slowly made her way into the lounge and sniffed wearily while Connor continued to bombard her with texts.

Why are you being so cold? Why do women always hanker after the immortal happy ever after? I can't promise something that doesn't necessarily exist, but I can promise to treat you well, and be faithful. Yes, I can be faithful when I choose to be! Give 'us' another chance?

Biting down on her lip, Eva closed her eyes taking a minute to compose herself before replying, *My feelings for you have grown over the months. I am not 'scared' or 'repressed' to admit that, but I think we both know 'we' won't work. I want a normal healthy relationship. If that means it fails, then so be it – I want to at least try!*

Connor's reply wasn't instant; it took him over an hour to text back, *Ok, I give in…*

Eva's heart sank. It looked like Connor thought rekindling their relationship would be a mistake. *Will you keep your promise regarding work?*

What? texted back Connor.

You said we would stay professional at work if our affair ended.

Ended??? I have just agreed to what you wanted. Why are you ending it?

It was Eva's turn to be confused as she replied, *What?*

Eva! Are you playing with me because it's not funny!

You're agreeing to a relationship?

Yes, we can give it a go…

Blinking down heavily at his text, it took more than a minute for his words to sink in. She then replied, *But you need to want to do this Connor because 'giving in' isn't good enough for me.*

I WANT TO TRY, EVA! he texted back.

So people will know we're a couple?

Yes, but at work you'll still be an employee. You can tell Roxanne and I'll speak to Ann. The other girls don't need to know straight away.

Eva's depression fell away like disrobing a heavy cloak. Excitement took over.

Ok ☺, Eva texted. She started to cry again – this time with joy.

Can I knock on the door now?

Gasping down at the screen, Eva realised Connor must have been sitting outside her house – for how long, she didn't know. *Yes*, she replied, hobbling to the front door.

'Hi,' said Connor smiling and holding twelve red long-stemmed roses tied together with a fancy bow.

With flushed cheeks Eva smiled. 'Are those for me?'

'Yes, but I want a kiss first.' Connor grinned and lowered his mouth to greet her lips while gently nudging the front door shut with his elbow.

Tasting his minty fresh breath, Eva's heart beat with joyous bliss as his tongue probed inside her mouth.

'Nice kiss.' Connor smiled, his erection pressing against the confines of his trousers. 'So how's the ankle?' he asked caressing her bottom.

Feeling his thick erection press against her hip, Eva grinned up at him lustfully. 'I've just taken some pain killers…'

'So you're not in any pain, then?' asked Connor, arching his brow.

'No.' Eva giggled, her pale cheeks deepening to dark crimson.

'I guess if I was really gentle with you, maybe we could have a kiss and a cuddle on your bed?'

Eva smiled coyly. 'Yes, I guess we could.'

Feeling his strong arms scoop her up like a weightless feather made Eva giggle. She found nothing more arousing than a handsome man carrying her to bed with the promise of a myriad of orgasms on offer.

Connor was gentle with his love-making. He supported his heavy muscular body with his strong sculpted arms and lay between her thighs while his hips rhythmically pushed back and forth plunging the full length of his large penis deep inside her.

Eva's orgasm stole the breath from her mouth as she dug her nails into his taut flesh. The unstoppable wave of ecstasy made her arch back and her swollen sex clenched the thick shaft of his penis.

'Eva!' panted Connor as she pulsated deeply around him, drawing his erection deeper into her body.

'*I love you*,' rasped Eva. As pleasure overwhelmed her senses, Connor feverishly slammed his hips between her milky-white thighs making her large breasts shudder beneath his powerful thrusts.

'*I'm going to come,*' he croaked. His breath hissed through his teeth as the bed shook violently before shuddering to a halt. Connor groaned incoherently as his orgasm left his body.

Eva felt his weight slump down on top of her and he slowly pushed in his penis once more before lifting off her and flopping down on the bed.

He lifted his arm so Eva could snuggle into to his body. She quickly draped her hand across his damp chest and looked up at him smiling.

'Are you going to tell Tommy?' she asked gingerly.

'He already knows,' said Connor, running the tip of his finger gently down her arm, creating a flurry of goose bumps on her skin.

'Does he? When did you tell him?'

'He knew I fancied you at your interview. So, of course, when I didn't fire you over Chu, or your rule-breaking performance,' said Connor, giving her a playful prod, 'he gathered something must be going on. I told him before I left this evening that I was going to see you.'

'What did he say?'

'It's not his place to say anything,' said Connor dismissively. 'I don't comment on his relationship with Roxanne.'

'He doesn't like me very much,' stated Eva sourly. 'I don't know why.'

'He thinks you're unpredictable and impulsive like Maria. Like your friend Susan—'

'Susanna…'

'Well, like her, she worries about you, and Tommy has got my back, too. He'll come round, I mean, what's not to like, eh?' He laughed and softly kissed the top of her head.

'Hmm…' Eva wrinkled her nose at Connor's prediction.

Within minutes Connor had fallen fast asleep.

A warm glow of happiness radiated around her as she looked across at a very exquisite, naked Connor. Snuggling close she felt his arm circle her shoulder as he stirred before gently snoring again. The smell and warmth of his body made her smile with contentment before she started to wonder, *how am I going to break the news to Roxanne that I'm in relationship with our boss who, in her words, is a 'womanising playboy millionaire who she's never known to be monogamous'!*

Chapter 20

'Eva…'

'Hmmm…what?'

'Its six thirty, baby. I'll see you later tonight,' said Connor, softly brushing the back of his fingers against her cheek.

'You're leaving for work early?' Eva said yawning.

'I've got an important meeting today with the council, so I won't be able to pop back at lunchtime. Why don't you invite Roxanne round to keep you company? I'd rather you tell her outside the club anyway.'

'Okay,' said Eva, blinking sleepily up at him.

He bent down to kiss her on the lips before walking out the bedroom with a waft of aftershave scenting the air.

Eva pulled the warm duvet up to her chin and fell back to sleep quickly until her alarm woke her at eight thirty.

Hi Roxanne, hope you're better? Do you fancy popping over today?

Hi babes, yes I feel much better thanx ☺ *Yes Ok, I'll be at yours for 11ish xxx*

Eva sat in the bath rehearsing what she was going to say to Roxanne. 'You know I said that I didn't like Connor, well…' said Eva, clearing her throat, 'm-my opinion of him has changed.' She paused to hold up her wet hand to her flushed face, cringing. 'Er… We are… *Oh shit, what am I going to say?*' cursed Eva, feeling sick at the thought of Roxanne's disappointment or, worse still, anger.

After her bath, she sat in her grey jogging bottoms and a white T-shirt staring at the beautiful bouquet of roses from Connor sitting in a vase on her lounge windowsill. A knock on the front door made her hold her hand against her stomach trying to abate the nerves dancing an Irish jig in her belly.

'How are you, babes?' asked Roxanne handing Eva a big box of chocolates. 'Ann said you'd sprained your ankle, but that's all really – how did you do it?'

'I fell down the stairs,' said Eva, closing the door and limping down the hallway towards the kitchen. 'I am so clumsy, but it's not as painful as it was. Connor said I could work in the casino until my ankle is properly healed, so I'll probably be back the week before Christmas.'

'Oh, so you've spoken to Connor, then?'

'Only briefly – tea or coffee?' asked Eva, averting her gaze to reach for two mugs.

'Coffee, please.'

'So Susanna got back okay?' asked Roxanne walking back down the hall, taking off her long black leather coat and draping it over the banister. 'Did you tackle her about the bruises?'

'Kind of, but she cut me dead. I don't want to lose her friendship – she's like a sister to me, so I didn't push it,' said Eva with a sigh before handing Roxanne a mug of hot coffee.

'Wow, what beautiful roses!' Roxanne gasped, walking over to her window and sniffing their sweet fragrance.

'Yes.' Eva blushed as her confession began to swell in her throat.

Turning around, Roxanne narrowed her eyes as a slow grin shaped her lips. 'I know who they're off.'

'Y-you do?' stuttered Eva, catching a dribble of milky coffee trickling down her chin.

'Your secret admirer! I remember Susanna saying you had one,' announced Roxanne, giggling.

'Okay…' Eva coughed feeling her cheeks darken.

'So…' probed Roxanne excitedly, 'who is this mystery guy? He must have money and taste looking at those roses, they're not your average supermarket bouquet.'

Eva lowered her gaze and started picking at her fingernails. 'Hmm…' she stalled, pushing a strand of hair behind her ear before clearing her throat. 'You know I value your friendship, Roxanne, don't you?' said Eva glancing up.

'Fucking hell, babes, I wouldn't grass to O'Neill if it's a punter. I know "thou shall not shag a punter" is one of the cardinal rules,' she scoffed, 'but I know for a fact Scarlett is seeing a member who's a married banker, so don't worry about me not keeping yours hush-hush,' she assured, sitting down on the sofa, not realising she had contradicted herself by divulging Scarlett's secret.

'You know him,' said Eva softly. 'We agreed it would just be a one-night stand, but then we agreed to start a relationship. We haven't been seeing each other long, it kinda just happened, but—'

'Eva,' pleaded Roxanne impatiently, 'you're rambling on, babes. Who are you seeing?'

'You're not going to approve. I am seeing C—'

'I don't believe it! Saved by the bloody doorbell!' she huffed. 'You stay there, I'll go and see who it is.'

'Who is it, Roxy?' called out Eva, hearing Roxanne speaking to a man with a broad cockney accent.

'It's a delivery for you,' shouted Roxanne, walking back into the lounge carrying a small square box.

'Delivery for me?' Eva frowned looking at the small package being placed in her lap. Ripping through the black plastic packaging, Eva stared down at the glossy brown box underneath.

'Gucci...nice!' Roxanne said with a huge grin.

Eva guessed straight away the identity of the buyer: Connor. She hesitated before opening it.

'A gift tag,' squealed Roxanne, hovering over her.

'To my sexy redhead, I want to see you wearing these, and only these, and lots of kisses!' read out Eva, dropping the gift card onto the arm of her chair.

'Gucci earrings!' Roxanne picked up one of the platinum and diamond droppers. 'Enough guessing – who's sending you beautiful roses and expensive jewellery? I'm jealous!'

Taking a sharp intake of breath, Eva looked over at Roxanne. 'Connor!' she blurted out, biting down on her lip.

'Connor who?' questioned Roxanne, shrugging her shoulders.

Eva blinked profusely. 'What?'

'Connor? I only know one Connor – the boss.'

The silence was deafening. Suddenly Roxanne's mouth fell open when she realised what Eva was telling her.

'I'm so sorry,' Eva said, sniffing, her voice weak and apologetic.

'*You* are seeing O'Neill!' screeched Roxanne, dropping the earring into Eva's lap.

With tears pricking her eyes, Eva watched Roxanne step away from her with a look of disgust.

'It just kind of happened gradually, I—'

'So all this time you've been pumping me for information about him, while secretly you've been seeing him – you've been using me!'

'No – I swear, Roxanne! You have to believe me!'

'Believe you!' snarled Roxanne. 'I don't think I even know you!' she roared. 'I told you things in confidence, and there you are sucking his dick and whispering in his ear. I always thought it was Tina who was desperate, but no – you've proved me wrong!'

'Desperate,' repeated Eva.

'Yes! Knowing what you know and you still want to be a notch on his bedpost. He is a womaniser, Eva. Didn't you hear what I said the other night? He has a string of women at his beck and call. I'm disappointed, I thought better of you.'

'I've fallen in love with him,' Eva said, tears starting to form.

'Love him? You don't even know him. How long has this *pathetic fling* being going on?'

'A couple of months,' croaked Eva. 'I know you're disappointed with me, and I deserve to lose your friendship over this. You have every right to hate me,' she said with a loud sniffle.

'*Hate* is a very strong word.' Roxanne's voice softened hearing Eva cry. 'I just can't believe you would go there, knowing what you know.'

'He makes me feel like no other man has ever done before.'

'You're not the first to fall in love with him. He's charming and charismatic for sure, not forgetting stinking rich. What woman wouldn't find all that a heady combination, but listen,' warned Roxanne, 'he has slept with hundreds of women over the years – could be thousands! Not one of them have found a ring on their finger, have they? What does that tell you?'

'He's been hurt in the past, so he's careful, I guess,' said Eva fidgeting in her seat.

'Be honest with yourself. Connor won't commit to one woman. He doesn't want marriage and babies – all the things you said you want. Are you going to waste your beauty and youth on a man who openly admits he doesn't want the life you visualise for yourself?'

Eva dropped her face into her hands. She couldn't challenge Roxanne's comments: they were all true.

Roxanne got up to leave and reached out for Eva's hand. 'Look, maybe I'm wrong, and perhaps he can change.'

'I know what you've said is right, but I can't help how I feel,' said Eva, lifting the latch and opening her front door.

'I'm still your friend,' Roxanne said compassionately as she stepped out into the cold wind. 'Phone me if you need a chat – yeah?'

'I will,' said Eva, letting her mouth form a weak smile.

'Okay then, see you soon.'

'Yeah, bye.' Eva closed the door and limped upstairs to bed. Emotional exhaustion quickly led her into a deep sleep.

* * *

Eva woke an hour later with Roxanne's words of warning making her heart heavy. *I know I want the fairy tale he said he can't give me, but maybe I can get him to change his mind,* she thought to herself. *I could make him fall so desperately in love with me that he'd want us to get married and have a child.*

Her mind raced with ideas how she could not only seduce his groin, but also his brain. She ticked the 'sexy in the bedroom' box, so now she could work on being 'a good cook in the kitchen'; after all, he enjoys his food and cooking. In with the healthy, home-cooked food and good wines and better coffee. She would please him every way she could.

She ran a bath and lay relaxing in the scented bubbles remembering Connor mentioning a meeting with the council. *I'll prepare a healthy, romantic meal,* she thought, shaving her legs. *I'll take an interest in how his meeting has gone – the perfect 'Stepford Wife',* mused Eva with a smile.

After getting dressed, she logged on to her computer and ordered ingredients to make Thai turkey cakes with a pepper couscous.

After vacuuming downstairs, she put fresh linen on her bed and waited for her groceries to be delivered. She had ordered a nice bottle of white wine and a selection of cheeses, which was much more sophisticated than a calorific dessert.

Her delivery arrived mid-afternoon. With all the ingredients laid out like she was auditioning for a cookery show, she followed the recipe diligently and was happy that her Thai cakes looked similar to the picture in her book. After putting them in the fridge to cook later, she went upstairs to change her clothes.

Wearing a black figure-hugging skirt and low-necked red chiffon blouse, she wanted to look demur and stylish; her lace-topped nude stockings added a touch of sexiness.

She texted Connor sat under a fragrant cloud of her favourite perfume to check what time he would be arriving.

Not getting an instant response, she hobbled over to the large bay window and pushed the curtains apart to peer outside into the street. With the only source of light coming from the streetlamp, she looked across at her new Mini sitting under its yellow beam. She couldn't wait until her swollen ankle had settled so she could drive her new car again. Letting the curtain fall back, she heard her mobile beep.

I'm about ten minutes away. Can you run me a bath and sort out some food? I didn't get time to eat.

Yes ok xxxx

She scented the water with chamomile and jasmine bath salts and put out a clean towel before touching up her make-up. By the time she heard a rap at her door there was a glass of chilled wine ready for his arrival.

Connor smiled as she let him in. 'Hi,' he said sounding tired.

'Busy day?' asked Eva watching him walk into the hall dressed in a smart pinstriped suit and carrying a large black leather briefcase.

'Yeah, what's to eat?' he asked, kissing her before going into the lounge.

'I've made Thai turkey cakes, so go and have your bath and I'll heat them up.'

'I could get used to this,' said Connor placing his briefcase on the sofa and walking over to her circling his arms around her waist.

Feeling his strong arms envelope her sent a shiver of excitement through Eva's body as he squeezed her bottom tightly. 'Go and have your bath, dinner will be ready in twenty minutes.'

'Yes, dear,' he mocked, releasing her from his tight embrace.

Popping the plump, juicy Thai cakes into a frying pan, the fragrant smell of lemon grass and herbs filled the kitchen, drifted into the hall and up the stairs like a fine sea mist.

'Hmmm… Something smells good,' said Connor walking into the kitchen with wet hair and wearing just a navy bath towel around his midriff.

'Well, it's ready, so you can take yours through. I've put a glass of wine on the coffee table.'

Connor happily took his tray and walked into the lounge barefoot with Mr Jingles hot on his heels.

Eva enjoyed watching him eat a meal she had prepared from scratch. She had to stop herself from repeatedly asking him if he was enjoying it. He didn't even screw his nose up after tasting the wine. *See, that wasn't too hard, was it?* she thought to herself.

'So, what was your meeting about?' asked Eva, blowing on a hot piece of Thai cake.

After finishing what he was chewing, Connor turned to her and frowned. 'It was about your old boss trying to ruin my club.'

'Booth! How can he ruin the Unicorn?'

'He wants to buy O'Brien's bar and turn it into a casino.'

'O'Brien's, on the corner of Park Lane?'

'Yes,' replied Connor bluntly. 'If he thinks he can take half of my business from under my nose, then he's very much mistaken,' he sneered.

Eva stopped eating and asked, 'Will it affect the club? I can't imagine the likes of old man Clark and Weaver slumming it in a tacky Vegas-style casino in their dinner suits – can you? Not when they have the grandeur and comfort of the Unicorn.'

'I've seen the plans for the new club and they're ambitious – it's more your top-end club, so the answer to your question is *yes*, if their proposal is accepted and he gets a gaming licence I could lose about sixty percent of my revenue.'

'What are you going to do?'

'First, I need to find out who's funding the project. Booth is just a front man for it, I'm certain. There's no way he could raise the capital to buy the bar then renovate it into a casino. Someone's bankrolling it.'

'Maybe it's St Clair?'

'He doesn't have the brains to orchestrate such a deal. It's true he hates my guts and is ravenous for wealth, but he's like Booth – a lowlife reprobate, an opportunist and a thug! Whoever's behind it must be idiotic to think I wouldn't oppose the plans, but I need to find out the puppeteers behind it, and quick.'

'Could it be corrupt?'

'It wouldn't surprise me,' said Connor reaching over for his glass of wine. 'If this deal was legit, then Booth and St Clair wouldn't be within an eight-mile radius of it.'

'Could it be a cover for drugs?'

'Money laundering or a drugs cartel, take your pick. They need to make it look legit, but for that to happen they need members – the Unicorn's clientele.'

'But your members just wouldn't abandon you, would they?'

'Eva, you're so naive,' patronised Connor. 'A degenerate gambler is like an alcoholic, they only care about their addiction. Why pay high membership fees when you can become a member for free? Loyalty is an empty word in my business.'

'Then why don't *you* buy the bar? I'm surprised you haven't thought of that already.'

'Don't you think I've tried? O'Brien won't sell it to me. I think he's been bought off, or warned.'

'Have you told the council all this?'

'I need to give them something I don't have.'

'And what's that?' quizzed Eva.

'Proof…'

'So find the proof you need, then.'

'And that's what I intend to do,' said Connor grimacing. 'Anyway, talking about Booth and St Clair has left an unpleasant taste in my mouth. What's for dessert?'

'Dessert?' said Eva, staring blankly at him. 'I didn't think you'd want anything sweet?'

'Well, I have a real fancy for something warm and sweet,' said Connor, putting his tray on the floor.

'*Do you?*' Eva giggled watching Connor slip his hand under her skirt. Shoving her tray onto the sofa, she bit her lip as Connor tugged down her knickers. She reached underneath his towel to eagerly find his thick erection.

Gliding her fingers up and down the shaft of his penis, Connor exhaled deeply as her touch stirred his desire. He quickly knelt on the floor and passionately gripped her hips, pulling her towards him. Eva slid down the leather cushion and let him control her body as he lifted her legs over his shoulders.

Feeling his tongue circle her clitoris made Eva pant; she wriggled her hips to push her sex closer to his mouth. Connor's tongue quickened with feverish hunger with every cry of pleasure from Eva's mouth. Calling out his name, she raked her fingers through his thick dark hair as her orgasm rasped out of her throat.

'Eva,' growled Connor urgently lowering her legs to his waist and lifting her in his arms.

She dug her nails into his bulging biceps. His muscles felt like steel beneath his taut skin while he effortlessly glided up and down her sex with the thick shaft of his large penis.

Releasing her hands from his neck, Eva arched her back as Connor lowered her shoulders down onto the sofa. With her arms bowed into a handstand, she felt his hands support her lower back and her body shuddered with each deep thrust of his hips.

'Not yet, Eva!' said Connor, hearing her groan with bliss due to her second orgasm starting to build.

Connor withdrew from her body and quickly flipped her over, making Eva squeal with excitement; he slapped her bottom and pushed her forward before plunging his erection back deep inside.

She dug her nails into the leather headrest and her knees sank into the sofa beneath her. Connor enjoyed the view of her shapely bottom while relentlessly slamming his hips against her soft flesh.

'*Fuck*,' he hissed through gritted teeth; intense pleasure started to swell in his balls and up into his penis. '*Baby I'm going to come*,' he cried, his breathing became deep and raspy. '*Evaaa…!*'

After uncoupling his penis from her sex, Connor gathered Eva's hair to the side and kissed her damp neck. 'That was the perfect dessert,' he whispered. His hot breath filling her ear sent a shuddering tingle down her back.

After taking a shower together, Eva went down to the kitchen to pour two glasses of wine when Mr Jingles came bounding through his cat flap.

'Hello, baby boy,' cooed Eva, wearing a Hello Kitty T-shirt. 'Does my baby want a biscuit? Oh yes you do.'

'I don't know what's more disturbing,' he said laughing and walking into the kitchen naked, 'you talking to your cat, or you thinking he understands what you're saying?'

'Well you should be careful,' said Eva looking at his flaccid penis, 'he has a fondness for small, wriggly things.'

'I should be perfectly safe, then,' boasted Connor modestly.

'Yes, you are,' agreed Eva, acknowledging that Connor had every right brag about his impressive manhood.

Eva finished her wine and tried to stifle a yawn. 'Time for bed, I think,' she said, glancing down at her watch.

'Yeah.' Connor got to his feet with a playful smile on his lips. He swiftly bent down and flipped Eva over his shoulder into a fireman's lift.

'Connor, put me down!' she squealed, but he was already carrying her upstairs.

'Your wish is my command,' he said, tipping her forward and letting her fall backwards onto the bed.

'Night, then,' she said softly, rolling onto her side and bringing her knees up to her stomach.

'Yeah, night,' said Connor, sighing heavily.

Pushing her face into the pillow, her eyes suddenly flicked open feeling the warmth of his body press against her back and his arm circle her waist. His soft lips kissed her bare shoulder. She turned her head towards him as her mouth found his lips.

'Night, gorgeous,' said Connor, holding her tightly.

A dreamy smile slipped across her face. 'Night, baby.'

Chapter 21

The loud reverberations from her mobile stirred her from a vivid dream. 'Hell-o...' she croaked, pressing the phone to her ear.

'Have you seen the snow outside?'

'Eh... What?' she said, rubbing her hand over her face.

'Are you still in bed?'

'Hi, baby, have you left for work already?' She yawned, rolling onto her side to see the empty space beside her.

'Yes – its half nine, sleepy head,' said Connor. 'Go and have a look outside.'

She threw back the duvet and shuffled over to grab her dressing gown before walking over to the window. Peering from behind her net curtains, she looked down at the carpet of white snow covering the street and parked cars.

'Wow, was it snowing when you left this morning?'

'Yes, but not as heavy.'

'Ask your butler to bring up your Land Rover if it's going to continue to snow. There's no way the Maserati is going to cope with weather like this,' said Eva.

'It's already on its way, "Brains",' he teased. 'Anyway, time to get up, lazy bones!'

Eva sighed and walked out of her bedroom. 'Yes, I'm up.'

'Good, see you later, beautiful.'

Eva smiled on hearing his compliment, 'Okay, see you tonight, and be careful.'

'I will... Bye.'

'Bye.'

Eva flicked on the fire and switched on the television to be bombarded with Christmas adverts that made her think about putting up her decorations. Her ankle was feeling much better, but she still didn't want to risk knocking it by clambering up into the loft to get her tree. *Hmmm... I could order a real one*, she thought, grinning excitedly.

'So can you deliver today...?' asked Eva, tapping on her laptop while on the phone. 'Yes, that's right, a six-foot blue spruce with an assortment of decorations... Great... You can – that's fantastic!' With a late afternoon delivery agreed, Eva continued her online shopping. With just a week until Christmas Eve, she wanted to buy Connor a special gift.

'Hmmm…not sure,' she mumbled, undecided whether to buy a pair of square gold cufflinks engraved with his initials or a fancy silver engraved fountain pen.

She had seen him wear a pair of platinum and black onyx cufflinks but couldn't afford platinum or twenty-two carat gold. Looking at the eighteen carat gold cufflinks, at a modest hundred and eighty-five pounds, she hoped Connor would like them and not think they were below his usual standard.

Her own dithering started to irritate her as she sat frowning at her laptop. '*Oh, sod it*, I'm going to get them,' she announced, clicking 'Place order'. The confirmation pinged through to her email. She was pleased with her decision imagining Connor wearing them with one of his handmade suits and a stylish Italian silk tie. It didn't stop there. She couldn't help herself buying a twelve-year old bottle of malt whisky for him, too.

She sat down to lunch and watched a festive film while listening out for her front door bell. She couldn't stop herself from smiling thinking that this Christmas was going to be so different from the last. No broken heart to nurse and no crying at the thought of being on her own on New Year's Eve. *This Christmas is going to be so magical*, she thought.

Her Christmas tree was delivered later that afternoon, and the kind delivery men placed it in her front room along with a huge box of decorations when she explained about her sprained ankle.

After cutting through the fine plastic mesh, she stepped back to avoid being hit by the branches immediately expanding out towards her. With a little trim she was happy with the shape, and after half an hour she had decorated the tree with red and gold baubles, a stream of clear lights, and finished it off with gold and red tinsel and bows. With the lounge light turned off, she switched on the tree lights and stood back to admire her artistic efforts.

'Look, Mr Jingles, doesn't Mummy's tree look beautiful?' she rambled on, kissing his furry cheek. Eva took his coincidental meow as a sign that he understood and agreed.

Hi, what time do you think you'll get here for? texted Eva.
Another hour if there isn't total gridlock on the roads!
Drive carefully. Missing you ☹
Yeah ok xxxx
She stared at the kisses on the end of his text feeling a rush of love.

An hour later an excited Eva rushed to greet him at the front door.

'Brrrr...' The snow is getting really deep now. I can't remember the last time it snowed so bad!' he said.

'Have you opened the club tonight?' asked Eva, brushing snowflakes of his coat and hanging it on the banister rail.

'No, London has come to a standstill. If it continues to snow like this it won't be worth opening the club tomorrow either.'

So, we might get to spend the whole day together tomorrow, then?'

'Maybe, so you'd better think of ways to entertain me because I can get restless if I'm not occupied,' he said suggestively.

'Don't worry, Mr O'Neill, I can keep you occupied all day,' fired back Eva, blushing.

Standing by the fire, Connor rubbed his hands together looking over at the Christmas tree with its lights twinkling in the subdued light.

'Well, do you like it?' asked Eva, wrapping her arms around his waist.

'Very festive,' declared Connor, leaning down to kiss her on the lips. 'Something smells good – what's for dinner because I'm absolutely starving?'

'I made a beef stew – I hope you like stew?' asked Eva in anticipation; it was a dish taught to her by her mother and had been simmering for the last four hours.

'I do.' Connor smiled and released her to grab the television remote before plonking himself down on the sofa.

The large bowl of homemade stew she brought in for him diverted his attention from the TV screen.

'Hmm, very good,' complimented Connor, chewing a tender chunk of beef.

His approval gave her butterflies; she flashed him a big smile.

After eating such a filling meal, they both lay bloated on the sofa in front of the warm fire feeling lethargic and drowsy.

'Right, I'm going to grab a shower, then go to bed,' said Connor, tapping her bottom playful as he got up.

'Yes, okay, I'll just clear everything away and I'll be up,' said Eva, switching on the news for the weather forecast.

With the risk of another heavy snow shower during the night, Eva's spirits were lifted as she switched off the TV and tree lights.

She slipped under the bed covers and saw a flurry of snowflakes fall under the yellow beam of the streetlamp outside. 'Hello puss-puss,' she cooed. Mr Jingles leapt up onto the bed and slowly padded his way up to her before rubbing his furry cheek against her pillow and curling up into a ball above her head.

Mr Jingles raised his head hearing the bathroom door open only to lower it again when Connor walked into the bedroom.

'It's started to snow again,' said Eva.

'Has it,' said Connor, peering out of the window before getting into bed.

'They say we've got it over the weekend now, until Monday. I can't remember the last white Christmas. Christmas Eve is next Saturday, I can't wait!'

'About Christmas, baby,' said Connor softly. 'I spend Christmas Day with my folks – sorry, I should've mentioned it earlier, but I'll fly out early Boxing Day morning and come straight here.'

'Oh...' said Eva, unable to disguise the disappointment in her voice.

'Maybe next year you can join me?' added Connor, hoping his invitation would dilute her disappointment.

'What, Christmas with your family?' asked Eva with excitement.

'Yeah, why not,' soothed Connor, wrapping his arm around her and kissing the top of her head. 'Actually,' he teased, 'because you have been such a good girl, Santa will have plenty in his sack to give you Boxing Day.'

His innuendo made her giggle as she snuggled into his chest. 'Sounds wonderful. So you're staying here next Friday, and we'll open our presents on Christmas Eve morning?'

Connor yawned sleepily. 'Yeah...'

Eva enjoyed the warmth of his body pressing against her. She kissed his chest and squeezed him tightly.

'Night, then...' said Connor softly.

'Night...' said Eva, lifting her head to meet his kiss.

It was the first night they had spent together without having sex. She wasn't sure if Connor was hoping she would initiate it, so she slipped her hand beneath the bed covers and trailed down the taut contours of his muscular stomach until they reached the soft pubic hairline of his groin. Holding her breath, she touched his flaccid penis.

'I'm tired, baby, I'll make it up to you tomorrow,' said Connor. 'Night, gorgeous,' he added quickly, sweetening his rebuff.

'Night...' said Eva, placing her hand back on his smooth chest.

Connor slept perfectly still, but Eva writhed around and suddenly woke from a vivid dream at three o'clock in the morning. Peering over her shoulder, she looked at Connor's silhouette and quickly rolled over to snuggle back up to him.

Her dream had made her feel anxious: Connor had jilted her at the altar, leaving Tina to tell her that he loved another woman – Cara!

* * *

'Hi, sleepy.'

'Hmmm…what time is it?' croaked Eva.

'It's just gone half seven. It looks like you're lumbered with me for the day. The snow must be at least eight inches deep,' said Connor, looking outside.

'I like the idea of being snowed in, we can cosy up and watch a movie.'

'Sounds good, but I've brought my laptop to do a bit of work,' said Connor. 'But…' he added, grinning, 'I've got time to take a shower – fancy joining me?' His tight black designer briefs showcased his impressive morning erection.

Eva flung off the duvet. Connor reached down and gathered her up in his arms to carry her masterfully into the bathroom.

'I'll go and start breakfast,' said Eva after their sexy shower. 'I really fancy a fry-up, but I can make you poached eggs on toast?' She said, slipping on her reindeer onesie. 'I think I've got some wholemeal bread in the back of the freezer.'

'I'll live dangerously, I'll have the same as you,' said Connor, unzipping a large tan leather holdall and pulling out a pair of black jeans and a charcoal-grey jumper. 'But I'll make sure we burn it off later.' He glanced up and winked at her.

'The weather forecast says there's the possibility of heavy snow starting Christmas Eve, what will you do if it does?' quizzed Eva when Connor came down to the kitchen.

'I'm sure all the airports will be gritted if they're expecting bad weather, we'll just have to wait and see.'

Eva wiped her hands on a tea towel and turned around to look up at him. His dark golden tan had faded making his blue eyes even more striking against his paler skin. She couldn't stop dreamily gazing at his high cheekbones and beautiful sensual lips.

'I was thinking maybe at the end of January we could take a break somewhere warm,' said Connor.

'Really?' squealed Eva giddy with excitement.

'Where would you like to go?' he asked, enjoying her childlike enthusiasm.

'Oh, I don't know. Er… Somewhere cultured like Italy or Venice,' she said tugging at his jumper.

'You mean somewhere with designer shops!'

'Maybe…' Eva laughed coyly and draped her hands over his shoulders. 'But I wouldn't mind where we go, even if it was Bognor Regis – as long as we're together,' she gushed.

'Is that so…' Connor smiled looking down at her dilated pupils staring back up at him. He brushed the back of his fingers across her pale cheek, then slipped his finger underneath her chin and tilted her face to meet his mouth.

Connor worked on his laptop for most of the day, only briefly stopping for refreshments and more home cooking. Not wanting to disturb him trying to keep on top of Booth's planning application, Eva lounged on the sofa pretending to watch TV but actually daydreaming about her future with Connor and, amongst many things, what their children would look like. The silliness of her fanciful thoughts made her heart beat with joy wondering if they would inherit her pale skin and red hair or Connor's dark looks. She even fantasised about names. *Erin Violet O'Neill, if it's a girl, and Oliver Andrew O'Neill for a boy,* she thought excitedly to herself. She frequently checked that Connor hadn't seen her inane grinning while pretending to watch turgid daytime TV.

That night as he made love to her, she couldn't hold back her emotions and told him again that she loved him as her orgasm overwhelmed her.

'Connor?'

'Hmm…?'

'Don't you think we fit together perfectly?' she asked subtlety as she lay in his arms with her cheek resting on his heaving chest.

'Yes, I guess so,' agreed Connor, cupping her left breast.

'Good,' said Eva beaming. She looked up at him before resting her head back down on his torso. 'I want to say something, but I'm worried about your reaction, so I'm just going to come out and say it!' she said, not having the courage to look at him again. 'I have never understood all the rules attached to dating. If you seem too keen, then men assume you're needy or desperate, which isn't fair – or true. I know you've been hurt badly in the past and it's hard for you to trust again, I know, because it's happened to me, too. So I can totally identify with your reservations about telling someone how you feel,' she added. 'I hope that you still believe in love, because I do. Actually, I think I've been gradually falling in love with you for some time, I'm not ashamed to admit my feelings,' said Eva. She inhaled deeply, then added, '*I love you Connor.*'

Holding her breath, she waited for Connor to reply. Every second of silence felt like she was being dangled head first from a cliff top looking down at the perilous drop beneath.

The sound of Connor's snoring made her head jerk back. She exhaled with frustration. Exasperated, she rolled away from him and flopped her head down on the pillow. She stared up at the ceiling not believing she had just declared her love for him while he was fast asleep.

It took an hour of restless tossing and turning before she finally drifted off, and even then she was woken an hour later by a chill down her back thanks to Connor taking most of the duvet.

Chapter 22

Connor left Eva's at nine thirty the next morning, leaving her to mope around the house like a grouchy teenager. Now able to put her full weight on her ankle and the bruising a lighter yellowy colour, Eva decided to go into work that evening.

She wore her long black cocktail dress with a sexy thigh-length side split that luckily displayed her good ankle, and her new platinum and diamond earrings.

Connor organised for Tommy to give her a lift in, which proved to be an awkward experience and convinced Eva that he was the last surviving Neanderthal due to his non-existent communication skills when she tried to pass the time with polite chitchat.

'Eva!' squealed Roxanne when she saw her friend walk into the dressing room. 'How's the ankle, babe?'

'Not too bad now,' said Eva, lifting the hem of her long dress. 'Most of the swelling has gone, it's just bruising now.'

'Oh, and I love the earrings, by the way,' added Roxanne, glancing over her shoulder, making Eva smile coyly.

'They're not real diamonds,' crowed Tina, wrinkling her nose.

Eva smirked proudly. 'Actually, Tina, they are!'

'You can't afford jewellery like that. They must be off a club member. You do know it's forbidden to take gifts, Connor would—'

'Before you go telling tales and spreading lies, they were a present from my boyfriend – Gucci platinum and diamond earrings, so go and suck on a lemon, Tina, there's no scandal to reveal,' said Eva, slightly blushing and looking over at Roxanne who raised her eyebrows and smirked.

'She wasn't saying there was any scandal!' said Donna, glancing over at Tina looking at her smartphone.

'Hmm…. Just over three grand! You don't have a boyfriend who would spend that amount on you! They're off a club member, probably that dirty old man Jenkins!'

'Fuck off, Tina,' said Eva, losing her temper.

'Oh, hit a nerve, have we? Very ladylike, I'm sure!' retorted Tina.

'At least I have a boyfriend who wants to buy me beautiful jewellery,' barked Eva. 'Can you remember the last boyfriend you had? You know a "real" one!'

'*Oh my God!* You're actually bragging that you have a better sex life than me,' scoffed Tina. 'All because some desperado has taken pity on you and decided that shagging you would be slightly better than a bad wank! You've got some nerve to crow over me!'

Eva narrowed her eyes as anger washed over her like a thick fog hearing Tina and Donna laughing at her.

'Why don't you ask me who my boyfriend is? Then we'll see who has the last laugh!' called out Eva with swagger in her voice.

'Why would I care?' Tina said followed by a high-pitched laugh.

'Oh, I think you will once you know,' replied Eva with a petulant a half-smile.

'Er, Eva,' said Roxanne, getting to her feet, 'let's go and have a cigarette, shall we? I think everyone needs to chill out.'

Tina sat smugly watching Eva and Roxanne walk towards the door. 'I know who your secret beau is,' she sneered. 'It's obvious now. It's your old boss – Booth! I must say, even for him, he's scraping the barrel!' she roared.

'Hilarious!' mocked Eva, 'Almost as funny as your budget-priced breasts and painted on tan. I bet your bed sheets look like the Turin Shroud when you crawl out in the morning. In fact, the last time I saw such a ropey looking body like yours it was charging a tenner for a blow job down Docket Lane!'

'Well, the last time I saw a body like yours they were trying to push it back out to sea!' shot back Tina.

'LADIES!' called out Ann from her office. 'I've heard enough! Eva can you make your way up to the casino, please? And, Tina, don't you have a private dance to get ready for?'

Eva gave Tina a snarling stare, flicked her long mane of red hair over her shoulder and slowly walked out of the dressing room.

Once inside the casino she tried to spot Connor amongst the sea of smartly dressed men.

'Can I help you?'

'Oh,' said Eva glancing up at the blond-haired man with dazzling blue eyes. She stopped struggling to edge her bottom onto the tall bar stool. 'Thank you.' She smiled warmly holding out her hand.

'It's okay. I've got her from here – thanks.'

Hearing Connor's deep Irish drawl made her instantly pull her hand back.

The slim, blond gentleman smiled weakly at Connor standing in front of Eva, eclipsing her body with his broad muscular frame.

'I said, I've got things here,' repeated Connor sharply, making the man feel uncomfortable with his glare. The man, looking awkward, walked away.

Eva smiled. 'Hi…'

Connor's deep frown indicated he was in a mood as he lifted her onto the bar stool.

'Have I done something wrong?'

'I don't know. Have you?' he snapped bluntly.

Eva didn't know if he was being flippant in a jokey way or if he was being serious. Either way, he was making her feel nervous; she quickly lowered her gaze submissively.

'I'm just under pressure with work, so take no notice of me,' said Connor softening his voice. 'Let's have a drink – yeah?'

'Yes, okay.'

'Darren,' called out Connor in a stiff and formal way. 'Whisky, and a vodka and lemonade.'

'Coming up, Boss!' shot back the barman quickly making up his order.

Eva took a large gulp of her drink in silence. Connor sipped at his neat whisky looking down at her.

'The earrings look nice!' he said eventually.

'I love them,' cooed Eva, touching the platinum and diamond droppers, making them glisten under the casino lights.

'Seeing as your ankle is on the mend you can work in the casino until the New Year, then come January it should be back to full strength,' added Connor, giving her a sexy smile.

Enjoying his softer tone, Eva nodded in agreement and discreetly reached for his hand. 'You know you mentioned taking a holiday in the New Year?'

'Yeah…' said Connor.

'Well, I've had a quick look online at some exclusive resorts. Do you prefer a beach holiday or a city break?'

'About the holiday, Eva,' he said reluctantly. 'We might have to postpone if the council delay or block my appeal against Booth's gaming licence.'

'Oh…'

'Sorry, it can't be avoided. But I do have a business meeting in New York at the beginning of February, so maybe I can take you with me.'

His offer may not have been presented in a 'Mills and Boon' manner, but being with Connor in New York created butterflies in her stomach and a large smile lit up her face. 'New York would be fantastic,' she squealed.

His gaze drifted away from her towards a heavy-set man with a large purple birthmark colouring part of his cheek and earlobe. 'I just need to speak to Councillor Williams for a minute,' he said, pulling his hand away from her.

'Okay,' said Eva, checking out his pert bottom as he walked away.

Within seconds Tina waltzed past with her nose in the air; Eva watched her like a bird of prey making a beeline for Connor and Councillor Williams.

What a bitch! thought Eva watching Tina discreetly slip her hand down the small of Connor's back.

Before she could take a step forward, Connor quickly turned around and glanced over at her, then brushed Tina's hand away.

Blinking hard, Eva breathed a sigh of relief. Her heart hammered against her chest with jealousy.

A few seconds later she muttered, 'What the fu—' watching Tina slip her hand around Connor's arm and push her fake boobs up against him. She then had the audacity to turn around to bait Eva with an obnoxious childlike laugh.

Eva, fuming and walking as quickly as her bruised ankle would allow, weaved her way over to Connor and Tina.

'Hello, young lady,' said Williams, glancing down at her breasts.

'Hello,' replied Eva, forcing a thin smile. 'Connor, can I have a quick word, please?'

'Mr O'Neill is *busy* with Councillor Williams,' scowled Tina, 'Why don't you go back to your seat and rest your ankle?'

'It's fine – *thank you*,' hissed Eva through gritted teeth.

'Tina's right, go back to the bar and sit down,' said Connor, looking annoyed at her interruption.

'I'll help her back to her seat, Mr O'Neill – it's no trouble at all,' said Tina, excusing herself with a disingenuous grin and cool insincerity.

Eva sucked in her cheeks as Tina linked her arm and pulled her away from Connor and Williams.

'What are you doing, psycho!' squawked Tina, releasing her arm. 'Connor's in the middle of a very important conversation! He's trying to block planning permission for a new casino which could ruin the Unicorn, and here you are with a face like a smacked arse interrupting everyone. I hope you're not going to do a "Chu" and disgrace Connor again!'

'*Why are you involved?* The meeting hasn't got anything to do with you!'

'Not that it's any of your business, but Connor asked me to join them, so fuck off and earn your wages by selling champagne – leave the important stuff to *me and Connor.*'

'*You and Connor!* You make it sound as if you're a couple!' growled Eva jealously.

'Everyone knows that Connor and I have history. We're like Richard Burton and Elizabeth Taylor,' boasted Tina. 'I don't expect you to understand, but we have a raw and passionate connection.'

'Burton and Taylor?! More like Wallace and Gromit!' Eva fired back. 'And we both know who the dog is!'

Tina's smile was unexpected. 'Nothing you can say can dampen my mood tonight, not even your twisted little fantasy. Everybody knows you have a sick crush on Connor, so listen up, my little fat friend, tonight me and Connor will take our relationship to the next level, so you and your warped infatuation can go and jump – preferably off a very tall building!'

'The next level, you're out of your mind,' scoffed Eva. 'You're going to spend the night with Connor – tonight?'

Tina smirked. 'Yes, he's so obviously out of your league, but not mine!'

'So you were actually awake when he agreed to this? You and Connor are going to spend the night together?'

'It's all in the body language, something you wouldn't understand.'

Eva laughed out loud. 'So he's said nothing, then?!'

'Laugh all you want,' hissed Tina. 'It will happen!'

'You know it's against the law to drug people, Tina. I actually feel sorry for you. You have a problem up there,' said Eva, pointing to her temple. 'Connor's not interested in you and never has been, and do you know how I know this?'

Tina smirked and folded her arm in amusement. 'You know nothing.'

Eva inhaled confidently with a triumphant smile. 'Connor is already seeing someone and when I say seeing someone, I mean in a relationship and has been for months – do you want to know who with?'

'Who…?' said Tina, narrowing her eyes.

'ME!'

Tina's smirk crumbled into an ugly gape. 'You're lying!'

'We both know I'm not!'

'Well let's ask *him*!' Tina turned on her heels and walked back over to Connor who was shaking Councillor Williams' hand.

Shaking with adrenalin, Eva watched her storm over. She felt sick seeing Connor lower his face so Tina could whisper into his ear. Within a split second he was glaring over at her, he then roughly pulled Tina to one side and growled something before releasing her arm and nodding over to Williams before storming past Eva. Her skin felt hot and clammy seeing Tina swagger back to her wearing a sneering grin.

'Connor wants to see us both upstairs. I hope you haven't unpacked your workbag because the truth will expose you for what you are: a fantasist and a liar. And you know what, Eva, I'm going to relish *every single second* of your humiliation!' jeered Tina, turning on her heels and leaving the casino.

Tina was nowhere to be seen as Eva made her way out of the casino. *She's probably already filling Connor's head with lies*, she thought. The lift couldn't reach the third floor quick enough. She felt physically sick knocking on the penthouse door knowing they would be finished for good if Connor renounced the truth in front of Tina. She would never forgive him if he humiliated her in front of Tina again.

'Come in and shut the door, Eva,' Connor snapped coldly.

Feeling apprehensive, she closed the door and looked at Tina standing with her lips pinched and arms folded.

'I am sick to death of this childish sparring between you both. If you can't act in a more professional manner, then I'm going to have to make a choice!'

'*She's* the one spouting off outrageous accusations. She said that you and her are in a relationship. Can you believe that?!' scoffed Tina, flashing Eva a look of utter contempt.

Connor inhaled deeply; his jaw twitched with annoyance. He had so much on his mind with Booth, St Clair and the local planning office that pandering to two hysterical women was very low on his agenda.

'*No!* You're the one with the warped obsession, not me! What I told you *is* the truth,' barked Eva, looking over to Connor for agreement.

Connor brushed his hand over his month as she stood in silence. He turned his back on both of them and walked over to a crystal tumbler filled with whisky.

Tina smirked at Eva and held up her middle finger.

'Connor?' croaked Eva, watching his shoulders lower while he exhaled loudly.

'Let me make one thing clear, *ladies*,' he said, turning around. 'While you're working in my club, you both follow my rules – understood! I don't have the time or interest to break up your constant juvenile spats. I pay you to dance and take your clothes off – period! If you feel you can't do that without tearing a strip off each other every night, then I will fire one of you!'

'Aren't you going to tell her the truth?!' questioned Eva with tears starting to build.

'There is no truth!' bellowed Tina. 'You made it all up to feed your sick little fantasy. I told you she was a weirdo, Connor, but now I think she's gone totally *mad*!'

Connor saw a tear fall from Eva's cheek. 'It's true…' he answered.

A second of silence hovered as his words slowly penetrated the air.

Tina's thin, vindictive smile dismantled instantly and she shook her head in disbelief. 'W-what…?'

'You heard what I said,' Connor said standoffishly. 'Both of you get back to work.'

Eva swallowed hard and wiped her eyes.

Tina laughed nervously. 'No! You wouldn't, *you couldn't*…not with her!'

'The subject is no longer up for discussion. I want you both back at work,' barked Connor, anger colouring his cheeks.

'I can't believe you would choose *her* over me! I have a twenty-four-inch waist and a body mass index of seventeen, what does she have? An arse full of cellulite and a Weight Watchers cookbook!' screamed Tina.

Eva opened her mouth to retaliate but was beaten by Connor. 'I have never pursued you, so I'm at a loss where all this nonsense is coming from?'

'Well, I must've read the signals wrong… *silly me*,' mocked Tina. 'Because when you had your hands down my knickers and your dick in my mouth, I thought you liked me!'

He quickly shot a look of fear at Eva, not knowing that she already knew about their sexual tryst. 'Well, when it's offered on a plate,' he said coldly, 'I guess a standing cock has no conscience – plus, I wasn't seeing anyone special then.'

'*She's* special to you, then?' seethed Tina, consumed with jealousy.

'My feelings for Eva are of no concern to you or anyone else. My private life is just that – private!'

'Connor, it's not too late to save what we had. I'm willing to forgive you if you get rid of that block of lard standing over there,' pleaded Tina, starting to cry.

'Block of what?!' roared Eva, taking a step towards her.

'Eva!' called out Connor, quickly blocking her path.

'From what I remember, it was a forgettable fumble at best. Now I don't want to discuss it any further – end of!'

'You cold-hearted bastard,' said Tina, her chin starting to tremble.

Connor inhaled deeply before replying, 'I'll give you that one because I probably deserve it.'

'You don't have a heart!' retaliated Tina, almost hysterical.

Eva knew she should relish her moment of retribution over Tina, but the coldness in Connor's voice and his dismissive manner made her wonder if one day she might be on the receiving end of his acid tongue.

'Perhaps I don't.' Connor shrugged, not showing any remorse for causing Tina's misery.

'Do you want to resign, Tina?' grunted Connor, pulling out his mobile phone and rudely checking his messages as Tina stood sobbing.

'Connor, please…' said Eva, pleading with him to show a little understanding.

'What?' Connor almost looked straight through her. 'You can go back to the casino; I'll be wanting a word with you later in private.'

'But shouldn't we—'

'Now, Eva!' he said, raising his voice, not lifting his gaze away from his phone.

After glancing at Tina, whose mascara lay in two thin lines down her face, she turned around and walked towards the door.

'Well, do you want to go or not? I haven't got all night.'

Eva looked over her shoulder at Connor's tense body language projecting his irritability and impatience while Tina continued to sob heavily.

Eva's mind was racing as she reached the lift. She started to worry about what would happen now they were on their own: Connor might take pity on Tina and comfort her, making her think he did care.

Then she realised she was being ridiculous. She had witnessed the cold indifference in his eyes; there was no mistaking his callousness to Tina and the situation.

Chapter 23

Back in the casino, Eva reached for an unfinished bottle of champagne on the bar and filled her glass before gulping back the entire contents.

'Well, I sure do like to see a lady enjoying herself!'

Mopping a dribble of champagne off her chin, Eva quickly turned around and gazed up at the weather-beaten American gentleman standing in front of her.

'Howdy, ma'am, let me introduce myself!' said the smiling, jovial man. 'Ted Marshall the third, at your service.' He held out his hand to her.

Eva looked at his infectious grin and white wide-brimmed Stetson sitting on a mop of white hair. He looked odd in his black jeans and checked shirt amongst the sea of tailored dinner suits. She guessed his age at sixty-three, but it was hard to tell with his tanned skin and deep lines creasing his eyes and forehead.

'Hi, my name is Eva – Eva Summers.'

'It's a pleasure to be acquainted with you. May I could be so bold and join you?'

'Please,' replied Eva smiling and motioning him towards the empty bar stool next to her.

Ted tipped the front of his Stetson. 'Thank you kindly, Miss Summers.'

'Please, call me Eva.'

'Then I will, ma'am,' he said, grinning and showing a set of very white teeth. Whether they were his own, Eva couldn't tell.

'So, Miss – sorry – Eva, do you work in this fine establishment?'

'Yes, I'm a dancer in the lounge downstairs, but I had a fall,' explained Eva, lifting the hem of her dress to show Ted her bruised ankle, 'so I won't be able to dance until the New Year.'

Ted nodded with interest listening to Eva explain she had only been working at the Unicorn since the summer.

'So do you live in Britain or just visiting?'

'I'm just visiting. Mr O'Neill is kind enough to let me dip in and out, so to speak.'

'Oh, you know Mr O'Neill personally, then?' asked Eva.

'Yes I do, ma'am. I've known your boss for about six years in total. We're both fond of a wicked lady called "poker". Whenever he's in Vegas we meet up, and I let him win.' He gave a chuckle. 'Actually that's a bold lie I've just told you, Mr O'Neill is a formidable card player for sure, I've never won a game sitting at his table.' He leaned in and whispered, 'His face is so deadpan, you'd think he was as dead as a mule lying in the desert.'

Eva laughed as Ted eyes twinkled regaling his anecdote.

'Yes, I heard he's a good poker player, but surely you must've seen him lose at least once in six years?'

'You're right, I have, only once,' confirmed Ted, in a serious tone. 'Three years ago in a private game he lost to what I can only describe as a ghost. This guy had no colour in his skin – I think they call them albinos.'

Eva's mouth parted in shock as an image of St Clair flashed in her mind. 'This other man beat Connor?'

'Yes, but I could feel something wasn't right between them before the game started. Bad blood has a smell of its own, little lady, and I could smell it that day.'

'What happened?'

'Well, when a man's blood is up like that, you take cover.'

'So they fought each other?' asked Eva, grabbing the half-empty bottle of champagne.

'Your boss accused the man of cheating, but I said you can't go accusing because Lady Luck ain't smiling down on you, but he was convinced the pale guy had cheated.'

'What happened?'

'Well, it might not be suitable for a lady's ear, but it got pretty nasty out there. If it weren't for security stepping in, they would've continued until one of them stayed on the floor, you understand what I am saying – until one of them didn't have the breath to get up. It was ugly to see two human beings having no respect for life, and I confess I'm in no hurry to witness anything like that again.'

'Were the police called?'

'No, you don't want the attention of the sheriff in your club, but I thought the albino came off worst, he looked pretty beaten up. Connor O'Neill takes no prisoners, that's for sure.'

Eva's eyes widened with interest. Ted's story enthralled her to the point where she didn't see Connor coming towards her.

'Ted, you old reprobate,' said Connor, extending his hand.

'C-Connor!' spluttered Eva. 'I was just com—'

'Good to see you, Connor.' Ted nodded and shook his hand firmly. 'I see you've met my newest dancer – what do you think?'

Eva felt her cheeks burn with embarrassment and quickly lowered her gaze.

'She is a credit to your club, sir, a true natural beauty.'

'Shall we go upstairs for drinks?' asked Connor, buttoning up his black dinner jacket.

'Will you be joining us?' asked Ted, smiling at Eva.

'Hmm... I—'

'Of course she is.' Connor clicked his fingers at Darren. 'Two bottles of Moet, have them brought upstairs straight away.'

'Shall we...?' said Ted, holding out his arm.

Connor seemed more than pleased with Ted's adoration for Eva; little did she know that he was the wealthiest client on the Unicorn's membership list. He owned one of the largest cattle ranges in Texas, so in terms of wealth he was ten times richer than Connor and, luckily for him, Ted enjoyed the company of good-looking women.

As they reached the penthouse, Eva was instructed to sit next to Ted with Connor on the opposite sofa as the champagne arrived.

'If you'll excuse me while I use the restroom,' said Ted getting to his feet, leaving Connor and Eva alone.

'Hello,' said Eva softly, quickly sitting next to Connor.

Letting her reach for his hand, Connor looked at her with a poker face expression.

'I know you're annoyed with me for telling Tina, but she was being so horrible to me. You didn't hear the things she was saying.'

'I told you not to say anything at work. I don't need the extra hassle.'

'Yes I know, and I'm sorry, but she was hinting that your feelings mirrored hers, so I just freaked out.'

'You heard the extent of our so-called relationship – an amateur blow job and a quick fondle.'

'So nothing happened once I'd left?' probed Eva.

'No. I've given her twenty-four hours to tell me if she wants to leave. I'll say this once more, so don't ask me about it again, Tina was purely a distraction at the time, nothing more.'

'So, what am I?' asked Eva anxiously, pulling her hand away and shuffling back in her seat.

'You were a surprise.'

Just before Ted returned to the room Eva jumped up from the sofa and quickly grabbed the champagne bottle and poured out three glasses of champagne.

Eva enjoyed listening to Ted's entertaining stories of his past. He had travelled extensively around Europe and the Middle East, and bought works of art for enjoyment and investment. His first wife divorced him twenty-eight years ago and took their two young children, and his second wife tragically died in a car accident six years previously.

'I don't think a man is supposed to journey through life on his own,' explained Ted, accepting a refill from Connor. 'He needs a mate. He needs the kindness of a woman to make him a better man.'

'So you still believe in marriage?' asked Eva, glancing over to Connor who was staring at her.

'I do, ma'am, I truly believe a man needs a woman and vice-versa. There's nothing in the world that can rival the feeling of true love. Money is nice, but love is a sweeter companion.'

Eva thought Ted's outlook on love was almost poetic; even in his mature years he was still searching for his next big love.

'So what about you, Miss Eva, do you believe in love?'

Blushing, Eva tried not to make her glances towards Connor too obvious. 'I do, I think life would be joyless without it.'

'Wonderfully put, may I say?' Ted smiled at Connor. 'So, Mr O'Neill, dare we ask what you think about love?'

Connor gulped down the reminder of his champagne. 'Haven't they proved it's just a chemical process? When we're infatuated with someone we release serotonin, then as the relationship progresses we release oxytocin, which produces the feelings of "love".'

Both Eva and Ted looked astonished at Connor's cold, biological explanation. He may have been correct in his factual evidence, but the way he portrayed his views were void of any warmth or emotion.

'Well…' said Ted before clearing his throat. 'I don't know about you, but I could eat the hind off a cow, Connor remind me, where's a good place to eat around here?'

'I'll book us a table somewhere,' said Connor.

Eva smiled politely at Ted while hearing Connor make a booking for five people. She wondered who else was joining them.

'Right, let's go,' said Connor breezily before making another phone call.

Connor's other two guests soon became apparent when she reached the lobby and found Roxanne and Tommy waiting.

After they said hello and shook hands with Ted, Connor threw Tommy his car keys and they set off.

'I hope everyone likes French?' asked Connor as Tommy drove them to the restaurant.

'I sure do, sir,' said Ted, resting his hat on his lap.

The La Petite Maison was nestled down a quiet side street with a luxurious red colour scheme oozed style and sophistication.

'*Soir, une table reservee pour O'Neill,*' said Connor fluently to the maître d' once they were all inside.

'Perfect French!' Ted laughed in a slightly teasing way.

Once they were seated and after the drinks were ordered, Roxanne winked over to Eva and announced she was going to the ladies toilets.

'Hold on, Roxy, I'll come with you,' said Eva, acknowledging her wink.

As they stood up, Connor and Ted rose to their feet before sitting back down again.

'So, how's everything going?' squealed Roxanne, pushing open the toilet door.

'Okay, until I opened my big mouth. I accidentally told Tina. Well, I guess it wasn't accidental, but she was being such a total bitch. Has she blabbed to the other girls yet?'

'I haven't heard anything. In fact, she hasn't spoken two words. It's fucking eerie not hearing her bellowing gob. It's like she's had the guts ripped out of her.'

Eva leant against the tiled wall. 'I didn't reveal the truth to destroy her. I know how it feels to be humiliated and have your dreams pulled out from under you, but she was being her usual vile self – so something just snapped. How long do you think it'll take for her to tell everyone?'

'Dunno…' Roxanne shrugged. 'I think Connor must've warned her to keep her mouth shut.' She smiled teasingly. 'Poor bloke doesn't seem able to control his staff at the moment.'

'Very funny,' said Eva dryly. 'But seriously, I'm going to be hated by the other girls – you won't turn on me, will you? I know you were annoyed with me for getting involved, but I don't think I could cope if—'

'Eva – you're my mate, right?' soothed Roxanne. 'And what do true mates do? They stick together through the shitty times and the good.'

'I don't deserve you, Roxy, you never seem to judge me,' said Eva, lowering her head in shame.

'Look, I just want you to promise me that you'll go into this with your eyes wide open. I honestly think Connor's forgotten how to love a woman. He can give them an orgasm with ease, but commitment – I'm not so sure.'

'Yes, I promise,' said Eva, nodding. 'And you're wrong about the "orgasm",' she said with a giggle, 'it's multiples, if you please.'

A cackle of laughter erupted which resulted in fevered hysterics as a grey-haired old lady came shuffling out of one the toilet cubicles wearing an I AM 80 TODAY! birthday badge.

'Come on, we'd better go,' said Roxanne sniffing and wiping her streaming eyes.

'Where have you two been?' asked Connor, noticing their schoolgirl giggles on their return.

'Yes, very cruel to take all the beauty away from the table,' Ted said to Connor whose gaze never left Eva.

With everyone's order taken, Connor turned to Tommy and whispered in his ear. Eva couldn't hear what was being said so looked over to Ted. 'Are you going back to America for Christmas?'

Ted reached for his glass of red wine. 'I plan to spend it with my son and his family.'

Eva nodded and took a large sip of her vodka and lemonade. 'I love Christmas. I bought a real tree this year.'

'Christmas can be a magical time. My late wife always enjoyed the holidays, but we aren't religious folk – are you a believer?'

'I'm not sure,' said Eva, taking another gulp of her drink, not offering any personal views on the subject.

'So, Connor, what are your plans over the holidays?' asked Ted as their starters arrived.

'Spend Christmas Day with my folks in Ireland, then back to London.'

Eva placed her napkin on her lap, then slid her hand over to Connor's thigh.

'And you, Miss Eva – is there a man at home to make your holidays special?'

Remembering what Connor had said about not broadcasting their relationship, Eva decided, for once, to do as she was told. 'No, I'm young, free and single.'

'You're single? Well shoot me with a ten-bore cos I'm struggling to believe such a beautiful young lady like you is without a mate. Perhaps I should steal you away for the holidays. I would treat you like a queen on my hundred-acre ranch,' boasted Ted.

The warmth of Connor's fingers tightly enveloping her hand prompted a large smile across her lips. Even though Connor's affection wasn't publicly displayed, it still created a honey-sweet feeling in her stomach.

As everyone chatted through their starter and main course, Eva continued to drink double vodkas like water.

'Is no one having a p-pudding?' Eva hiccupped, feeling greedy that she had just eaten a large meal of seared duck and seasonal vegetables swathed in a calorific creamy-laden sauce.

'If you want a desert, then have one,' said Connor, handing her the menu.

A drunken daydream of Connor's perfect body covered in sweet milk chocolate while her eager tongue licked off every morsel from his beautiful, sculptured abs made Eva start giggling to herself.

'What?' Connor smiled.

'Nothing...' said Eva, looking at him dreamily.

'Just order, simpleton,' said Roxanne, 'and I'll share it with you.'

Eva pointed down at her menu and said, 'That.'

The waiter nodded. '*Tres bon, chocolat et orange gateau.*'

'Yes – with two spoons, please.'

'How big is your pud, love?' Roxanne, also now merry, asked the waiter.

Eva sniggered into her fancy cotton napkin, which encouraged Roxanne to burst out laughing as well.

'It is...er...big...large – yes?' said the poor waiter looking bewildered as every word he spoke created an even louder burst of laughter from Eva and Roxanne.

Ted, Tommy and Connor all sat looking equally perplexed at the girls' wild fit of giggles.

Once their cake arrived, Connor stopped Eva and Roxanne from asking the same waiter for cream.

'Bill, please,' said Connor, clicking his fingers at the waiter and reaching for his wallet.

'I've already taken care of it,' said Ted, putting down his empty brandy glass.

Connor nodded and helped Eva get to her feet.

As the cold fresh air washed over her warm cheeks, Eva wrapped her arms around Connor's waist; his spicy aftershave found the tip of her nose.

'Hel-lo,' she hiccupped, grinning up at him.

'I think someone is drunk,' said Connor looking down at her and raising his eyebrows.

'Nooo… Who?'

'Ted, it might be best if you sit upfront. I'll climb in the back and try to keep my staff under control,' mused Connor.

'Let's go clubbing!' squealed Eva.

'I don't think so. It's a glass of water and bed for you,' said Connor.

'Hmm, let's skip the water…' Eva slipped her hand between his legs.

Releasing a sharp cough, Connor gently moved her hand away from his groin. Roxanne giggled and turned away.

'If you can drop Ted at the club first, then we'll drop off Eva,' instructed Connor quickly stopping Eva's hand wandering towards his groin again.

'Can we play I Spy?' said Eva in a huff.

'No…' said Connor softly.

'Can we p-play Name That Tune, then?' Eva said, hiccupping.

'No…' said Connor shaking his head.

'Well, w-what can we play?'

'Who can be the quietest for the longest,' Connor retorted.

Eva pressed her finger up to her lips and gave a silly grin. 'Did I win?'

'You were only quiet for a second?' scoffed Connor.

Roxanne and Ted started to laugh.

'Ohhhh…' moaned Eva, 'that game is boring, let's play another!'

'No…say goodbye to Mr Marshall, he's leaving now,' said Connor, leaning across Roxanne and shaking Ted's hand.

'Bye-bye, Mr Ted,' said Eva.

'Not goodbye, but as the French say it, *au revoir*! I hope to see you again real soon, Miss Eva,' said Ted, reaching into the back of the car and kissing her hand. 'But until then, sweet lady – good night.'

As Ted shut the door, Connor told Tommy to pull away and slipped his arm around Eva shoulders letting her snuggled into him.

'Aah, Ted is such a sweetie. Isn't he, Roxy?'

'I think he's got the hots for you.'

'What? No, he's a gentle-man,' said Eva, hiccupping again.

'He does,' agreed Connor.

'Stop it…' said Eva, flapping her arm up and down. 'He is just a nice old man, y-you lot just have filthy minds!'

Connor smiled and kissed the top of her head. 'Go to sleep.'

'But I want to dance.' Eva exhaled deeply. 'I know!' she bellowed, sitting up. 'Can we go karaoke singing, pleaseeee?'

'Thanks, Tom,' said Connor as they pulled up outside Eva's house. 'Can you pick me up at half seven tomorrow?'

'Yeah, okay,' said Tommy, glancing in the rearview mirror watching Connor gather Eva into his arms and lift her out of the car.

'Ohhh, are we home already?' sulked Eva, draping her arms around Connor's neck.

'Night, babes!' called out Roxanne.

'N-night,' she called back, raising her hand in the air and waving.

Once inside, Connor carried Eva straight to bed. 'I'll go and get you some water.'

'Okay, *my prince*.' Eva giggled and lifted her head off the pillow after he left the bedroom. She rolled her body across the bed and stumbled over to her dressing table.

'Er…hello?' said Connor, coming back in holding a large glass of water. 'I meant sleep,' he added, looking down at Eva sprawled in a dodgy porn pose wearing a pair of sheer nude stockings with a long ladder snagging one leg.

'D-do you like t-them?' mumbled Eva, running her hand over her matching nude satin bra and knickers.

'Yes, very nice, but it's time for sleep.'

'But t-this is much more fun.'

Connor put the glass down on the small bedside cabinet and sat on the bed smiling at her. 'Sleep, madam – now.'

'Have you gone off me already?' quizzed Eva, trying to sit up and looking at him watery-eyed.

Connor reached over to touch her cheek. 'Don't be silly. Anyway, you've old man Marshall after you now – I'm a pauper next to him.'

'I don't c-care about money, like Ted said, it can only b-buy you stuff,' Eva rambled, flopping back down on the bed. 'I would rather have you than ten million pounds.'

A wide smile curved Connor's mouth. He leant over and kissed her on the lips; she suddenly pulled him on top of her.

Feeling his tongue probe her mouth sent a quiver of excitement through her body as she reached for his belt buckle.

'Eva,' whispered Connor, holding down her hands, 'drunken sex doesn't do anything for me – sorry.'

'Oh…' sulked Eva, pulling her hands free.

Her petulant frown amused him. He pulled the duvet from underneath her bottom before covering her with it. 'Now, are you going to be a good girl and go to sleep?' asked Connor.

'No, I want to be a bad g-girl and stay awake!'

Connor stood up and laughed at her grouchiness.

Feeling disappointed at the lack of bulge protruding through his trousers, Eva conceded, 'Okay, but tomorrow, then!'

'And every day after that – promise,' said Connor, softly kissing the tip of her nose.

'Don't forget Mr Jingles…' Eva yawned. 'Call him in and lock the cat—' Before she could finish her sentence, she fell into a deep, drunken sleep.

Connor watched her for a second. He thought how drunk she looked, but also how incredibly beautiful with her red hair lying in big loose curls on her pillow.

He called out for Mr Jingles in the back garden; his breath created a smoke-like vapour in the freezing night air.

'Mr Jingles,' he called out again, trying to peer through the pitch-black dark. Looking over towards the snow-covered fence, he couldn't hear anything apart from a car driving past, so he decided to try a different approach. He went back into the kitchen in search of a box of cat biscuits. Shaking the box, he called out again, 'Mr Jingles, come on boy,' followed by another rattle of the box.

As the cold wind gnawed at his face, he heard a faint meow in the distance when he shook the box for a third time. With relief, he smiled to see Mr Jingles come bounding over the fence and dart straight through his legs into the house and upstairs to the bedroom.

He shut the cat flap and left the box of biscuits out on the kitchen top before switching off the light and going up to bed.

He found Eva's drunken snoring testing and had to stir her four times during the night.

Chapter 24

Connor woke up tired the next morning. He had a shower and wrote Eva a note while sipping on an unsweetened black coffee. On hearing Tommy tooting outside, he left the note by the kettle and poured Mr Jingles some milk before he left.

'Eh...' grunted Eva, slowly opening one eye as Mr Jingles' tail brushed against her face. She glanced over towards the window and cursed, 'Oh my bloody head.' Quickly gobbling down the tepid glass of water Connor had left her, she swung her legs out of bed and moaned, 'Oh God.' Everything was an effort. She held on tightly to the wooden banister and gingerly made her way downstairs. Feeling nauseous, she picked up the note from Connor.

Hi sleepy,
If you wake up to the sound of a pneumatic drill then don't be alarmed, the noise will just be your head LOL (impressed with my wit...eh?). Look, I think it's best to let things settle down with Tina, so give it a couple of days until you come back. Will phone you later sexy!
PS I've taken your spare door key again.
PPS I'll go to the chemist to buy some earplugs and a cricket bat – both to silence your snoring! (more wit!)

Eva stood and blinked slowly with her throat parched like a dry riverbed. She literally poured down a glass of cold milk and was thankful that Mr Jingles' bowl had been filled so she didn't have to bend down: her head wouldn't have been able to cope. She took two painkillers and shuffled into the lounge to lie on the sofa only to curse out loud hearing her mobile ringing the kitchen. 'For fuck's sake...' she whimpered. 'Yeah...?'

'Someone sounds rough,' Connor answered, laughing. 'I'll go easy on you. What are your plans today? Apart from nursing your hangover.'

'Don't know, why?'

'How about some retail therapy, my treat?'

'Well it's very generous of you, but I don't really need anything.'

'You're definitely a one-off, Miss Summers. I've never known a woman like you.'

'Good...' said Eva, tasting a stinging burp in the back of her throat. 'But I have to go now and be sick.'

'Alluring. I think you need to detox for a couple of weeks – speak to you later!'

'Yes – bye,' grunted Eva before quickly running into the kitchen to throw up.

She felt relieved that Connor had suggested taking a few days off work as there was no way she could face Tina with her raging hangover. Trying to rehydrate her body, she lay on the sofa for most of the day craving greasy food.

Watching the six o'clock news with a family bag of Maltesers in her lap, her mobile beeped, the screen read, *On my way – fancy a takeaway?*

Without a second's hesitation she replied, *Oh yes please!* Large amounts of saturated fat, sugar and salt was just what she needed.

'Hi, it's me, I got a Chinese,' called out Connor from the hall, jolting Eva from a deep sleep.

'Great, I'm starving.'

'Have you been on the sofa all day?' quizzed Connor, handing her a large white plastic carrier bag.

'Yeah…' said Eva, sniffing the aromatic smells wafting through the lounge.

'I don't care that Chinese food fattening,' she announced, carrying the takeaway out to the kitchen to plate up.

'Well, everything in moderation, Miss Summers,' called out Connor. 'You shouldn't eat too much of one thing – well, maybe with one exception.' Connor chuckled at his joke.

'Was that an innuendo?' said Eva walking back into the lounge carrying two plates.

'Yes it is, and if you're feeling better later I'd like to take you through the finer points of it.' He smiled, slipping his suit jacket off his broad shoulders.

A big smile spread across Eva's lips at the mere thought of him giving her oral sex. 'I'm sure after this I'll be ready for anything,' she flirted back, much to Connor's delight.

Eating quickly, she glanced over at Connor on his laptop and eating at the same time.

'I'm done, so I'm going for a shower,' announced Eva, taking her plate into the kitchen.

'Yeah…okay,' said Connor, engrossed in his work.

In the shower she daydreamed about Connor's sexy muscular body and deliciously large penis. With a flutter of excitement she knew within the next hour she would be gasping in pleasure under his expertise love-making. While drying her hair she pondered on what to wear and was undecided between her sheer nude stockings with a baby-blue negligée, or a pure white lace knickers and bra set.

'I'm just going for a shower, Eva,' called out Connor on the landing.

'Okay,' said Eva, still deciding what to wear.

Once dressed she sat at her dressing table and dabbed a little scent behind her ears and between her breasts sitting pert under the flimsy negligée fabric.

'Wow,' said Connor walking into the bedroom naked with his damp hair combed back.

'Do you like?'

'Come here, sexy.'

Swaying her hips, she sauntered over to him unable to resist lowering her gaze to his long, erect penis.

'You don't have to dress up for me all the time, you know,' said Connor, slipping his arms around her waist.

'Oh...I thought you liked it?'

Hooking his finger gently under her chin, he tilted her face up to meet his gaze and stared into her vivid green eyes. 'I do like it and I appreciate the effort, but all I'm saying is you don't need to dress up to turn me on – just being you does that.'

Staring up at him through a haze of lust and love, Eva felt her heart miss a beat; she found him very captivating and entrancing when he was loving and charming.

'Do you want me to take them off?'

Connor grinned. 'It's a shame when you've gone to the trouble of putting it on.' He slipped his hands under the hem of her negligée.

The sex was lustfully hot and sticky. Having enjoyed three blissful orgasms, two through oral sex and one through penetrative sex, Eva lay exhausted next to Connor on the bed.

'I love you,' purred Eva, snuggling into his side and glancing up at him.

Connor looked down at her dilated pupils and swallowed hard. 'I—' He stopped to cough. 'I have strong feelings for you, too.'

A sharp pinch of disappointment pierced her heart. She lowered her head back down onto his chest and thought as they lay in silence, *will he ever fall in love with me? Is he even capable of true love?*

Declaring her love for him so soon into their relationship now made Eva worry she was in danger of scaring him off. With fear taking over, she pressed her fingertips into his smooth skin and held onto his chest tightly.

'Night, Eva…' said Connor, brushing his fingers down her long silky hair before draping his arm over her shoulder.

'Yes, night…' replied Eva, not having the confidence to lift her head for a goodnight kiss. Doubt had robbed her of a sweet kiss that night as she blinked back tears of anxiety.

Chapter 25

There was a real buzz of excitement in the club the evening before Christmas Eve. The lobby looked elegantly festive dressed in luxurious green garlands dressed with poppy-red velvet bows. A huge seven-foot tall Christmas tree stood by the reception desk decorated with beautiful glass baubles and red and green tartan bows.

'Don't open it until Christmas morning,' said Roxanne handing Eva a small square box wrapped in silver paper with a large white bow tied around it.

Eva eyes widened looking down at the securely taped parcel before passing Roxanne a wrapped bottle of Dior perfume. 'And here is yours.'

'What have you got planned for tomorrow, then, some last minute shopping?'

'Well, I've always had to work Christmas Eve, so it'll be strange not working.'

'We never have. Connor knows most of the girls have little ones, so he only opens the casino and shuts the club early.'

Eva glanced over at Scarlett who was trying to eavesdrop and said quietly, arching her hand over her mouth, 'Connor is coming over to mine tonight as he's flying out early tomorrow for Ireland, then coming back on Boxing Day.'

'Oh right,' mouthed Roxanne. 'Next year I guess you'll be going with him, then?'

Eva smiled excitedly. 'Hope so!'

Roxanne winked at her before walking back to her dressing table.

'I'll see you break time, Roxy,' said Eva, spraying her hair before heading out to the casino.

Eva guessed with only about twenty club members milling around that the predicted heavy snowfall must have put many off from venturing out. After an hour of sitting alone, her face plainly displaying her boredom, she sighed heavily checking the time. She hadn't physically seen Connor that evening, only briefly speaking to him on the phone because he was in the penthouse with Tommy going through the books.

'Hi,' Eva said to Roxanne walking in the casino. 'Are you looking for Tommy?'

'Nah – I've just spoken to him because it's dead downstairs. Connor said the girls can go early, so I've come up to see if it's any livelier in here!'

'No, it's dead as well, but I do have this,' said Eva reaching over to a nearly full bottle of champagne.

An hour later, with an empty bottle of champagne sitting on the bar, both girls were merry and telling each other silly jokes.

'I've got one,' said Roxanne, giggling. 'What did Adam say on the day before Christmas? It's Christmas, Eve!'

Eva spat a small spray of champagne out of her mouth as she laughed. 'Me next…Who is never hungry at Christmas?'

'Hmm…dunno?'

'The turkey – he's always stuffed,' bellowed Eva.

'Oh God, that is seriously bad!' Roxanne sighed and shook her head. 'Oh, that might be Tommy,' she said, handing Eva her glass hearing her mobile ring.

'Hi babes… Yeah… Right… Okay then…' Roxanne nodded. 'Five minutes? Yeah – okay.'

'What's happening in five minutes?' asked Eva, handing back her glass.

'Neck it back, Connor said we can go. We've got to meet them out front in five minutes,' said Roxanne, gulping down her champagne.

A swirl of excitement bubbled in Eva's stomach thinking about the romantic night she had planned with her Mrs Santa outfit.

Standing outside the main doors smoking with Roxy, Eva saw Connor walking towards them in a thick black overcoat pulling a large black leather suitcase. She kissed Roxanne goodbye and glanced up at Tommy who had his bah-humbug face on.

'See you Tuesday then, Eva – Merry Christmas!' said Roxanne, kissing her cheek.

'Yes, Merry Christmas, Roxy.' Eva waved and followed Connor to his car.

'Can we open one present each tonight, then the rest tomorrow morning?' asked Eva, her voice full of excitement as he drove out of the car park.

'I know I won't get any peace until I agree,' said Connor reaching over to playfully squeeze her leg.

'I can't wait! Are we giving our main present or a just a stocking filler?'

'Who said I've got you more than one?' replied Connor deadpan, suppressing a smile.

'Oh you!' scoffed Eva, trying to mask her fear of disappointment.

Connor started to laugh and glanced over at her. 'You have a few,' he confessed, securing a playful slap on his leg.

Once back at the house, Eva spotted Mr Jingles lying on the sofa headrest and switched on the Christmas tree lights. 'Shall we have a drink?' she asked. 'I've got a new bottle of Baileys in.'

'I'll just have a tea.'

'Okay,' she said, thinking his choice of tea was slightly boring. She opened the kitchen door and lit a cigarette waiting for the water to boil.

'You've just had a cigarette,' moaned Connor at the waft of smoke scenting the air. 'Maybe that could be your New Year's resolution?'

'I might think about it – anyway,' said Eva walking in with his tea, 'present time!'

Connor opened his case and took out a small bag of gifts.

'Where are all your clothes?' she asked, noticing there weren't many packed.

'I have stuff over there, so I'm just taking over everyone's presents.'

'Oh.' Eva sat down by the tree, waiting excitedly.

Connor rummaged through the bag of gifts on his lap. 'Here you go – Merry Christmas, baby.'

Practically snatching the gold wrapped box from Connor's hand, Eva tore into the paper and gasped seeing a Chanel jewellery box. 'Oh my God!' she gushed. 'Isn't this the one from the auction?'

'Yes, the very same.'

Her mouth gaped open momentarily before saying, 'It's beautiful, just as I remember.' Her chin gave way to a slight wobble. 'It's absolutely perfect,' she added with tears of joy.

'Do I get a kiss, then?' said Connor, enjoying her exhilaration.

She shuffled over on her knees and wrapped her arms around his neck still holding her gift. 'Thank you, I absolutely love it!'

Feeling his tongue slip into her mouth, she closed her eyes for their passionate kiss. Mr Jingles watched, then flopped back down on the headrest to resume his sleep.

'Now yours!' said Eva, breaking away from his kiss and reaching under the Christmas tree.

Connor looked down at the glossy red wrapping paper and read out the message written on the tag, 'To my gorgeous Irishman, Merry Christmas, lots of love Eva and three kisses.' He looked up and smiled. 'Gorgeous, eh?'

Eva impatiently watched him slowly peel back the tape and unfold the paper. She had ripped open her gift like a five-year-old child; there he was tentatively opening his present without a making a single tear.

'Wow…' said Connor looking down at the pair of gold cufflinks.

'Look!' said Eva, pointing excitedly. 'I had your initials engraved on them. I know you wear platinum, but I couldn't afford that, so I—'

'Eva,' interrupted Connor. 'I wear gold, too. They're great – thank you,' he said, giving her a genuine smile of appreciation.

'I have a little something upstairs as well,' said Eva blushing and taking hold of his hand.

'Oh yeah, are you going to give me any clues?'

'Well, it's very short and very sexy.'

'Exactly want I asked Santa for.' Connor chuckled being led upstairs.

She quickly changed into her Mrs Santa sheer negligée with a white fluffy trim in the bathroom as Connor waited in bed.

'Fuck me.' His thick, swollen penis lay across his thigh as he sat up.

'Well that's the plan,' said Eva, raising her eyebrows.

The wide smile on Connor's lips sent a shivering pulse of excitement through her body as she swayed over to him and lay on the bed.

His fingers brushing up her thigh reaching for the top of her white lace stocking gave her goose bumps.

'You're so beautiful, Eva,' he whispered in his soft, velvety Irish drawl.

Eva exhaled deeply as his fingertips probed inside her knickers, quickly finding her clitoris. 'Aaah…' She gasped feeling his middle and index fingers slowly enter her.

'Oh, baby, you're so wet,' croaked Connor, easing his fingers in and out. 'I want to taste you,' he said, throwing the pillow off the bed and lying on his back.

Lifting her leg, Eva straddled Connor's handsome face; her soft breasts pressed against his toned stomach as she guided his thick penis towards her open mouth.

Feeling her lips envelop his penis quickened Connor's tongue, making Eva groan from his firm strokes and flicks.

'Baby,' said Connor, enjoying her hand caressing the shaft of his erection as she sucked and licked with eagerness. '*Fuckkk...*' he growled, quickly shielding his penis from her mouth not wanting the embarrassment of ejaculating so soon.

Feeling her clitoris swell with a surge of unstoppable pleasure made Eva sit bolt upright. She groaned and pressed down further onto Connor's mouth as she came. 'Con-nor!' she rasped while he continued to lick her relentlessly, smearing her orgasm over his lips and chin.

Pressing her hands down onto his hard stomach, she swung her leg over his head and sat on the bed with a rosy flush.

'Take this off,' instructed Connor, flicking the hem of her Santa dress.

She immediately complied and pulled it over her head and let it fall to the floor.

'*Jeszzus!* Connor looking at her intensely. 'I really want you to fuck me hard!' He grabbed her waist and pulled her onto his thighs. '*Baby...*' he growled lustfully, reaching eagerly underneath her, plunging his large erection deep inside.

'Aaah,' she groaned, digging her nails into his chest. Rocking her hips back and forth, she looked down at Connor. He looked so breathtakingly sexy with his blushed cheeks as warm breath billowed out of his mouth.

'*Eva...* fuck me hard!' pleaded Connor, his breath hissing through his teeth with urgency.

Pushing down hard on to him, small beads of perspiration clung above her top lip as she rode him like a champion jockey.

'*Baby, I'm near...!*' cried out Connor, his words tailing off into a breathless gasp.

'Ohh...' murmured Eva, feeling his hard penis plunge deeper and faster into her.

'Fuck, *yeahhh...!*' shouted Connor as an orgasm shot from his body.

'Con-nor!' panted Eva, in stunted gasps, climaxing with him.

'Shit, that was intense!' said Connor, quickly trying to catch his breath. 'I don't think I'll ever tire of you fucking me, Miss Summers,' he added with a beaming smile.

'That's good to hear!' She rolled off his thighs and lay sprawled out on the bed next to him.

'I'll have to put in more hours at the gym to keep up with you,' he said with a smirk, brushing his hand across his damp chest.

'So…' said Eva coyly, 'are we only opening one present tonight?' She rolled onto her side and brushed her hand over his rippled abs.

Connor raised an eyebrow and smiled down at her. 'Yes, you have no patience whatsoever, do you?'

Eva laughed. 'Nope.'

'Do you have any beers in?'

'No sorry, but I've got some wine and Baileys?'

'Go on then, I have a glass of wine,' said Connor, kissing the top of her head.

'Coming right up,' said Eva, climbing off the bed.

'Well, give me a couple minutes,' said Connor, glancing down at her shapely bottom as his penis twitched.

Eva laughed walking out of the bedroom. 'I'll hold you to that!'

Pouring two glasses of wine, she glanced up at her kitchen clock and wondered if Connor was going to stay in bed or come down to watch some TV with her. *Maybe I could talk him into opening another present!* she thought.

She took the wine upstairs only to be greeted by Connor's snoring. With a content smile she quietly backed out of the room.

Back downstairs, she grabbed her coat off the banister and went outside for a smoke. The moon and stars shone like diamonds on a carpet of black velvet. Even though Connor hadn't verbally told her that he loved her, all the signs were there: his attentiveness, big gestures and gifts all spoke to her of his pending love. *You spend hundreds on a jewellery box and thousands on earrings for someone you love, or hoping to fall in love with, not a 'fuck buddy'*, she thought through a haze of pure happiness.

After finishing her cigarette, she hung her coat back on the banister and went upstairs. Connor's gentle snores echoed around the room; she quietly tiptoed over to her chest of drawers and out took a pair of knickers and vest top. She turned around and watched him sleep for second before closing the door and going back downstairs.

Sitting cross-legged on the floor, she ran the tip of her fingers across her neat stack of DVD's. 'Hmm, do I fancy a comedy, a thriller or a horror?' she said to herself. Pressing 'Play', she lay on the sofa with the remainder of the prawn crackers from their takeaway and sighed contentedly watching, for about the two hundredth time, *Pride and Prejudice*.

She plunged her hand into the bag of crackers, grabbed the largest she could find and shoved it into her mouth. She then narrowed her eyes in curiosity at the bag of presents left by Connor's suitcase. The anticipation of not knowing what was hidden beneath the brightly wrapped paper was proving impossible to ignore.

Maybe I could peel back the paper and just take a peek? she thought, with half the cracker still in her mouth. She stopped chewing and turned down the TV to listen for any noises coming from upstairs. Satisfied there was no movement, she licked her fingers and wiped them down her vest top before kneeling down in front of the bag. Her fingers trembled with excitement as she carefully reached inside and pulled out a small box wrapped in gold and red paper with a matching tag saying, *To my beautiful Eva, Merry Christmas, Connor xxx.*

Suppressing a squeal of joy, she gingerly picked at the corner of the paper like a sneaky five-year-old. But the only thing she could make out was the colour of the box inside.

With a deep sigh she debated if she should remove more of the tape or not. *You only have to wait a few more hours, Eva!* she reasoned. Blinking heavily, she nodded to herself and taped up the corner again before placing it back into the bag. She then wondered if he had a 'secret' present for her in his suitcase. For a second she let her imagination run away with her as the image of a large diamond ring consumed her senses. She slowly unzipped his case and peered inside. Connor was telling the truth: along with a pair of black jeans, black T-shirt and a wash bag were his Christmas gifts.

Picking up a heavy square box wrapped in purple wrapping paper, Eva read the gift tag, *To Mum, wishing you a wonderful Christmas, love Connor xx.* She smiled and placed the gift back in his case before picking up a white envelope with a blue bow stuck on it. *To Gabriel, Merry Christmas from Connor,* it read. Eva remembered his brother from the charity gala night. 'Hmm, a cheque,' she muttered, giving it a good shake before putting it back.

Yawning, she went to close the case when a small wrapped box caught her eye. It was covered in the same glossy red paper used for her gift with a matching bow. *Maybe this is my secret gift?* With a nervous flutter and eyes wide in anticipation, she moved the bow to one side and read the message on the small gift tag, *To Cara, Merry Christmas, Connor xxx.* She laughed nervously staring down at Connor's handwriting; shock tightened her throat. She read the message again.

Her hands began to tremble and a wave of nausea washed over her as the box tumbled out of her fingers. With her mouth void of moisture, she glared at the package lying on the floor beside her. She struggled to breathe. She snatched it back up and tore at the red paper. With her fingers hovering over the lid, she closed her eyes and swallowed hard.

'*Oh God!*' she whimpered, staring down at a beautiful pair of half-carat diamond stud earrings. A searing pain gripped her chest; bile stung the back of her throat. Through a haze of despair, she felt disoriented as though she were drunk. Letting the box drop from her hands again, she reached over and grabbed Connor's mobile sitting on the coffee table in front of her. It took all her composure to stop the tremor in her hands as she scanned down his list of contacts.

'What the hell are you doing?'

Instantly dropping his phone, Eva gasped in shock at Connor standing in the lounge doorway wearing just a pair of black boxer shorts.

'I SAID, what the *hell* are you doing going through my phone?!' he barked, his cheeks ablaze with rage.

Catching her breath, her eyes stung with tears as she let out a deep breathless cry. 'YOU LIAR!' she screamed up at him. 'Oh God.' She slammed her clenched fist against her chest. 'Jesus Christ, it's all been lies!'

'What the fuck are you going on about?' cursed Connor, bending down and snatching his mobile off the floor. 'Have you been through my SUITCASE as well?!' he bellowed, looking down at the diamond earrings shimmering in their box next to Eva.

'You're a fifthly cheat!' she cried, getting to her feet.

Fear washed over Connor's face as he attempted to reach out to her. 'It's not what you think!'

'DON'T TOUCH ME,' yelled Eva, now screaming hysterically. 'GET OUT! GET OUT!'

'JUST CALM DOWN AND LET ME EXPLAIN,' Connor shouted back. 'It's not what you think. I bought those months ago, they don't mean anything!' he pleaded before dodging the flight path of the earring box as it came hurtling towards him.

'LIAR!'

'I *have* finished with her. There's no hidden meaning behind them. I thought I couldn't give them to you, so she might as well have them. I don't hate her – God! She has done nothing to be hated for – they mean nothing, she means nothing!'

'OPEN YOUR PHONE!' demanded Eva trembling with rage, her face contorted with hate.

'What?'

'You heard what I said. OPEN YOUR PHONE!' she screamed with watery, wide eyes.

'STOP screaming at me!' warned Connor, his piercing blue eyes darkened with fury. 'I am telling you the truth. Throw them in the fucking bin if you want to, they mean NOTHING to me!' he added, raising his voice.

'Give me your phone, then!' seethed Eva, her heart pounding against her chest.

'Why? What are you hoping to find? Texts full of betrayal? I am telling you the truth,' he said. 'Yes, okay,' admitted Connor restlessly running his fingers through his hair, 'I admit, it could look a bit suspicious, but I promise you, I'm not lying. There's nothing still going on between me and Cara!'

'Believe you!' Eva grimaced, shaking her head. 'The truth would choke a man like you!'

'I AM NOT GOING TO ADMIT TO SOMETHING I HAVEN'T DONE!' he hollered, clenching his fists down by his side.

His vociferousness made Eva quickly step back from him.

Realising his temper was frightening her, Connor softened his tone. 'She is an old acquaintance, as you know. A fuck buddy, whatever you want to call her. She is just one person in a circle of friends that I will be seeing on Christmas Day at a family gathering. I am not going back to see her with any romantic inclinations, whatsoever!'

'PROVE IT – SHOW ME YOUR PHONE, CONNOR!'

'NO! You either believe me or you don't.'

'I DON'T!' wailed Eva. 'I want you to LEAVE!'

'Don't do this, Eva,' implored Connor, his voice low and anxious. 'Baby, I swear you have nothing to worry about. You can trust me one hundred percent. You're wrong. I promise I'm telling you the truth!'

Eva sniffed loudly before composing herself. 'I want you to leave, please.'

'If I go, then we're finished for good,' croaked Connor, his voice tight with emotion.

'Yes, I understand,' said Eva coldly. 'I still want you to leave. I am not going to give my love to another lying cheat – I won't!' she cried, desolation making her hunch over with pain.

'For fuck's sake,' said Connor, his eyes watering and full of despondency. 'I won't go to Ireland, then. I'll cancel my flight. I won't see her. We can talk all night if you want?'

'It's too late!' said Eva, her back now rigid and straight. 'My heart is lying next to those earrings on floor. You've ripped it out, Connor – there's no putting it back. You put her gift in your case, so the least you can do now is to make sure she receives it!' she sneered bitterly.

'Shit, Eva,' said Connor in despair, 'please tell me how I can make things right between us. I don't want to lose you over a thoughtless mistake!'

'How apt! You're the thoughtless one, so that makes me the *mistake*, eh, Connor?'

'Stop talking like a crazy woman and twisting my words – you know what I mean!'

'You led me to believe that you cared about me. Tina was right, you don't have a heart!'

'*Oh God!*' Connor laughed. 'Do you think I'd put up with all your shit if I didn't care?' he said nastily.

'Yeah, maybe while your dick is inside me, but when it's not I'm just a forgettable fumble,' sneered Eva, quoting the spite-flavoured words he so viciously said to Tina.

'I'm not having this!' roared Connor, picking up the earring box and throwing it at the wall with such force that the earrings flew out of the box. 'You're REALLY pushing me to my limit!' he continued. 'You want to finish this – yeah?' he baited, his eyes flared and wild. 'Then say it, Eva… SAY in front of me that we're finished for good because once you say it, I promise you here and now that you will not exist to me once I walk out that door!'

Eva could barely speak trying to choke back her tears. With her legs feeling as though they would buckle at any second, she stared up at Connor as she composed herself. 'W… We are f-finished,' she mumbled passively.

'*Jesus Christ,*' murmured Connor, his voice hoarse and trembling. '*You have no idea what you've just done to me.*'

With her whole body trembling, she watched Connor walk over to his suitcase in silence and drop it down by the front door before going upstairs. A couple of minutes later he came back down, reached into his pocket and threw the spare door key on the stairs. Without a backwards glance, he grabbed his coat and picked up his case before slamming the door behind him.

Eva flopped onto the sofa, wrapped her arms around her body and rocked gently as emptiness engulfed her.

Chapter 26

Christmas and Boxing Day passed in a blur of tear-filled drunkenness. Eva listened to soul-wrenching music, playing Toni Braxton's 'Unbreak My Heart' on loop. With her hair unwashed and clothes stained, she didn't recognise the unkempt woman staring back at her in the lounge mirror. Reaching for another glass of wine, she loudly slurred the words to Aerosmith's 'I Don't Want To Miss A Thing' surrounded by empty wine bottles littering the lounge floor.

During a breather of her one-woman karaoke session, she saw her mobile screen flash. She gulped down the entire contents of her drink and tried to focus her blurred vision.

OMG – I've just heard that you and Connor have split up – do you need to talk? Roxanne xxxx.

Eva sighed heavily, dropped her phone on the sofa and cranked up the volume of her stereo before pouring herself another large glass of Merlot. She couldn't hear Mrs Simms knocking on the front door or Roxanne's second text pinging through to her mobile; she was completely cocooned in a dark tomb of misery and pain. No one could help or comfort her until she pieced back the shattered pieces of her heart, which meant more alcohol and an endless playlist of sad songs.

* * *

'Eh…' croaked Eva, her eyes flickered open lying face down on the hallway floor surrounded by a pool of vomit.

'Eva!' screamed Roxanne, peering through the letterbox. 'Hold on, I'm coming!'

With a loud bang Eva's front door shuddered and the letterbox clattered loudly.

'Boot it in, Tommy!' Roxanne cried out from the other side of the door.

With another loud thud the door flung open.

'Eva!' shouted Roxanne, throwing her handbag on the floor and falling to her knees.

'M-mum,' Eva groaned.

'Babe, it's Roxanne, you're okay now,' she soothed, lifting her head out of the pool of sick. 'Tommy, I need you to carry her upstairs so I can clean her up!' she cried.

Shoving the door shut Tommy turned around and looked down at Eva. 'Roxy, she's covered in puke,' he said, wrinkling his nose. 'I'm not touching her.'

'You have got two choices, Tommy Jakeman, you either carry her upstairs or you can live the rest of your life as a *monk*, so choose!' shouted Roxanne, glaring up at him.

'Fucking hell!' he cursed, turning his face away from the pungent smell as he lifted Eva into his arms.

'No – the bathroom!' Roxanne barked seeing him head towards a bedroom. 'Sit her up, don't lie her down on the cold floor!' she ordered.

'OKAY!' Tommy shot back. 'Jesus – my best mate has gone AWOL, and here I am pandering to the cause of his disappearance – you couldn't write this shit!'

'Oh shut up, Connor has texted you!'

'I had one text on Christmas Day telling me they'd finished. He didn't catch his flight to Ireland. I've had his mum phoning me every five minutes going out of her mind with worry. I should be out looking for him, but, instead, I have to deal with *this*.'

'He'll turn up, he always does. He's probably nursing his ego with some tart while my friend lies here choking on her own vomit!'

'She's fine,' moaned Tommy, turning his back when Roxanne started to remove Eva's dirty clothes. 'She's just hammered, that's all. After she's slept it off she'll be fine. Whereas Connor has disappeared off the face of the earth!'

'Have you checked with his Irish tart, what's her name…that fucking Cara!'

'She hasn't heard from him either. That's what I'm saying, no one has seen or heard from him for three days!' Tommy remained turned around when Roxanne held Eva under the shower and washed her.

Roxanne dressed Eva in a clean T-shirt and put her to bed on her side bolstered by pillows to stop her rolling over.

'Can you nip back home and get me some clean underwear and my phone charger, please,' asked Roxanne on their way back downstairs.

'What?' Tommy said frowning. 'You're not coming home tonight?'

'Of course I'm not. I can't leave her on her own.'

'Oh fucking great!' complained Tommy. 'I knew this would happen.'

'What would happen?'

'I told Connor not to hire her, but would he listen?! She's just like his ex Maria, and look how that ended!'

'What, you think Connor had something to do with her death?'

'Would you blame him if he had? He lost two years of his life for that cheating bitch. She nearly drove him mad with her fucking mind games and lies.

'Eva's nothing like her!' snapped Roxanne, turning around with an arm full of empty wine bottles and a scowl.

'Ha!' mocked Tommy, shaking his head. 'Maybe not the cheating, but she whacked Chu, then Black drops down dead alone with her. None of the other girls like her after she made Connor tear a strip off Tina, and now she's pulling you away from me!'

'And now for the truth!' said Roxanne dryly, placing the empty bottles down on the coffee table. 'Chu tried to molest her while Connor, *your best mate*, stood back and did nothing. Yes, Black died of a heart attack, but you forgot to mention one crucial fact, Black was morbidly obese and one AA meeting away from being a chronic alcoholic. So that just leaves Tina, where shall we start? Tina has been obsessed with Connor since the day she started there. She's spiteful, vindictive and jealous of Eva in every possible way because Eva is everything she's not – beautiful, kind and has Connor lusting after her like a dog on heat!'

Tommy stood towering over her with a furrowed brow and relented. 'So just some underwear and your phone charger, then?'

'Yes, that would be great – thank you.'

'Can I have a kiss before I go?' he asked, in a sulk.

'Yes, if you want one.'

'Well, I do,' huffed Tommy, lifting her three feet off the floor to reach her mouth.

'I don't like it when we argue,' he said, his eyes wide and full of need.

'Then stop always taking Connor's side. Eva's a nice girl who's had her heart repeatedly broken by shitty men, so until both of us know the facts, we won't judge either – yes?'

'Yeah, okay,' agreed Tommy glumly, hugging her tightly.

'Now put me down before you squeeze the life out of me.'

'Love you baby…' said Tommy, hovering by the lounge door.

'Love you too, Mr Jakeman,' said Roxanne. 'See you in half an hour.'

With Roxanne's declaration of love lifting Tommy's spirits, he smiled contentedly before walking out of the lounge.

***

'W-what time is it?' muttered Eva, finding herself in bed with Roxanne beside her.

'Hi babe, how are you feeling?'

'Like hell!' grumbled Eva, rolling onto her back.

Roxanne got out of bed and drew back the curtains a little before returning her attention to Eva. 'You don't look well, babes,' she said, noticing her sallow complexion. 'You frightened the life out of me yesterday. I dread to think what would've happened if we hadn't found you. Tommy had to kick your door in. He's repaired it the best he can.'

'Sorry, I just needed oblivion.'

'Do you want to talk about it?'

Eva sighed. 'I'm sure Tommy must know all the facts.'

'No one has seen Connor,' explained Roxanne, shoving a pillow behind her back as she got back into bed. 'He didn't catch his flight to Ireland. Tommy received a text Christmas Day saying you had split up, but that's the last he heard from him.'

'I'm surprised he isn't with his *tart*, the lying snake!'

'Who, Cara?' asked Roxanne softly.

'Yeah,' said Eva, her swollen eyes glistening with tears. 'He bought her a pair of diamond earrings for Christmas. What a lovely romantic gesture, don't you think?' she snarled, wiping her tears away.

'How did you find out?'

'I found them in his suitcase. They weren't even hidden!' she scoffed miserably. 'Of course, he denied anything was still going on. He just said he bought the earring months ago, and it didn't feel right to give them to me, so he decided she might as well have them.'

'Perhaps it was a "goodbye" present?' reasoned Roxanne delicately.

'And if Tommy had done the same?'

Roxanne lowered her gaze realising, in the same situation, her actions would have mirrored her friend's. 'I don't know what to say.'

'*I told you so?*' said Eva, a tremor of despondency making her chin tremble. 'I should've listened, so now I'm paying the price for falling in love with a lying, heartless bastard.'

'You did nothing wrong, babes!' assured Roxanne. 'Connor is a heartless shit for doing this to you. I honestly don't know what's going on in his head. Tommy only said a couple of weeks ago that there's been a real change in him. He seemed really happy and content, so this callousness doesn't make sense.'

'Christmas Eve had been perfect up to that point,' stated Eva. 'THEN BANG! My world came crashing in. I asked him to show me his phone to prove he was telling the truth, which he wouldn't do of course. Do you know what he said?' jeered Eva, curling her top lip. *'That I should believe him without him having to prove his innocence!'*

'Well, I still can't believe what he did,' said Roxanne simply. 'Surely if he wanted *her*, why didn't he go back home to Ireland to be with her?'

'Perhaps she's flown out to be with him.'

'No…' added Roxanne, shaking her head in disagreement. 'Connor's mum has been phoning Tommy – she's really worried. Perhaps he's genuinely heartbroken and gone away to lick his wounds.'

'Yeah,' mocked Eva, with a weary smile. 'Heartbroken! That would mean he has a heart, which we both know he doesn't!'

Roxanne exhaled deeply. 'What about work – are you coming back to the Unicorn?'

'Of course,' Eva said sharply. 'I've spent my life running away from heartless bastards, but no more. Fuck men, and fuck Connor O'Neill!'

Chapter 27

'God, you look rough!' said Donna with a grimace glancing at Eva and Roxanne walking into the dressing room.

'We went to a party last night, so what?' snapped Roxanne.

'No punter is gonna pay to look at her tonight – no matter how much make-up she slaps on!' added Donna curtly.

Ignoring Donna's attempts to provoke her, Eva slumped down at her dressing table as a wave of nausea swept over her. She was sick before leaving the house and felt as if she needed to throw up again. She rushed to the toilet and heard Roxanne knock against the cubicle door.

'Babe, are you okay?'

'I feel as sick as a dog,' mumbled Eva, opening the door and wiping her mouth with a handful of toilet tissue. 'I have a really sharp pain in my side?' She frowned, rubbing her hand over her pelvic bone.

'Right, I'm taking you home!' insisted Roxanne. 'You can't work like this. I'll tell Tommy to drop us back at yours.'

Eva didn't offer any resistance hearing Roxanne argue with Tommy down on phone.

'Roxy...' croaked Eva, 'I'll get a cab!'

Roxanne pressed her mobile to her chest and held out her other hand. 'Tommy can take us – end of!'

Eva, in no position to argue, put down the loo seat and sat with her head in her hands.

'Oh, so he's alive then...!' said Roxanne loudly, pacing the floor.

Eva lifted her head listening to Roxanne's conversation.

'Where's he been? Eh... That figures! Okay, I'll see you out front in five.'

Scarlett stopped curling her hair seeing them both walk back into the dressing room. She looked over at Donna and nodded. 'Is she going home? You do know Tina's called in sick and Vicky's booked a holiday – who's going to cover her shift?'

'It's dead out there tonight,' sniped Roxanne, slipping her arm around Eva's waist. 'I'm sure between everyone you can cover our shifts!'

'She's not even ill!' piped up Donna. 'She's drunk! It's a good job Ann isn't here, but I guess when you're screwing the boss, the rules don't apply – do they!'

'Get a life, Donna, or get out of the one you're in!' fired back Roxanne on their way out of the dressing room.

With a heavy frown advertising his mood, Tommy stormed over to Eva and Roxanne waiting in the lobby. 'Let's go!' he said, glancing down at his watch.

They led Eva down the black granite steps. The cold, blustery wind made them gasp as it crawled at their warm cheeks.

'I hope she isn't gonna be sick everywhere!' snapped Tommy, unlocking his car.

'I just feel dizzy,' reassured Eva, climbing into the back, quickly lying into a foetal position.

'So you must be happy to hear your best buddy is *alive*?' whipped Roxanne.

'I'm not talking about this now,' said Tommy, reversing out of the club's car park.

Roxanne glared over at Tommy with pursed lips before glancing over her shoulder at Eva. 'I'm going to stay with Eva again tonight. I'm really worried about her.'

'I gathered you would be!' Tommy replied sulkily.

'Oh, drop the attitude, please!'

'Attitude!' Tommy widened his eyes and released a mocking laugh. 'I have to spend another night on my own because of *her*! It's like looking after a bloody toddler!'

'You'd do the same for Connor!'

'He would never burden his mates with his so-called "feelings". He's an adult!'

'Correct me if I'm wrong, but isn't he the creator of all her misery? He's the reason why you're sleeping alone tonight, Tommy Jakeman!'

'No, she—'

'I don't want to discuss it any further!' barked Roxanne. 'Just drive, please.'

Tommy cursed under his breath and slammed on the accelerator making the car jerk forward. Not long into the journey he flashed his headlights and shouted at a cyclist who had to swerve into the gutter to avoid them.

'Let's try not to kill anyone tonight – shall we!' fumed Roxanne.

Tommy jolted the car to a halt after pulling into a petrol station, sending Eva across the back seat and earning Tommy another scathing glare from Roxanne.

'Do you want anything?' growled Tommy, getting out of the car.

'No, but if they're selling personality transplants, treat yourself!' said Roxanne before quickly looking at Eva and offering her the sweetest smile. 'Not long now, babes.'

'I've got no energy?' whimpered Eva.

'Well, you've put your liver through the mill over the last couple of days. Your body needs to detox, babes,' explained Roxanne, seeing Tommy walk back to the car.

'Here.' Tommy threw a packet of cigarettes into Roxanne's lap as he reached for his seatbelt.

Thanks,' said Roxanne raising an eyebrow. His gift was an obvious plea for a truce because Tommy hated her smoking and always refused to buy her cigarettes unless he was trying to soften her mood.

Roxanne glanced over her shoulder at Eva fast asleep as they pulled up outside her house.

'Can you—'

'Yes, I know the drill!' fumed Tommy, flinging open the driver door and getting out.

'Arrrgh!' shrieked Eva.

'Tommy – you're not grappling a bloody punter!' seethed Roxanne, watching him grab Eva by the ankles and roughly jerk her towards him.

Holding Eva in his arms, Tommy grimaced like an unenthusiastic groom while Roxanne rummaged for the front door key.

'Take her straight upstairs, please,' instructed Roxanne.

'You're coming up too, aren't you?' asked Tommy quickly.

'Why are you acting so weird?'

'I don't like being alone with my best mate's ex-girlfriend! I don't want Connor thinking I've taken her side.'

'Oh grow up! I don't care what Connor may or may not think!'

'Argh! I can't talk to you when you're like this,' moaned Tommy, stomping up the stairs carrying Eva. He flopped her onto the bed like a sack of potatoes, then went back downstairs to the kitchen where Roxanne was making a drink.

'Did you cover her up?'

'No…' sulked Tommy shaking his head, 'you never asked me to.'

Roxanne gave a huge sigh and handed him a cup of coffee.

'I'd better get back to the club,' he said, glancing down at his watch before taking a sip of his drink. 'I'll phone you later – yeah?'

'Yeah, okay.' Roxanne nodded watching him put down his mug and walk down the hall.

'Love you!' called back Tommy, turning to face her as he lifted the door latch.

'Love you too, moody arse.' Roxanne smiled but then winced when he slammed the door making the letterbox clatter behind him.

* * *

'Eva…'

'Hmm…?'

'It's midday, babes. I've made you some toast.'

'I'm not hungry…' Eva sighed, pulling the bed covers over her face.

'Just have a couple of bites for me, please?' pleaded Roxanne, hovering over her.

Peering from behind the duvet, Eva's eyes looked puffy and red against her colourless complexion with clumps of hair stuck to her warm face.

'When you've finished, maybe you can take a shower and get dressed? You'll feel better.'

'Yeah, okay,' said Eva with a nod. She sat up and struggled to swallow her toast. After her shower she went into the kitchen.

'I've fed your cat and made us a drink.' Roxanne smiled and handed her a mug of milky, sweet coffee.

Eva frowned taking a sip. 'Ugh, I think the milk is off!' She wrinkled her nose smelling the hot steam.

'Mine's okay,' said Roxanne having a sniff at her own drink.

Eva poured it down the sink, then winced as a sharp spasm pinched her groin. 'If this pain doesn't go within the next day or so I'll have to go to the doctors,' she said, shuffling out of the kitchen and down the hall.

'I'll google your symptoms, babes?' called out Roxanne from the kitchen.

'Okay,' said Eva, making her way upstairs to the bathroom. She looked at her pasty appearance in the cabinet mirror and groaned. After opening the small mirrored-door she stared in horror at the unopened box of tampons sitting on the second shelf.

'*Oh shit… Roxanne!*'

There was a loud clatter downstairs before Roxanne burst into the bathroom shrieking, 'WHAT IS IT?'

'This is unopened!' cried Eva.

Roxanne looked at the box in her hand, then at Eva. 'So?'

'I bought them over a month ago! My period should have been THREE WEEKS AGO!'

'Are you sure?'

'I need to sit down,' muttered Eva, gripping onto the edge of the sink.

'Don't fucking panic!' wailed Roxanne, starting to panic. 'Er…why don't you lie down for a minute,' she said, raising her hand to her brow. 'I'll go to the chemist and get you a pregnancy test. You could just be late?'

'Yes, you're right,' said Eva, her voice quivering.

'Are you normally late?'

'No, I'm never late! I haven't missed a pill, or noticed anything strange!'

'Look, I'll be ten minutes,' said Roxanne, dashing out of the bathroom and downstairs.

Hearing the front door slam shut, Eva's mind started to race recalling Connor's repeated warnings: *I don't want any accidents complicating my life – I can trust you, can't I, Eva?*

'It's just a false alarm,' mumbled Eva, trying to reassure herself as she walked into her bedroom. 'I'm just late,' she added, before lying down and disappearing under the duvet. She closed her eyes and repeated these words like a mantra until exhaustion and fear lead her into a restless nap.

'Eva – I'm back!' shouted Roxanne.

'Eh…' Eva jerked, opening her eyes.

'Where are you, upstairs?'

'Yes!' called out Eva, flinging back the bedding and leaping out of bed.

Roxanne joined her in the bathroom. 'I got two.'

'Right…' Eva inhaled nervously pulling down her jogging bottoms and underwear.

'You have to wee on the stick, then wait for three minutes,' added Roxanne, reading the instructions on the back of the box.

A cluster of nerves tightened in her belly. 'I can't go!'

'I'll get you a glass of water,' said Roxanne, racing out of the bathroom.

Feeling nauseous again, Eva lowered her head into her hands waiting for her.

Roxanne shoved a tall glass of water in her hand. 'Right, drink all this.'

Eva gulped down the water in loud, snorting breaths, then handed back the empty glass.

After a long, agonising five minutes, Eva managed to pee.

Roxanne took a large intake of breath. 'Now we wait,' she said anxiously, perching her bottom on the rim of the bath.

'Three minutes, you said?' asked Eva, getting to her feet and flushing the loo.

'Yes...' Roxanne answered, tapping her fingers against her thighs.

'I can't sit here and wait,' said Eva. 'I need a cigarette!'

Leaving the tester on the bathroom windowsill, they went downstairs into the back garden.

'My mum lives in Spain, and I don't have any other family nearby. I have no support!' explained Eva, inhaling deeply on her cigarette.

'You have me,' soothed Roxanne with a sympathetic smile.

'I know and I'm so grateful,' said Eva, starting to well up. 'But I can't keep it.'

'Look,' reasoned Roxanne, gently brushing away her friend's tears, 'I know the situation isn't perfect, but I'm sure Connor would provide for the child financially – you wouldn't be destitute. It'd be more beneficial for him to arrange a private agreement than going through the CSA.'

'But that'd mean I'd have to tell him!' said Eva, sniffing.

'Of course,' replied Roxanne as a billow of smoke left her mouth. 'You've got to tell him if you are.'

'I'm not keeping it,' whimpered Eva. 'Look at the mess I've made of my life. I would be a useless mother.'

'Stop talking nonsense, you'd be a great. You're kind, caring and will find the strength from somewhere, even if you have to move to Spain to live with your mum.'

'Let's hope I don't have to make that choice!'

'There's only one way to find out,' said Roxanne, stubbing out her cigarette. 'Let's go and find out if you have Connor's baby growing in your belly!'

Eva stood outside the bathroom. She took a deep breath trying to steady her jelly-like legs. 'You look, Roxy,' she croaked.

'Okay...'

Eva waited anxiously for Roxanne to call out her fate.

'Roxy?' There was still silence. 'Roxy, what does it say?'

Walking slowly out of the bathroom holding the white and blue pregnancy tester, Roxanne lifted her gaze. 'You're pregnant...'

'No, you're wrong!' cried Eva, shaking her head. 'It's not true!' A soul-curdling cry leapt from her mouth. 'It can't be true!'

'I'm sorry, but it's true – it says two weeks, so according to the leaflet it means you're four weeks pregnant.' Roxanne started to sob handing her the pregnancy tester.

After an hour of resting in bed, Eva heard Roxanne's raised voice coming from downstairs. She sat at the top of the stairs to listen.

'I told you she isn't coming in tonight… She isn't well, Connor!'

Eva's body jerked hearing his name; she crept down to the middle of the staircase.

'Well, it's tough, can't you ask one of the other girls to entertain Marshall. I don't care if he has asked for her, *she isn't well*! I swear on my life if you storm round here and cause a scene, I *will* stop you from entering the house. Read into that what you will, Connor. It would take a bigger and better man than you to get past me. What? No, she isn't just drunk! Is that Tommy in the background?' barked Roxanne. 'Tell him we'll be having words later!'

Eva started to chew her fingernails when Roxanne went quiet.

'What… Tommy hasn't said anything? Hmm… Anyway, Eva isn't coming in tonight… Bye!'

Eva felt uneasy making her way into the lounge.

'Argh…the conceited, narcissistic, bas—' Seeing Eva made Roxanne jump. 'Oh… How are you feeling, babes?'

'Okay, I guess – who was that on the phone?' asked Eva innocently, sitting down on the sofa with a blanket wrapped around her shoulders.

Roxanne dropped the mobile into her bag and shook her head. 'Fucking PPI. God knows how they got my number!'

'I heard you say Connor…' Eva said softly.

'Oh… Sorry – I just thought you didn't need any more stress today.'

Eva managed a faint appreciative smile. 'What did he say about Ted?'

'Ted's at the club asking for you.'

'Can you phone him back and tell him that I'll be in work tonight, please?'

'But you're not well enough,' argued Roxanne.

'Not for dancing, I know, but I can sit with Marshall. I'm still going to need my job.'

'But Connor's in vile mood. He'll be on your back as soon as you go in. Can you handle seeing him so soon after finding out…you know?' asked Roxanne, glancing down at Eva's belly.

'What? That I'm carrying his child – yes.'

Roxanne shook her head in despair and took out her mobile. 'I'll tell Tommy to pick us up at six thirty, then.'

Tommy beeped his horn outside at six thirty on the dot.

Eva felt nauseous in the back of the car. Tommy and Roxanne sat in silence. She was relieved when they finally pulled into the club's car park.

She took a deep breath walking through the lobby. Two of the staff refilling the bar and three topless barmaids stared over at her and whispered indiscreetly.

'What are you doing back? I thought you were supposed to be *ill?*' sniped Donna, nudging Tina.

'And a Merry Christmas to you, too!' mocked Roxanne, displaying a spurious smile, following Eva into the dressing room.

'Just going to the loo,' said Eva, dumping her handbag on her dressing table.

'Connor's in a foul mood tonight,' stated Tina. 'Personally I think he's come to his senses and is embarrassed that he even *went there*,' she added, giving Eva a toxic stare.

'Put a cork in it, Tina,' said Roxanne, shoving her handbag into her locker. 'No one is interested in what you think or have to say.'

Tina inhaled deeply. 'Well...' She paused to flick a long strand of bleached blonde hair over her shoulder. 'He's not the only one to come to his senses. I've decided that he doesn't *deserve me*,' announced Tina conceitedly.

'Tina,' scoffed Roxanne, '*no one deserves you!*'

'Someone is chucking up their guts in there!' said Scarlett, wrinkling her nose as she came out of the toilets.

'Whatever she's got, it better not be catching!' Donna grimaced and held a tissue under her nose. It's New Year's Eve tomorrow, and I have a party to go to. I don't want to get sick.'

Roxanne quickly made her way to the loos. Ann was already in there.

'I just want a word with Eva in my office, if you don't mind, Roxanne.'

Eva rinsed her mouth and looked at Ann's pinched lips and arched brow.

'Is this about me and Connor?' asked Eva simply.

'Yes...'

'Roxanne knows everything.'

'Well then, shall we all go into my office?' said Ann, holding open the toilet door.

Eva and Roxanne both walked in silence wondering what fresh 'drama' was coming next.

Sighing heavily, Ann sat down and motioned for them take a seat. 'I don't know who I'm more disappointed with, you or Mr O'Neill?' stated Ann, removing her glasses and rubbing the two red indentations on her nose.

'Is he going to sack me?' asked Eva bluntly.

'He can't sack her, can he?' butted in Roxanne.

'Stop,' said Ann, holding out her hands. 'No one is getting fired. Mr O'Neill has spoken to me about the "situation".'

'*The situation*,' scoffed Roxanne, shaking her head.

'Indeed,' said Ann curtly, slipping on her glasses and reaching over for a piece of paper on her desk.

'Mr O'Neill is opening another club in the West Midlands and thought Eva might want—'

'He wants me to relocate?' said Eva wearily.

'This is horseshit!' snapped Roxanne, getting to her feet.

'Let's just take a minute here.'

'Considering the intensity of the *situation*, working in such close proximity is going to be uncomfortable for both parties. You may feel, Eva…' said Ann softly, 'that you're being banished from the Unicorn, but you have a good opportunity to become the principal dancer at this new club. Mr O'Neill acknowledges that you're a good dancer – he has never tarnished your ability or creativeness.'

'When does he want my answer by?'

'What?' seethed Roxanne staring down at Eva who sat expressionless and calm.

Ann's silence spoke volumes; Connor wanted her answer that night.

Eva got to her feet. 'I'll let you know by the end of my shift.'

Ann nodded. 'Okay, it would be a new start for you, Eva. Think carefully before you give me your answer.'

Walking back to her dressing table, Eva was aware that Roxanne was talking but couldn't unscramble the words to make sense of them: shock had anaesthetised her mind. She went through the motions of applying her make-up oblivious to the whispers and stares circling her like a pack of wolves.

'See you at nine, babes,' Roxanne said warmly, accompanied by a frown of concern watching Eva walk straight past her table.

Eva left the dressing room wondering if she could reach the casino without being sick.

Chapter 28

Dressed in a figure-hugging black velvet cocktail dress, Eva's hair was pinned up highlighting a pair of purple diamanté drop earrings. Such a vision of elegance secured her with the attention of a large group of men standing by the casino entrance.

'Evening, beautiful,' called out one of the men.

Eva pretended not to hear and tried to find Ted through the sea of black dinner jackets. A group of men moved away from one of the circular tables clearing the way to see Ted in his white Stetson next to Tommy. Also stood there was Connor.

Anguish and sadness took the strength from her legs; she swallowed hard and unconsciously placed her hand on her stomach.

'Miss Eva!' bellowed Ted, noticing her standing awkwardly in the centre of the room. 'Come and join us!'

Her chin trembled with apprehension; she forced a smile and willed her legs to move.

'Merry Christmas, Miss Eva!' said Ted adoringly. 'May I be so bold and say how utterly bewitching you look tonight.'

'Thank you,' said Eva, her voice faltering.

She couldn't help herself glancing up at Connor whose face was expressionless. He kept his gaze high to avoid her stare.

'Your boss here has intrigued us all by not revealing how he came to get such a scratch on his face. Maybe you can enlighten us, or get him to reveal the story behind it,' said Ted with a chuckle.

Eva couldn't see what he was talking about.

'Show the lady,' said Ted, bemused by Connor's reluctance to indulge them.

Eva muffled a faint gasp when he turned to his right and revealed an angry raised scratch tailing down his cheek.

Eva thought it looked like a deep fingernail mark. 'What happened?' she asked.

Connor's refusal to acknowledge her question caused even more interest than the mysterious wound itself.

'Well…' said Ted, tasting bitterness in the air, 'Miss Eva, let me get you a drink – champagne?'

'Just a soft drink for me please.'

'Partied too wildly over the holidays – eh?' Ted laughed and offered a warm smile. 'So what shall we do? Play the slots or blackjack?' he asked, securing the attention of one of the waiters.

With a stutter of hesitation Eva swallowed hard. 'Er... M-maybe later, if you don't mind.'

Connor exhaled deeply and quickly turned on his heels and left the group. His anger had quite the opposite effect to the one he had intended; his displeasure had given Eva her first genuine smile for over five days.

'Are you okay, Miss Eva,' probed Ted, offering his hand as she clambered up onto a high stool.

'Actually, I haven't been well over Christmas, so I feel a little out of sorts – sorry.'

'Don't apologise. Is there anything I can do to ease your discomfort?'

Eva gave Ted her second genuine smile of the evening. She thought if only he was thirty years younger and banished his love of rhinestone, he would be perfect for her.

'Excuse me, Mr Marshall,' said Tommy, producing a rare smile that transformed his normally unappealing features into a rather rugged and attractive appearance, 'can I just have a quick word with Eva?'

Eva kissed Ted's cheek and followed Tommy out into the casino foyer.

'What are you playing at?' hissed Tommy, his face returning to its usual sour grimace.

Feeling tired and irritable, Eva snapped back at him, 'I'm not playing at anything, so get off my back!'

'Have you forgotten why you're here? Marshall is worth over eighty million, so he can afford to lose a little loose change tonight. Stop treating him like your sweet little grandfather and guide him over to the roulette tables!'

'If you want his money so badly, why don't you just steal his wallet and be done with it?!' snarled Eva.

'Look at you...' He stepped back looking her up down under an obnoxious frown. 'Don't take the moral ground with me, you're nothing special,' he growled viciously.

'What is your problem, Tommy? Can't bully a strong woman?!'

'You're not strong. You're one of those women who break hearts and rip friendships apart for sick kicks. You've alienated all the other dancers with your high and mighty attitude. You've caused rows between me and Roxy with your "*poor me*" routine.'

'What?' said Eva, blinking back tears.

'I can't believe Connor has fallen for the empty allure of such a heartless bitch. *Again!* Do you know what it took for him to trust another woman – do you!' seethed Tommy. 'Thanks to you, he took his eye off the ball and stands to lose this place if your *old flame* Booth opens a new club a hundred yards from the Unicorn!'

'THAT'S ENOUGH!'

Eva spun around hearing Connor's voice booming behind them.

'Go upstairs, Eva, I want a word with Tommy in private,' ordered Connor, glaring at Tommy. 'MOVE!' he roared.

His strident voice made her jump and run towards the lift. Too frightened to look back, she slammed her hand against the lift button while Connor and Tommy exchanged a barrage of angry words. She rushed inside and averted her gaze to the floor waiting for the doors to slowly close. Eva looked into the mirrored wall and was shocked to see how withdrawn she looked. Even with heavy make-up she looked gaunt from not eating for the last five days. Another wave of nausea washed over her as she stepped out of the lift and approached Connor's apartment.

'What are you doing up here?' quizzed Eva seeing Tina close the door.

'W-what?' said Tina looking startled and nervous. 'Nothing. Ann asked me to bring up Connor's post.'

Eva blinked in astonishment at Tina's civil reply. There was no sarcasm or bitter attack, which was totally out of character for her. 'Right…' she said, watching Tina dash towards the back stairs. Eva's mobile suddenly ringing distracted her.

'It's nine o'clock, babes, where are you?' asked Roxanne.

'I'm outside the penthouse waiting for Connor.'

'Why – what's happened?'

Eva sighed wearily. 'I'll tell you later.'

'Do you need me to come up?'

'No – I'm okay, but you know what? The more I think about the Birmingham job, the more I think it would be a good idea. I need to get out of this fucking place.'

'Don't decide any ye…?'

'Get off the phone, Eva!'

Spinning around, with her mobile still pressed to her ear, Eva stared up at Connor storming past.

'I'll speak to you later,' whispered Eva, quickly turning off her phone and dropping it back into her bag.

'Shut the door after you.'

Eva complied and clasped her hands tightly in front of her.

'Did Ann mention the Birmingham club?'

'Yes.'

'So?' he barked coldly, dabbing his two-inch weeping scratch with a white handkerchief.

'I-I might, I haven't decided yet,' stuttered Eva.

'You should take it. I think I'm being more than fair.'

'Fair?'

'Yeah, considering how you've treated me,' sniped Connor, walking over towards a concealed drinks cabinet in a wooden globe.

'The way *I* treated you?' Eva laughed and shook her head in confusion.

'Why, don't you think you've treated me badly?' said Connor with his back to her pouring himself a large double whisky.

'Can you at least turn round and look at me, please?!' she demanded. 'I think you must've banged your head as well as your face because I think you'll find it was *you* who's treated me appallingly. I loved you, and you betrayed me for a second time with the same woman – Cara!'

'I told you,' yelled Connor, turning to face her, 'that I wasn't lying, and I wasn't! She's an old friend who I enjoyed sex with from time to time.'

'Actually, I believe you,' said Eva blankly, letting her hands fall down by her side. 'I don't think you're capable of loving another woman – Maria took your heart to the grave with her.'

'Ha!' Connor laughed in bewilderment. 'Why does everyone assume I'm still hung up on her? Every ounce of feeling I had for her died when she fucked St Clair – that's the truth. I don't forgive,' fired back Connor bitterly.

'I believe you,' replied Eva wearily.

'I don't lie and I *despise* being called a liar,' said Connor. 'Okay, so I've fucked a lot of women, so what. Who cares? But when I'm accused of doing something I haven't done, I can't forgive. I told you if I left, then you wouldn't exist to me…' Connor paused, raking his hand through his thick black hair. 'I promised that I wouldn't fire you if things didn't work out, so here I am honouring that promise. You can have the Birmingham job. I call that fair!'

Eva looked away from him desperately trying not to cry. 'So what happens now?' she croaked.

'You'll be issued with a new contact if you decide to take the Birmingham position,' said Connor, taking a mouthful of whisky.

Eva sniffed and straightened her back. 'What if I won't go?'

'Let's just hope that you do decide to take it, Eva,' Connor said callously.

Covering her mouth to silence her whimpering, Eva felt each word wound her like a storm of hailstones pelting against her body.

'Here, take this,' said Connor, pulling out a clean cotton handkerchief from his pocket.

Eva snatched it from him and pressed it against her face; the smell of his aftershave sent a stab of pain straight to her heart.

'Thanks,' said Eva, handing it back now mascara stained.

'Keep it,' said Connor dismissively.

'I don't want anything of yours,' declared Eva, dropping it on the floor and making her way towards the door.

As her hand hovered over the door handle, her heart begged her to turn around and search Connor's face for any remorse, or hidden love.

'Bye, Eva,' said Connor, without a trace of empathy in his voice.

Staring at the door, with tears stinging her cheeks, she let it click shut behind her. Once inside the lift she burst into deep sobs; her heart lay in pieces where she had stood in front of Connor. Of course she wouldn't be able to erase the memory of him until she terminated his baby growing inside her. Feeling numb, she didn't know how she got back to the casino but somehow managed to compose herself enough to find Ted.

'Why, you look upset, missy?' asked Ted.

'I'm fine,' said Eva sniffing.

'No you're not.' Ted frowned noticing her smudged eye make-up and red tear-stained cheeks. 'Don't be thinking under this weather-beaten exterior is an old fool. I know when a problem is weighing someone down.'

'I'm worried that you'll judge me,' Eva whispered.

'Well,' said Ted, shaking his head, 'I don't know a single soul who hasn't done something they haven't regretted, or at least should – no one is perfect.'

'I could get into trouble by telling you.'

'I promise I'll take your secret to the grave. You have my complete trust on this.'

Eva sat and smiled over at Ted. His eyes, deeply lined by the hot Texas sun, were bright and warm.

Ted saw the hesitation in her face and suggested they leave the club for an hour or so.

'Connor will never allow that,' said Eva.

'O'Neill isn't going to refuse this old cowboy – I know my worth to him,' said Ted, smiling. 'I'll offer to cover his costs, unless you feel uncomfortable with my suggestion? Be sure, Miss Eva, I will be a perfect gentleman – you have my word on that.'

Eva answered Ted with a smile and a nod.

'I'll be back shortly. Shall we meet in the lobby in ten minutes?'

'Yes, okay,' said Eva accepting Ted's hand as he helped her down from the barstool. She made her way back into the dressing room and tapped on Ann's door.

'Mr Marshall has asked me to accompany him to dinner. I think he's speaking to Connor now.'

'Yes, I've just been speaking to Mr O'Neill,' said Ann, swinging around in her chair. 'He isn't happy about you leaving the premises.'

'Oh…'

'Mr O'Neill was quite adamant with his reason for refusing,' said Ann with a deep intake of breath.

'What did he say? You don't have to spare my feelings.'

Ann pondered for a second. 'Well, Mr O'Neill said he isn't offering an escort service and, while I think his response is a little insensitive and crass, I do think Mr Marshall's request is more than a little inappropriate.'

'Mr Marshall is a perfect gentleman—'

Ann sighed as her office phone rang out. 'Wait a moment.'

Eva stood silently as a dull pain in her abdomen made her stand rigid.

'Mr O'Neill has apparently changed his mind,' announced Ann, putting down the phone, 'so if you're agreeable, you can go. But he did stress you're under no obligation to entertain Mr Marshall off the club's premises.'

'Yes I know.' Eva nodded and imagined Ted must have flavoured his request with more than a sprinkle of blackmail to get Connor to agree.

'Mr Marshall has been a member with us for some time, so while I'm not overly concerned about his intentions, I would still like you to phone me at the end of your shift,' instructed Ann.

'Yes, okay,' agreed Eva, walking towards the door.

Eva waited for Ted in the lobby with her coat wrapped tightly around her.

'Sorry for keeping you waiting, Miss Eva. My driver should be just pulling up outside.'

Offering Eva his arm, they both walked down to the waiting black limousine.

'Where we go is entirely up to you,' said Ted beaming and sitting down next to her.

'How about a drive around London,' suggested Eva. 'It's so pretty this time of the year, plus I'm worried we might be overheard somewhere more public because Connor knows so many people.'

Ted nodded and instructed his driver through the intercom.

'So, Miss Eva, what's making you so unhappy?' asked Ted with genuine concern.

Inhaling deeply, Eva pulled a tissue out of her handbag. 'I've been an idiot.'

'Well, can I join your club?' said Ted, 'I've probably done every stupid thing in the book!'

'Have you ever got pregnant with your boss's child?' she asked, wiping her eyes.

Silence hung in the air as Ted digested her confession. 'Are you sure? Does he know?' he asked softly, seeing her distress.

'No, and he mustn't find out either!'

'I won't breathe a word, but won't he notice if you decide to keep the child?'

'What, from Birmingham? He's packing me off!'

'To Bir-ming-ham?' said Ted, in his broad accent. 'I'm confused, were you his mistress or girlfriend? O'Neill isn't married, is he?'

'Our relationship was a casual affair to begin with – a one-night stand,' said Eva blushing, hoping Ted wouldn't judge her too harshly. 'I was apprehensive, of course. Connor's my boss and has a reputation for being a womaniser, but he assured me that I wouldn't lose my job if I entered into a relationship with him, so I guess in that respect he's kept his promise.'

'Did he cheat?'

'Yes – I must admit I don't remember asking Santa for a broken heart,' said Eva with a hint of humour in her reply. 'Obviously, he denied that he had.'

'Oh, I see now,' said Ted, 'and now he wants you banished?'

'If he could ship me off to the moon, I'm sure he would!'

Ted paused for a moment. 'I could help.'

'Help – how?'

'Eva, I'm sixty-four years old and have enough money to live my life many times over, but I'm lonely.'

Eva indiscreetly tugged down on the hem of her dress.

'Don't be uneasy with me, I'm not proposing anything improper here. I don't expect there to be any sexual closeness between us, what I'm proposing is companionship. I would be more than happy to care for you and your child.'

'I-I don't know what to say,' stuttered Eva. 'Are you asking me to move to America with you?'

'Yes, I am. It's a genuine offer. I'd make sure everything was legal. You and your child, if you choose to keep it, would be financially taken care of during my life, and after my death.'

'What would your family and children say – I'm sure they wouldn't approve?'

'Well, the way I look at things is I'm entitled to a life of my own. I've always provided for all of my children and will continue to do so. I am not about to hand over my entire fortune to you, you understand,' said Ted chuckling. 'But I enjoy your company, and I think we could offer each other a sincere, respectful and platonic relationship.'

'I am flattered, Ted, but wouldn't you want a psychical relationship with a woman?' asked Eva, blushing again. 'Doesn't a man need to be intimate with a woman?'

Nodding, Ted smiled. 'Yes I believe a man does need the physical touch of a woman. But you see, Miss Eva, I had prostate cancer three years ago and it took away that need from me – excuse my frankness. So a platonic relationship is what I'm offering you.'

Eva raised her eyebrows in disbelief at the enormity of his offer. Ted offered his phone number and told Eva to take as much time as she needed before adding, 'Forgive my asking, but do you love O'Neill?'

Eva turned her face away and inhaled deeply trying to abate further tears flowing. 'I did – I guess it takes a while for your heart to catch up with your mind. I wanted a life with him, but it was a schoolgirl dream. You see, Connor doesn't want marriage or babies, so…'

'I know it's not in my own interests, but I think you should tell him that you're carrying his child. A woman can soften a man and show him a better way of living his life when she presents him with the prospect of becoming a father.'

'And how about if he wants me to have an abortion?'

'Then you walk away from him and never look back,' Ted said simply. He tried to lift the mood talking about his ranch in Texas and how she would want for nothing.

Eva listened and sporadically looked through the car window watching a flurry of snow gracefully settle on the historic streets of London.

'You look tired,' he acknowledged noticing Eva muffle a yawn. 'I'll tell Morris to head back to the club. You need to rest and decide what you want to do next.'

'Will you be in the club tomorrow for New Year's Eve?' asked Eva.

'I will, I fly back in a couple of days – I can always book another seat,' Ted said, grinning.

Eva smiled and thanked him for helping her out of the limousine before saying, 'Well, I'm working in the casino tomorrow, so I'll see you then.'

'You definitely will, and take this…' said Ted shoving a large bundle of notes into her hand.

'That's too much, are you sure?'

'Yes I am. I was told I'd have to pay for your time, which I'm more than happy to do.'

Eva gave Ted a small peck on his tanned cheek and made her way back into the club.

The dance lounge was full of inebriated men whistling and cheering at Scarlett and Donna's erotic lesbian floorshow.

Eva made her way into to the dressing room feeling tired yet grateful for Ted's listening ear.

'Hi,' said Roxanne sitting in just a pair of black lace knickers. 'Did everything go okay with Marshall?'

'Why are you given preferential treatment?' screeched Tina on cue.

'Preferential…eh? Someone must've received a dictionary for Christmas,' mocked Roxanne, giving Tina a wide-eyed glare.

Tina jumped to her feet. 'Why is she allowed to swan around London with Old Snakeskin!' she protested.

'Mr Marshall is a perfect gentleman, unlike the object of your desire – an Irish fuckwit!' said Eva.

Tina smirked, folding her arms under her fake breasts. 'Oh, so it's true, then?'

'What is?'

'That Connor's dumped you. I knew it wouldn't last. You were just a curiosity for him. I imagine he hasn't shagged many fat women before.'

'You know what, Tina,' said Eva, not knowing how she could have found out so soon, 'I actually felt a little sorry for you when Connor basically told you your "fellatio" skills were seriously below par.'

'Fellatio?' Tina frowned and glanced over at Donna.

'Short dictionary, then?' added Roxanne with a sarcastic laugh. 'Blow job, dimwit!'

Clamping her teeth together, Tina's cheeks flushed vivid red. 'Don't you dare fucking pity me, Eva! You're the one who fell for his fake charm. I had a lucky escape. Plus, before you crow over me, just remember…who laughs last, laughs longest!'

'Meaning?'

A sly, malevolent sneer spread across Tina's face. She flicked her long mane of hair over her shoulder and remained annoyingly silent.

'Take no notice of her,' Roxanne called out. 'I think she's losing the plot! Anyway, how much did old man Marshall pay you? I think he has a soft spot for you!' she teased.

'I told him it was too much,' explained Eva, counting the bundle of fifty-pound notes. 'Shit, there's three grand here!'

'Told you, the Yankee Doodle Dandy fancies you!'

'I'll take this through to Ann, then shall we go for a cigarette?'

'Okay,' said Roxanne, intrigued by Eva's wide grin.

Once they were both outside in the courtyard, Eva confessed Ted's proposal to Roxanne.

'Companionship? Dirty old man!'

'No, honestly it's not seedy at all. He can't do anything,' said Eva, pointing down to her crotch. 'He had cancer and now it doesn't work,' she mouthed.

'Could you really give up your life here and any thoughts of a sex life to move in with an old guy who lives on the other side of the world? It's creepy, Eva. You need to think about what you'd be accepting,' warned Roxanne. 'You may be escaping from your problems here, but I think you'd be creating just as many new ones if you take him up on his offer.'

'He said I should tell Connor about the baby.'

'Well initially I thought that, but thinking it over I'm not too sure now.'

'Why?'

'Because I think he'd tell you to get rid of it.'

'Well, I haven't decided what I'm going to do yet.' Eva sighed. 'My head is all over the place, so until I'm sure I won't be agreeing to anything, or telling anyone!'

Struggling through her shift, Eva felt tired and emotional when it was time to clock out. The cold wind gnawed at her face as she and Roxanne ran around to the club's car park. With little conversation, Eva sank deep into her seat as Roxanne drove her home.

'Are you sure you don't want me to stay over again tonight?' asked Roxanne, pulling up outside Eva's house.

'No, honestly I'm fine. Thanks for the lift. I'll see you tomorrow,' said Eva, reaching for the door handle.

'Okay, babes – night.'

As Eva watched Roxanne drive away, she felt an eerie feeling creep over her, like a ghost touching her skin, as if someone was watching her. She turned around and peered into the darkness when a sudden screech of car tyres roaring past made her jolt on the spot. She quickly went indoors and slipped on the door chain. She called out for Mr Jingles who came bounding down the stairs.

After washing her face, she brushed her teeth and went straight to bed. She fished out her mobile from her bag and typed 'pregnancy terminations' into Google. She read in horror the stark information about abortions. Rolling onto her side, she brushed her hand across the empty space next to her while slipping her other hand down to her stomach. Heartache would again keep her from her sleep that night.

Chapter 29

'Happy New Year's Eve,' she muttered miserably to herself on the way into work seeing hordes of drunken revellers already out in force.

She walked into the dressing room but didn't see Roxanne sitting at her table as usual. 'Scarlett, is Roxy in?'

'Yeah, she's about somewhere…' mumbled Scarlett, having difficulty squeezing her curvy figure into a tight red PVC catsuit.

Stripping down to a black G-string, Eva reached for her short black velvet cocktail dress draped over the back of her chair.

'Evening, ladies!' bellowed Connor, striding into the dressing room.

Eva gasped in shock and snatched her dress to quickly cover her naked breasts. Even through Connor had caressed and kissed every inch of her body, she now felt exposed and vulnerable in his presence.

Connor waltzed past her to Ann's office without even a sideways glance.

'Oh shit!' cursed Scarlett, holding a piece of broken zip in her fingers.

Eva quickly stepped into her velvet dress and yanked up the side zipper. While she was pinning up her hair, her whole body stiffened when she heard Connor's booming voice from behind.

'I want everyone ready in five minutes, Ann – don't keep me waiting.' He walked back through the dressing room and let the door swing shut behind him.

'Eva, have you seen Tina or Donna?' asked Ann quickly walking over to her table.

'No, I haven't seen Roxy either?'

'Roxanne's outside in the courtyard having a cigarette, so can you go and hurry her along, please,' fretted Ann.

'Yeah, okay,' said Eva, spraying her pinned hair before getting to her feet.

'Tell her Mr O'Neill wants everyone in the casino in five minutes! A group of his friends have come over from Ireland, so no dawdling! Right?' Ann huffed when she reached the dressing room door. 'Where the hell are Tina and Donna?!'

'Hi, Ann told me you were out here?'

'Just having a fag. How are you?'

'Surviving, I guess,' replied Eva, looking down at the smouldering cigarette between Roxanne's fingers. 'Can I nick a drag?'

'Should you be smoking?'

'It's only you and nicotine that are keeping me sane.'

'Tommy hasn't been very forthcoming about where Connor went over Christmas.'

'I don't care,' said Eva, taking a long drag. 'We've all been summoned up to the casino. Apparently the father of my child has guests over.'

'Eva! Roxanne!' bellowed Ann from behind the fire exit door. 'Mr O'Neill is waiting – move it!'

'Bloody hell,' whinged Roxanne, linking arms with Eva as they walked back into the club. 'Bloody New Year's Eve's and we have to sodding work!'

As soon as they walked into the casino, Eva saw Tina and Donna standing by the bar with Connor and four other men. Taking a deep breath to steady her nerves, Roxanne told her to grit her teeth and ride it out. With a forced, wide smile she followed Roxanne over to the group.

Connor glanced over at Eva nonchalantly before taking a large mouthful of neat whisky. 'This is Roxanne and Eva,' he announced to the group. 'To my right are Jack March, William Lang and Lewis Mannford, you both know my brother, Gabriel,' he added, glancing over towards his younger brother.

Eva smiled over to the man Connor introduced as Jack. He stood short next to Connor's six-foot-two frame and was very handsome with gelled brown hair and oval hazel eyes. William, who was taller and plainer in looks, had a slightly hooked nose and receding hairline. But it was Lewis Mannford who stood out from the crowd. His pursed mouth and effeminate stance along over-waxed eyebrows screamed 'diva'.

'Hello again.'

'Hello, Gabriel,' said Eva warmly.

'How is my much *older* and *uglier* brother treating you?' said Gabriel, enjoying Connor's frown. 'Is he a good boss, ladies?'

'Do you expect us to answer that truthfully with him standing two feet away from us?' scoffed Roxanne.

'I bet he's wicked,' said Lewis offering Connor a teasing pout.

Feeling a wave of nausea take her breath away, Eva turned away from the group to see a slender blonde woman approaching them.

'Cara, come and have a glass of champagne,' said Connor, offering her a fluted glass filled to the brim.

Roxanne's mouth fell open. She turned to look at Eva before glaring back up at Connor.

Eva swallowed hard and stared up at the tall, elegant woman whose wavy blonde hair trailed down her back. The faint lines around her eyes and a small crease in her brow were the only signs of her age. Her red cocktail dress was demure and sophisticated, but Eva wondered why Cara wasn't wearing the diamond earrings that were the catalyst for her and Connor breaking up.

'So, Cara,' asked Gabriel with a huge smile, 'what do you think of the Unicorn?'

'Very opulent and grand,' answered Cara. Her own wide smile displayed a row of perfect, white teeth. 'But then again, I wouldn't expect anything less, would I, Connor darling?'

'Very opulent and grand – a bit like his ego, then!' added Gabriel, earning himself a scathing stare from Connor.

'So, ladies,' said Jack, looking at Eva, 'can you guide us round and help us bankrupt your employer?'

'The pleasure will be all ours!' said Roxanne, looking Cara up and down.

'So...' said Cara, with a sneer, 'you take your clothes off while dancing – do you?'

'You can say the word – *stripper*.' Roxanne grimaced. 'Connor has built his empire on men paying handsomely to see young, beautiful women dance for them. Of course, there is a sell-by date,' she added curtly, flashing a disingenuous smile, 'no punter wants to see a sour-lipped, titless thirty-something floundering around – don't you agree, Connor?'

'I think...' said Connor sternly, 'that we should move over to the roulette table.'

Cara flashed Roxanne a look of animosity as the group moved away from the bar; she then moved her gaze over to Eva who returned her condescending stare.

'I'm just going to the toilet,' said Eva, her voice trembling with emotion.

'Give me a minute and I'll join you,' seethed Roxanne, glancing over her shoulder at Connor.

Watching her friend walk solemnly towards the casino lobby, Roxanne turned around and looked in disgust at Connor. 'Excuse me,' she snapped, prodding Connor's arm sharply with the tip of her finger, 'can I have a word in private, please?'

Frowning down at her jabbing him, Connor bared his teeth and hissed down at her, 'Can't it wait!'

'No, I don't think it can.'

'I am busy, *Rox-anne*.'

'We can either talk here in front of your delightful friends or in private. I don't mind which, you choose, *Con-nor*!' she growled back.

His face consumed with anger, he challenged her unflinching stare.

'*I've got all night...*' snarled Roxanne, widening her eyes.

'Two minutes!' said Connor, clenching his teeth and storming out of the casino. 'So, what's so important?' he barked, turning to face her when they reached the lobby.

'You're a cruel bastard, Connor,' wailed Roxanne, shoving her hands on her hips.

Curling his lips into half a smile, he baited her, 'You called me out just to tell me that! Why – you should've just sent me a text.'

'Don't fuck with me! You're purposely trying to hurt Eva by bringing *her* here.'

'I didn't have you down as being unintelligent, Roxanne,' said, Connor, sighing with boredom. 'I believe you know I own the Unicorn; I think that entitles me to invite whoever I wish.'

'You didn't have to bring her here. You could've gone anywhere in London tonight, but you wanted to wound and belittle Eva – that makes you a cold-hearted bastard!'

Connor stood with his teeth clenched but didn't offer any protest to her character assassination.

His silence and raised eyebrows mocking her sharp words made her bite back again, this time harder, 'You know what, Connor...' said Roxanne with swagger in her voice, 'you may be able to fuck as many women as you want, but you'll never find another woman like Eva. She's kind, loyal and wouldn't mind if you didn't have a penny to your name. You're so blinded by your ego and conceited principals, you can't see what you could've had – you're such an asshole, you don't deserve her.'

The smug grin instantly dropped from his lips. He hissed through his teeth, 'I want to remind you, *Miss Meadows*, that I employed you first to take off your clothes in a pleasing manner, and second because Tommy fancied you. You weren't hired to dictate your views on how I should live my life – know your place!'

'Know my place – fuck off!' fired back Roxanne, her eyes flared with anger.

'Watch your mouth, or you'll be joining Eva up in Birmingham!'

'I would gladly go, if only to escape putting up with your horseshit,' bellowed Roxanne. She was about to turn on her heels when she heard a blood curling scream coming from the ladies toilets.

'EVA!' cried out Roxanne, slamming open the toilet door and seeing her lying crumpled on the floor.

'What's wrong with her?' asked Connor, joining Roxanne who was crouching over Eva.

'Eva, wake up!' panicked Roxanne, shaking her.

'She's out cold,' said Connor, placing his hand on her forehead.

'This is all your fault,' barked Roxanne, pushing his hand away.

Connor got to his feet and rubbed his face. 'We need to get her upstairs and call a doctor.'

'Shush…can you hear that?' Roxanne cocked her head listening to muffled noises coming from Eva's phone. 'She's talking to someone!'

Connor reached down and gently prized Eva's mobile out of her fingers. 'Hello – who is this?' he asked, looking down at Roxanne placing a wet paper towel across Eva's brow.

'She's starting to come round!' gasped Roxanne. She lowered her head to listen to Eva's incoherent rambling.

Connor frowned. 'Pardon? Can you say that again?' he asked, looking down at Eva.

'Who is it?' probed Roxanne, fanning Eva with her hand.

'Her friend Susanna is dead?' he said, pressing his palm against the mouthpiece.

'Fuck off!' cried out Roxanne, her mouth dropping open.

'S-Susanna is dead,' rasped Eva, starting to hyperventilate, 'someone has murdered her!'

'Shitting hell!' wheezed Roxanne. She rocked Eva in her arms as her screams bounced off the tiled wills.

'What shall I say?' whispered Connor, holding the phone away from his mouth.

'Who's on the phone?' asked Roxanne.

'He said he's Susanna's brother, Kurt.'

Roxanne snatched the phone out of his hand and told him to take Eva up to the penthouse.

Connor carried Eva shaking and sobbing towards the lift.

'Where's Roxanne?' croaked Eva, blinking up at Connor as he lowered her down onto one of the white sofas in his private suite.

'She's talking to Susanna's brother, so just lie there – you've had a massive shock,' he said, propping up her head with a cushion.

'Ouch!' whimpered Eva, plunging her hand down between her thighs and suddenly propelling herself forward.

'What is it?' asked Connor, stepping back.

'Ahhhh…' Eva cried out, doubling over.

'For God's sake, what's wrong?'

'*Oh God, no!*' she howled, looking down at her blood-smeared fingers. 'Get Roxanne!' she screamed.

'Yeah, okay.' Connor quickly turned around hearing a loud knock on the door.

'All right, Boss,' said Tommy. 'Shit, what's going on?' He gasped hearing Eva wailing.

'Get Roxanne, quick!' shouted Connor. 'She was in the casino lobby.'

Connor looked on helplessly at Eva sobbing uncontrollably. He wanted to comfort her, but every time he went near she screamed for him to stay away.

'Eva!' cried Roxanne, literally bursting into the penthouse.

'She won't tell me what's wrong,' explained Connor, his eyes wide with confusion.

'Will one of you carry her to the lift? Now!' shouted Roxanne.

'She just got her period, hasn't she, babe?' asked Tommy, glancing over at Connor who returned his look of bewilderment.

'What? Yes!' babbled Roxanne, swinging open the door to let Connor carry Eva to the lift. 'But she's just been told her best friend's been murdered!'

'Murdered?' repeated Tommy, lowering his voice.

'I tell you something, I'm gonna need fucking therapy after this!' cried Roxanne, running out of the lift and through the lobby with Connor two steps behind her.

'Are you taking her home?' asked Connor.

'Yes…' lied Roxanne, knowing she was taking Eva straight to hospital.

'I'll come with you, babe,' said Tommy, running over to her car.

'No!' barked Roxanne. 'Sorry, babe, she'll just want me with her.'

'Do you want me to do anything – phone anyone?' Connor asked, lowering Eva into the passenger seat.

'Oh, believe me, Connor,' shot back Roxanne, buckling Eva's seatbelt, 'you've done quite enough already!'

***

After leaving the hospital Roxanne drove Eva home. 'How are you feeling now, babes?'

'Like I'm stuck in a living nightmare,' muttered Eva with smudged mascara blackening her swollen eyes.

'At least the baby's okay. The doctor said your ultrasound was fine – just a breakthrough bleed?'

'Yeah…' Eva started to sob again. 'I just can't believe Susanna has gone. I can't think about anything else, not even the baby.'

'I know, my brain can't take it in,' said Roxanne, shaking her head. 'We only went out clubbing together a couple of weeks ago, and now she's…' Roxanne glanced at Eva.

'Her brother said she was found strangled in an alleyway!' Eva lowered her head into her hand as her deep sobs became deeper and prolonged.

'Maybe the killer is a punter with a grudge?' suggested Roxanne, lowering the car window and flicking out a cigarette butt and promptly relighting another. 'Or that thug of a boyfriend! I'm sure the police won't leave any stone unturned.'

'It won't bring her back though, will it?' whimpered Eva.

'Perhaps the story will be on the news, you know, a Brit killed abroad,' said Roxanne. 'Why would anyone want to kill her, Roxy? She's never hurt anyone in her life.'

Not having the answers to stem her outpour of questions, Roxanne felt emotionally exhausted when they finally arrived at Eva's house. She helped her out of the car and slowly led her to the front door. 'Sorry, babes, but I need a drink?' announced Roxanne, kicking her shoes off in hallway.

'Pour me one too,' croaked Eva, 'I'm going to check if there's any coverage on the news.' She sat transfixed in front of the TV scanning the news channels. 'ROXANNE!' she shouted, quickly turning up the volume. 'Susanna's on ABC News!'

'Fuck!' gasped Roxanne, rushing into the living room with a bottle of vodka and two glasses. 'What are they saying?'

'Shush, it's on now!'

'The LVMPD today are still investigating the murder of a twenty-five-year-old British woman Susanna Curtis, whose body was found in the early hours of December twenty-sixth in her apartment on Twenty-First Street. Miss Curtis, a known prostitute on the Las Vegas strip, was last seen leaving the renowned Palazzo Hotel casino hours before her death with a man the LVMPD would like to question in connection with her murder. The Palazzo Hotel have released security footage to the police in the hope it will help catch who is responsible for Miss Curtis's death.'

'*No way!*' said Roxanne; the bottle of vodka falling from her hand.

Eva quickly started to record the news bulletin. She sat speechless and wide-eyed watching the CCTV footage in horror; she instantly recognised the image of the man who had forcefully knocked Susanna to the ground. Both women felt the oxygen being choked out the air as raspy breaths stuck in their throats.

'R-Roxanne...' stuttered Eva, turning to her for validation of the image they were both staring at.

'Jesus...fucking...Christ!' Roxanne mumbled in shock.

'It can't be!' cried Eva.

'I-I didn't say anything because you said you didn't want to know where he was,' rambled Roxanne, 'but Connor was in Vegas!'

'He was there that night... It's him pushing Susanna!' Eva jumped to her feet, letting the TV remote clatter to the floor, and ran into the kitchen to throw up in the sink.

'Holy shit,' muttered Roxanne, falling to her knees. 'It *is* Connor...'

'PHONE HIM!' screamed Eva, rushing back into lounge, her eyes ablaze with rage.

'I can't stop shaking!' Roxanne scrambled to her feet; her hands trembled over her mobile which then started to ring. 'Wh-who is this?' she wailed, pressing her phone to her ear. 'Tommy, is that you? Oh my God, Connor is on the news! The police want to speak to him about Susanna's death?'

'WHAT'S HE SAYING?!' yelled Eva.

'Shush – I can't hear!' Roxanne cried out. 'What? Someone from the hotel named Connor as the man who left with Susanna!'

'He killed her! He killed her!' repeated Eva, pacing up and down, her fingers pressed against her temples.

'Connor has been taken to Savile Row Police Station for questioning,' explained Roxanne.

'How does he know Susanna?' cried Eva. 'What was he doing there, why did he kill her?!'

Tommy heard Eva cry out her questions and quickly explained to Roxanne that a woman inside the Palazzo Hotel had propositioned Connor. He didn't know this woman, and she was acting crazy so the hotel security stepped in and removed her. As he left the hotel she propositioned him again, and then attacked him when he refused her advances. He thought the woman was a drug-crazed hooker desperate for money. Tommy assured Roxanne that Connor wasn't involved in her murder, but did admit he pushed her to the ground outside the hotel.

'So are you at the police station with Connor?' asked Roxanne, glancing over at Eva. 'You're waiting for his lawyer... Okay. Well let me know what happens. Eva's going out of her mind here. Speak to you later... Love you, bye.'

Eva slumped down onto the sofa staring ahead in a vacant, hypnotic gaze.

'Well I can't believe Connor killed Susanna,' Roxanne said fervently, dropping her mobile on the coffee table. 'What do you think?'

'I don't know. Did they ever find out who killed his ex?'

'What do you mean?'

'We only have his word about what happened to Maria, and now he's connected to Susanna's murder. He could be a serial killer for all we know,' said Eva, getting to her feet. 'I could be carrying a murderer's child!' she cried, becoming hysterical.

'Wait!' said Roxanne, reaching out and cupping Eva's hands. 'The cops investigated Maria's death and found no evidence linking Connor to her murder – plus, what motive would he have to kill Susanna?'

Eva took some comfort from Roxanne's analysis, but she still felt incensed at Susanna being portrayed on the news as a cheap whore with a drug habit; that was not the Susanna she knew and loved.

'Why was Susanna looking for punters in a casino? She had her regulars. None of this makes sense,' Eva argued.

'All we can do is keep watching the news and wait for Tommy to phone back with more information,' said Roxanne wearily, feeling exhausted by Eva's grief.

Both women sat watching the news all night, and then, with no emotion, pictures of London's skyline ablaze with New Year's fireworks after Big Ben struck midnight.

Eva sighed and announced, 'I'm going to bed.'

'I'm going to sit up awhile,' said Roxanne, refilling her wine glass. 'See you in the morning.'

* * *

The next morning Eva woke up feeling sick. She made her way downstairs into the lounge and found Roxanne lying on the sofa.

'How are you feeling?' asked Roxanne, sitting up.

'Numb…'

'Me too, if I'm honest.' Roxanne exhaled loudly. 'I'll go and make us a coffee.'

'Not for me – the smell of milk still makes me heave. Have you heard anymore from Tommy?' asked Eva, following her into the kitchen.

'Just a text saying the police kept Connor in overnight. Apparently they can keep you in custody up to ninety-six hours without charging you, if it's a serious crime. Connor's brief is confident he can get him out on bail this morning.'

'Oh… Well, this is a great start to the New Year!'

'Look – I was thinking, maybe it might be a good idea to call your mum. I think you need someone to be here with you – you need your family.'

'Maybe…' said Eva, her eyes shadowed with fatigue.

Just before noon, Roxanne received a phone call from Tommy saying Connor had been bailed and that he wanted to speak to Eva at the club within the hour.

A short while later Roxanne drove them to the Unicorn. Eva silently stared through the car window not sure if she could bear to be in the same room as him, but knew she had to hear his account of events.

'Eva…' said Roxanne, breaking the heavy silence between them. 'I phoned your mum on your mobile and told her what's happened – sorry. She's catching the first flight out of Spain today.'

'It's fine,' she muttered, her chin releasing a small tremble. 'My mum really liked Susanna.'

Eva glanced over at Connor's green Range Rover when they pulled into the club's car park; her stomach rumbled through a lack of food and apprehension. On their way to the front entrance she gazed up at the brass sign that only six months ago had stirred so much excitement, but now only evoked bleak and melancholy thoughts.

'How do you feel, babes?' asked Roxanne as they stepped into the lift.

'There aren't any words to describe how I feel. I just want to find out what he has to say, then leave.'

'Well, if it's any consolation, they wouldn't have granted him bail if the evidence had stacked up.'

'I'm sure Connor has the best lawyer money can buy,' replied Eva, brushing her hand over her stomach when they reached the third floor. 'We may never find out the truth.'

After knocking on the door it immediately swung open, startling both women.

Tommy quickly reached out for Roxanne, lifting her off her feet and hugging her tightly. 'I've missed you so much, baby.' His voice raspy as Roxanne wrapped her legs around his waist.

'Come in, Eva!' Connor called out.

Averting her eyes away from Tommy and Roxanne, Eva walked into the penthouse to find Connor standing by a roaring fire with his hand resting on the white stone mantel staring at the hypnotic amber flames.

'I want to speak to Eva alone,' said Connor, not moving his gaze from the fire.

'Eva, I can stay if you want me to?' asked Roxanne, ignoring Connor's request.

'It's okay, I'll be fine – thanks, Roxy.'

Hearing the door click shut, Connor turned to look at Eva. Against a backdrop of almond-shaped eyes and high cheekbones he looked breathtakingly handsome, if not tired and unshaven.

'I didn't kill your friend,' stated Connor bluntly, glancing back towards the fire. 'I've done many things that have tarnished my name, but murder isn't one of them.'

'I need to sit down,' said Eva walking over to one of the white sofas flanking a stone-based coffee table. 'I want to know everything that happened that night,' she added, brushing away a tear and sniffing heavily.

'I went straight to the airport when you told me to leave Christmas Eve. As you might've heard, I didn't go home to Ireland. I needed to forget about "us" for a while, so I went to Vegas to gamble. Christmas Day I stayed in my room and drank all day. Boxing Day I played poker for most of the day and got drunk. I went back to my room and slept for about three hours, then had a shower and went out again. I was in the middle of a game when this woman came out of nowhere. She reeked of alcohol and had a cut lip and a bruise under her eye.'

'Susanna…' murmured Eva, averting her gaze from Connor.

'I had no idea who she was, or why she'd made a beeline for me. She seemed hell-bent on securing my attention.'

'What did she say to you?'

Connor stepped away from the fire and sat opposite her. 'Are you sure you want to know?'

'Yes,' replied Eva, meeting his stare.

'She asked me if I wanted to go back to her apartment for sex. I didn't know your friend was a hooker,' said Connor frowning.

'She was a high-class escort!' snapped Eva.

Connor looked at her with indifference. 'She offered me sex in exchange for money. I told her I wasn't interested, which seemed to propel her into a verbal attack. I folded my hand of poker and went to get up when security marched her out of the casino. I played another couple of games, then decided I'd go for a walk and clear my head – I admit I'd been drinking whisky for most of the day. When I left the hotel I saw her screaming into her mobile, then she stared over at me. I started to walk in the opposite direction, but she came running towards me yelling if she didn't earn some money then her pimp was going to beat her up. I just wanted to get rid of her, so I went to reach for my wallet, but she lunged at me and tried to kiss me.'

'What did you do?'

'I threw her to the ground. I thought she was going to stab me or something! I don't make a habit of manhandling women, but she was crazy!'

'Is that it?'

'Pretty much – I managed to grab a cab and went to a bar. Of course…' said Connor curtly, 'I don't expect you to believe me. We both know you think I'm incapable of telling the truth.'

'Did you look back towards Susanna?'

'No,' replied Connor coldly.

Eva got to her feet with tears streaming down her face. 'I'm sure the police will uncover the truth, but I promise you here and now, Connor, if you're lying…I will personally burn down your precious club, with you in it!' she threatened before turning on her heels and leaving Connor sitting in stunned silence.

Chapter 30

'Did he explain what happened?' asked Roxanne, waiting in the lobby. 'Tommy told me what he said in his statement, but I wonder if we've heard the same version?'

'Well, he didn't confess to it, if that's what you mean?' Eva said wearily.

'So you think he did it, then?' pressed Roxanne.

'As you said, there's one thing missing…motive.'

'Hand on heart, Eva, I don't believe he did it, but there's something very suspicious about the whole thing.'

Roxanne's comment made Eva stop dead in her tracks on the pavement outside.

'Why did Susanna only proposition Connor? There must've been hundreds of men in that casino that night, so why only him?' added Roxanne, unlocking her car.

'She might've spotted his platinum Rolex, or seen how much he was betting and winning and assumed he was wealthy?' Eva suggested.

'I don't buy that, also who was she talking to on the phone? She could've pulled off a trick in the street or in a bar, but no – she wanted Connor. Why?'

'I don't know,' said Eva, slumping down into the passenger seat. They sat in silence on the journey back to Eva's until her mobile pinged. 'It's my mum. She's about thirty minutes away.'

'Okay,' said Roxanne, pulling up outside Eva's house.

Both women sat on Eva's sofa absorbed by the continuing news coverage.

A knock at the door jolted Eva. 'Mum…' she said as she answered it.

'Why didn't you phone me, Eva!' said Patsy, blustering into the hallway carrying a large grey suitcase. 'I can't believe the mess you've got yourself into,' she rambled on, putting down her case and slipping off her coat. 'Pregnant with your boss's child who, might I add, is being questioned by the police over the murder of your best friend!'

Eva turned to look at Roxanne. 'You told my mum about the baby as well?'

'Sorry,' mouthed Roxanne, 'I thought she needed to know *everything*.'

'Of course she told me!' argued Patsy, brushing a strand of red hair away from her flushed cheeks. 'You should've told me, Eva – I am your mother!'

'I'm not even sure that I'm going to keep it, Mum!' fired back Eva, storming into the lounge.

'Eva Summers!' Patsy shouted, quickly following her. 'You're in no fit state to make such a decision.'

'I am not giving birth to a murderer's child!' snapped Eva, turning to face her.

'There's no proof that Connor is actually involved,' added Roxanne, noticing the similarities between Eva and her mother – and that they were both stubborn and outspoken.

'Sorry, love, you must be Roxanne?' Patsy softened her tone and smiled.

'Yes, Hi…'

'Thank you so much for calling me. If it was left to my daughter here, I'd be none the wiser,' sniped Patsy, returning her attention back to Eva.

'Mum!' said Eva in exasperation, 'I would've phoned you, but my head's been all over the place – sorry.'

Patsy shook her head and exhaled deeply. 'Do I get a hug from my daughter?'

A soft smile of affection spread across Eva's face as she wrapped her arms around her mother's shoulders. 'I'm stuck in a nightmare, Mum,' she said, beginning to sob.

'I want to know everything about this O'Neill person,' demanded Patsy, releasing Eva from her embrace.

'Okay…' said Eva, sniffing.

'Do you think he's guilty?' asked Patsy sternly.

'I don't know. He did meet Susanna – we know that much because there's evidence. There's footage showing them outside a hotel, and his account of what happened seems to add up…' Eva prepared herself for the inevitable reaction to her next revelation. 'But this isn't the first murder Connor has been connected to. His ex-fiancée was murdered and found in a canal.'

Patsy's eyes widened in horror. 'Good Lord!' she gasped. 'What kind of people are you associating with?'

'I can explain everything. It's not as black and white as it sounds – I promise.'

An hour later Patsy knew everything.

Eva, exhausted from going through every last detail and answering endless questions from her mother, went upstairs to bed.

'Eva, I'm going to shoot off now because Tommy's home,' called out Roxanne from the foot of her stairs.

'Yeah, okay, phone me if you hear anymore news!' shouted Eva from her bedroom.

'Thanks for all your help, Roxanne,' said Patsy gratefully. 'Can I ask a question? What do you think Connor would do if he found out Eva was pregnant with his child?'

'Do?' quizzed Roxanne, just about to go through the door.

Patsy peered upstairs and lowered her voice to a whisper. 'I want to take Eva back to Spain with me. Do you think he'd come looking for her?'

'In what way?'

'To bully her into having an abortion, or hurt her?'

'I've known Connor for four years, and my partner Tommy has known him the best part of twenty years – neither of us have witnessed him be violent towards a woman.'

'But he has been violent in the past?'

'Connor is a self-made man. He wasn't born with a silver spoon in his mouth. He doesn't pretend to be saint. I personally don't believe he had anything to do with his ex's murder or what happened to Susanna after the hotel incident. I know for a fact that Connor liked Eva, but I also know marriage and kids don't interest him. Would he try to talk her into having an abortion? Maybe. Would he physically hurt her? Never.'

'Good,' replied Patsy with a nod. 'Because I'm determined to persuade Eva to keep my first grandchild and to come and live in Spain with me and Dennis.'

'I doubt she'll want to go anywhere until Susanna's killer is found.'

'Well, we'll have to wait and see.'

Roxanne smiled walking out onto the porch step. 'Eva has my number if you need to speak to me.'

'Thanks again, Roxanne. I really appreciate all the help you've given Eva.' Shutting the door, Patsy thought how she was going to persuade Eva to move to Spain and keep her baby.

* * *

'What time is it, Mum?' asked Eva being shook gently and the smell of bacon and eggs filling her bedroom.

'Quarter past ten, love,' said Patsy. 'You need to eat some breakfast.'

Eva, for once not greeted by morning sickness, sat up and ate the delicious food placed in front of her.

Patsy watched her daughter with a weak smile and faint frown line.

'Say what's on your mind,' said Eva, knowing exactly what that face meant.

'Well,' started Patsy and then clearing her throat, 'me and Dennis were wondering if you would like to come and live with us for a while, just until you decide what you're going to do about the pregnancy.'

'I need to be here until the police find out who killed Susanna.'

'It wouldn't make any difference if you were here or in Spain, darling. I'm sure Roxanne would let you know if anything happened.'

'My job is here and my home. I still need to pay the bills.'

'You could rent out your house to cover your bills? I'm sure you'd be entitled to compassionate leave after what's just happened and considering your boss is implicated in the case. Perhaps I should speak to him directly.'

Eva slammed down her knife and fork and glared up at Patsy. 'No, Mum!'

Patsy tutted. 'His mother must be sick with shame!'

'Mum, I don't want to talk about moving, Connor or the baby anymore!' shouted Eva, slouching back on her pillow.

'Why couldn't you have got a nice, normal job in an office?'

'Oh – not this again,' said Eva sharply.

'I don't know why they call those sorts of clubs "gentlemen" clubs – a gentleman would never set foot in them.'

'Thanks for that!'

'You know what I mean. I wasn't exactly over the moon when you told me you were going to be a stripper, and now look at the mess you're in. Everyone knows dating your boss is asking for trouble, but you seem content on making the same mistakes!'

'Are you finished?'

'I'm only saying this because I love you, Eva. I want you to be happy, so please think about moving to Spain. I'll help you raise your baby.'

'How many times do I have to tell you? I'm not sure I'm going to keep it!'

With the tension escalating, Patsy's frustration manifested into shock when Eva informed her that she was going into work that evening. Unable to persuade her daughter to change her mind, Patsy conceded as long as she could drive her to and from the club and have regular phone calls to let her know she was okay.

* * *

'So, this is the place?' said Patsy pulling on the handbrake. 'The Unicorn Gentlemen's Club?'

'Yes,' replied Eva, reaching for her workbag sitting on the backseat of her Corsa. There was no way she could bring herself to drive the Mini knowing it could have been bought by a murderer!

'Remember what we agreed,' warned Patsy.

'Yes – I'll phone you on my breaks and what time to pick me up – see you later!' huffed Eva, glad to get out of the car.

Watching Eva go into the club, Patsy glanced across the road and noticed a car parked on double yellow lines. The hazy light from the streetlamp didn't offer a clear view of the two men sitting inside, especially as they quickly lowered their heads when they noticed her staring. Patsy made a mental note of the registration number before driving away.

For work that evening Eva had grabbed the first thing to hand from her wardrobe, a cream satin mini dress with chiffon sleeves and beaded cuffs. Pulling open the heavy lounge doors, she draped her heavy winter coat over her arm and walked through the lounge carrying her small work case and handbag. She approached the dressing room door with a deep breath to steady her nerves.

'Here she is!' said Donna, attracting the attention of the other dancers. 'Is it true the police have taken Connor in for questioning over the murder of a prostitute?' she asked with enthusiasm.

'Who told you?' snapped Eva.

'I can't remember,' snarled Donna dismissively. 'So is it true?'

'Ask Connor,' said Eva, walking over to her locker.

'Donna is asking *you*!' argued Tina, wearing a smug expression. 'There's also a rumour that *you knew* the woman. *Is that true?*'

'It's none of your business. I don't want to talk about it,' Eva fired back before quickly wiping away a tear from her cheek.

'All this happened in Las Vegas, didn't it?' added Scarlet, glancing at Tina and Donna before returning her attention to Eva. 'What was Connor doing in Vegas with a cheap hooker?'

'SHE WASN'T A CHEAP HOOKER!' roared Eva, turning around. 'You know nothing about her, so just shut up!'

Tina raised her eyebrow in amusement and a Machiavellian smirk shaped her lips. 'I guess we are being a little insensitive, girls,' she said with an even more pronounced pout than usual. 'Poor Eva must be in such turmoil discovering her lover is trawling the streets of Vegas looking for a twenty-dollar hooker! We should pity you on your choice of lover, and friends. What was her name – you know, your *dead* hooker friend?'

Tina's eyes widened in terror at Eva launching herself towards her. With both women screaming at the top of their voices, the other girls stood back and watched Eva claw at Tina's long hair extensions.

'What the fuck is going on?' yelled Roxanne walking into the dressing room. 'Eva! Ann is just coming! She'll sack you on the spot!' she cried out, rushing over to separate them.

Roxanne grabbed Eva and dragged her backwards with Tina's legs flailing around trying to kick out at her.

As Tina ran her fingers through her hair, torn out extensions dropped to the floor. 'You crazy, fat bitch!' she wailed.

'What did you call me? You ugly, emaciated slag!' sneered Eva, lunging forward again

'Stop!' pleaded Roxanne, wrestling Eva back. 'Can everyone just chill the fuck out?!'

'I was only asking her about her dead friend, then she attacked me!' bawled Tina.

'How the hell did *you* find out?' quizzed Roxanne as Eva tugged her shoulders free.

'Ask no questions and you'll be told no lies,' crowed Tina. 'I know everything!'

'Well, I'll tell you something for nothing, Tina. Both you and Eva are on a final warning, so I'd sit down and get ready for work before Ann comes through that door!'

Tina bent down and snatched a handful of hair extensions off the floor and threw them onto her table as the dressing room door swung open.

'Everything okay, girls?' asked Ann, noticing the eerie silence.

'Yeah…fine…' said Roxanne, forcing a smile while a hiss of chatter filled the awkward atmosphere.

'Good,' said Ann, glancing at Eva sitting with a sour scowl blemishing her pretty features. 'Let's keep it that way, shall we?' she added, walking towards her office.

'Eva, are you ready?' said Roxanne, shoving a lighter and a packet of ten cigarettes into a small clutch bag. 'Let's make our way up to the casino.'

Eva got to her feet and followed her out of the dressing room.

'What are you doing?' said Roxanne, standing at the bottom of the stone stairs. 'You're pregnant and picking fights!'

'How did Tina find out about Susanna?'

'I honestly don't know,' Roxanne said wearily. 'I just want one night without any commotion.'

'Sorry,' murmured Eva. 'I'm dragging you through my nightmare, it isn't fair.'

'I want to help and be there for you, but I'm struggling with all this fucking misery and suspicion. Mind you, there is something you should know.'

'What about? Susanna?'

'No, Cara's here,' revealed Roxanne, reaching for the fire exit door to the second floor.

'She's welcome to him,' scoffed Eva. 'I haven't got the energy to be jealous.'

'Have you heard from Ted?' probed Roxanne, seeing Eva's eyes fill with tears.

'I think he's gone back to Texas. He's given me his number, but I won't be calling him. Like you said before, Ted isn't the answer to my problems.'

'I agree,' soothed Roxanne as they approached the casino doors.

'A calm night,' said Eva, forcing a smile and slipping her fingers around Roxanne's hand. Eva swallowed hard entering the casino and spotted Connor over by the bar with Tommy and Cara.

'A bottle of Moet,' said Connor, clicking his fingers at Darren who nodded and quickly nestled a bottle of champagne into a large ice bucket.

Eva stood slightly out of view using Roxanne's body as a shield to block Connor and Cara. Cara, on the other hand, displayed no such coyness and brazenly moved into Eva's eye line and stared at her with resentment and suspicion.

'Mr Marshall sends his regards,' said Connor, cocking his head so he could see Eva.

Eva kept her gaze lowered to the floor and acknowledged his comment with a small bob of her head.

'Who's Mr Marshall?' asked Cara, noticing Connor's gaze lingering on Eva.

'He's the club's wealthiest member,' stated Roxanne.

'Well done...' sneered Cara. 'You've caught the eye of an old man,' she said giggling.

'My mother used to say...' started Roxanne with a smirk, 'better to be an old man's darling, than a young man's slave.'

'I wouldn't know. Myself and Connor are the same age, aren't we, darling? But I do feel sorry for you, Eva,' Cara purred with disdain, 'being seen as an object of folly. I worry what'll happen to you once your youthfulness fades.'

'Don't worry, Cara,' said Roxanne in a sarcastic tone. 'Eva will be married long before then. As you can see, she's beautiful and has a body most women can only dream of – no, she won't end up a desperate old spinster waiting for her emotionally stunted lover to pop the question. Even *strippers* find love, you know,' whipped Roxanne, securing a big grin from Tommy.

'Shall we move over to the roulette table,' said Connor in a deadpan tone.

'Okay, darling,' said Cara, reaching down to his inattentive hand hanging down by his side.

Eva lifted her gaze and saw Connor slip his arm around Cara's waist. Witnessing this small gesture of affection plunged her heart into darkness thinking about his child growing inside her. 'At least he didn't kiss her in front of me,' she said, holding back a flood of tears. 'I know it's an awful thing to say, but I hope he is found guilty because men like him don't deserve to be adored. I doubt even *she* would wait twenty years for him.'

'He is being cruel bringing her here,' sympathised Roxanne, reaching down for her hand and gently squeezing her fingers. 'But I'm pretty sure the cops won't find any evidence, babes.'

'That's if they even bother to search the club,' said Eva, narrowing her eyes in thought. 'I'm just popping to the loo if anyone asks where I am,' she added, quickly walking towards the casino lobby. Eva looked back as Roxanne re-joined Tommy, Connor and Cara. She saw Connor still had his arm draped around Cara's waist.

She raced towards the lift with hatred boiling in her blood, her heart pounding with adrenalin, and slammed the palm of her hand against the button. Once on the third floor, her fingers trembled as she recalled the security code to open the penthouse door.

The faint aroma of Connor's aftershave greeted her when she walked inside. She tiptoed across the cream carpet and paused briefly to survey the plush furnishings. She opened drawers and cupboards with care, making sure not to leave any trace of her prying. She ground her teeth in irritation when she couldn't find anything that looked remotely suspicious.

Her eyes darted around the room in search of divine intervention. Then, on a circular table under one of the large domed windows, she spotted a small black and jade Japanese lacquered trinket box with a mother-of-pearl lid. She walked over and picked it up. After gingerly lifting the lid, she let out a stifled gasp and her eyes widened in disbelief at a red and pink woollen braided wristband with small brass letters looped through the frayed wool spelling out SUZY AND EVA 4EVER FRIENDS.

She stared down at the child's friendship wristband. Tears fell onto her powered cheeks as she picked it up carefully, as though handling the crown jewels. She raced out of the penthouse and burst into the dressing room, startling the other dancers, and sprinted over to her locker quickly snatching her handbag to find her mobile.

'What's up with you?' called out Scarlett watching Eva grab her coat and dash out as quickly as she'd entered.

'Mum, come and pick me up now!' Eva shouted down the phone. 'MUM! Stop asking me questions. I need to go home!' she cried out running into the lobby.

Within fifteen minutes Eva heard the screech of car tyres speeding down the road.

'What's he done!' shrieked Patsy when Eva jumped in the passenger seat.

'Just drive, Mum!'

Patsy crunched the gearstick into first and sped off down the road, her face ashen-white with fear.

'Are you going to tell me what's happened?' wailed Patsy.

'Just let me think for a second,' said Eva, her voice trembling. She didn't say another word until they got back to her house.

'Eva!' bellowed Patsy chasing her up the garden path. 'Have you found out something?'

'Wait here!' instructed Eva. She ran up to her bedroom while Patsy stood anxiously in the hall listening the sound of her daughter's heavy footsteps echoing above her head. Then suddenly Eva came stomping back down the stairs. 'Look, Mum!'

Patsy stared down at her open hand. 'What are they?'

'They're friendship bands.' Eva started to weep. 'Susanna made a band for both of us when we were twelve!'

Patsy blinked in confusion. 'Where did you find hers?'

'It was hidden in a box in Connor's apartment!'

'You need to p-phone the police. He *needs* to be arrested!'

Eva curled her fingers around the two woollen wristbands and held them tightly. 'I know…' she croaked before walking into the lounge and slumping onto the sofa.

'Eva, we must phone the police immediately – there's no time to sit and ponder!'

Shaking with disbelief, Eva reached for the TV remote. She didn't know why she wanted to watch the hotel security footage again, but something compelled her to play it. Even though she had just wished Connor would be found guilty, she was now faced with the fact that he would be. Her mind couldn't process the incriminating evidence sitting in the palm of her hand.

'Why are you watching TV? Didn't you hear what I said – we need to call the police!'

'I will, I just want to watch the news report I recorded one last time so I can believe it.'

Patsy frowned and sat down next to Eva. 'What more is there to see?' she asked with a huge sigh.

'I'm not sure, but…'

'Oh, there's Susanna,' said Patsy, starting to cry. 'I'm not sure I can watch it again.'

'Shut up, Mum!' barked Eva, quickly pressing rewind. 'Fuck – why didn't I see that before?!'

'What have you seen?' asked Patsy, staring at the TV.

Eva jerked forward in her seat as she hit the pause button and glared at the flickering image on the screen.

'No – it can't be!'

'Eva, what is it?' implored her mother.

'I'm sure that's Booth's reflection – look! The reflection in the glass door there!' Eva shouted, unable to blink for fear her mind was playing tricks on her.

'I'm not sure. I've only had the displeasure of seeing him from afar. Do you think it could be him?'

Eva knelt down in front of the TV. 'I'm sure it's him, but what was he doing there?'

'Coincidence?'

Eva narrowed her eyes studying the grainy image. 'I'm going to find out why he was there.'

'What?!' said Patsy, watching Eva get up and rush out of the room. 'Wait – where are you going?'

'To speak to Booth!'

With a rasping breath, Patsy gave chase and slammed her body against the front door. 'You're not going to confront him, Eva! We're going to phone the police and tell them what you found in Connor's apartment and seen on the CCTV footage.'

'Something isn't right here, Mum, and I suspect that Booth knows something! Perhaps he saw the real murderer but won't come forward because of his hatred for Connor? If I can persuade him, or even trick him into telling me what he saw that night, then—'

'Eva!' argued Patsy. 'You're overlooking one major piece of the jigsaw – you found Susanna's bracelet in Connor's club!'

'Connor isn't a stupid man. Why would he hide evidence in his place? Plus, he said Susanna invited him back to her apartment, but he refused. How did he get the bracelet? The last time we wore our friendship bands we were at school – Susanna wouldn't have been wearing it on the night of her death – nothing adds up.'

'And those are all questions the police will be asking O'Neill when we phone them! Challenging Booth direct will get us nowhere – we need to call the police.'

'He'll wriggle out of their questions, Mum,' argued Eva. 'I'm going to the Rodeo to confront him, and that's final!'

'Eva Summers!' shouted Patsy. 'I forbid you to leave this house!'

'Mother, I'm twenty-five not twelve!' Eva fired back. 'I'll phone you when I've spoken to him!'

'Stubborn!' yelled Patsy, her brow furrowed. 'Well, I'm not going to let you go alone – I'm coming with you!'

'Fine,' snapped Eva. 'Just wait here while I get something from upstairs.' Rushing back downstairs after a few seconds, Eva grabbed her coat and handbag before slamming the front door shut behind them.

Chapter 31

'When we get there let me do the talking, Mum,' said Eva driving through a light dusting of snow.

'I still think—'

'MUM!' bellowed Eva, hitting the steering wheel with the palm of her hand. 'Are you listening to what I'm saying? We need to stay calm and get him to talk!'

'Okay, I won't say anything!' promised Patsy, quickly firing off a text to Roxanne and Dennis.

Eva sat brooding. She needed to get a plan straight in her head and hold her nerve.

Looking out of the passenger window, Patsy looked up at the large neon sign of a naked woman straddling a bucking bronco.

'Ready, Mum?'

Patsy nodded slowly, trying not to give away how anxious she felt. 'I've texted Roxanne and Dennis, so if anything happens they'll know where to come looking.'

'Mum, this isn't an episode of *Spooks*. Nothing is going to happen apart from a few insults and hopefully Booth confessing why he was there.'

Patsy said nothing and slipped her mobile into her coat pocket as they walked towards the main entrance.

'All right, Eva?' said a man in a broad Liverpudlian accent standing next to three other bouncers.

'Hi, Paul, how things?' said Eva with a bright and breezy exterior but inside her stomach was churning.

'Yeah, not too bad – how about you? You're looking gorgeous as ever,' he said with a smirk, revealing a gold tooth.

Eva offered a flirtatious smile and casually asked if Booth was in.

'Yeah, but I doubt he'll want to see you, pet.' Paul laughed and lit a cigarette.

'Actually, I was just passing and wondered if Tammy and Charmaine were working tonight? My mum's visiting and knows Tammy, so I wondered if we could pop in and say hello?'

Paul glanced over at Patsy and released a long line of smoke. 'Billy…?'

'Yeah,' said the stocky ginger-haired man wearing an ill-fitting black dinner suit.

'Tammy's on tonight, isn't she?'

'Yeah, I fink so...'

'Great, so can we nip in and say hello? I promise I won't be two minutes.'

Paul looked Eva up and down. 'Maybe we can go for a drink sometime? You know, catch up?'

'Yes, why not,' she said, having no intention of honouring their agreement because he was married with four kids!

'Go on then, gorgeous – five minutes!'

'Thanks, Paul,' said Eva, flashing another teasing smile before swaying past him, instantly dropping the façade once inside the dimly lit lobby.

Eva could almost taste the sweat and strong alcohol walking through the rowdy mass of drunken men in the dance lounge.

'Mum, this way,' said Eva, leading her down a long, narrow corridor. Eva hovered outside Booth's office; her skin pricked hearing the familiar rattling cough echo behind the door.

'I still think this is a bad idea,' whispered Patsy, grabbing Eva's arm. 'I think we should go!'

'We're here now,' growled Eva, 'I'm not leaving until I've spoken to him.' With her heart hammering beneath her chest, she brushed her tongue across her dry lips. She raised her hand and rapped her knuckles against the door. With no answer, she listened for a lull in Booth's coughing and knocked again, holding her breath.

'Yeahhh!'

Eva glanced over to her mother as she pressed down on the door handle and walked inside.

'Well, well...look what the cat's dragged in!' bellowed Booth, slouching back in his chair. 'What the fuck are you doing in my club?' he sneered. 'If you've come here begging for your old job back, then you can get on your knees and suck my cock for it!' He laughed creating a deep rattle of phlegm in his throat.

'What a disgusting thing to say to a young woman,' retorted Patsy, taking a step forward towards Booth's desk.

'It's okay!' snapped Eva, reaching out for her mother's arm.

'Who's the old tart?'

'Old tart!' shrieked Patsy with a gasp.

'*Mum*,' pleaded Eva, giving her a wide glare. 'We haven't come here for an argument. Mr Booth has an acquired sense of humour, that's all,' added Eva nervously.

'Mother, hey?' Booth sniffed loudly giving Patsy the once over. 'So tell me, have they locked up that Irish bastard yet?'

'You've seen the news, then?' probed Eva.

'Everyone's heard about him killing that hooker in Vegas. It's a shame they don't hang murderers anymore!' taunted Booth as he broke wind in front of them.

'He hasn't been charged, only questioned,' corrected Eva.

'It's just a matter of time,' added Booth, lighting a cigar. 'So why are you souring my evening – what do you want?'

With a cloud of white cigar smoke drifting over his desk, Eva discreetly slipped her hand into her coat pocket.

'Have the police questioned you yet?'

'Why would they want to question me?'

'You were there, weren't you? You're on the hotel's CCTV footage.'

Booth's chair creaked as he sat forward. 'So what if I was?' He shrugged and reached over to a half-empty bottle of Scotch sitting on his littered desk. 'It's got fuck all to do with me, but if the police want a character reference on O'Neill, then I'd be happy to give them one. I mean, what is he? A fraudster, a liar, a woman beater! Yes, I could paint the cops a very colourful picture of your scumbag boss,' he said, enjoying every reproachful word tumbling out of his mouth.

Patsy blinked and looked at Eva in shock. 'Woman beater?'

'Didn't your daughter tell you?' Booth tutted. 'He beat his ex-girlfriend to a pulp and killed her unborn child. He's a fucking animal! He needs putting down like a diseased dog!'

'Of course, that's your version of the story!' challenged Eva, noticing the utter horror etched on her mother's face hearing such a barbaric account of Connor's dark past.

'I guess he fed you a pack of lies while fucking you up the arse, did he!' snorted Booth, revealing a row of yellow, rotten teeth. 'You must've made his balls tingle swallowing that bullshit! Well I must say, I'm disappointed in you Eva; I thought you had a little more nous than that!'

'Who's to say he was lying? The only two people who can reveal the truth is Susanna and her killer, but if I can find a witness—'

'O'Neill is guilty and that's that! Has he sent you here to try and persuade me to lie for him? Cos I'd rather cut out my own tongue than say a good word about that bastard. He'll get twenty-five-years when the cops find the evidence,' said Booth, smirking.

Eva narrowed her eyes. *'Find the evidence?'*

Booth fidgeted in his seat; a pile of cigar ash tumbled down his already stained shirt. 'I er… I mean, they're bound to find some evidence, aren't they?!'

'That's not what you said, or implied,' said Eva. 'You said *the*, which implies you're certain there's something to be found!'

'You're twisting my fucking words!' barked Booth, stubbing out his cigar. 'That Irish bastard is going down for twenty-five years for killing that slag, and there's nothing or no one that's gonna stop it from happening!'

'You seem pretty confident of his guilt,' argued Eva. 'I think you saw something that night but won't say!'

Booth glanced over towards the partially closed door before glaring back at Eva. 'Well, where's your proof he's innocent?!'

'Where's your proof of his guilt?' Eva baited.

'You just wait and see,' roared Booth. 'The police will find something that'll leave them in no doubt he killed that whore!'

'What – something like this?' said Eva, holding up Susanna's friendship band.

With Booth's sweat-sodden skin erupting into purple blotches, Eva took a step back seeing his whole body tense with rage.

'What the fuck have you done!' he yelled. '*Jesus Christ*, you've just signed our death warrants, you stupid bitch!'

'We're going, Eva!' cried out Patsy, grabbing her arm.

'*You're not going anywhere,*' came a deep voice rising above the sound of the door creaking open.

Panic widened Eva's eyes as she shuffled backwards, pulling her mother towards her.

'Who are you?' cried out Patsy to the tall figure emerging from the shadows.

'I'm your worst nightmare, old woman.'

'St Clair…' croaked Eva.

'You cannot keep us here against our will. I-I'll phone the police!' yelled Patsy, plunging her hand into her handbag, feverishly rummaging for her mobile.

'Be quiet!' barked St Clair, lunging forward and snatching the mobile out of her hand.

'*Oh God,*' whimpered Eva when St Clair quickly blocked the doorway with his body.

'You've ruined months of planning with your prying and meddling, you brainless bitch!' sneered St Clair, baring his teeth at Eva.

'She's got the bracelet!' panicked Booth. 'What we gonna do now? I ain't losing my fucking head over this,' he wheezed. 'Perhaps we can tell the Murphy brothers the truth and replant the evidence?'

'Everything has been set for tonight. That evidence was supposed to be found by the cops! Without it, O'Neill won't be charged and he'll carry on fighting our gaming licence, and we both know what'll happen if we don't get it!' shouted St Clair. 'The Murphy brothers have paid us upfront to fucking launder money out of the new casino, there's no turning back. Either O'Neill goes down or we'll find ourselves in a shallow grave!'

Booth swallowed hard thinking about the consequences facing them. 'Can't we try and delay the raid?'

'Tina planted it!' mumbled Eva, squeezing Patsy's hand, her mind racing to recall the night she saw Tina leaving the penthouse with the excuse of dropping off Connor's post.

'We can't delay, you fool! Johnny has given me the nod. It's fucking happening tonight – everyone's been paid off,' barked St Clair.

'It was your idea to kill that stupid girlfriend of yours and frame O'Neill! I wanted to keep it clean and kill the Irish cunt but no, you wanted a more elaborate plan and look where it's got us!' yelled Booth.

'You speak to me like that again, and you'll be joining her!' sneered St Clair.

'What?' snapped Booth, 'I'm the one who brought you into this deal. You forget, Patrick, I know your past. If anything happens to me, my lawyer has a detailed letter explaining who killed O'Neill's ex and Susanna – you!'

'I'll rip that tongue out of your head if you don't shut the fuck up!' cursed St Clair, scowling at Booth. 'Get Jenkins on the phone and tell him to bring the van round in half an hour, plus get Tina here and give her this,' he said, snatching the woollen braid from Eva.

'You killed Susanna just to stop Connor opposing your gaming licence?' asked Eva, in a slow hypnotic tone. *'You're the boyfriend!'*

St Clair gave Eva a slow, malevolent grin. 'Can you imagine my surprise finding out you knew Susanna – ha!'

'You followed her that night when I saw you in the nightclub.'

'I didn't want to risk the sulky bitch going AWOL over a couple of bruises. Without her, we would've had to alter our plan.'

'Your plan,' cried Eva, *'to kill her.'*

'There are always casualties in business – she was expendable.'

'She was a human being,' pleaded Eva.

'No, she was a whore – but I'll concede, a very profitable one.'

Eva wished she had a knife to stab St Clair straight through the heart. She always thought monsters only existed in children's stories, but what stood in front of her was a real-life monster; one that she needed to snare, and the only way she could do that was by shutting down emotionally and getting St Clair to reveal everything.

'How did you know Connor was going to be in Vegas over Christmas?' asked Eva, blinking back a flood of tears.

'I guess it won't matter now if you know the truth – you won't be telling anyone after I've finished with you,' St Clair said coldly. 'I knew O'Neill would be attending the annual Wynn Fall Classic Poker Championship on the twelfth of January, but imagine my delight when my good friend here saw your man on Boxing Day. Bringing forward our plan meant we had more time to put things into place. So after a little *physical* persuading, Susanna agreed to lure him back to her apartment thinking I was going to steal his wallet – she didn't know who he was,' he said dismissively.

'But Connor didn't go back to her apartment.'

St Clair grimaced with annoyance. 'She couldn't even manage that. The only thing she did well was die!'

Booth released a chilling laugh as he pressed his mobile to his ear.

'You look pretty brainless, so I'll simplify the facts. My plan was like a game of Cluedo,' gloated St Clair. 'I had a venue, a body, and a suspect who was drunk and had previous – it was almost *too* easy.'

'So you took something from Susanna's apartment and gave it to Tina who then planted it in Connor's apartment,' persisted Eva, swallowing hard.

'Actually, Tina came to us,' said St Clair. 'She hates you!' He chuckled. 'She came here looking for dirt on you and practically wet her knickers at the chance to bring O'Neill down. Everything was in place until you went fucking snooping!'

'Please don't hurt us,' begged Patsy. 'We won't tell anyone – I promise! Eva can put the bracelet back – can't you, Eva?'

Booth's mobile ringing stirred Eva out of her trance-like state.

'Jenkins is outside with the van,' said Booth.

'Right, enough questions,' said St Clair, glancing down at his watch. 'What time is Tina getting here?'

'She'll be here in ten minutes,' wheezed Booth, heaving his huge bulk out of the chair.

'Right, let's get this done.'

'People know we're here!' screamed Patsy, watching in horror as St Clair took a step towards them. 'There'll be here any minute!'

Eva squeezed her mother's hand tightly before reaching into her coat pocket with her other hand. She stared wide-eyed at both men, then snatched a glimpse of the door. 'MUM, RUN!' screamed Eva, pulling a small can of hairspray from her pocket and aiming the stinging mist towards St Clair's face.

With hysterical screams, pandemonium erupted. St Clair stumbled backwards clutching his face roaring for Booth to stop them leaving.

Eva pushed Patsy in front of her out of the office and they both started running down the narrow corridor.

Hearing Eva scream behind her, Patsy slid to a halt and turned to see Booth forcibly restraining her daughter by her hair. 'Let her go!' roared Patsy, clawing at Booth's face until he released her.

St Clair yelled expletives and threats behind them; Eva kicked Booth in the groin making him drop to his knees.

'Run towards the lobby!' instructed Eva, hot on her mum's heels.

'PAUL!' St Clair shouted to one of the bouncers, his eyes streaming with tears. 'Don't let them leave!'

Looking startled, Paul turned around to see Eva and Patsy charging out of the lobby screaming at the top of their voices. He held out his arms to block their path.

'MOVE!' roared Eva, holding out her car keys and striking Paul hard across his cheek.

With blood pouring from the deep wound, he stumbled down the entrance steps while the ginger-haired bouncer lunged forward and knocked Eva down onto the pavement.

Eva and Patsy's loud screams instantly secured the attention of passers-by. A group of young men came running over and pulled the heavy-set bouncer off Eva, with one of the men punching him in the face.

'Eva!' cried out Patsy, reaching down to help her off the pavement.

Fear widened their footsteps as both women sprinted up the street; a chorus of car horns beeped at them running carelessly across oncoming traffic.

'EVA!'

'Eh?' gasped Eva, her face flushed crimson and dripping with sweat.

'Roxanne!'

'Eva, we're here!' screamed out Roxanne, swerving into the kerb in Tommy's black Audi.

'Oh, thank God,' sobbed Patsy, hurling herself into the back of the car. 'They were going to kill us!'

Eva dashed into the car and panted in the backseat trying to catch her breath. 'Drive, Roxanne!' she screamed.

Roxanne sped away with her foot flat on the accelerator. 'Sorry, I've only just got your text!' she cried, glancing into the rearview mirror. 'Why did you go to the Rodeo, Eva?'

'Because she saw Booth on the CCTV footage,' said Tommy calmly sitting in the passenger seat.

Eva gasped. 'You know?'

'Of course – Connor's legal team have studied every second of the tape. Connor has people working on why Booth was there.'

'Well, I can save him the trouble,' stated Eva.

'What do you know?' asked Tommy, turning to look at her.

'St Clair confessed to killing Susanna and Connor's ex Maria! He killed Susanna to frame him so he couldn't oppose their gaming licence. He thought we wouldn't be alive to tell anyone, so he revealed everything.'

'Who's behind the deal?'

'The Murphy brothers, he said. And Tina's involved, too. She helped them plant a bracelet of Susanna's at the Unicorn, which I found. Apparently the police are going to raid the club tonight.'

'And St Clair told you all this?'

Eva nodded, her eyes swollen with tears. 'Roxy, please take me to the nearest police station,' she asked, sniffing.

'It'll be your word against theirs.' Tommy frowned reaching for his phone to call Connor.

'That's why I recorded everything on my mobile,' replied Eva, taking it out of her coat pocket. She played St Clair's confession.

Jesus Christ…' uttered Tommy, his eyes wide and serious. 'Rox, get them to the police station quick because St Clair will have his men crawling around London looking for them, especially if the Murphy brothers are involved. Booth and St Clair will know they're on borrowed time.'

Eva felt drained sitting in the police interview room listening to St Clair's confession for a third time. The police had all the evidence they needed to arrest both men for the premeditated murder of both Maria and Susanna, and the attempted murder of Patsy and herself.

'We'll be in touch soon, Miss Summers,' said Inspector Mossop. 'This will secure a long custodial sentence for both men,' he said, holding up her mobile with his chubby fingers.

On her way out, Eva noticed Connor leaving another room with two detectives. His warm smile pinched her heart as he walked straight over to her.

'It was incredibly dangerous and also very courageous of you to confront Booth and St Clair on your own,' declared Connor.

'I wanted justice for Susanna,' said Eva, dabbing her eyes with a crumpled tissue. 'How do you feel discovering that St Clair killed Maria, too?'

'I guess at the back of my mind I always thought he was involved but didn't have the proof. He'll get twenty-five years, if not more,' explained Connor, knowing the lengthy sentence would not really ease Eva's pain.

'I can't believe I'll never speak to her again,' cried Eva. 'She was such a beautiful person; she didn't deserve to die in such a horrible way.'

'Look, I want you and your mother to stay at the club with me tonight,' pleaded Connor, 'you're not safe until Booth and St Clair are caught.'

'Roxanne said we can stay with her, but I need to go home and get Mr Jingles and some clothes.'

'Sorry, Eva, but I must insist that you stay at the club. The whole place is wired with CCTV and alarms. I'll take you home to get your cat – I insist,' said Connor.

'Okay, if you think we'll be safer there. What about Tina?'

'The police have already been to the club and arrested her. The club will be closed for the next couple of days.'

'Oh, Eva, I still can't believe what's happened,' sobbed Patsy, walking over to her and Connor. 'I won't sleep soundly until those murdering thugs are caught and locked up!'

'Once the Murphy brothers find out their plan has been foiled, they'll want to contain the damage – that means making Booth and St Clair disappear. I reckon the Murphy brothers will go underground until everything settles down,' said Connor.

'I guess it takes the mind of a corrupt man to understand another!' said Patsy.

'Mum...' said Eva wearily.

'My daughter has told me all about your character and morals, Mr O'Neill,' added Patsy with a furrowed brow. 'You might be able to charm young impressionable girls with your looks and money, but that won't work on me. I can see through all your finery and inflated ego. Why, you're not much better than the two thugs who murdered poor Susanna!'

'MUM,' snapped Eva, her cheeks flushed crimson. 'Connor has said we can stay at the club tonight – it'll be safer than staying at Roxy's.'

'It's the least he can do!' said Patsy, holding Connor's stare, her five-foot frame under his shadow.

As they left the police station, Roxanne insisted that she and Tommy escort Eva home with Connor in case St Clair's henchmen were lurking around her house.

The mood was sombre in the back of Connor's Range Rover. Eva looked out towards a large group of rowdy, intoxicated revellers staggering down the street. A few stragglers were wandering carelessly into the road as police sirens echoed in distance – a typical night in London.

Turning into her road, Eva saw her next-door neighbour Mrs Simms and her husband, Stanley, standing outside on her garden path talking to two police officers.

'They've been here already!' cried out Eva, pushing open the door when Connor pulled up.

'Eva, dear!' called out Mrs Simms. 'We heard the sound of glass breaking, so Stanley went to take a look and saw two men in your back garden!'

'I told Doris to phone the police immediately,' interrupted Stanley, standing in his tartan dressing gown and slippers. 'I called out to them that the police had been called, and they ran down the side alley.'

'Oh God!' cried Eva, fumbling for her front door keys as a young female police officer approached her.

'Excuse me, madam, are you the owner of this property?'

'Yes I am,' said Eva, shoving her key into the front door lock.

'Madam, you cannot enter the property until I or my colleagues have checked inside.'

'They might have hurt my cat!' shrieked Eva, nudging past her and storming into the hallway.

'MR JINGLES!' Holding her breath, she stood still and waited to hear his brass bell ring but was only greeted with silence. Fear quickened her step as she ran into the lounge, then into the kitchen where splinters of broken glass crunched under the soles of her boots.

'Please don't touch anything,' said the female officer joining her in the kitchen. 'It looks like they tried to force the lock before smashing the glass, but it doesn't appear that they entered the property – thanks to your neighbour.'

'I know exactly who tried to break into my home. You need to speak to Inspector Mossop,' called out Eva, quickly sprinting upstairs.

'Mum, I can't find him!'

'Eva!' Connor called out from the hallway. 'I'll go outside and call him.'

Eva felt despondent and frightened walking back into the lounge with Patsy.

'Eva,' announced Connor a couple of minutes later, 'is this what you're looking for?'

Spinning around, Eva screamed with joy seeing Mr Jingles being held tightly by Connor. She snatched him out of his arms and burst into tears bombarding her beloved cat with kisses. 'He's unhurt,' Eva said with relief.

'Miss Summers,' interrupted the female officer. 'I've spoken to Inspector Mossop and he's confirmed your break-in is probably linked to an ongoing investigation regarding a…Mr Booth and a…Mr St Clair,' she said reading from her notepad. 'Do you have somewhere to stay tonight?'

'Yes, they're staying with me,' said Connor, picking up Eva's small overnight case.

Roxanne stared at Eva. 'You know you can stay at mine, babes – you and Patsy.'

'It's already been agreed, they'll stay with me tonight. So let's go,' said Connor in a sharp, direct tone. 'I'll get my maintenance guys to come over and make your house safe,' he added, slamming her front door shut.

'Is Cara back at the penthouse?' asked Eva, walking down her garden path.

'No, she's staying in a hotel,' Connor replied dismissively.

'Can we lock the doors, please?' asked Eva, holding Mr Jingles tightly and climbing into the backseat of Connor's Range Rover.

'No one is going to hurt you with me here,' Connor stated firmly.

'All the same, I'd feel safer if the doors were locked.'

'Okay.' Connor did as she asked to calm her.

'I still can't believe St Clair was Susanna's boyfriend – you couldn't write this shit,' blurted Roxanne sitting in between Eva and Patsy.

'I don't know how I'm going to get through the funeral,' confessed Eva, her voice tight with emotion.

'You won't be on your own,' soothed Roxanne, 'me and your mum will be there to support you.'

'We can all go, if you want?' added Connor looking at Eva through his rearview mirror.

'I'll be fine with Mum and Roxanne,' replied Eva, resting her head on her friend's shoulder, closing her eyes with exhaustion.

Approaching the club's car park, Eva lifted her head and peered out of the window. 'What if they're watching us – lying in wait?'

'You see that guy over there in the black bomber jacket?' said Connor. 'And the guy in the navy coat? I've hired them to keep a look out.'

Eva glanced over at the men. Holding Mr Jingles tight to her chest, she stayed close to Connor as they all walked through the main entrance. He quickly ushered everyone into the lobby before locking the double doors behind them. Eva felt emotionally drained as they entered the penthouse suite.

'Why aren't you at the hotel?' asked Connor indignantly, seeing Cara sat on the sofa watching TV.

'I wanted to make sure you got back safely, darling,' explained Cara, quickly getting to her feet and joining him.

'I'm fine. I'll get Tommy to take you to the Hilton.'

'I'd rather stay here with you,' said Cara, looking down at Eva under a frown of jealousy.

Not having the strength to return Cara's childish glares, Eva asked Connor if she could lie down in one of the bedrooms.

'Yes, of course,' fussed Connor, 'do you need or want anything?'

'If I could have a glass of water?'

'Oh…?' said Cara. 'Is everyone staying here tonight?' she moaned. 'Why don't you offer my hotel room to Eva and her friend?'

'I'm Eva's mother,' Patsy said frostily.

'Eva and her mother are staying here tonight' explained Connor in a stiff and formal manner. 'Tommy will take you to the Hilton. End of discussion.'

Patsy glared at Cara as she wrapped her arm around her daughter. 'So, where can Eva rest?'

Roxanne sensed the building tension. 'I'll show you,' she offered.

Latching herself onto to Connor's arm, Cara watched Eva, Patsy and Roxanne walk away under a repugnant frown. She sullenly watched Connor go over to the drinks cabinet for a bottle of mineral water.

'Go and pack,' snapped Connor, becoming increasingly irritated by her shadowing his every move.

'Will you be joining me at the hotel?' asked Cara, her voice soft and pleading.

'No…' replied Connor before walking off.

Knocking on the first bedroom door, Connor stood holding the glass of water until a disgruntled Patsy opened the door.

She took the glass and hissed under her breath, 'Get rid of *her*, haven't you got an ounce of compassion for my daughter's feelings?!'

Connor frowned. 'I didn't intend for them to meet,' he said, lowering his voice.

'Once those two murdering bastards are locked up, I will personally make sure you never see my daughter or your…' Patsy stopped herself before blurting out Eva's secret. 'Just get rid of that tart!' she added sourly, shutting the door in his face.

Both women stayed in their room all night despite Connor's efforts to speak to Eva alone.

Chapter 32

It was late morning when Eva and Patsy were woken by a loud knock on their door.

'The police are here. They want to speak to the three of us together,' stated Connor from outside the bedroom.

Eva flattened down her hair and walked into the lounge with Patsy close by her side. There stood two police officers.

'Have you found them?' asked Patsy, sitting down.

'Two bodies have been found in Battersea Park at eight o'clock this morning,' answered the older policeman. 'The descriptions match that of Mr Booth and Mr St Clair.'

For a second Eva sat in shock. She glanced over at Connor.

'I am *not* sorry to hear that. It may sound inappropriate to rejoice, but both men got what they deserved – they were evil murderers,' announced Patsy without a flicker of remorse.

'Do you know how they were killed?' asked Eva.

'Both men were shot at point-blank range,' added the Indian police officer.

'I'm assuming those so-called Murphy brothers shot them?' added Patsy.

'We cannot confirm who was involved at the moment.'

Connor's silence made Eva wonder whether he had any involvement in their timely deaths; she knew he had people on the ground trying to 'resolve' the situation.

'So what happens now?' asked Patsy.

'We have their recorded confession, so Mr O'Neill will no longer be questioned over Miss Curtis's death, but I need to ask each of you to confirm your whereabouts at three o'clock this morning?'

'Why? Are we being accused of shooting them?' scoffed Patsy. 'Does it look like either myself or my daughter could overpower two hardened criminals. The notion is ridiculous.'

'Mum!' said Eva blushing. 'They just need to establish where we were last night. We were here all night, officer,' stated Eva truthfully.

'And were you both alone?'

'No, I was here, too,' said Connor.

'Is there anyone that can corroborate your story, sir?'

'Yes, his girlfriend was here as well,' added Eva.

'She *isn't* my girlfriend,' said Connor. 'I had a friend here, but she left at one o'clock this morning – her name is Miss Cara Dickson.'

'Is there any way we can contact Miss Dickson?'

'Yes, but we parted on bad terms. She's staying at the Hilton. You can check the club's CCTV. Neither Miss Summers, her mother or myself left the club all night. I have the disc here,' said Connor, reaching into his jacket pocket and pulling out a CD case.

The older police officer nodded for his colleague to take the disc and continued to write on his notepad.

'And what about Tina, what will happen to her?' asked Eva, getting to her feet.

'Miss Jackson will be charged with conspiracy – she willingly planted evidence against Mr O'Neill in the attempt to secure his arrest.'

'Will she be locked up?'

'The person in question will be looking at a custodial sentence – yes.'

Eva sighed as she looked down at Connor. She was sure Tina's love must have been so deep for him that when it turned to hatred, she was willing to take such a major role in his downfall.

Eva watched the police leave and turned to Connor. 'Do you think the Murphy brothers will come looking for us?'

'I think they'll go to ground, so no. There's too much heat on them to go looking for further reprisals.'

'Why am I not surprised that you'd know how a criminal's mind works,' scolded Patsy. 'Behind all your finery, you're cut from the same cloth!'

'Mum, please,' said Eva, sighing. 'So, we can go home now?'

'Your door hasn't been fixed. My guys are doing it this afternoon.'

'Oh...'

'Do you need something from home?' asked Connor. 'I can go and get whatever you need?'

'No, but I am hungry.'

'I can book us a table at The Grosvenor?'

'I just meant a snack or something. The Grosvenor is a little grand for a sandwich and a cup of coffee,' replied Eva.

'Sorry... I just thought we could have a nice lunch,' said Connor, sounding crestfallen at her dismissive tone.

A ping of awkwardness washed over her as she realised her reply had been delivered so ungraciously. 'Sorry, yes, The Grosvenor would be nice. I need to take a shower and freshen up first.'

'Of course, I'll get out of your way, then call back for you in an hour,' said Connor, his spirits lifting on hearing her conciliation as he left the apartment.

'Let me run you a bath and we'll have a chat, love.'

Eva narrowed her eyes. 'Chat about what?'

Patsy turned on the taps and reached for a bottle of scented bubble bath. The smell of jasmine and lemon quickly filled the bathroom.

'Chat about what, Mum?' repeated Eva, dropping her clothes on the floor and stepping into the warm scented bath water.

'I won't be a minute, I'll fetch you some clean clothes,' soothed Patsy. With a set of clean underwear, a pair of white jeans and a dark green jumper, Patsy walked back into the bathroom. She pulled down the loo seat and sat down. 'Can we talk about the baby?'

'Mum, we've spoken about this,' said Eva, submerging her shoulders under the water. 'How would I manage? I can hardly look after myself.'

Glancing down at the pretty pink satin bra and knickers sitting on her lap, Patsy inhaled softly. 'But you wouldn't be on your own if you moved to Spain. I would help you raise the child. Dennis would love a little one running about the place. The move wouldn't have to be forever, just until you're back on your feet.'

'I'd have to tell Connor if I did decide to keep it.'

'Why? He has no desire to be a father.'

'It wouldn't be right to keep it from him.'

'Are you expecting him to suddenly become a doting father?' What would be crueller? Telling him about the child and waiting for him to abandon you both before the child reaches its first birthday, or not giving him the chance in the first place?'

'Maybe an abortion is the only option, then,' said Eva, resigning herself. 'At some point our child will want to know about its father. I don't think I could bear him rejecting our child.'

Sensing she had approached the subject in the wrong way, Patsy quickly changed tack; she was desperate for Eva to keep her first grandchild and if that meant telling Connor, then so be it. 'Perhaps you're right,' she assured, grabbing a large bath towel. 'Maybe you should tell Connor, then move out to Spain. It will give you both time to get used to the idea. You could rent out your house and bring your cat with you?'

Eva glanced through the open door to look at Mr Jingles sleeping quietly on the bed. 'But what if he's repulsed by the idea of becoming a father?'

'Then we'll cross that bridge when we come to it,' reasoned Patsy.

'I need to think about it,' pondered Eva, dunking her head under the water and rinsing off a layer of white suds.

Patsy held out the bath towel for Eva as she stepped out of the bathtub. 'The bar is doing well, so there'll be a job for you whenever you want. And don't worry about childcare, me and Dennis will babysit whenever you want a break or need time to yourself,' offered Patsy, following her into the bedroom.

'Mum, enough, you're giving me a headache. I said I'll think about it, and I will.'

Patsy went to answer a knock on the door leaving Eva to finish getting dressed. 'Oh, you're back,' said Patsy, looking up at Connor's handsome face. His piercing blue eyes and perfectly symmetrical features held no allure for her.

'I've booked us a table,' said Connor, trying to peer around the door to catch Eva's attention, 'so I'll bring the car around in twenty minutes.'

'Okay, I'll tell Eva,' said Patsy, slamming the door in his face again.

Connor quickly jerked his head back. He knew he was going to have to work hard to win over Patsy – her disdain for him seemed resolute.

'We're ready,' said Patsy, finding Connor sitting in the lounge.

Eva looked down at her white jeans. 'I feel underdressed.'

'You look great,' said Connor, giving an admiring smile.

'Shall we go?' snapped Patsy, not happy with Connor's extended glances towards her daughter.

Unlocking the lobby doors, Connor smiled at Eva again as she walked past him. She lowered her gaze and bit her lip; his handsome features and seductive scent tortured her heart.

'Dennis!' cried out Patsy seeing a black cab pulling up and Dennis's large frame clambering out of the back. 'Thank God you're here!' she said, running over to him.

'This is my mother's partner,' said Eva, watching Dennis quickly walk over towards her and Connor.

'Step away from my stepdaughter!' barked Dennis, pulling back his fist.

Eva gasped in horror as Connor swiftly blocked his punch.

'I don't want to fight you!' warned Connor, baring his teeth, his cheeks flushed with anger.

'Eva, go to your mother!' sneered Dennis.

'I'm not in any danger, Connor didn't kill Susanna!' pleaded Eva, watching Dennis draw back his fist again, this time hitting Connor in the mouth.

With panic and hysteria surrounding them like two screaming toddlers, Connor grabbed Dennis by the throat and raised his fist.

'CONNOR, PLEASE DON'T HIT HIM!' cried out Eva, clinging onto his arm.

Gritting his teeth, Connor lowered his fist and pushed Dennis down onto the pavement.

'Get your hands off my husband!' demanded Patsy marching over to Connor. 'Dennis, for God's sake – get up!' she ordered.

Dennis, with a small graze on his forehead, got up and stared at Connor with abhorrence.

'Mum, did you tell Dennis that Connor has been cleared?'

'I was going to explain everything once he got here.'

'Mum!' growled Eva, widening her eyes.

'I'm sorry! I didn't know Dennis was going to hit him.'

'Eva, let's go!' insisted Dennis, reaching out for her arm. 'Get in the taxi!'

'Don't shout at her!' Connor fired back, wiping the back of his hand across a small, deep cut on his bottom lip. 'Eva, you don't have to leave. I'd like us to talk privately. Maybe just the two of us can go for lunch?'

Eva glanced up at Connor. It was the first time she had ever seen him looking vulnerable and sad.

Dennis looked on with irritation and fists clenched down by his side.

'I think I should go,' said Eva, trying to blink back imminent tears. 'Perhaps you should go and fix things with Cara?'

'Eva…' started Connor. 'I don't love her, I lo—'

'Eva, come on!' called out Patsy. 'Let's go back up to get your things and Mr Jingles – the taxi is waiting.'

'*Eva*…' implored Connor, touching her hand but struggling to retain composure.

'Eva – come on,' insisted Patsy, walking over to them, forcefully leading her daughter away towards the lift. 'A leopard never changes its spots, love,' she added coldly. 'I think it's best to make a clean break.'

'I know in my heart that I still love him, Mum.'

'I know it's hard to be strong and walk away. He's handsome and rich for sure, but he's also arrogant and self-centred. You can't change those traits in a man, Eva, because if you could, every woman would have her "happy ever after", wouldn't they? Don't be blinded by false hope that you'll be able to change him. Men like that stay single for a reason – they enjoy the lifestyle, the women, the power, and the ability to disregard the feelings of others who don't play by their rules.'

'Rules?' said Eva as they reached the third floor.

'Yes – no commitment, no demands and no obligations. So if you're happy to live within those constraints, then he's the man for you.'

Patsy glanced at her disheartened daughter knowing her words had been delivered unsweetened and with conviction. She wanted Connor out of Eva's life for good, and she intended to make that happen.

Eva packed her bag, picked up Mr Jingles and followed her mother out of the penthouse with her mum's words of admonition playing on her mind, '*No commitment, no demands and no obligations.*'

'Eva, can I speak with you in private, please?' implored Connor, forcibly blocking her path as they stepped back into the lobby.

'Sorry, but we don't have time,' Patsy said aloofly, stepping in front of Eva to obstruct Connor's beseeching stares.

'Mum, take Mr Jingles and wait in the taxi with Dennis, please.'

'But—'

'Please, Mum!' snapped Eva, shoving Mr Jingles into her arms.

Waiting for her mother to walk out of earshot, Eva pulled her coat tightly together and looked back up at Connor. 'Here, take this,' she said, taking a tissue from her handbag.

'Please can we go somewhere to talk?' asked Connor, dabbing his lip. 'I want you to stay on at the Unicorn – forget the Birmingham job. It was just a knee-jerk reaction to us splitting up. I knew I wouldn't be able to deal with seeing you every day, so I wanted to send you away.'

'Mum has asked me to move to Spain until all this dies down. They have a bistro and she's offered me a job.'

'But you have a job here,' argued Connor. 'I swear on my life no one will hurt you if you stay.'

'Do you include yourself in that promise?' asked Eva, her eyes watery and pupils dilated.

'I know my behaviour has been unkind at times, but don't they say you hurt the people that you care about the most?'

'In that case, you need to stop caring about me because my heart can't bear any more pain – I'm on my knees with grief for Susanna.'

'Tell me what I have to do to make you happy again, and I'll do it!'

Eva brushed her lips together and lowered her gaze. 'You have to let me go…' she whispered.

Connor suddenly stepped back looking dejected. He quickly turned away to brush a tear from his cheek and took out his mirrored sunglasses from his shirt pocket.

Eva knew she had every right to rejoice in his misery but took no pleasure from his despair; she couldn't exult in his wretchedness because she still loved the man, if not the person. 'Sorry, we want different things in life. We couldn't survive trying to live in each other's lives.'

'Are coming back?' asked Connor, swallowing hard.

'I don't know.'

'Can we at least stay in contact?' pressed Connor.

'Eva, we must go now!' called out Patsy from the back of the taxi.

'Eva,' said Connor quickly, 'I-I…'

Eva paused briefly as Connor struggled with his pride. 'I have to go, I guess we'll see each other at Tina's trial,' said Eva before walking towards the waiting taxi.

'Nineteen Normandy Close, Hackney, please,' said Patsy, shuffling across the backseat to make room for Eva.

Eva looked across at Connor standing motionless on the pavement as the black cab pulled away.

'You've done the right thing, love,' soothed Patsy, wrapping her arm around her shoulder.

Eva sat back in her seat with tears streaming down her face. Heartache chilled her bones like an arctic wind while her mind cruelly recalled Connor's smile and touch. Eva's heart and true feelings were plunged into an abyss of desolation and misery.

Chapter 33

Three weeks later Eva had rented out her house, and she was living in Spain with Patsy and Dennis. She kept in contact with Roxanne who confessed that Connor was struggling with her sudden departure. Even his associates and friends were noticing his excessive drinking and wild, uncharacteristic behaviour.

Tina's trial was taking place in a month's time at the end of May. Eva had received a message from Connor, via Roxanne, asking if she would be willing to meet up before the hearing. Eva had been hesitant to reply. She had decided to keep their child and would be nearly six months pregnant by then, so he would obviously notice her weight gain if they saw each other. Also, she didn't want to risk the feelings she had buried under the bitterness of his betrayal with Cara resurfacing again.

'Mum, I'm just going for a walk,' called out Eva, picking up her sunglasses and sliding open the back door of Patsy's whitewashed villa. A warm breeze swirled her lime-green summer dress making it billow out like a ship's sail as she stepped out onto the terracotta patio.

She'd only just reached the black iron gates at the end of the drive when she heard Patsy call out, 'Eva – lunch is in twenty minutes, so don't walk too far up the beach!'

'Okay,' she called back, smiling at Mr Jingles circling her mother's feet.

Patsy picked up Mr Jingles and went back inside the villa after watching Eva cross the road towards a narrow flight of steps leading down to the quiet and uncrowded beach.

She slipped out of her white flip-flops to feel the warm powdery sand under her feet. Connor's baby softly kicking inside her made her smile. She stared out towards the deep turquoise sea with a deep, contented sigh.

She hummed a tune as she continued to walk up the beach. Apart from an elderly man throwing a ball for his brown wiry-haired dog, there was no one around until she saw a tall man dressed in white shorts and a blue T-shirt staring over at her. She squinted trying to focus in on him when he started to walk directly over to her.

Suddenly feeling uneasy, she scanned the beach and wondered if her cries would be heard by the man walking his dog or the elderly woman who she could now see walking with a young boy towards the gentle waves of the sea.

'Miss Eva Summers?'

Eva took two steps back and protectively placed her hand onto her rounded stomach. 'Who are you?'

'Are you Eva Summers, madam?' repeated the tall man holding a large white envelope.

Not answering his question, Eva glanced back to her mother's villa.

'There's no need to fear me, madam. I have a letter for a Miss Eva Summers.'

'A letter?' asked Eva.

'Yes,' confirmed the man, holding out the envelope.

'Who is it from?'

'I cannot say until you confirm you're Miss Eva Summers – sorry.'

Eva studied the middle-aged man, then nodded.

'I've been hired by Mr Connor O'Neill to give you this.'

'How did you know where to find me?' Eva quizzed nervously, checking the beach again. 'Is he here?'

'No, madam – my instructions were to find you and give you this,' said the man, handing her the envelope before turning and walking away.

Eva's heart thumped against her chest looking down at the neat handwriting. She walked over to a small cluster of rocks and tried to make herself comfortable. Her fingers hovered over the sealed flap before checking who was around. She peered inside and saw a letter and a CD. Taking a deep breath, she reached inside and took out the disc which simply said 'play me' written in black maker pen. Eva dropped it back inside and took out the letter.

Dear Eva,

I hope this letter finds you well. This is the first letter I've written to a woman confessing my feelings, so please forgive my inexperience in expressing myself in an articulate manner, and for the high-handed manner in which this letter has found you.

In truth, I was upset and angry when Roxanne told me that you didn't want to meet up before the hearing – why? I couldn't bear it if you feared me – do you?

I've replayed the moment you left a hundred times and each time cuts me as deep as the first. I apologise if my feelings are unwelcome, but I wanted to let you know how I felt and still feel.

Christmas – I handled the situation badly, I can see that now, but I still insist that I was telling the truth. I do not love Cara! I should have fought harder to reassure you of this, which I regret and always will.

Putting yourself in danger by confronting Booth and St Clair made me feel less of a man. I should have told you that I had people working on getting evidence – I would like to apologise for withholding this information from you. It was of course apparent to all apart from myself that I suffer with selfish pride. I've lived the last twenty years of my life in conceit and arrogance. I haven't cared for anyone's feelings but my own, until I met you. I guess I'm paying for my pomposity now because I no longer taste joy in my life now you're absent from it. What I'm trying to say – very ineptly – is I have fallen in love with you, Eva.

Why should you believe me? It's true, I tried to ignore my feelings for so long but 'love' I've come to realise, is like a game of poker. You try and hide your hand until the stakes are too high, then you have no choice but to lay your cards on the table – this is what I'm doing. I love you, and hope one day you will forgive me and reclaim my heart from the depths of misery in which it dwells.

Until that day, all my love Connor xxxxxxxxx

PS Hope you play the CD x

With tears cascading down her face, large watery droplets splashed onto the letter smudging the ink.

She had not heard such heartfelt and soul-baring words from a man before. Such sentiment choked the breath from her throat. The pain of his betrayal – which she had successfully suppressed until now – had, without warning, instantly melted away, and her mind flooded with joyous memories of their passionate and lustful affair.

Eva wiped her fingers across her cheek and pushed the letter back in the envelope.

'Eva!'

'Mum!' she turned around shocked hearing her mother's voice.

'I got worried when you didn't return for lunch. What are you doing hiding away here? Have you been crying?'

'No...' replied Eva, hiding the envelope behind her. 'I'm fine.'

'Well, let's go and have lunch?' said Patsy, holding out her hand.

She had no pockets in her dress and there was no time to stash the envelope in her underwear, so she dropped it behind the rocks and slowly walked back to the villa with Patsy.

Connor's love letter had dulled Eva's appetite as she sat looking at the chicken and vegetable pasta meal in front of her.

'What's a matter, darling,' fussed Patsy, looking at Eva's untouched food.

'Actually, I've got a headache. I might go and have a lie down.'

Patsy looked on with concern when Eva excused herself and went into her room.

Eva lay on her bed thinking about Connor's letter. She had tried to reconcile her new life without him, but now Connor was all she could think about; her memory bombarded her mind with vivid glossy images of his sexual, predatory stare and seductive mouth.

She jumped to her feet, grabbed her flip-flops and raced out of her room.

'Where are you going, love?'

'Just need some fresh air, I won't be long.'

'But you've only just come back from your walk?' stated Patsy, looking concerned. 'You seem agitated, is everything okay?'

'Yes, stop fussing, Mum,' said Eva, rushing out of the villa. She headed to the beach and quickly walked back towards the rocks.

'Shit!' she cursed out loud, scanning the area for Connor's envelope and not seeing it. Looking up and down the beach, she saw a man with a litter cart making his way past the bank of sand dunes.

'Hello!' she bellowed, waving her arms in the air. 'HOLA!' She managed to catch up with the man sprinting as fast as she could cradling her swollen belly. 'Do you speak English?' asked Eva breathlessly.

'*Un poco*... A li-ttle,' replied the man in broken English.

'I dropped a letter on the beach, have you seen it?'

'*Carta?*'

'A big white envelope?' said Eva, drawing a large square in the air.

'*Que?*'

'Oh never mind,' said Eva, peering into his rubbish cart.

The rubbish collector looked on in amusement as she sifted through the cartons, bottles, wrappers and tissues covered in food debris he had collected.

'Here it is!' she cried snatching the slightly stained envelope from amongst the rubbish. 'Thank you! *Gracias!*' she squealed.

Eva rushed back to the villa, took out the CD and folded the letter so it wasn't so visible to prying eyes.

'You sure you're okay, love?' asked Dennis, looking at Eva's flushed cheeks. 'Your mother's worried about you.'

'Yes, I'm fine,' Eva said dismissively. 'Would you mind if I borrowed your laptop, Dennis?'

'Of course not, but what do you need it for?'

'Just to email a friend,' rambled Eva.

'Eva, you're home!' said Patsy, appearing from the lounge. 'You feel clammy, love.' She flapped around feeling her cheeks. 'Perhaps we should call the doctor?'

'I feel fine, I swear,' snapped Eva. 'I'm just borrowing Dennis's laptop to email Roxanne.'

Sitting cross-legged on the bed, she slipped in the disc and put on her headphones. She didn't know whether Connor had recorded a message for her, but her heart skipped a beat instantly recognising the song's intro thanks to her love of 80s music. The poignant words gave her palpitations as she sobbed through Foreigner's 'Waiting For A Girl Like You'.

'So long. I've been looking too hard, I've been waiting too long.
Sometimes I don't know what I will find, I only know it's a matter of time.
When you love someone, when you love someone.
It feels so right, so warm and true. I need to know if you feel it too.
Maybe I'm wrong, won't you tell me if I'm coming on too strong.
This heart of mine has been hurt before, this time I wanna be sure.
I've been waiting for a girl like you to come into my life.'

She scanned down the photos on her mobile and found her favourite of Connor sleeping in her bed. With his arms above his head, his dark hair framing his tanned face and his strong jaw line made him beautiful in her eyes. Adonis came a close second next to Connor's sculptured, powerful physique.

She played the disc for a fourth time and reminisced about the passionate sex they had enjoyed before sending Roxanne a text, *Hi Roxanne, can you tell Connor I got his letter and disc xx*

Within minutes Roxanne replied, *Hi babes, I'm assuming Connor must have hired someone to find you then? He has plagued me for weeks to give him your address, as you know. I feel sorry for him though because he looks so unhappy, but I would never betray you. I always say if a man truly loves you, then he'll move heaven and earth to prove his love…*

Is that what he's doing? Eva typed back.

I think so. He's told Tommy letting you go was the biggest mistake of his life. I believe he's in love with you. What are your feelings?

My head is still a mess if I'm honest. I thought he loved Cara!

Actually, she turned up at the club last night and they had a massive showdown in the lobby in front of me, Donna and Tommy! He basically told her that he never loved her and that he'll never see her in private again. She was crying and screaming, saying that she loved him and that he had used her! He physically marched her out of the club and slammed the door in her face – it was fucking brutal!

I don't know what to do? Shall I text him?

Only you can decide what's best for you. Cara is definitely off the scene and I doubt now she was ever on it. Maybe you should speak and clear the air?

Eva took a deep breath and replied to Roxanne's text, *Can you give him my new number then?*

Ok xxxx

Connor rang within ten minutes. Hearing his voice tightened the knot of nerves in her belly, making her feel nauseous.

'How are you?' asked Connor.

'Good, thanks… You?'

'Existing, I guess…'

Eva felt her cheeks burn feeling wired, apprehensive and in love. 'Is the club doing well?'

'Did you believe what I wrote in the letter?'

Taking in a deep breath, she fidgeted on her bed, her heart beating like a drum beneath her chest. 'Yes…'

'So you believe that I love you?'

'Love is so much more than a four letter word…'

'Give me another chance to prove myself, that's all I ask,' begged Connor, his voice breaking with emotion.

'It's not that easy, we need to talk.'

'I can get a chartered flight out of the UK and be with you in a couple of hours? Just say the word.'

Eva briefly moved the phone away from her ear, needing a moment to think, feeling anxious at his urgency. 'I need to prepare myself to see you again. Can we meet tomorrow – midday?'

'I would rather we seized the moment today, but I'll agree to what you want – I'll do anything you want, Eva.'

Eva blinked back her impending tears and tried to compose herself. 'I'll see you tomorrow, then.'

'You will,' replied Connor. 'I love you…'

'Okay, bye…' said Eva before quickly clearing her throat and hearing the line go dead.

She went out onto the patio and took a deep breath looking at Dennis and Patsy sitting in the sun drinking wine.

'Mum…'

'Do you want something to eat, darling?' said Patsy, immediately putting down her glass and getting to her feet.

'No, thanks.' Eva swallowed hard. 'I have something to tell you and Dennis.'

'What is it? Is it the baby?' fretted Patsy.

'No…' reassured Eva before pausing briefly. 'I've heard from Connor.'

'What do you mean *you've heard from Connor*? He doesn't know where you are.'

'He hired someone to find me. He wrote to me saying he loves me.'

A heavy silence hung in the air as Patsy looked down at Dennis. 'Words are cheap, Eva, ignore him,' said Patsy. 'His floozy has probably dumped him, that's all!'

'Your mother is right. You need to move forwards, not backwards, love.'

'Connor's flying out tomorrow. I've decided to tell him about the baby.'

'You're making a huge mistake!' warned Patsy, her face etched with worry. 'He will hurt you again and run a mile when he learns about the baby.'

'Then I'll deal with it,' Eva said adamantly. 'He's going text when he lands.'

'But—'

'No, Mum – I've made my mind up!'

Eva went back to her room where she stayed all evening ignoring the numerous protests from Patsy and Dennis to come out and discuss the situation further.

Chapter 34

Eva got up early the next morning after only managing a couple of hours sleep. After her shower she decided to wear a loose-fitting red summer dress, she curled her hair and applied her make-up all the while imagining how her life would look by the end of the day.

'What time is he flying in?' asked Patsy curtly, placing a plate of toast in front of Eva.

'I don't know, he said he'd text.'

'You can bring him here to the villa. Dennis and I will sit out on the patio,' added Patsy, pouring Eva a glass of orange juice.

'I want to go to the beach and talk there.'

Patsy exhaled with frustration and stared over at Dennis to intervene.

'Let her do it her own way,' said Dennis, knowing it would be fruitless to argue with his strong-willed stepdaughter. 'But keep your phone on,' he warned, getting up and planting a kiss on the top of Eva's head. 'Your mother only worries because she loves you, so do I. Call if you need us.'

'I will,' said Eva. 'I promise.'

It was approaching ten thirty before Eva received a text from Connor saying his flight had just landed and that he was on his way in a taxi.

'Connor should be here in twenty minutes – I'm going to wait for him down at the beach,' said Eva. 'I have my mobile, so I'll see you later,' she added, letting her mother hug her tightly.

'Don't be taken in by empty promises, that's all I'm going to say,' Patsy said softly.

'I won't. See you both later.'

Eva walked down the drive and closed the iron gates behind her. Patsy and Dennis watched until she went out of view.

A bout of nerves made Eva heave as she stepped onto the beach. Her legs felt as though they would buckle at any moment. She decided to meet him at the cluster of rocks where she had read his letter the day before. In between checking her mobile every couple of minutes, she played numerous scenarios in her mind of what Connor's reaction was likely to be hearing she was pregnant with his child.

Hi, I'm here – where are you? xxx

Eva's mouth went dry and her cheeks flushed with apprehension. She steadied her hand to let him know where she was. Holding a large white and red striped canvas bag against her swollen stomach, Eva felt as if her heart was going to burst through her chest.

'Eva!'

Hearing Connor's broad Irish accent boom behind her made her spin around and her heart miss a beat.

He walked towards her dressed in faded denim jeans and a white short-sleeved T-shirt. He gave her a large dimpled grin; his eyes were wide with joy as he quickly joined her.

'Oh…' said Eva, looking up at the large bouquet of red velvet roses. 'They're lovely – thank you.'

Connor stood anxiously trying to judge her mood. 'Shall we go for a walk?' he asked, offering his hand.

The warmth of his strong hand enveloping hers and the light breeze carrying the scent of his aftershave sent a quiver down her spine. She held her bag across her bump as they walked side by side up the beach.

'You look wonderful,' said Connor carrying her heavy bouquet of roses.

'Thank you,' said Eva, smiling up at him nervously.

Feeling her uneasiness, Connor gently squeezed her hand and linked his fingers through hers.

'I need to tell you something,' croaked Eva, averting her gaze to the horizon.

Hearing the seriousness in her voice made Connor stop and turn to look at her. 'Are you going to rip my heart out – again?' he asked, his voice cracking with fear.

'Maybe…'

'Then just say it,' said Connor, releasing her hand and inhaling deeply.

Eva lowered her gaze to the sand and held on tightly to the handles of her oversized beach bag. 'I just want to say it wasn't planned, and you're under no obligation morally or financially to support me or—'

'Under no obligation?' questioned Connor, not able to unravel her puzzling comment.

She dropped her bag to her feet and placed Connor's palm on her swollen belly before announcing, 'I'm pregnant.'

Staring down at his hand, Connor stood mute and wide-eyed.

'I can support myself and the baby, so…'

Connor frowned. 'How many months are you?'

'The baby *is yours*, Connor,' Eva said defiantly. 'I'm twenty-one weeks.'

'But how did it happen?'

'I can promise you it wasn't planned. I wasn't going to tell you, but after your letter I changed my mind – plus, you would've noticed at the hearing, so I—'

'I'm going to be a father,' interrupted Connor, removing his hand then reaching up to cup her face.

Eva blinked staring up into his deep blue eyes. 'Yes…'

'So if you want me, then you have to want our child, too – we come as a package.'

'Well…' said Connor, running the tip of his thumb across her bottom lip, 'I *want* the woman standing in front of me, and I *want* what we've made together – *our baby.*'

Eva burst into tears hearing his words and trembled under his loving gaze. 'I've been so scared to tell you!'

'Being away from you, Eva, has finally made me realise what I want in my life. I want you, and now I want my baby, too,' confessed Connor, wrapping his arms around her.

'And you're sure? Because if you're not, then this won't work.'

Connor smiled. 'I am sure.' He reached down to kiss her.

Feeling his warm lips brush against her mouth sent a surge of love straight to her heart, making it quicken with happiness and sheer bliss.

'I have a scan tomorrow if you want to come along,' said Eva softly, breaking away from his passionate kiss.

His almond-shaped eyes shone through genuine happiness; his pupils dilated like two pools of ink. 'I wouldn't miss it for the world.'

A soft rose blush coloured Eva's cheeks as happiness radiated from every pore. 'I need to speak to my mum and Dennis. There's no pretending they'll approve of our reconciliation.'

'Perhaps I should go and speak to them alone?'

'No, I think I should break the news to them.'

'If you're sure. I'll walk back with you and wait outside.'

Eva gave an anxious smile and nodded as Connor reached down for her hand. Carrying her beach bag and roses, he could not stop smiling down at her as they walked hand in hand up the beach to Patsy's villa.

'I like the name Darcy if the baby is girl and Jack for a boy,' said Eva as they reached the sandy stone steps leading up to the road.

'I've always liked the name Kyla as a girl's name?' said Connor grinning, squeezing her hand gently. 'I guess we'll know for sure tomorrow.'

With a childlike joy filling her soul, Eva felt as if she were walking on air; her world had been turned upside down, but this time in such a joyous way. Connor loved her and was happy about the baby – perhaps she was going to get her fairy tale prince after all?

'I'll wait here, then,' said Connor, frowning with concern holding Eva tightly. 'If I hear things getting heated, I'll come in whether I'm welcome or not. I don't want you getting upset.'

'Okay, but remember their approval is important to me. I would like their blessing.'

'I promise to be on my best behaviour,' he quipped, cupping her bottom playfully.

'Mum!' called out Eva, sliding shut the patio door.

'What's happened?' asked Patsy, quickly walking into the kitchen with Dennis behind her.

'We talked, and I told him about the baby – he's happy about becoming a father.'

Patsy looked at Dennis, then back to Eva. 'So he wants to be involved in the child's life?'

'He wants us to be together – him, me and the baby – a family.'

'Well, words are cheap,' scoffed Patsy.

'At least give him a chance, Mum. Not everyone is like my father. I believe Connor is genuinely happy about the baby – he won't abandon us,' said Eva, hoping that Connor's love and enthusiasm wouldn't wane under the pressure of such a massive change to his life.

'I agree,' added Dennis. 'We have to give him a chance to prove himself.'

'I see I'm outnumbered,' Patsy said curtly. 'I suppose he wants to take you back to London with him.'

Seeing her mother visibly upset made Eva feel awful. 'We haven't discussed where we'll live, but I suppose with the club and his other businesses being in the UK it would make sense to live there. I still want you there at the birth, Mum – I still need you,' assured Eva, walking over and giving her a warm hug.

Patsy sniffed, wiping a tear from her cheek. 'Where is he?'

'Waiting outside.'

'Bring him in, I want to speak to him alone, please.'

Eva swallowed hard and did as her mother asked.

Sitting outside with Dennis, Eva got up and slowly paced the patio with her baby kicking relentlessly. After a long, tense fifteen minutes, Connor emerged from the villa.

'Dennis and I are going out for lunch,' said Patsy, stepping out onto the patio.

'Are we?' Dennis looked surprised at Eva then back towards his wife.

'Yes, Connor and Eva need time to talk alone.'

'What did my mother say to you?' asked Eva after Dennis and Patsy had left for their impromptu meal out.

'Only that I wouldn't be able to physically father any more children if I didn't look after you. Actually, she's missed her vocation, I'm sure the army could learn from her interrogation skills,' he said, smiling. 'I assured your mother that I have no intentions of letting you walk out my life again. I'm not perfect, but my love for you and my unborn child is at least pure and honest. I have never loved anyone more than I love you and our bump,' added Connor, gently caressing her rounded belly. 'I promise on my life I will never let either of you down. I want to be a devoted partner and a protective father.'

Such chivalry made Eva melt; a shudder of lust gave her goose bumps. 'Shall we go to bed?'

'If you're sure, I don't want to rush you,' Connor said softly. 'I expected you'd make me wait before we became intimate again.'

Blushing with coyness, Eva looked up at his handsome face. 'Do you want to wait? My body has changed, so if you don't—'

'Shush,' soothed Connor. 'My desire for you is unchanged. And contrary to what women believe, if a man is in love with a woman, the superficial stuff doesn't matter. There's nothing that could dampen my lust for you, but maybe leave him outside?' He smiled looking down at Mr Jingles meowing loudly at his feet.

Connor's words of love and tenderness allayed any fears she had about her body; Eva let him carry her masterfully to her bedroom.

With gentle caresses and attentive probing, Connor's tongue quickly delivered Eva's first orgasm within seconds. At his insistence that she didn't hide her body under a nightshirt, Eva quickly straddled his thighs and enjoyed every blissful plunge of his erection into her body. He groaned breathlessly beneath her softly brushing his hands over her tender breasts and down to her rounded belly.

'I love you,' murmured Eva, quickening the motion in her hips.

'I love you too, baby,' croaked Connor, lifting his pelvis to push deeper inside as her orgasm pulsated in spasms around the length of his penis.

After their mutual cries of ecstasy had subsided, he slowly positioned Eva's body so they lay spooned together.

She felt the warmth of his breath on the nape of her neck and his taut body curve around the soft contours of her bottom before he gently lifted and parted her legs.

'I love you so much,' whispered Connor, penetrating her with his thick erection.

Eva enveloped his embrace and turned her head to reach his mouth.

The bed rocked with the motion of Connor's body as he quickly came inside her.

'I wasn't too rough, was I?' he asked, withdrawing from her body.

'No, it was wonderful,' gushed Eva, turning around and snuggling into his muscular chest. 'But…'

'What is it?' Connor asked anxiously, rolling onto his side so he could meet her gaze.

'I keep on wondering if all this is a dream. I'm scared to close my eyes because I don't want this feeling to end.'

Connor, sighing with relief that her worries were unfounded, kissed her forehead. 'If you're dreaming, then I'm dreaming the same wonderful dream, too – one that I never want to wake from,' he whispered.

A deep love consumed each other as they lay together in pure bliss.

*　*　*

The next morning they woke in each other's arms. Eva felt Connor get out of bed but rolled over with a sleepy grin and went back to sleep. Waking an hour later, she noticed Connor had not returned.

'Where's Connor?' asked Eva scratching her head on her way into the kitchen.

'He had to pop out, love,' replied Patsy, glancing over to Dennis and sipping on a hot coffee.

'Go where?' asked Eva, suddenly feeling anxious.

'Don't worry, he said he wouldn't be long.'

'Do you think he's changed his mind, Mum?'

'Well, he said he'd be back by one, in time for your scan,' explained Patsy. 'Sorry, that's all he said.'

Not feeling able to stomach any breakfast, Eva took a shower and tried to stay calm by reassuring herself that Connor would return at the time he said he would.

'It's quarter to two, Mum!' shouted Eva. 'He's not coming back, is he?'

Feeling her daughter's anxiety, Patsy told Eva to give Connor until two o'clock.

Eva sat in the lounge alone feeling despondent and weeping. She stared at the clock – it was five to two.

'Eva…' called out Patsy from the kitchen, 'can you come in here, love?'

Eva dabbed her eyes and walked into the kitchen. 'You came back!' she cried, looking at Connor who was kneeling down on one knee.

Patsy and Dennis quickly stepped outside, sliding shut the patio door behind them.

Eva slowly walked over to Connor with even more tears streaming down her face.

'Sorry I took so long, I wanted to find the right one,' explained Connor.

'I thought you'd left us,' said Eva, sniffing.

Connor grinned holding out a navy blue ring box. 'Not a chance,' he said. 'It's not the romantic setting I would've planned, but, Eva Summers…would you do me the honour of becoming my wife,' he added, a pink hue colouring his tanned cheeks.

Eva giggled nervously. 'Yes, I will!' she squealed, lifting the lid of small square box. 'Oh my God, it's beautiful,' she gasped, looking down at the platinum four-carat square diamond engagement ring shimmering up at her.

She squealed again with joy letting Connor slip the ring on her finger. Patsy and Dennis stepped back into the kitchen.

'You knew what he was planning to do, and you didn't tell me,' she scoffed.

'He made us promise – congratulations, Eva,' said Patsy, crying and hugging her tightly.

'Yes – congratulations,' said Dennis, wiping a tear from his cheek. 'Connor has promised your mother and I that he will take care of you, and we believe he will,' added Dennis, glancing over at Connor with a small nod.

Connor held out his hand to Eva. 'I never break a promise.'

Quickly grabbing his hand, she stood on her tiptoes and lifted her chin so Connor could reach her lips.

'Yes, well...' Patsy let out a small cough. 'We must get going otherwise we'll be late for your scan. We'll take my car.'

Even though it only took twenty minutes to get to the hospital, it felt like an age to Eva.

'Miss Eva Summers,' called out a slim pretty nurse in perfect English.

'Will it be okay if my partner and my mum and dad come in, too?'

The nurse nodded warmly. 'Of course.'

Eva took a deep breath and lay down before lifting her top above her bump. Connor sat in a chair next to her.

'So, you're twenty-one weeks – yes?' read the nurse from her notes.

'Yes,' said Eva, glancing down at Connor who gave her a big smile.

'Okay, so let's have a look at baby,' said the nurse smiling and smearing gel over Eva's stomach. 'First, let's check baby's heartbeat.'

Connor sat wide-eyed hearing the strong *ba-dum, ba-dum, ba-dum* and promptly squeezed Eva's hand.

'Then we check baby's measurements. I'll turn round the screen so you can see in a moment,' added the nurse staring into the monitor. 'Would you like to know the sex of the baby?'

Eva stared down at Connor. 'Do you want to know?'

Connor grinned. 'Do you?'

Eva gave the nurse a quick nod and glanced over at her mother who was trying unsuccessfully to hold back tears of joy.

'You understand we cannot guarantee a hundred percent, but let's see if baby is shy or not,' she said, turning the screen so everyone could see. 'I think...' she said, moving the handheld device around Eva's belly, 'that you have a...little...girl.'

Hearing Eva was carrying his daughter produced a sudden outburst of emotion from Connor; he wept openly before reaching for her hand and kissing it tenderly. He couldn't hide his happiness as they left the hospital and tucked a photograph of his unborn daughter into his leather wallet.

When they were back at the villa, Eva agreed that she would follow Connor back to the UK the following week.

'I'm not sure I can bear being parted from you for a week,' muttered Connor as they embraced in the departure lounge like two love-struck teenagers. 'I'll phone Father O'Donnell when I get back to see how quickly he can marry us at my family parish.'

'What will he say when he sees I'm pregnant?'

'I've been funding the maintenance of my local church for the last ten years, so I expect a raised eyebrow, then silence,' mused Connor nonchalantly.

A voice over the speaker system announced that his flight was boarding. Connor wrapped his arms around Eva and kissed her passionately, securing raised eyebrows and whispers from bemused onlookers.

'Go…go or you'll miss your flight! I promise I'll be on the plane next Friday,' said Eva standing on her tiptoes to kiss his cheek.

'Promise me you'll take care of yourself and our daughter,' implored Connor, cupping his hand over her swollen belly. 'I want you to rest, understand?'

'Yes, okay, I will,' Eva said beaming. 'Go on, hurry, this is your last call.'

'I love you, Eva Summers!' called out Connor.

Eva stood waving. 'Love you more!'

She instantly felt sad seeing Connor disappear through the terminal. 'Just one week until we see daddy again,' she whispered, holding her hand over her bump.

Eva arrived back at the villa forlorn and already pining for Connor as she sat scanning the photos on her mobile.

* * *

Early that evening Eva went for a lie down and fell fast asleep as soon as her head touched the pillow. A couple of hours later Patsy popped her head around Eva's bedroom door to ask, 'Did you want a hot chocolate?'

Eva stirred from her slumber. 'I didn't realise the time!' she said before emerging from underneath the duvet. 'I was supposed to phone Connor,' she moaned, quickly firing off a grovelling text, *Sorry, I fell asleep! Can I phone now? XXX*

Her phone pinged immediately, she smiled reading Connor's reply, *I wonder if the baby sleeps when you do x*

Eva quickly rang his number. 'Our daughter kicks me all the time, so I don't think she does much sleeping,' she said with a chuckle. 'Is the club busy?'

'Quite busy, your admirer has lost about thirty-five thousand pounds tonight.'

'Are you crowing over his misfortune, by any chance?'

'Yes,' Connor replied simply.

'That's mean. I see money is still your first love?' she teased.

'No…but I need my businesses to be profitable so I can provide for the copious amounts of babies you'll probably want from me.'

'Hope you don't mind, but Roxanne told me about your showdown with Cara.'

'I didn't want to tell you because she means nothing to me. She left me a parting gift though – she keyed my car, so I have a nice repair bill.'

Eva gasped. 'Did she?!'

'Yeah – I did wonder if she'd spoken to your mother,' said Connor. 'She wrote "bastard" in massive letters.'

'My mum doesn't think that – well, not now,' said Eva, glancing down at her beautiful engagement ring. 'So Cara doesn't know about us or the baby?'

'It is none of her business, but I guess she'll find out through mutual acquaintances – my mother has told everyone she knows.'

'So you've told your family, then?'

'Of course, and they're delighted. They want to throw a party for us next weekend.'

'Here you go, love,' said Patsy, placing a mug of hot chocolate on the kitchen table.

'Well, I'd better let you get back to sleep,' said Connor.

'Okay.' Eva sighed before adding, 'Four more sleeps until we're back together,' she cooed. 'Phone me in the morning?'

'Of course, love you both.'

'We love you too – night.'

'Night, baby…' whispered Connor.

Smiling like a child on Christmas morning, Eva picked up her hot chocolate and carried it to her room. 'Night, Mum. Night, Dennis!' she called out before shutting the bedroom door.

Lying in bed, she couldn't remember being so happy and content. She was going to be Connor's wife and the mother of his child – her schoolgirl dream had come true.

After finishing her drink, she quickly fell asleep again and had the most wonderful dream about her and Connor settling in Ireland with a brood of children. Her dream definitely entailed a 'happy ever after'.

* * *

Eva reached out for her mobile ringing by her bed. She frowned when saw the time was 3:42 a.m. 'Hello…?'

'Eva…!'

'Roxanne? I can barely hear you!' said Eva, raising her voice slightly. 'Hello…' she repeated, sitting up and switching on a small bedside lamp. 'Roxanne speak up, is there something wrong?'

'E-VA, can you hear me!'

Eva threw off the bed covers in a panic and started to pace the floor. Her raised voice quickly brought Patsy and Dennis to her room.

'What's wrong?' asked Patsy, noticing Eva's agitated state.

'Shush, Mum, I can't hear what Roxanne's saying!' she cried. 'Roxy, speak up, what's going on? Is Connor okay?'

Releasing a loud cry, Eva stared over at her mother.

'What's happened?' screeched Patsy.

'The club is on fire…' explained Eva in a monotone voice; shock making her whole body tremble.

Patsy looked on dumbfounded. 'Where's Connor?'

Swallowing hard, Eva struggled to answer. 'T-trapped i-inside…' she mumbled, dropping her mobile as she fell to the floor.

All the news channels covered the story, and what transpired that night truly shocked the country. It seemed Cara wasn't going to disappear quietly as Connor had hoped. Armed with bottles of flammable liquid and a box of matches, Cara was hell-bent on retribution for Connor's unrequited love. Her reprisal would add yet another chapter of scandal to the history of the Unicorn.

* * *

With her heels sinking into the soft grass, she looked at the gleaming white carved headstone in front of her. Placing her hands on her swollen belly, she read the name on the gravestone: Connor Andrew O'Neill.

She stepped back hearing her mother call her. A bee hovered around the freshly laid flowers sitting by her feet.

'The service was lovely, Eva,' said Patsy, joining her.

'A whole century of Connor's family have been married and buried here,' said Eva.

'It's a beautiful church, but looks like we might be in for a light shower,' she said, glancing up at sky. 'Shall we go, love?'

'Yeah, I won't be a minute,' said Eva, wafting the bee away with her hand. 'I'll catch everyone up.'

Gathering a handful of her long dress, Eva carefully stepped back onto the gravel path.

'Have I told you how beautiful you look?'

Turning around, Eva brushed her veil over her shoulder and smiled. 'I didn't know you were named after a family member?'

'My father had a twin brother who was knocked down and killed when he was eight,' explained Connor, resting his hand on a brass-handled walking stick. 'I was named after him.'

'How sad…' said Eva, glancing back at the gravestone.

'Yes, it is, but today is a happy day,' said Connor beaming and kissing the tip of her nose. 'For today, I married the most beautiful woman in the world – *just*!'

'I don't know what I would've done if you hadn't managed to escape,' croaked Eva, her eyes brimming with tears.

'Luckily Tommy and I knew about the secret passage from the cellar that leads out to the old Victorian waterworks. I know Cara lost her life trying to take mine, but I can't rejoice in her death.'

'I'm just so thankful that it was Cara, and not you,' said Eva with tears starting to form. She brushed her hand gently across the inch-long scar trailing down from his right eye.'

'Do they put you off – my injuries?' whispered Connor, holding her close.

'Somebody once told me, if you're in love with someone, then the superficial things don't matter,' she replied, quoting his words. 'I love you with all my heart…'

'And I love you with all mine …' said Connor, reaching down to kiss her.

The End

Printed in Great Britain
by Amazon